SACRED SWORD
A NOVEL ABOUT THE INQUISITUON

by Mayer Abramowitz

Copyright © Mayer Abramowitz
Jerusalem 1991/5751

All rights reserved. No part of this publication may be translated, reproduced, stored in a retrieval system or transmitted, in any form or by any means, electronic, mechanical, photocopying, recording or otherwise, without express written permission from the publishers.

Cover Design: Maya Art Studio

ISBN 965-229-079-3

Edition 9 8 7 6 5 4 3 2 1

Gefen Publishing House Ltd.   Gefen Books
POB 6056, Jerusalem   POB 101, Woodmere
91060 Israel   N.Y., U.S.A. 11598

Printed in Israel

Dedicated to

Rachel

Prologue

When several of us at the university volunteered to work on an archaeological dig, I went along. It was the cheapest way to get a vacation in Mexico.

Our first evening in Mexico City, we were in the home of Senora Margarita de Cordo, the dig's sponsor and a descendent of one of Mexico's pioneer families.

Despite her frail appearance, Senora De Cordo, who was probably in her eighties, proved to be marvelous raconteur recalling her personal contacts with Roosevelt, Churchill, and Stalin. We bombarded her with questions and her answers were as exciting as her stories. Graciously, she halted our questions asking each of us about ourselves.

When she called on me, I told her I spent last year, my junior year, at Hebrew University in Jerusalem.

"How is your Hebrew?" she asked.

"Not great," I replied, "but I can read it fairly well."

She slowly rose and, excusing herself from the group, quietly asked me to follow her. She led me to the library where she removed a blue velvet bag from an ornate desk. Untying the bag's worn tassels, the Senora carefully took out a leather-bound book. She handed it to me.

"Last year after my brother's death," she explained, "I found this Hebrew book in his library. At the time, I thought it was just another one of the rare books he collected. When you mentioned your year in Jerusalem, it occurred to me that you could read this book. Would you tell me what it is about."

I carefully opened the musty book. The finely-lettered Hebrew script was rather easy to read. But, the contents made no sense. I read the title, mouthing the words, "Espida Segruda".

"Read that again," she said.

"'Espida Segruda'," I repeated the meaningless syllables.

"Espada Sagrada," she corrected my reading and added, "it means 'Sacred Sword' in Spanish."

"This Hebrew text is without vocalizations," I said, adding that whoever wrote this, used Hebrew phonetics for the Spanish language. "You have to imagine variant pronunciations to the words. I mouth them because I don't understand them and I don't know how to pronounce them."

I read the opening sentences, pausing after each phrase, waiting for her to write the Spanish idiom on a piece of paper. When I finished the first page, she clenched her fingers to her lips and, stifling a cry, read,

> *"Esta es la historia de mi vida.*
> *Una vida sobra las espada sagrada*
> *La cual he sobrevido solo por la gracia divina.*
> *A vosotros mis descendientes*
> *Os dejo esta herencia para que sepais de donde*
> *llegaste a estas costas.*
> *A vosotros, las generaciones por nacer,*
> *Os llego mis bendiciones paternas."*

The senora grasped my hand and translated the Spanish text:

"This is the story of my life
A life of terror, under the sacred sword,
Which only by the grace of God have I survived.
To you, my survivors, I leave this legacy
That you may know whence you came to these shores.
To you, unborn generations, I bequeath
My paternal blessings."

Sacred Sword

"Mr. Banner," she said, after reading the text to herself several times, "Would you explore this book instead of working at the dig?"

It was a command, not a request. Naturally, I accepted.

She dialed the phone and spoke in Spanish. Then she said, "That was Rafael, the curator of our museum. He's quite proficient in English. Work with him as you and I have done translating the first page."

And so I did.

Michael Banner
Margate U. '89

1

I am now called Alberto.

I am a converso, hounded and hated, suspected and spied on. I am barely twenty-two but no trace of my youth remains. Since the tragedy befell us, all my normal behavior has vanished. Even my stride is abnormal as I walk the streets of Cordoba to attend to the sick. My shoulders hunch forward as if I am buffeted by a wind. I look neither right nor left, my head bowed down, greeting no one. I return no greetings. No laughter or even tears are left in me. I am a lifeless shell. Like a hermit, I shun all associations, avoiding all social overtures.

My isolation is my security.

I learned the bitter lesson conversos must live with to survive: any person — peasant or prince — may ensnare us into the clutches of the Inquisition. And anyone we befriend may become its victim. This fear keeps me from my Maria. She could be destroyed because of our love. To protect her, I resolved to stop seeing her. She scorns my resolve. She is convinced that the daughter of the renowned Count de Trastamara is beyond the Inquisition's reach. I know she is wrong. I must protect her from her own naivete. Although my life is unbearable without her, I can not act otherwise for to come near her would threaten her existence.

Even as I write these cryptic lines, I know that I endanger my life as well as the lives of those whose names appear in these pages. For my life I care not; physical existence no longer concerns me. I have lived for so long under Satan's sword that death would be a reprieve not a punishment. My only thought now is to record the misery of our lives.

The story of the Inquisition must be told. Keeping it secret would perpetuate its treachery.

I take some comfort knowing that hatred did not always rule in Spain. Spain was once glorious.

Don Isaac Abrabanel, Treasurer to Their Majesties Ferdinand and Isabel in the days when the Moors were finally driven from Spain, was a most prominent personage in Toledo's royal court.

He was my father. A tall, robust man with ruddy cheeks and a well groomed beard, he always dressed impeccably. Once a teacher told me I looked like my father and I felt it a supreme compliment. I, too, was tall for my age, with a full head of jet black hair and a ruddy complexion. Father's prominence and Their Majesties special treatment of him brought honor to our family and to Spain's Jews who saw him as their leader.

Spanish Jews, like all Spaniards, are a proud people. We take pride in educational or business accomplishments, in military or political honors. But the Spaniard's highest source of pride is *linaje*. The Hebrew counterpart is *yihus*, family lineage.

Thus, our pride is the distinctive Abrabanel genealogy which can be traced to the dawn of Spanish history. Father was proud his family had come to Spain with the conquering Roman legions. He never denied the rumors that he was a descendant of the biblical King David. I, too, was fiercely proud of our *linaje* and of father's role in the Iberian Peninsula's political history. The name Abrabanel loomed large in Portugal as well as in Spain.

I am named after my great-grandfather, Samuel, a member of the Cortes of Seville, who emigrated from Spain to Portugal and became Counsellor to King Juan I. Father grew up in Portugal and also became a familiar figure in the royal court. In one of his books, father describes his childhood playmates in Lisbon as "the children of the House of Braganza, the most powerful of Portugal's noble families."

Early in his life, father proved exceptionally talented in commerce and trade. He attained high political stature in the royal court by uniting various noble families behind the Braganzas.

As Royal Treasurer, father succeeded in reconstructing the Portuguese economy, thereby securing the rule of the Braganzas and establishing Portugal as the leading trading country in Europe. For many years, 'Don Isaac Abrabanel' was synonymous with Portugal's financial success.

Father's wealth grew with the empire he helped shape. He became one of Portugal's richest men. Then, at the height of his career, he abruptly withdrew from commerce to devote himself to scholarship. He devoured all the books which had attracted his wide interest and attained his life's ambition: he became a writer. I recall the celebration in our home when he published his first scholarly essay, "The Form of the Elements" which earned him instant recognition as one of Portugal's serious philosophers. He studied Greek and Latin and kept writing.

His reputation as a philosopher established, father turned to Judaic subjects, writing commentaries on the Bible and Hebraic lore. He maintained the social contact with the royal family, but shunned political appointments.

My mother was never happier. She shared the management of the family's far-flung business with my three brothers, relishing the idea that father was no longer troubled by political intrigue. She also could give her personal attention to being a competent hostess to friends and family.

Our home was a happy one until father had to give up his books and once again return to serve the royal house.

King Alfonso summoned father's help in the political crisis following his protracted wars with Castile which drained Portugal's economy. Out of friendship with the king, father could not refuse the summons. Within a relatively short time, father recruited the nobility to subsidize the king's armies thus restoring the economic bases of the realm. However, the House of Braganza paid a heavy price. It yielded suzerainty over vast lands to nobles who supported the armies. Despite this cost, the king greatly honored father because Portugal's economic stabilization ushered in an era of peace.

But that peace was short lived. Three years later, Alfonso died while on a military campaign in Africa, bringing Juan II to the throne.

Juan was a bad person and a bad king. He begrudged the costly royal patrimony to the nobles and ruthlessly pursued them with his mighty army until he reclaimed all lands King Alfonso yielded. His avarice knew no bounds. His sword was swift and his terror deadly.

Father knew that his wealth put his life in jeopardy.

Yet, he was ordered to remain at his court post because he alone kept all the records of the crown's possessions. When a high-ranking count of the House of Braganza was executed for treason, suspicion was cast against father whose Braganza's ties were well known. Soon, he, too, was summoned to appear before King Juan II for a summary trial.

I shall never forget the night before he was to appear. I was only nine, but I was allowed to attend that critical family gathering. Father said to us that someone close to the king assured him that the crown desired only our property and that, if father fled, the family would not be harmed. Father then announced he was escaping to Spain where we would soon be reunited.

That night, he crossed the Castilian border. His business associate, Diego de la Fuente, arranged father's stay in Segura de la Orden, a border town. Several days later, King Juan issued a death sentence against father and, as he predicted, our holdings were confiscated. Yet, no action was taken against us.

Despite father's assurances that we would not be harmed, we lived in constant fear, awaiting our flight to Spain. My mother kept our spirits up and went about her affairs with reasonable normalcy. Somehow she kept in touch with father. Her surreptitious contacts with palace insiders enabled us to finally make the perilous trip, stealthily reaching Segura de la Orden.

Sacred Sword

We stayed at Diego de la Fuente's ramshackle house. He gave father a certificate of residence issued by the Spanish Monarchs granting the Abrabanels permission to reside in Spain. Father read the official document and predicted he would soon have to pay for this privilege because "royalty give away nothing for nothing".

De la Fuente did everything to make us comfortable in the cramped quarters we shared with his family. My two married brothers tried in vain to find adequate homes for their families in the small village. Father's new poverty forced us to remain there, despite the strain and inconvenience.

About a month later, a high-ranking general, Don Carlos de Santa Fe, arrived as King Ferdinand's emissary. He summoned father to an audience with the Queen Isabel and King Ferdinand. Father showed no surprise. He jestingly asked the general why the king had waited so long.

"Since I am summoned to present myself to Their Majesties, I have no choice," father said. "If, however, the purpose of this summons is to burden me with affairs of the realm, I shall have to respectfully decline. I am too old for political responsibilities."

Don Carlos, who was fifteen or twenty years younger, ridiculed father for referring to himself as old.

"But you are correct about Their Majesties' intentions," Don Carlos said. "I am empowered to transmit their offer to appoint you Royal Treasurer of Spain."

"I shall have to respectfully decline," father repeated, saying he would not accept the appointment even if permission to live in Spain were withdrawn.

Don Carlos did not press. He simply stated he would relay father's reply to Their Majesties and he remained with father describing the latest developments of the Reconquista, the war to liberate Spain from the Arabs.

Later, at dinner, Don Carlos told us had recently been promoted to the rank of general, commanding the Palace Guard.

To me, he did not even look like a general. He was short, a head shorter than father, stout and almost totally bald, with a round boyish face and light-blue eyes. Instead of the stern traits I imagined a general should possess, he had an excellent sense of humor. Throughout the meal he was affable and pleasant, paying attention to my brothers and to me as though he were a life-long family friend. I liked him instantly.

I still recall something he said to me that night. I remarked how exquisite his medal-bedecked uniform looked.

"A uniform can cover up many blemishes," he said. "What's under the uniform is far more important than the braid on it."

"You don't sound like a military man," father remarked. "You sound more like a thinker than a warrior."

"If I were a thinker," Don Carlos replied, "I could understand your refusal of Their Majesties' appointment to the Council of Ministers."

"I have lost faith in the integrity of the crown," father said, quickly adding that he was referring to royalty, in general, not to Ferdinand and Isabel, in particular.

Don Carlos expressed sympathy with father's feelings about royalty, especially in view of his recent narrow escape from Juan II. Then, begging father's indulgence, Don Carlos detailed Spain's financial problems.

"The prolonged wars with the Moors is a financial disaster for Spain. The crown's treasury has no money for the army or for investments in our African colonies."

Father said nothing as Don Carlos went on to explain that father's reputation had spread throughout the Spanish Royal Court. When King Ferdinand learned of his escape into Spain, the king initiated plans to enlist father's help in saving Spain from economic ruin. Don Carlos assured father he would be handsomely rewarded if he decided to help Spain.

Father smiled and reminded Don Carlos of his earlier promise to relay father's refusal to Their Majesties.

Don Carlos shrugged, saying, "You can't blame me for trying."

"Nor can you blame me for refusing," father said, explaining that he could not go back to the turmoil of court life and wanted only to return to his books, as he had done earlier.

After dinner, Don Carlos and father went out to the small portico. They agreed to lay aside court issues and discussed the merits of the academic life, Spanish art, and current trends in philosophy. They talked until my mother called them in for refreshments. Sitting in the salon, they acted like close friends, joking, amicably arguing, calling each other by first name. I had never seen father so relaxed nor heard him laugh as much.

Suddenly the laughter stopped. Father said, "I do not intend to remain long in Spain. I appreciate the hospitality of your Sovereigns, but I have great fears for our safety here."

I was startled and frightened. I could not believe my ears. I can still see him, sitting in a tall-backed chair, tapping his finger on one of its arms, lecturing Don Carlos that before long the Inquisition would firmly establish itself throughout Spain. He was certain it would soon turn against Spain's royal house, rendering it powerless. He did not say what his plans were.

I was even more frightened when Don Carlos agreed with father about the expanding, ruthless power of the Inquisition. However, he repeated his assurances that the army would guard against the Inquisitors. Father waved him off saying that Carlos did not know the Inquisition's true goals.

"How can I convince you?" Don Carlos asked.

"You can't," Father replied. "You are a military man, and you overestimate the army's power. The Inquisition is a church matter, not a military one."

"Then, would you be willing to discuss this with Spain's leading churchman?" Don Carlos asked.

He suggested a meeting with Father Hernandez, Tomas de Torquemada's former assistant who later became papal nuncio to the Spanish Monarchs. Father was refused, stating he had no desire to engage in a religious debate with a prelate of the church. Only when Don Carlos said the meeting would take place in Toledo did father agree.

My mother jestingly warned that Carlos was luring father to Toledo, a city whose legendary beauty fascinates and finally captivates the visitor. Yet, father consented. After the harrowing experiences in Lisbon and the strain of living in the border village, father explained, he wanted the family to relax in Spain's Imperial City.

I could hardly contain my excitement.

Don Carlos arranged father's visit with the precision of a military campaign. Every function in court and every tour of the city was planned in minutest detail. Once, he even admitted that his intention was to bring father to Toledo so that the city's fabled grandeur would entice him. Don Carlos fully realized father had accepted these visits only to entertain his family. After a few days in Toledo, father even told my mother he was not interested in meeting Father Hernandez but could not disregard Don Carlos' elaborate plans.

They met in the archbishop's office in the Cathedral of Toledo. I was allowed to stay in the room because I could not keep up with my brothers who were touring the great Cathedral. As I settled in a corner of the elaborately furnished room, father exhorted me not to interrupt. I was not nettled because I expected that remark from father.

After Don Carlos made the introductions, father said he was deeply impressed that the prominent priest travelled the long distance from Cordoba, the capital of Andalusia, just for this meeting. Father Hernandez replied that he would have travelled even to India to meet father, a writer he so admired.

Their quiet discussion, steeped in philosophy and theology, intermittently put me to sleep. When I awoke, the priest was stressing the point that the office of the Inquisition had existed for hundreds of years to guard against heresy within the church. He repeated over and over again that, as a papal institution, the Inquisition was only an academic body promoting faith.

Father argued that the Inquisition had ceased being only an academic institution. He questioned the elderly priest about the endless riots incited by the Inquisition, about its network of spies, about its torture chambers. Father Hernandez charged these were excesses of the populace or of misguided local zealots. The Inquisition, as conceived in Rome and, as seen by Hernandez, was primarily a theological institution within the Church.

"In Spain, apparently, the Inquisition has become much more," father said. "Under Torquemada, it is becoming a militant organization using terror as its tool."

"Torquemada is not the church; the church is not Torquemada," Father Hernandez replied.

"What will the church do," father asked, "if the Inquisition ascends to power and acts against Spain's Jews as it purports to do?"

My fright at the question increased when Father Hernandez stood up, agitatedly paced around the room, and then turned to father saying, "You ask, if the excesses of the Inquisition cannot be halted, who will protect the Jews? I reply, men like me, men with influence in the church will stand by your people. But we will need men like Don Carlos whom the Monarchs will heed."

Don Carlos interjected, "King Ferdinand wants to appoint Don Isaac as Royal Treasurer."

"With you in the Council of Ministers, the Jews of Spain will be safe," Father Hernandez said, "Torquemada will have little chance to subvert the Holy Inquisition."

I walked over to father and, tugging at his sleeve, whispered that he should unite with the priest to protect us. They laughed at my pleading while father patted me on the head. My fears vanished at the end of the meeting when father quietly announced he would reconsider the king's offer. Father Hernandez embraced father repeatedly assuring him of his support.

After our delightful stay in Toledo, Don Carlos returned with us to Segura de la Orden and waited several days for father's decision. They engaged in lengthy conversations about matters of state. But in his free moments, Don Carlos joshed with me, telling me hair-raising military adventure tales, teaching me swordsmanship, and improving my horseback riding. He told my parents he would like to have a son like me.

Before the week was over father accepted Ferdinand's offer.

We went back to Toledo where Don Carlos installed us in Casa Floridiana. The beautiful 20 room mansion stood on the banks of the Tajo River, near the St. Martin's Bridge, far from the densely crowded city. A high wall surrounded the house and its sprawling gardens. My mother protested that it was far too luxurious, too sumptuous, for her tastes but I knew that inwardly she liked the elegance and comfort of our new home.

Father, too, was pleased and soon the mansion became the hub of the community's social and civic activities. Through the years, we celebrated many family milestones in the Casa Floridiana which accommodated a great number of guest quite comfortably in the house and gardens.

From the very first day, father assumed prominence in the royal court. The two other financial advisors to the Monarchs, Abram Senor and Luis de Santandor, accepted his leadership and sincerely welcomed his appointment. They readily deferred to him in financial matters. Spain's old and well established Jewish community also immediatelyacknowledged him as their leader. Such was his magnetism.

The ceremony inducting father as Treasurer to Their Majesties was one I would never forget.

It was held in the Palace of Seville where the Royal Pair had often hosted official affairs of the realm. My mother, my brothers, their wives, and I were ushered to the Room of the Crystals, a reserved section of huge grand ballroom. Amid glittering furnishings, we awaited King Ferdinand and Queen Isabel. The hall was filled to capacity with eminent dignitaries and their ladies. I was awed by the splendor of the palace and by the large assemblage of Spain's ranking noblemen all dressed in formal attire befitting a royal coronation. Coronets blared and the chamberlain then announced the entrance of the king and queen. We all stood with bowed heads as Isabel and Ferdinand mounted their gilded twin thrones. She was beautiful and adored by her countrymen. The chamberlain called out father's name announcing the commencement of the induction ceremony of the Royal Treasurer.

I was thrilled when the chamberlain called out father's name: "Don Isaac Abrabanel, grandson of Don Samuel Abrabanel, Royal Treasurer of Seville, by order of his Majesty, Enrique de Trastamara."

As father stepped forward, my mother whispered that the legendary King Enrique de Trastamara, under whom grandfather Samuel served, was Isabel's great grandfather. I was named after my great grandfather, Samuel and I felt a lifelong attachment to him, an ancestor I had never known but always revered.

I remember little of the long speeches praising father or the actual induction ceremony, but I shall never forget his introduction: "grandson of Samuel Abrabanel, Royal Treasurer of Seville".

For our family, father's induction ceremony was a homecoming. We sincerely believed that Spain was where we really belonged, and we were glad to be back.

For me, coming to Toledo also meant finding new family. My cousin Asher, two years my senior, came to live with us because his parents had died. My mother treated him as a fifth son. Orphaned at an early age, he was shy and withdrawn. A speech impediment, a lisp he could not overcome, further pushed him into loneliness. Only I could make him feel at ease. Alone with me he would talk freely, lisping, but relaxed.

Asher filled a special need for me. Throughout my boyhood, my much older brothers treated me as the "baby". They were preoccupied with their families and with father's business so that I was never their equal. Father encouraged this annoying disparity always calling me *chico*, small child. So Asher and I gravitated to each other. We became inseparable over the years. He needed me; I needed him.

He overcame his lisp while we were playing, skipping flat stones on the Tajo River. Our favorite playground was a small island connected to the shore by a narrow marshy land bridge jutting into the river. The marshy strip was difficult to navigate, so our island was always deserted. From that tiny island, we would skip stones on the river's surface counting aloud as the stone bounced over the water. Once, Asher counted seven jumps. In his excitement he shouted: "Look! I scaled the stones seven times!" without a trace of a lisp.

"Say it again," I shouted back.

Asher, more startled by his linguistic accomplishment than by his stone-scaling success, repeated flawlessly, "I scaled the stone seven times".

"Now you can say our drill phrase," I shouted again.

"'A serious student studies; a simple student sleeps'," Asher clearly and triumphantly repeated the drill phrase we had invented.

Asher and I would also spend hours away from our other friends and even from our doting elders in our secret hiding place, a dry well. We prepared elaborate rigs of twine and cord to slide down and to climb out. Asher liked the well so much I often found him there when I needed him. We remained close to one another until he left our house several years later to study in a rabbinical seminary.

Father's unique relationship with Don Carlos enabled him to

make rapid progress in solving Spain's pressing financial plight. When they were together, often working late into the night on Spain's costly wars, they were like brothers discussing a family problem. Don Carlos was a bachelor and my mother eventually gave him the bedroom next to mine.

One day, while waiting for father, Don Carlos came in my room and entertained Asher and me with an adventure story about a Spanish warrior fighting gallantly against the Moors. When Don Carlos finished, father, who walked in during the story-telling, ridiculed the hero criticizing Don Carlos for repeating "such nonsense".

"These types of military adventures brought about the ruin of Spain's economy," father chided. "Individual military battles undertaken by local noblemen may make good children's stories, but they impoverish Spain by destroying precious crops and farm lands."

Guided by father's analysis of Spain's needs, Don Carlos forbade local militias to fight the Moors without a previously-approved resettlement plan for liberated areas. That meant no battle could be undertaken unless Spanish peasants stood ready to come in and cultivate lands seized from the Moors.

Asher and I accompanied father to his meetings of the Royal Council and I can recall the day he told the king's ministers, "The casualties of unplanned wars are not only dead soldiers, but dying farms."

Don Carlos, leading the relentless war against the Arab invaders, became the hero of the peasants who, with spades and pitchforks, trailed the marching armies. The troops' unswerving loyalty to Don Carlos was equaled only by the adulation the young general received from the peasants.

As a result of father's 'war against little wars', Spain moved quickly towards full economic recovery. Fewer battles were fought but more land was retaken from the Moors. When Don Carlos was promoted to Commander of the Royal Army to lead the 'Reconquista', he publicly acknowledged that his sucscess was due to father's brilliance.

Father's mission — the strengthening of Spain's economy — required lengthy trips throughout the realm in order to enlist the nobility into a closer alignment with the crown. I fondly recall those journeys when I would have father all to myself. I chafed every time he introduced me as his *chico*, but I felt fully compensated when we were alone and he would share with me stories of our great family or would relate bible tales in his own inimitable style.

When I was seventeen years old something happened which demonstrated Queen Isabel's regard for father.

Luis de Santandor, the queen's counsellor, invited a ship captain, Cristobal Colon, to meet father privately. The captain proposed to sail westward to India eliminating the expensive and time consuming voyage around the African Cape. Colon had asked Queen Isabel to finance the project but she refused. Desperate, Captain Colon was about to leave for France to present his plan to King Charles.

Father, who knew little about navigation, invited the captain to make his presentation to some of father's friends at our house. The gathering included Spain's leading merchants, traders and cartographers. The leader of the group, Emilio Manzano, father's partner and friend, was convinced that the plan was sound and that Spain must take the lead so that France should not grab a commercial advantage. Together with Manzano, father led a delegation to Queen Isabel on behalf of Colon's mission. To fortify their argument, they collected 750,000 Marvedis, about one third of the amount requested by Colon. Father's enormous popularity with the crown, combined with this financial backing, convinced Isabel to finance the sailing. Several days later, I accompanied father to Emilio's home where the original sponsoring group gathered to fete Captain Colon before he left Toledo.

1492 was an important year for Spain. In April, the Moors

were finally driven out of Granada. All of Spain was now celebrating the decisive victory which assured the Christian unity of the Iberian Peninsula. The 'Reconquista' was complete. The Moors had been driven from their last stronghold and for the first time in 400 years the Spanish peninsula was free of Arab domination. Don Carlos became hero of Spain, a beloved figure greeted throughout the realm with tumultuous parades.

Father had a share of glory as King Ferdinand and Queen Isabel prepared to honor him for his signal role in financing the nine-year siege against the Moors.

That fateful spring came early to Toledo. Magnolias burst forth heralding the first breath of spring. Home owners replaced heavy shutters with colorful awnings; drab winter garments gave way to light capes; open carousels were bedecked with lavish floral wreaths. The sombre colors of winter capitulated to the gay greens of spring.

This festive April mood also characterized the gathering at our home, the Casa Floridiana. My mother always opened our home to our far-flung family and to the community. But, at this event, oddly, father was not at the entrance greeting his guests. It also seemed strange that the guests were family members from all over Spain, not just from Toledo. My uncle Reuben arrived from far away Santiago. Cousin Gerson Di Modena came in from Malaga. I was overjoyed to greet Asher who, at 22, was already the rabbi of Segovia. We had not seen each other in more than two years.

"You're so big and tall, I don't recognize you," Asher said backing up and staring at me as though seeing me for the first time. "You're not a *chico* anymore."

"Well, is the serious student still studying?" I said, reminding him of scaling stones into the Tajo River.

"More serious than his simple minded mentor," Asher replied handing me one of his bags to carry up to my room.

"Hey Asher, what do you have in these bags? Marble from

the quarries of Segovia?" I asked.

"Just a few books," Asher said.

"Not enough books here?" I asked, pointing to father's library.

"What about reading during the trip?" He replied.

"There's a world beyond the world of books," I said. "Mountains and meadows and trees, towns and villages. You can't let them pass you by."

"I'm probably more concerned with the Creator than with what He's created," Asher quipped.

We became engrossed in conversation trying to catch up on each others' lives. He again referred to my manly appearance, but I sensed he had another motive for telling me how handsome and mature I was. When I questioned him, he reminded me that I was already 18 soon to be 19. He asked if a marriage was being arranged for me because, if not, he knew of a beautiful girl in Segovia. I replied that no marriage was being discussed and as far as father was concerned, I was still his "little boy." Asher noticed my resentment and lectured me about the respect I owed father, assuring me that before long father would acknowledge my maturity.

We sat in my room most of the morning, until my mother passed by. "So that's where you are," she said embracing Asher. "It's time for lunch and we're not starting without the learned rabbi and his devoted disciple."

The day was glorious. The sun was warm and a mild breeze wafted the fragrance of honeysuckle and jasmine through the high-arched portico where our group had gathered. My mother, was attentive to her guests and, in her inimitable way, circulated amongst them like a butterfly flitting over flowers. She was absolutely adorable. To the family she was a combination of a mother fretting about everyone's welfare and a younger sister playful with young and old. A babel of voices and the hearty sound of laughter filled the portico. Father still had not arrived for the noonday meal but my mother ordered lunch to be served without him. She explained that father was attending a meeting of the Royal Council at the palace where a unique honor was to be bestowed upon him, and that he did not want it to be divulged until his return.

When someone asked my mother the reason for this celebration, she replied, "It was simply Isaac's wish that we come together today. It's a time to be happy."

"There must be something very big looming at the Palace," Reuben from Santiago called out from his seat near the head of the table. "After all, our Don Isaac was responsible for the victory of Granada. He's probably being honored for his part in it right now."

"An honor to Isaac Abrabanel is to the glory of all our people," Asher added.

I sat next to my favorite aunt, Benevita, who recently moved from Toledo to Cordoba to be with her son Alfredo. A robust cheerful woman, her face always sparkled with an infectious smile. That day she radiated happiness about her return to Toledo.

"What's been happening to you since I left?" she asked me.

"Good news!" I replied, "I had my first interview with Don Alfonso, the court physician. He accepted me as his apprentice."

"Listen, everybody," Benevita called in her shrill voice, attracting everyone's attention tapping her fork on a crystal water pitcher. "There's already a happy occasion for us to celebrate. An Abrabanel, our own little Sami, will be the physician to the Royal Court."

Everyone knew that Benevita exaggerated, but they cheered the news, congratulating me. "No, no, not yet," I called out trying to quiet them. "I am merely being considered for apprenticeship to Don Alfonso. But, as far as my our beloved aunt is concerned, I'm already a court physician."

"Not just an ordinary court physician, but the handsomest doctor in all of Spain," Benevita said and, in her raucous laughter, added, "He's going to attract the finest ladies of the court as his patients even before they get sick."

The more I protested, the heartier Benevita bellowed, bringing on more toasts, more praise, and louder cheers, "to the greatest physician of Spain". Finally, I joined in the merriment. Draping a spare red tablecloth over my shoulders as a cape, holding the serving ladle as a scepter, I proclaimed myself a "Royal Physician to the Court of Toledo!" In jest, Benevita curtseyed before me and proclaimed a couplet which stayed with me for many years:

"The illustrious and noble family Abrabanel
Have a crown-jewel in their youngest Samuel."
Alfredo, Benevita's son, added:
"And, like his father, he will excel".

I felt very close to Alfredo who managed father's holdings and whom I always called, "Uncle". When father's commercial interests in Spain expanded, Alfredo transferred from Toledo to the southern province of Andalusia. He lived in Cordoba, where he became prominent in the cortes, the city's ruling body.

Inwardly, I was pleased that Benevita made my appointment public. I felt the recognition would bolster my relationship with father. Like my successful brothers, I was eager to emulate him in the world of finance. However, much as I tried, I could not generate even an interest in, much less the mastery of, the intricate field of commerce with its fluctuating markets, foreign trade and currency exchange. I had to admit defeat; I would not follow in father's footsteps.

As an apprentice to the famed Don Alfonso, I would no longer be father's "little boy". I was determined to excel in medicine as he had in finance. I wondered if Alfredo realized how much his simple addition to the couplet, 'And, like his father, he will excel', meant to me.

When the meal was over small groups of guests settled themselves in various corners of our house and garden to await father's return. Asher and I headed toward our boyhood island playground. The River flowed in a horse shoe shape around the city, forming a natural moat separating it from the surrounding villages. Toledo, perched on a hill rising towards the Alcazar, glistened like a gilded dome in the afternoon sun.

As we crossed the main highway, we looked in the direction of the Palace but there was no sign of father's ornate carriage. We continued the sharp descent to the river's edge, drawn to the small islet. Dropping our jackets and shoes on the bank, we crossed over to the islet and relived our boyhood games and pranks. We scaled stones over the water, counting the hops and shouting, "a serious student studies." Before long we were racing along the water's edge and competing in acrobatics.

From the very beginning, I could tell that Asher was in no physical shape to keep up with me. He tired easily during our games. When we climbed the steep hill homeward, we had to stop several times for him to catch his breath. At one time, while he was leaning panting against a fence, I lectured him about his poor physical condition. I recalled the days we would swim the entire length of the river around the city when we were boys.

"Even a rabbi must take care of his health," I said.

"Benevita was right," Asher scoffed. "You're already a doctor."

"Never mind Benevita. I'm worried about you," I said, "and forget the 'doctor' title."

"I can't forget the 'doctor' title," Asher replied. "Sure I've changed. But so have you. Your face glowed with excitement at the very mention of your becoming a physician. You even enjoyed Benevita's exaggeration."

"Was it that obvious?" I asked.

Asher did not reply but when we finally sat down under a tree in Casa Floridiana's gardens, he said again, "There's a tremendous change in you."

A sudden chill in the air sent most guests indoors. A few rested under shawls on the portico. Alone in the garden, neither

Asher nor I minded the cool breeze. We were still overheated from our long walk.

"Seriously," Asher asked, "have you definitely decided to study medicine exclusively?"

"What do you mean 'exclusively'?"

"Well," he said, "if you're going to be a physician, you won't earn a livelihood. You'll always need your father's help"

He did not realize how that statement irked me.

"What makes you so sure I can't make a living?" I said.

"Simple," Asher replied, "every physician I know, here and in Segovia, has some other occupation which earns his living. Nobody makes a livelihood exclusively as a doctor."

"Alfonso does quite well 'exclusively' as a physician," I retorted.

"Alfonso!" Asher exclaimed. "Only one Don Alfonso in all of Spain. Not everyone can be an Alfonso."

"Why not? I can see myself," I began, but I stopped when I realized that I sounded like a bleating braggart.

"Don't ever be embarrassed in my presence," Asher said. "Your most charming asset is your delightful sense of self-confidence. I believe in you. I don't fault you for believing in yourself.

"Someday you will become as great as Alfonso."

"Sure," I said, "Just ask Aunt Benevita."

Asher put his hand over mine and said, "Tell me, what made you decide to be a physician?"

"Nobody ever asked me that," I said, after thinking about his question for a long time, "and I have never tried to analyze it. I suspect it's also father's doing."

"How can that be?" Asher challenged me. "You never even spoke to him about it. You told me you wanted to prove to everybody and to yourself that you can become an apprentice to Alfonso without your father's help."

"But, indirectly, father helped me decide," I replied. "Once, on one of his trips, he told me that he regretted not having studied medicine."

"Your desire to be a doctor may very well be your father's influence," Asher said, "but it's not as simple as that."

"What do you mean?"

"I think you chose to be a physician because you can't be in commerce," Asher said, "so, you chose medicine, where you can become as well known as your father. And, there's nothing wrong with that."

I readily confessed that he was correct. I explained I could not admit it to myself because I still felt guilty for not following in father's footsteps like my brothers. Asher began to explain what my attitude should be, but it turned even colder and we hurried back to my room. Before we had a chance to continue our conversation, we heard father's carriage driving up the path. From my window we saw my mother waiting at the foot the stairs to meet him. Asher and I quickly ran to the pathway, arriving just as the coachman opened the door.

An unforgettable shock overwhelmed me when I saw father stumble out, bedraggled, wobbling down the few steps of the carriage.

His eyes were red, his head swayed from side to side. His bearded chin rested on his chest as though his neck could no longer support his massive head. As Asher and I helped him climb the few stairs into the house, my mother sent for Don Alfonso. Father leaned on my shoulders dragging his unsure feet.

We carried him into his bedroom where servants had already prepared the towels and basins of water my mother had ordered. Father collapsed on the bed.

My mother began washing the grime and blood from his face. A few moments later, he weakly motioned to Asher. His words slurred as he told Asher to assemble the guests. My mother pleaded that he was in no condition to meet anyone. She told him she had sent for Don Alfonso. Father finally agreed to wait. He slumped back on his pillow, helpless, gazing at me with a fixed stare.

Fear was etched on my face as I stood there. He had been the tower of strength, and now he lay like a broken reed. I wanted to help my stricken father but could do nothing. He stared at me pathetically, as though begging me to forgive his incapacity. I was relieved when Don Alfonso arrived. He applied a salve to reduce the swelling of father's bruised face and head. Ordering us out of the room, Alfonso remained with father for quite a long time.

At last, father called us. When we entered, we noticed his color had returned and he was sitting up propped on his pillow. In response to the questions my mother asked, Don Alfonso only replied that father was completely cured.

Don Alfonso was slender and tall. He appeared stern and severe, yet he spoke tenderly to my mother, assuring her that father was in no danger. When my mother thanked him, Don Alfonso replied in jest saying that soon she would not need to call him since I could do as well when I became a doctor. As I saw him to the door, I thanked him for helping father and for accepting me his apprentice.

When I returned to the bedroom, father again called Asher to assemble the guests in the Reception Room. My mother still begged him to postpone the meeting but to no avail. Father reminded her that the doctor pronounced him well.

2

The Reception Room, the largest room in our house, had a high arched ceiling and cathedral windows of artistically cut stained glass. The dull-red tile floor sharply contrasted with the gold and blue velvet curtains and the richly colored tapestry on the walls. The gilded chairs and the marble mantelpiece over the fireplace were the only furnishings in that large room.

On gala occasions, it was our ball room. That afternoon, it seemed more like a mausoleum.

The guests were quiet, somber and grave. Most had seen father when he arrived; others were told about his stricken condition. They were seated in a semi-circle facing the fireplace when father entered flanked, by my mother and my brothers. He had changed from the formal fur-lined gown he had worn at the palace to a short waist-high green and gray jacket. He looked refreshed and composed with his shoulder-length hair swept back and his beard well groomed. A touch of pink had returned to his cheeks, revealing no trace of his earlier condition.

He greeted each guest with his customary warmth and, although his demeanor was grave, he managed to smile at one or two of the elderly relatives who expressed concern for his health. Father placed himself in the center of the semi-circle, sitting in a throne-like chair facing the family. He asked me to sit beside him and patted me on the lap assuring me his health was restored.

"What I have to tell you is not good," father began, but halted in his speech.

Talking was obviously difficult for him. His breath was short and his words were somewhat garbled, but he refused to listen to suggestions that he lay down. He nervously kept tugging at the fringes of his sleeve, as though searching for the proper words.

Father began by stating his motto: "To be prepared for any eventuality is the surest means of surviving any crisis."

Then the words flowed clearly and loudly. He related every detail of the events he called, "the most terrifying experience of my life."

I shall never forget anything that transpired that afternoon, nor any of the words he spoke with much pathos:

Father had been summoned to the palace for an audience with the Royal Monarchs, King Ferdinand and Queen Isabel. The special presentation honoring father and Don Carlos de Santa Fe in the presence of the royal court was to be the beginning of a year-long victory celebration over the conquest of Granada. But, when father's carriage entered the outer court of the palace, Don Carlos sprang onto the carriage, taking father by complete surprise.

"Isaac," Don Carlos gasped, "Tomas has succeeded."

Tomas de Torquemada, the Inquisitor General of Spain, had been pressuring the queen for the past six years to expel all Jews from Spain. Each time, father blocked Torquemada's edict.

"Isaac, Tomas has succeeded," Don Carlos repeated. "He is calling for the expulsion of the Jews."

"He's tried before and gotten nowhere. He'll get nowhere now," father replied.

"When I came to the palace this morning," Don Carlos continued, "I learned Tomas had been with the queen since dawn. He gave her a draft of the Edict of Expulsion demanding that it be proclaimed as part of the victory celebrations."

"He's submitted the same edict before," father said.

"He threatened to resign as her confessor unless she does his bidding," Don Carlos said.

"He has resigned before, several times," father said recalling the dates of his threatened resignations.

"But this time, she agreed," Don Carlos interrupted.

"Isabel agreed!" father asked with disbelief.

Don Carlos nodded.

"It's unthinkable that the queen would issue an edict of expulsion now," father said. "If the purpose of this audience is to honor us, how could Tomas succeed in bringing up the Edict of Expulsion?"

"Perhaps there is something we don't know about de Torquemada," Don Carlos said, shaking his head and looking at father who remained silent.

Tomas de Torquemada, Confessor to Queen Isabel, was well known to the royal court. Father considered him a sincere, but hostile fanatic. He often said Tomas was the most incorruptible man in Spain, an ascetic repelled by the glitter of the Court, openly scorning its lust and luxury. To demonstrate his revulsion of opulence, Tomas de Torquemada refused to accept the papal appointment as Archbishop of Toledo.

He would have become the highest ranking churchman in Spain, but he would then have had to participate in the protocol of court life which he so detested. He preferred his monk's cape to a Bishop's cassock and proudly wore his tonsure as his crown of thorns. Under Tomas Torquemada's direction, the Inquisition had become the supreme authority in all matters of faith. It fact, it had become even more.

Since the Holy Tribunals had the power to recommend confiscation of a heretic's property and since the crown became the beneficiary of all such confiscated properties, the Inquisition had become an institution of finance as well as of faith.

As soon as Don Carlos and father entered the Palace's vestibule they heard their names called by the chamberlain who signalled them to approach the throne. The king and queen sat in the double throne, resplendent in their ceremonial royal garb. Ferdinand, bored, as usual, with court protocol, fidgeted as though he could not wait for ceremony to be over. Isabel, who appeared tired, told the large assemblage of royal ministers that she had kept a nightly prayer vigil during the Lenten period. She scorned the ministers for not observing the rites of Lent.

"It is our wish," King Ferdinand interrupted, "to extend royal felicitations to General Don Carlos de Santa Fe and to Don Isaac Abrabanel for the victory at Granada."

The king continued reading from a scroll which listed their accomplishments. He commissioned Don Carlos as the Royal Knight of Granada and presented to father a gold chain bearing the Royal Insignia, designating him as the King's Minister of the Royal Court. The queen descended from the raised dais and touched her scepter over the bowed heads of the two honorees. The assembled guests applauded. Father breathed a sigh of relief when Ferdinand signalled the end of the ceremony and turned to leave the Throne Room.

"We wish to communicate an urgent me matter to you," the queen called out asking the ministers to remain as she unfurled a scroll.

"Since the victory has been given to us by God, it is now our desire to acknowledge God's gift by obeying His will," the queen read from the scroll and, raising her voice, she proclaimed, "We shall order the expulsion of the Jews from Spanish soil."

Her words struck father like a hot iron branded to his chest. He would have collapsed had Don Carlos not caught him.

"As we proudly defend our noble lineage, and protect our land from those who would destroy it," the queen continued her reading, "so must we safeguard against the defilement of our faith. To allow believing Christians to be swayed by the Jews is a defilement; to allow the Jews to pervert the faith of the converso is a defilement. In the name of God, we issue this Edict of

Expulsion. It is not only a royal act but a righteous act; righteously inflicted upon a sinful people."

"Isabel reads her lines well," Don Carlos whispered to father. "Those are Tomas' exact words."

When she concluded reading her proclamation, the queen instantly reverted to her warm, compassionate nature which has so endeared her to her subjects. She embraced father, kissing him on his cheeks.

"Upon my word, dearly beloved Isaac," she said, "no harm shall come to you or to your family. I swear it. You will be specifically excluded from the Edict of Expulsion. You will continue to be under our personal protection so that no suffering will ever come to you."

Father stood motionless; his head was bowed, his eyes fixed on the floor. He could not listen to her declarations of concern for him. He had to collect his thoughts, to plan some way to avert her decree. Once before, when he had defeated Torquemada's edict, she had cried out with childlike ennui, "Oh Isaac, why did you have to be a Jew!"

When Isabel stepped back to the dais, father looked to Ferdinand hoping that, as so often in the past when the queen made some impulsive statement, the king would announce, "the queen's proposals will be taken under advisement by the Royal Council of Ministers". Now, the king remained silent; father knew that this time Ferdinand could not be relied upon.

Father had to block the queen's edict alone.

Father knew Ferdinand was far more concerned with temporal than with spiritual matters. The king would subjugate himself to the Inquisition only for financial gain. The queen, on the other hand, saw in the Inquisition her means of salvation.

Father recognized the finality of the situation. He could appeal to Isabel's natural kindliness by describing the suffering of the women and children an expulsion would cause. But, he reasoned, that would be futile. Her religious fervor obliterated her humane feelings. There was a cold-blooded savagery in her voice when she proclaimed the closing phrase of the edict: 'This expulsion is an act of righteousness, righteously inflicted upon a sinful people.' It was Torquemada's hue and cry which she had fully adopted.

Father concluded no argument would prevail when a diabolical scheme is clothed in saintly trappings. The best he could hope for was to effect a delay. What was needed now was time: time to quell Isabel's religious zeal, time to split the unity between the Royal Pair, time to find a solution, time to avert an impending doom. He needed an excuse, any excuse, even a ruse, to delay the issuance of the Edict of Expulsion. Since he could not bank Isabel's fires of faith, he decided to appeal to Ferdinand's zeal for money.

During the nine years father served the Royal Pair, he discerned their antithetical personalities. In every way, Ferdinand was different from his Castillian queen. His temperament was cŏld and reserved; Isabel abounded in tenderness and sentimentality. Ferdinand was both irreligious and impious; Isabel was devoutly dedicated to the church. Ferdinand regaled in ostentatious wealth, bedecking himself with outlandish jewels; Isabel preferred simple dress, acquiescing to wear her jewels only when protocol dictated. Isabel was just seventeen years old when her historic marriage to Ferdinand took place, ending centuries of warfare between the kingdoms of Aragon and Castile. Married to an unfaithful husband, she found solace in her church. Ferdinand needed no solace, only money.

Father approached the throne and said to Ferdinand, "If the king possessed three hundred horses and someone drove them out of their pasture, the king would obviously sustain a loss of three hundred horses." Ferdinand smiled and asked father to explain.

"Your Majesty now is the sole owner of three hundred thousand Jews who live in your realm," father replied, "and when they are driven out of Spain, the king will sustain a loss of an enormous amount of property."

Ferdinand, who stood beside the queen as she read the Edict, now sat down, a clear indication that he was interested.

"What a vulgar comparison, equating Jews and horses," father thought, "but if it saves the Jews from disaster, the vulgarity might well be a virtue."

To get Ferdinand to act, he had to think like Ferdinand. Father reminded the king of the feudal law establishing the Jews as *servii cameri*, servants of the chamber. They belong to the Ruling Monarchs; liens Jews might possess on anyone's property, juridically, belonged to the Monarchy. On more than one occasion, Ferdinand had used such 'Jewish' liens to discipline an errant nobleman.

"An expulsion of the Jews may prove to be an irreparable loss to the crown and a total forfeiture of a substantial amount of indemnified property," father concluded.

When Ferdinand asked about the disposition of these properties, father responded he would need time to study the problem and to suggest appropriate action. Isabel violently shook her head saying she recognized father's attempt at postponing the edict and denied father's request for more time. Ferdinand did not pursue the subject.

Father felt defeated.

"If it please your Majesties," Don Carlos said in the awkward moment of silence following the queen's objections, "permit me to speak about the honor of Spain. We have recently concluded a peace treaty with the Moors in Granada."

He reminded the king and queen that the peace treaty stipulated that those Moors who chose to stay in Spain would be permitted to remain. "This guarantee," Don Carlos argued, "was extended to all the people in the Kingdom of Granada, Jews and Arabs, who have resided there for hundreds of years."

Ferdinand reminded the queen that Don Carlos was both a celebrated general and a popular folk-hero. His recommendation could not be treated lightly, even by the queen. Ferdinand looked away from her and proclaimed, "We must study the treaties to determine whether they included the Jewish inhabitants. The Edict of Expulsion will be postponed."

A postponement! Father was inwardly ecstatic but could not show it. Grateful for Don Carlos' help, he allowed himself to smile toward his friend.

"General Carlos," the queen commanded in a shrill voice, "present the necessary documents this afternoon, so we can proceed with the issuance of the Edict of Expulsion."

"This afternoon?" Don Carlos implored.

He got nowhere with his plea. She abruptly stood up and left the chamber with the king trailing after her.

Father remained at his place, his hands crossed at his chest, his head bowed. When several ministers approached him with words of encouragement, he thanked them but told them the situation was now hopeless. Carlos stayed after everyone else left. He promised to examine the treaty to find some wording which would help. Father shook his head reminding Carlos that they both drafted the treaty and that it mentioned nothing about the Jews.

Father walked out with Don Carlos but entered his carriage alone. When the coachman asked for instructions, father did not reply. He could not return to his home, nor could he waste precious time at the palace. He felt cornered, like a trapped animal.

Suddenly he ordered his coachman: "To the casa of Don Abram Senor."

Abram Senor was old. No one knew his age. Some said he was past ninety, some even said he was more than one hundred.

But, all agreed he had lost none of his brilliance. He served many years as Ferdinand's financial counsellor when the king ruled Aragon. The aged Abram Senor was short, lean with a very thin, fragile-looking face. His watery blue eyes were deeply set into his bald head.

"I sense this is not a social visit," Don Abram said, greeting father at the door. "What emergency brings you here?"

Father apologized for disturbing him, sat down facing his colleague, and related his experiences at the palace. He recalled, almost verbatim, the Edict of Expulsion and told of the brief postponement gained from Don Carlos' challenge.

"Abram," father said, "we are at an impasse. The monster is loosed upon our people. They will wail and mourn when they learn about the Edict."

"Wailing may soothe the anguished heart," Abram said, "but it could also dull the mind."

The aged Abram walked slowly to his wine chest and selected father's favorite Malaga. He poured a glass for father and one for himself.

"The Edict of Expulsion has been drafted by Torquemada," father said sipping the wine, "and this afternoon it will be proclaimed by the queen. We are on the brink of a tragedy.

"Come, come, Isaac," Don Abram said "You and I have overcome similar threats before. Ferdinand is still a very practical man. We can work with him."

"This time, the saintly queen is our problem not the devilish king," father replied.

"Then we'll come up with an offer to the queen," Don Abram said with a twinkle in his eye, "an offer she will find difficult to reject. I'm certain there's a solution. All we have to do is search for it. We've never failed before and we're not going to fail now."

Abram Senor was weak and frail but his optimism trickled through to father like raindrops on parched soil. Father felt better just sharing his burden with Abram. They sat, thinking in silence.

"It's a religious issue," Don Abram finally said. "We now have to contend with Isabel's missionary zeal."

"That rules out the usual offering of a monetary gift as a solution." father said.

"Not if the gift is religious and big enough to excite them," Don Abram said cryptically.

"They're in the flush of victory. I have seen to it that Ferdinand will acquire virtually all the wealth of Granada and will not have to give away too much to his nobles." father said.

"We're not concerned with Ferdinand," Don Abram reminded father. " Isabel is our problem. What, exactly, did she say about the Jews in her edict?"

"She said that they sway loyal Christians from their religion," father replied.

"And you mentioned Spain has three hundred thousand Jews," Don Abram said and sank back in his chair. "What if you offered Isabel 300,000 gold escudos as a gift from her Jewish subjects?"

"It's a fantastic sum for anyone, but not for Isabel. No amount of money would impress her," father replied dismissing the suggestion with a wave of the hand.

"Let me finish," Abram said. "What if you offered Isabel the 300,000 gold escudos for the specific purpose of building a cathedral in her honor, the greatest cathedral on the continent, second only to St. Peters in Rome?"

"For 300,000 gold escudos, you can build three cathedrals," father replied, "each greater than St. Peters. Money is not the issue with the queen."

"Isaac, our problem is a religious one and only a religious solution has a chance. The number three hundred thousand represents the number of Jews in Spain. The offer of 300,000 gold escudos is significant only because of its symbolism. Think of it as Isabel would:

'My Jews, all my Jews, are building a cathedral for me'."

"Every Jew in Spain thus becomes a patron of Isabel's Cathedral," father said following Abram's line of reasoning. "That ought to counter her charge against us."

"And, your analogy of three hundred horses will not fail to impress Ferdinand," Abram said. "There is enough in this sum to excite his imagination."

"You are right," father said, "but we must also contend with Torquemada. "Will he accept?"

"We can do nothing about that," Don Abram said. "But what about our own Jews? Would they agree?"

They both realized many would be opposed to building a cathedral. They would equate it with idolatry. Father agreed that such a proposal would spark heated arguments which might even endanger raising the required funds. He began formulating appropriate responses.

"All this is important but, premature," Don Abram said. "The only issue now is to gain time. If Isabel accepts the 300,000 escudos for her cathedral, we will have accomplished our immediate goal."

"If Isabel accepts the 300,000 escudos," father repeated Abram's challenge. "But, how can we be sure of that?"

"We can't," Don Abram said. "But, we have no other choice."

They calmly examined the facts. Father said he knew the treaty with the Moors did not mention the Jews, so Don Carlos' stab at a postponement would fail. Don Abram recalled the king's request for a plan to insure against the loss of Jewish property.

"Ferdinand will probably ask you again about that," Don Abram stated. "You must respond, but not to him. Don't be drawn into a conversation with him. You must address the queen, not the king."

They discussed the issue of Jewish property at length and agreed that any amount would tantalize Ferdinand but no amount would sway the queen. They studied every detail of their Cathedral plan, even rehearsing the exact words father would use to make the offer to Isabel.

"You have a good proposal for the queen," Don Abram said, accompanying father to the carriage. "Address yourself only to her. Disregard Ferdinand. Remember, today Isabel is not 'Her Highness', she is the 'High Priestess'."

Father relaxed in the carriage, confident the queen would accept his offer and certain that, once again, he would frustrate Torquemada's scheme. Riding through the narrow streets of Toledo, he enjoyed the sights of the beautiful capital. But, he was hungry; he had eaten nothing the whole day. The wine made him somewhat dizzy, yet he felt sure neither hunger nor dizziness would affect his critical presentation.

He waited most of the afternoon at the palace. The hunger pangs began to grow and, for a moment, he considered returning home to eat. He quickly dismissed the thought. He would do nothing to endanger his crucial meeting with Isabel.

When she finally arrived with Ferdinand, the queen convened the special session by calling on Don Carlos to report the specifications of the treaty with the Moors. When he indicated that the treaty contained no guarantees for Jews of Granada, the issue was summarily dismissed. The queen triumphantly declared no further obstacle would delay the implementation of the Edict of Expulsion. She dismissed the ministers.

The king immediately raised his hand ordering them to remain. The queen chafed but, before she could begin her protest, the king called on father to suggest means of transferring liens held by Jews against Spanish property.

Father approached the throne and, disregarding the king, he faced Isabel. She sat rigid, almost motionless like the scepter she tightly grasped in her fist. She wore a severe expression, her eyes staring over the heads of the grandees.

"Isabel of Castile," father called out, raising both his hands towards heaven, "it is by the will of God that you are today sitting on the throne of Spain ruling over a united kingdom which stretches from the Pyrenees to the Mediterranean. You have united your people not only by the power of the sword but by the power of God Who selected you to be His Queen.

"Isabel of Castile, blessed be you, above all women. You rule not only by Divine Right but with Divine Righteousness."

The queen turned and gazed intently at father who again pontificated, "Isabel of Castile! You rule not only by Divine Right but with Divine Righteousness."

A radiant glow and a faint blush brought life to her face which betrayed a trace of a smile. She looked at Ferdinand then to the ministers nodding her approval.

Father continued, "The Jews of your realm have been accused of perverting your faith. We, who number three hundred thousand souls, will present you with three hundred thousand gold escudos to erect a majestic cathedral here in the Royal City of Toledo. We hope the Church will allow it to be called the Cathedral of Isabel. Such a cathedral will make this city the center of Christendom second, only to Rome. I repeat our tribute: three hundred thousand gold escudo. One escudo from each Jew in your realm, to build a cathedral in your honor, the Cathedral of Isabel."

"Cathedral of Isabel," she repeated several times, clapping her hands with childlike glee.

She did not even try to conceal her enthusiasm. She thanked father for the example he set to all Spaniards, demonstrating the importance of giving "money for God not for armies."

"We are favorably disposed to accept your munificent offer," she said.

"Madam," father asked, "what about the edict, the Edict of Expulsion?"

"I shall be inclined to accept this gift from the Jews and consider it a repudiation for what they've been accused of."

A murmur of approval arose from the ministers whose spontaneous applause grew louder as the queen descended from the throne to thank father. When she returned, he whispered to Don Carlos that he felt as though a dark cloud has been lifted from his head. As Don Carlos embraced him, tears of joy welled in father's eyes.

Ferdinand and Isabel remained in the Throne Room greeting members of the royal council. An air of good will pervaded the hall as everyone congratulated father on his victory.

Suddenly, the door from the queen's chambers flew open. Tomas de Torquemada burst into the Throne Room and, routinely bowing to the king and queen, he demanded to know what was happening.

"My revered Father," Isabel cried out, "our three hundred thousand Jews will contribute three hundred thousand gold escudos to build the Cathedral of Isabel in our Royal City. Our Jews have proven their innocence."

While she spoke, she was oblivious to his growing rage. Torquemada repeatedly shifted his eyes from the queen to father. The priest then turned his back on her with his arms folded over his chest.

"You, as my Father Confessor, will supervise the building of the Cathedral of Isabel."

"Me, an accomplice to Don Isaac's devilish scheme?" he railed, backing away from her to the very edge of the raised platform. "Never!" he breathed with rage.

His eyes darted around the room, his facial muscles twitching uncontrollably. He stepped off the dais clutching his black onyx crucifix which bore a silver figurine of Jesus — the queen's gift to him. It was the only bejewelled ornament he had consented to wear. He yanked it from his neck and threw it toward her. It skidded on the marble floor and smashed into several pieces dislodging the Jesus figurine, which spiraled to rest at Isabel's feet.

"Judas betrayed the Lord for thirty pieces of silver," he shouted. Pointing his finger at her, he thundered, "You, Madam, you now betray Him for three hundred thousand gold pieces. Shame on you!"

Without waiting for her response, he stormed out, slamming the door behind him.

Isabel remained motionless, like a boulder in a raging river, her eyes transfixed on the door Torquemada had slammed. She dropped her head to her chest sobbing bitterly and kneeled to pick up the pieces of the shattered crucifix. She clutched the broken onyx shards in her palm squeezing the jagged stones so hard they cut her clenched fingers, oozing slow drops of blood onto her gown. She remained on her knees refusing the extended hands of those who rushed to help her.

Finally, she stood up. She walked to the desk which held the unsigned Edict of Expulsion. Still clutching pieces of the broken cross in one hand, disregarding the stream of blood branding the scroll, she dipped the feather quill into the ink well and signed the document.

Looking at neither Ferdinand nor father, she ran towards the slammed door bitterly crying, calling for her Father Confessor.

King Ferdinand dismissed the Council of Ministers and departed. No one spoke to father. Don Carlos alone approached with words of sorrow, but Father stood impassive, unresponsive. The young general squeezed father's shoulder and left him alone in the glittering empty throne room where drops of Isabel's blood stained the floor.

A strange sensation came over father. He knew he was in full control of his faculties; he understood what was happening, he could think. But, he was physically stricken, unable to move his feet. Motionless he stared at the empty throne. Finally, he staggered to the courtyard where his feet buckled under him and he collapsed. Falling, he rammed his head against the stone abutment of the massive gate.

Several guards rushed to his side as blood spurted from his head staining his face, his beard, and his robe. They called for his coachman and together lifted him into the carriage.

My family reacted with shock when father finished his story. My mother sobbed; others openly cried, wringing their hands in grief. Aunt Benevita was tearing at her hair as her son, Alfredo, struggled to arrest her hysteria.

I reacted quite differently. I waited for father to continue. I waited for a sequel, expecting him to tell how he reversed the tragedy and saved the situation by adroit maneuvering at the palace. I could not accept father's failure. He always displayed such wisdom, such courage. Where were they now? I thought of his motto: "to be prepared for any eventuality." Surely, having faced Torquemada all these years, he would have been prepared for this.

My illusions were quickly dispelled when he quietly announced, "Nothing further can be done."

He explained that we had two choices: remain in Spain as converts or go into exile.

"Although the Abrabanel family will be excluded from the Edict," he said, "we will join our brethren in exile."

No one questioned his decision.

That night, I did not sleep. None of us did. We sat up talking about father's experience. Like everyone, I was shocked but, unlike the rest, I questioned father's judgment. I said he was hasty in announcing that we would leave Spain with the exiles. I told my brothers that father should continue to press for the Edict's withdrawal rather than encourage Jews to be exiled.

"Maybe the injury to his head affected him?" I asked my mother.

My brothers angrily ridiculed me. I did not argue further with them, but the following day, I went directly to father to question his decision to capitulate to Torquemada. He had no time for me then or in the days following. Whenever I approached him, he was busy with communal affairs, working until late each night. When I finally managed to talk to him, he did what I feared most: with a wave of his hand, he disregarded my objections telling me I was too young to grasp the gravity of the situation.

But I was not to be put off. Several days later, when he went to discuss the disposition of communally-owned property with Abram Senor, I asked to come along. I planned to confront him in the presence of Don Abram, whom I deeply loved and who had often praised my penetrating mind.

When we entered Don Abram's casa, I kissed his hand and bowed my head for his blessings. He, as always, tussled my hair and patted my face. He congratulated me on my selection as apprentice to Alfonso, the Royal Physician, expressing regrets that I would have to forego this great opportunity. I did not reply. Quietly, I waited for the right moment to speak my piece.

"I have two simple questions," I finally spoke up when I saw father fold up his papers ready to leave. "First, why are you accepting the Expulsion as a fait accompli? The Edict will not take effect for four months? Father, you told us that when you were faced with the Edict, all you wanted was to gain time to block Torquemada's plans. Well you have it, four months from the day the edict will be announced. Why are you planning an 'orderly exile' when you should be planning to fight the Edict of Expulsion?"

"What is your second question?" father asked.

"Do you believe that all Jews will follow your example and leave Spain?" I asked. "I think not. I think most will remain even after the Edict. They will feel that it's only a matter of time until Torquemada burns himself out. If that's true, many will remain and they'll need the protection of the Palace, which only you can provide. You told us that the royal decree excluded you from the expulsion. And, that's my second question: Why have you so hastily and, forgive me, so arbitrarily, decided, 'the Abrabanel family will join their brethren in exile'?"

Father looked at Don Abram, inviting him to answer. The old man smiled saying, "The boy is asking some serious questions and he deserves forthright answers."

"Torquemada will not burn himself out," father began. "And the Inquisition will continue long after he is gone. As soon as the Edict goes in effect, Spain will be caught in the vise of the Inquisition. No one will be free of its power."

I retorted, "Torquemada is not the first to stir up hate. We've always been able to ride out the storm."

"There is no comparison between Tomas de Torquemada's plans and anything in the past. The Inquisition is the result of two hundred years of war to reconquer Spain from the Arabs."

Father gave a lengthy dissertation on the Reconquista, saying it must be viewed as Christendom's attempt to free the Iberian Peninsula from Islam's dominance. With the Arab invasion, Islam's influence had penetrated every segment of Spanish civilization. The Reconquest of Spain meant not only the ouster of the Arabs from Spain, but the purging of alien contamination from Spanish faith. "And to Torquemada," father said without rancor or hate, "Jews and Judaism are a contamination and, as such, a serious threat to the purity of Christianity."

"Torquemada didn't issue the Edict; the Queen did," I persisted. "You were always able to convince her. You did so when she refused to finance Captain Colon's sailing. You did so many other times before. Why aren't you fighting her now?"

"Isabel is not only a child of the church, she is a religious zealot," father said. "She's Torquemada's puppet. And that dooms our survival."

"But, the fact is that we have survived even the Martinez riots in Seville. Haven't we?" I asked.

"Comparing the Martinez rioting in one city with Torquemada's demonic plan for the entire realm is not only naive but dangerous," father calmly replied. "The Inquisition will devour everything, including the Spanish Monarchs. As for the

Jews, we will survive. But not in Spain. Anyone remaining in Spain after the effective date of the Expulsion will cease living or will cease living as a Jew. That is why, Sami, I have deliberately, not arbitrarily, chosen an orderly exile."

"And," Don Abram added, "you are mistaken if you believe many Jews will remain in Spain. Our reports from various cities show otherwise."

I wanted to continue, but Don Abram was tired, so we got up to leave.

"My dear boy," Don Abram said as we were getting into our carriage, "I agree with your father's analysis and, of course, with his decision. You may now consider it hasty or arbitrary but one day, when you grow up, you will realize how tragically correct your father is about the power of the Inquisition."

I resented being told again and again that I was young and and not yet grown up. So, when father and I were alone in the carriage, I challenged his 'orderly exile' stating that the two words were mutually exclusive. An 'exile' was a catastrophe — there could not be an 'orderly' catastrophe.

Father said again, "When you grow up, you will understand."

"Assume for a moment that I'm fully grown," I protested. "Make believe that I'm as old as Don Abram and I asked you the same simple question: Don Isaac Abrabanel has beaten Torquemada ten times before, why can't he do it again?"

"You're not only fully grown," father sarcastically said, "but you're fully committed to becoming a physician." I was too hurt to answer father's sarcasm. We sat in silence the rest of the trip.

"Spain is not the only place where you can learn to be a physician," he said when we reached Casa Floridiana. "Wherever we resettle, you will find a physician who will take you on as an apprentice."

"Do you really believe that my desire to study medicine has blinded me?" I asked.

"You are more qualified to answer that than I," said father, walking ahead of me into the house.

All night I thought about our confrontation. I became more agitated by father's reaction. He not only continued considering me immature but he accused me of being selfish, indifferent to our plight. In the morning when my mother came into my room to ask which personal belongings I wanted to take with me when we left Spain, I angrily blurted that leaving Spain was a mistake. She scorned me for saying so and for my temper. I asked her the same questions I had asked father the night before. She replied that she understood my anguish and that was all she would say. But, when I came down from my room, she suggested I go to Segovia to discuss my problem with Asher. I welcomed her suggestion because I sensed she agreed with me. I was convinced Asher would also understand my agony.

Ever since my boyhood in Lisbon, I liked horseback riding. Later, under Don Carlos' training, I excelled in horsemanship and enjoyed the sport. I even won several awards in riding competitions. However, my ride to Segovia that day offered little pleasure. The thought of enlisting Asher to help me confront father was embarrassing. The long, hard ride took from early morning until late afternoon. I stopped only once to rest my horse.

When I arrived at Asher's home I was thrilled to see him in the courtyard but annoyed when he said, "I have to attend several meetings but I'll soon return."

Before riding off, he asked me to make myself comfortable in his home, promising that we would spend the entire evening together.

I was shocked by his small, bare apartment. The sitting room held neither a table nor chairs; the kitchen had only a few dishes and pots. Even the bed where I lay down had no sheets or pillow cases. I had not realized that Asher's existence was so Spartan.

When he returned, I asked, "Why is your home so bare?"

"I'm leaving Segovia tomorrow," he replied.

"When are you coming back," I asked.

"Coming back?" he replied. "I'm getting out of Spain."

"So, you're also preparing for an 'orderly exile'," I said and, without waiting for his response, I pelted him with questions: "Why are we rushing into exile? Why isn't father fighting Torquemada to get the Edict withdrawn? What will happen to the Jews who will remain in Spain? Who will care for them? Has no one questioned the wisdom of father's plan?"

"Your father's appraisal of the finality of the situation and his plan for the immediate exile of the Jews from Spain were unanimously agreed to at our Council of Elders," Asher replied.

"'Unanimously agreed'," I mimicked him. "Who would dare to disagree with Don Isaac Abrabanel! Father's opinion is law. His voice is the voice of Sinai."

When Asher did not respond I pleaded that I had a problem with the decision to go into exile and that he was the only one I could talk to about this matter. I reminded him of the days we shared intimate secrets.

"Asher, don't be overwhelmed by father's awesome power," I pleaded. "Talk to me like we used to talk."

"You are still bothered by your father's power," Asher taunted.

I resented the insinuation. Neither of us spoke for several anguished moments.

"Well, there are three options open to us," Asher broke the long silence. "One. We can submit to conversion. Two. We can die as martyrs. Three. We can leave Spain forever."

"But there's a fourth," I angrily countered, "we can stay on and fight Torquemada."

"And in the process we'll have thousands of martyrs and hundreds of thousands of converts?" Asher challenged.

"If Don Isaac Abrabanel remains in Spain, there will be neither converts nor martyrs," I retorted.

"The Abrabanels are no guarantee," Asher said. "They had their share of converts, like Samuel Abrabanel, your great grandfather."

"What! Samuel Abrabanel, a converso!" I shrieked.

"Yes," Asher replied, "Your great grandfather, whom you're named after, Samuel Abrabanel, former Royal Treasurer, was converted during the Martinez rioting in Seville. He was living there as a marrano until his escape to Lisbon."

"My great grandfather, a marrano!" I protested. "I never heard that."

"It's a well kept secret. Your father still considers it a stain on the Abrabanel family." Asher embraced me saying he realized this came as a shock. He quietly assured me that my great grandfather had reverted to Judaism immediately upon arrival in Portugal. I sat down on the edge of the bed hurt and confused by Asher's revelation. I was not attentive to Asher's continued assurances about my great grandfather's motives.

"Your father is right," I heard Asher say. "He wants to avoid a repetition of the tragedy which occurred in Seville."

"Yet the Jews of Seville survived the Martinez riots," I calmly responded, "and the respected Jewish families of Seville are still thriving there, a hundred years later."

"What's blinding you, Sami?" Asher said in desperation.

"Nothing, Asher," I said, looking at his empty home, "For the first time, I'm beginning to see the situation more clearly."

"What are you talking about?" Asher asked.

"Father's decision was faulty," I replied. "He ordered the Jews into exile because he was ashamed of his grandfather's conversion. Under these circumstances, father couldn't possibly judge the situation objectively."

Asher ridiculed my theory, chastised me for my disrespect for father, and sternly commanded me, "You must follow your father's advice."

"His judgment was flawed," I shot back, "If my grandfather

were a marrano, I also couldn't be objective."

"Do you know how much I trust your father's judgment?" Asher said, "At his request, I'm leaving tomorrow to contact other European Jewish communities in Europe to seek help in resettling our exiles."

"You're going into exile even before the Edict is proclaimed!" I sneered. "Have you given up entirely on our ability to survive as we have so often done in the past?"

"There's little time left, and there's much to do," Asher replied. "Your disloyalty to your father does not alter the hard facts of the impending danger."

He abruptly put an end to our conversation, pointing to a sofa where I was to sleep and leaving me alone in the room.

I slept well for the first time since the problem with the Edict unfolded. That night, I decided to make my own plans without fearing father or being ashamed of opposing him.

That morning Asher and I parted for the last time. He embraced me and, holding back tears, said, "Remember, you are an Abrabanel. Never blemish our name."

I turned my back on Asher even before he drove off in his carousel. I felt like shouting, "I don't want to be an Abrabanel."

When I returned to Toledo, I decided it was useless to argue any further with father. Instead, I headed for Don Alfonso's dispensary. Alfonso greeted me, surprised that I was not preparing to leave with my family. I told him of my discussions with father and Asher. Much to my pleasure, he agreed with me, shrugging off the Inquisition as a passing phenomenon. He said that father had always exaggerated its power. To prove it, Don Alfonso noted that, though he was a known heretic, he was untouched by the Inquisition. Its agents had never invaded the sanctuary of his dispensary.

"As long as you are serious about becoming a physician," he

said, "you may stay at the dispensary with the other apprentices. You'll be safe."

A few days later, on the first of April, the Edict of Expulsion was made public. Copies of the royal proclamation were posted on the doors of every synagogue. That day, schools were closed, shops were abandoned, all social and civic activity came to a halt. There were no tears, no despair, no grief, only an eerie bustle in the streets and alleyways in the *juderia* as people were on the move selling, bartering, or packing their belongings.

Father began disposing of his property early and in public so others would see and follow his example. He repeatedly said he wanted to make certain that, on the effective date, four months later, no one would be held back by a pending transaction. He travelled the length and breadth of Spain announcing that the fate of Jews who would remain in Spain would be catastrophic. The aged Abram Senor, though feeble, stood at father's side to emphasize that the Edict of Expulsion would be final and that no one should jeopardize his life by clinging to false hope.

The exile became an instant reality. It certainly was orderly.

I observed, with annoyance, how families were trading their possessions for anything movable. A house was traded for a horse, a vineyard for a wagon, a bed for a bundle of clothing. Since gold was specifically prohibited, the exiles exchanged their property for anything portable.

Everyone followed father's example. Everyone, except me.

I began my apprenticeship with Don Alfonso soon after the Edict was proclaimed. His encouragement helped me overcome any doubts I may have had. I feared only the moment when I would have to face father with my decision.

On the Festival of Shavuoth, when we read the Ten Commandments in our synagogue, the exhortation, "Honor thy father and thy mother," stung me. The following day, I walked into father's library and, as I entered, I heard him say to someone, "It is all finished, then. We shall leave in the morning."

Father introduced me to the nobleman from Cordoba who had just purchased our home. The new owner graciously thanked father and then turned to me, saying, "What beautiful memories a boy like you must have, growing up in so beautiful a home."

"Well, it's all arranged," father said to me after he escorted the nobleman to his carriage. "Tomorrow we take our first steps out of Spain."

"Ten weeks before the final date?" I asked.

"It will take that long to make the trip," he said using his finger to trace the route along a map spread on his desk. "We head from Toledo to the port of Valencia, and board a ship to Italy."

He pointed to several stop-over points where he had arranged for us to stay on our way across the peninsula to Spain's east coast.

"Father," I said as my last appeal to him, "there are still ten weeks. Can't something be done to fight the Edict."

Without looking up from the map, father waved me off.

"Father," I asked again, putting my hand on his and looking straight into his eyes, "could I take advantage of the specification in the Edict of Expulsion which excludes you and your family from expulsion."

"You can't be serious!" father replied, stroking my hand. "I know what it means to be uprooted, but I received permission from the Cortes of Naples to live there and also arranged for a home. I doubt it will be this kind of a home, but it is safe in Italy."

"I will be safe in Spain, too," I replied. "I will claim exemption from the Edict."

He grasped my hand; I felt him tremble. Withdrawing my hand from his, I announced, "I'm not leaving Spain."

He was probably as shocked hearing these words as I was speaking them. The confrontation was strange and unfamiliar for both of us. He stared at me for a long, agonizing moment. He did not rail at me, did not exhort me, did not denigrate me. He looked at me as though he saw me for the first time.

"I have been so occupied preparing for everybody's orderly exile, I neglected my own son," father said.

"An 'orderly exile'," I interrupted, stressing the words which had become so odious to me. "That's exactly what I've been trying to talk to you about since you first ordered it."

"The queen ordered it," father said, "Not I."

"You might as well have," I said. "You accepted the Edict without a fight, before it was even published. Asher left before it was even proclaimed and you're leaving before the effective date. You didn't even appear at the Cortes of Toledo when it was brought up. The Cortes would have helped you plan some counter measures against the Inquisition."

The relative ease with which I spoke surprised me but father's reaction surprised me more. He came to my side of the table, put his arm over my shoulders, and took me back to his side of the desk. He spoke as though he were teaching a class and responding to a single student who had simply asked an academic question. He spoke softly without ridicule.

"You ask about the Cortes," father said pointing to the map, "Here, at Teruel, the Council closed the city gates to the oncoming Inquisition mob. Here at Aragon, the Cortes actually organized armed resistance and declared a state of siege against the Inquisitors. In Seville, members of the Cortes joined with the powerful barons in an alliance against the Inquisition."

His fingers criss-crossed the map of Spain as he pinpointed the march of the Inquisition.

"Everywhere the story was the same," he concluded. "The opposition of the Cortes, even with the help of the nobility, melted away as the Inquisition asserted itself. Today it is the supreme power in Spain. The Edict was issued by Isabel in her religious zealotry, but it is not an ordinary royal proclamation. It is the Inquisition's bellowing roar of victory over the Royal Monarchs."

"Yet the same Monarchs gave you immunity from the Edict."

"Yes, I know what you're thinking," father said. "You asked me several times why I could not stay behind to help Jews who will remain in Spain."

"That's right," I said, "why don't you use the queen's guarantee of immunity."

"Listen to me, my son, the good will of a monarch is a as secure as stem of this flower," he said, snapping a stem he yanked from the vase on the table. "God willing, we will soon be safe from this rage."

"If God exists," I asked, "why does He do this to us."

I walked over to the large bay window and looked out at the landscaped terrace.

Nothing stirred except a huge philodendron leaf nodding before a passing breeze. All was calm in the garden, but inside of me turbulence raged against God, against father.

"Let me try to answer your question," father said. "First, it is the deeds of man, not the act of God, that brings evil into the world. Second, your question is valid. It's even found in the Bible, 'O God, my God, why hast thou forsaken me?' It is a legitimate cry, a challenge to God's apparent injustice."

"'O God, my God, Why hast thou forsaken me?'" I repeated, "That's it! That's what I'm asking."

"My son," father replied, "there is no answer. Faith cannot be reduced to logical formuli. But, merely asking the question does not mean that God has, in fact, forsaken us."

When I told father I could not follow his reasoning, he began an explanation, but I interrupted him, "What about your grandfather, Samuel? Why did he convert?"

Father acted as though he did not hear the question. He continued expounding on the existence of good and evil. I pressed on, accusing him of allowing the shame of his grandfather's conversion affect his decision to chose exile instead of resistance to Torquemada.

"Father," I said, "I am not joining you. I am convinced that the Inquisition will pass before long and, with or without God, Torquemada will be defeated."

"Sami, I plead with you. I beg you. Come with us. Your life is at stake."

"It is not!" I retorted. "Alfonso assures me that his dispensary will be my sanctuary against the Inquisitors."

"Don Alfonso is an outstanding physician," father said, "but he knows little about the Inquisition and less about the looming political upheaval."

"You have exaggerated the power of the Inquisition because of Samuel Abrabanel," I repeated.

"Stop! Stop this debate," father begged. "You will not survive in Spain, with or without the immunity clause."

Tears welled up in his eyes. I had never seen father cry. He suddenly seemed weak, beaten. He moved to embrace me but I withdrew.

"I shall be as safe here in Toledo as you will be in Naples," I said quite calmly. "And, thousands like me will remain here. We will not be driven away by fear."

"I beg you, Sami, come to Naples with us. If my assessment is wrong, we will return to Toledo in three months."

"Under no circumstance will I go into exile, father," I said. "But I promise you, at the slightest hint of danger, I will make my way out of Spain."

My mother walked into the library and heard what I was saying. She burst into tears. She too pleaded with me, but I steadfastly refused to submit. To allay her fears, I said that Don Alfonso assured me he would bring me to Naples if my life were ever imperiled. I hugged her and kissed her, repeating Don Alfonso's assurance.

When she realized my mind was made up, she surprised me by helping pack my clothing. Then, she accompanied me to the dispensary where she confronted Don Alfonso and made him repeat his promise to look after my safety.

She stayed a while with me at the dispensary, reviewing my needs with Don Alfonso. He recognized her anxiety, assuring her that no harm would come to me because the Inquisition had never invaded the privacy of his clinic. He promised that at the first hint of danger, he would personally escort me to Naples.

I was proud of Don Alfonso, proud of the way he assured my mother. His repeated guarantees made parting from my family much less stressful. A few days later, father came to the infirmary to inform me that he postponed his departure to contact Don Carlos, who was with the troops in the north of Spain. Father asked him to look after my safety. Don Carlos' response was that my well-being would be his responsibility. Before leaving, father also told me he spoke about me to his friend, Emilio Manzano, suggesting that I should maintain contact with him and his family.

Thus assured by Don Alfonso, by Don Carlos, and by some of father's close friends, my parents left Spain convinced of my safety.

Sacred Sword

3

I was safe for exactly ten weeks.

Then, on the first day of August, the Day of Terror burst upon the city.

The once-peaceful city of Toledo became a boiling cauldron. Its serene gentry turned into a religiously-crazed mob roaming the streets in a maddened search for Jews. No one, neither father's friends nor even the militia, could withstand the terror unleashed by the Inquisition.

On the effective date of the Expulsion, the *juderia* was emptied of Jews. Only a handful of the sick and elderly remained. They literally threw themselves at the doors of the churches begging to be baptized.

I had spent the morning away from the dispensary and, because of the sudden outbreak of rioting in the street, I could not make my way back.

When I asked father's closest friend, Emilio Manzano, who helped launch Captain Colon on his mission, to let me hide in his barn, he turned away saying I was a marked man. He feared he would jeopardize himself by helping me. Another friend of father's even tried to hand me over to the authorities to ingratiate himself with the Inquisition. I secretly made my way to Don Carlos' home where I was told he was with the troops in the south of Spain and where I learned that the king's militia had become an extension of the Inquisition.

I could not move freely; it was dangerous for me to be seen in the streets. Alfonso was my only hope. I stealthily made my way to the dispensary but, as I came close, I saw there were more Inquisition agents milling about that area than anywhere else. I did not dare get closer. Obviously, Don Alfonso's clinic was no longer a safe sanctuary.

I then decided I would have to make my own escape.

I hurried to the river bank and hid in the tall weeds near a bridge hoping to flee through the farmlands. But, from afar, I saw that the militia heavily guarded the bridge. At about midnight, I made my way to the small islet where Asher and I once played. Fortunately it was deserted. I shed my coat and shoes and, plunging into the water, began to swim to the other side of the river. When I neared the shore, I heard sentries shouting to one another to seize me. I frantically made my back, luckily without being discovered. I was exhausted but could not stop. I ran aimlessly away from the river bank.

Then, I remembered the dry well where Asher and I used to hide. I ran toward it with wild abandon, quickly scaling down to its bottom, hoping that I was not discovered. Hearing no one around the well, I fell asleep, utterly exhausted. I remained hidden in it for more than a week, coming out only at night to search for food.

On one of those nights I succeeded in meeting Don Alfonso outside the home of a patient he regularly visited. When he spotted me, he told me to remain hidden until he returned with his closed carriage. At last, he transported me to his home without being noticed by the agents. That night, he gave me the first meal I had eaten in ten days. As I gulped my food, he told me that he could offer me no sanctuary nor could he deliver me to Naples as he had promised my parents. He admitted his strong guilt at being unable to help me get out of Spain.

"I can only let you stay here tonight," he said.

"I tried get to Don Carlos," I said, "but he's away with with the troops."

"Well, at least, I can help you with that," Don Alfonso said.

"I can contact Don Carlos and apprise him of your predicament."

Alfonso was in his late sixties and although his hair was completely grey, he appeared much younger. He was tall, thin, with a swarthy gypsy-like complexion. His scraggly moustache and small pointed beard gave him an austere appearance. An intense person, he always gave the impression that he was eager to get on with whatever he was doing, that he had no time for talk or trivia. He was harsh with subordinates, and would readily insult them with biting criticism. He displayed this impatience even with the nobility, many of whom he knew intimately. Only when he was treating the sick was he gentle and compassionate, and his warmth would shine through his steel-grey eyes.

That night, he treated me as a patient. He was sympathetic and friendly. We talked much of the night about the dreadful changes in Spain. He reminisced about his rise to his present position, proud that it had little to do with his noble family in Valladolid. He claimed he earned his reputation as a skilled physician by achieving spectacular medical results. His healing procedures, especially his surgery, had become legendary and his dispensary had become Spain's most renowned medical institution. If he could not help to unite me with my parents as he had promised, he said, he would help me to become a good physician. Despite my fears, I was glad he said that, telling him that I was most eager to emulate him.

I felt very close to Alfonso until he showed me to my room where he quietly said, "In the morning, you will turn yourself over to the Inquisition."

"What!" I cried with disbelief.

"You will go there to seek confirmation of your immunity from the Edict of Expulsion," Alfonso ordered. "I have taken up your problem with important personages and with the Minister of Justice. I know that your request will be fully supported by the

Council of Ministers. When you get that immunity, you can continue as my apprentice."

I knew he would not have suggested such a dangerous course unless he had assurances of the "important personages".

Don Alfonso awakened me before dawn and, under the cover of darkness, drove me in his carriage to the Fort of Madrasa, the Inquisition's headquarters. Before leaving me at the outer gate, he again assured me he had alerted the Minister of Justice and would also contact Don Carlos. He turned me over to a sentry who nodded to Alfonso as though he had been expecting me. Without being told who I was, the sentry called my name and ordered me to follow him. For a moment, I wondered whether Alfonso had also contacted the Inquisition.

The sentry lead me through the old Moorish fort, across a quadrangle, through an alley into a magnificently landscaped courtyard separating two buildings.

The garden that filled the courtyard had tall cypress trees surrounding a pool with a huge statue of a bronze dolphin spouting water into the pool. On the left stood a church with a massive Byzantine arch inscribed in gilded lettering, "Church of Christ the Redeemer". The Moors had probably erected its two towering minarets as a mosque hundreds of years earlier. Now, the minarets were capped by mammoth silver crosses which shimmered in the early morning haze.

The fortress-like building on the right bore the sign: "Supreme and General Council of the Inquisition". It was the supreme religious authority in the realm, called 'Suprema' by the populace. The building housed the offices of Tomas de Torquemada, the Holy Tribunal of the Inquisition, and prison cells for those awaiting trial.

Ordinarily hundreds of people would be waiting to be interrogated by the Inquisition but, because it was early, the compound was deserted.

The sentry led me into the Inquisition building where a

hooded monk, seated behind a long wooden table, called my name saying, "We've been expecting you."

"I have come to receive confirmation of my immunity from the Edict of Expulsion," I replied with as much confidence as I could muster. My voice echoed eerily in the large empty hall.

The monk did not reply. Instead, he ordered the sentry, "Stand behind the prisoner so that he will not try to escape again."

"I protest being treated like a prisoner," I announced. "I came here on the advice of Don Alfonso, the court physician, and of my own free will."

The monk did not even look up. He continued writing into an open ledger.

I called out again with an even greater tone of authority, "The Abrabanel family is excluded from the Edict of Expulsion. I should be allowed to remain in Spain. I request written confirmation, so that I may work as apprentice to my master physician."

The monk again said nothing.

When he finished writing, he ordered the sentry to put a blue band on my right arm and place me in a holding cell "until his case will be decided by the Holy Tribunal."

The sentry led me out of the building, through an archway, down a long flight of stairs, and along a narrow subterranean corridor. He opened the door to a dark cell and shoved me in. Then I heard the clanging of the door shut behind me and the clicks of the bolted lock.

I shouted to the sentry that he need not lock the cell since I expected to be taken out of there soon by the Minister of Justice.

I surveyed the cell thinking of prisoners who had probably languished there. The bare room had a low ceiling with a muddy clay floor. A streak of daylight, entering from a slit in the shuttered window, was its only source of light. A cave-like opening on the opposite side was blocked by an iron gate. I paced the cell, waiting to be called to the Holy Tribunal. Certain that Don Alfonso had arranged for my immunity, I remained standing rather than sit on the muddy floor. By late afternoon, my feet grew weary and I tried to attract attention by climbing up to shout through the window. I saw no one.

Towards evening, I began to worry: Could some official have misplaced my request? Was Alfonso so occupied at the clinic that he neglected to make the necessary arrangements? Did he forget to contact Don Carlos?

An entire day had passed; still I had not been called. It turned dark. The light from the overhead window had long vanished. I was losing my confidence and my strength. I slipped down to the soggy floor and tried to sleep but in addition to my tears, hunger now gnawed my stomach. As the night wore on, I searched for a dry spot on to stretch out but no matter where I lay, I was awakened by seeping water. I crawled around most of the night, futilely searching for some place to rest my body. Then I forgot my pain, my hunger, and my discomfort when it occurred to me that not only had I become a prisoner of the Inquisition but that this might be my permanent punishment: to be left to die. When daylight streaked in from the window slit, I was thoroughly exhausted.

A loud crashing noise coming from the direction of iron gate startled me. A tall man, in uniform, was clanging the heavy iron chains opening the gate to my cell.

"Hey," he shouted, motioning me to come forward, "you're lucky. Your case comes up to the Tribunal today."

I tried to stand. My feet were unsteady and I had difficulty balancing. The soldier propped me up, helping me to my feet and leading me through a labyrinth of corridors to a windowless grotto where the only light came from the burning torches in wall brackets. I followed the soldier into the dungeon, where hands stretched out of narrow openings in rows of cells to receive the morning meal. When a guard passed me carrying a pot of food, its smell sharpened my hunger and I pleaded for something to eat. My guard paid no attention, hurrying me on through other corridors.

He reminded me that my case might be heard any moment.

Thus encouraged I strained to keep up as he marched me up and down various passage ways. But I was ravishingly hungry. When other guards passed carrying prisoners' food, I reached for a slice of bread and immediately felt the sharp snap of a whip across the back of my hand.

"Don't tamper with other people's food," the guard bellowed pulling me away from the pile of food. "Come, we can't keep the judges waiting."

Staggering and dizzy, I followed him through an endless maze of dark halls and up and down stairs. At the time, I thought of reporting this treatment to the the Minister of Justice. The hope of getting to the Tribunal kept me going beyond my strength. When I stumbled and fell to the floor, several guards helped me to my feet forcing me to march on. I finally collapsed.

I heard the guards talking to me, but I could not understand them. They revived me by pouring cold water over me and — wet, muddy, hungry, and exhausted — I stumbled behind them. At last, they brought me into a large room where the sudden bright sunlight blinded me. I could vaguely discern the features of three judges seated on a raised dais. One of them read the charges against me, but his voice sounded hollow. I could neither understand nor comply with the shouted orders to stand and face them. Two guards lifted me up but the moment they let go, I collapsed, my body draped over the iron railing between me and the dais. I remained in that position, my head almost reaching the floor.

In my drooped position, I felt the blood rushing back to head. I tried to sort my thoughts. Who were they? What was I doing here? What am I supposed to say?

"You have forfeited your life," I heard someone say. "The penalty for any Jew still in Spain beyond the first day of August, is death."

I mumbled something and the guards again lifted me and helped me stand erect.

"You are a Jew, are you not?" a voice called out to me. I

looked around. Suddenly I remembered the cell, the sleepless night, even my hunger.

"You are a Jew? Are you not?"

I heard the question a second time but now I saw the speaker — a judge in ecclesiastical robe. Three of them were seated at an elevated rostrum draped with a banner bearing the Inquisition's insignia. Seated below, not far from me, another person nodded to me, encouraging me to reply.

Coming out of my stupor, I called out, "I am the son of Don Isaac Abrabanel. And, by the queen's decree, I have been excluded from the Edict of Expulsion."

My response gave rise to a heated debate between the judges and the person sitting next to me, whom I finally recognized as the Minister of Justice. I could not follow the legal argument but I heard one judge state, "It cannot mean anything else. Only if Don Isaac had remained in Spain, would members of his family be entitled to immunity from the Edict of Expulsion. Since he is no longer here, no one, not even his son, can lay claim to that exclusion."

The minister argued, "If a civil court orders payment to two claimants and should one of them absent himself, or die, or disappear, surely the remaining claimant cannot be denied his share of the payment."

"What is applicable in a civil court is not applicable in a specific royal decree," the judge replied intimating that the Minister of Justice had no status in such a case.

The minister insisted that in every case coming before the Holy Tribunal, secular officials were authorized to argue the legal aspects for or against the accused.

They kept arguing until the presiding judge ruled that this legal point would require clarification by the queen. He declared a recess in the proceedings to allow a review of my case by Her Royal Highness.

As I was led out of the court room I passed the Minister of

Justice who whispered to me that Don Alfonso sent him. He patted my hand and said, "You are now safe."

The guard lead me into a small room adjoining the court, where I was fed and ordered to await the court's decision. I fell asleep on the narrow bench grateful to Don Alfonso and confident again of the outcome of my case.

At dawn, Don Carlos suddenly stormed into my room and roused me from sleep. He ordered the sentry to leave and then informed me that the queen was coming back to Toledo in order to conclude my trial.

"By tomorrow morning," Don Carlos said, "you will be declared guilty of remaining in Spain beyond the expulsion date. You will be condemned to die."

I began to repeat the argument I had earlier heard in court but he cut me short. I saw in him no trace of the friend and mentor I once thought him to be.

"I'm not here to debate with you," he said sternly, "There's very little time. You must save you life."

"How," I asked

"Convert!" he barked out, "I have it all set up."

I was stunned. I sat immobile, not knowing what to say. I thought of my great grandfather, Samuel, of my discussion with Asher, of my father's warning that no Jew could survive in Spain.

"Move!" Don Carlos commanded and when I remained sitting, steeped in thought, he pulled at my shoulders and, slapped my face several times to arouse me out of my seeming lethargy, he shouted, "On your toes."

He hurried me down a flight of stairs and across the courtyard to the Church of Christ the Redeemer where he called to the old priest to proceed with the conversion. The priest shuffled slowly past the general explaining that the ceremony of conversion requires time but that he would try to hasten it.

Don Carlos waited patiently while the priest performed the conversion and, as part of the rites, asked me to state my new

Sacred Sword

name. Don Carlos, in turn, asked the priest for his name.

"My name is Alberto, Alberto di Cadiz," he replied

"That's his new name, Alberto," Don Carlos said.

Pleased with the choice, the priest signed the baptismal certificate with a flourish. Don Carlos snapped the document and hastened me out of the church. Outdoors, I noticed the first streaks of daylight pierced the darkened skies.

"Where are we going?" I asked trailing behind Don Carlos.

"To Torquemada," he replied.

When I hesitated for a moment, he turned around and grasped my hand jerking me forward. He strutted past the statue of the dolphin into the Suprema building and asked the monk in the outer corridor for Torquemada's office. The monk quickly escorted us up the stairs and knocked on the door of an office. I was surprised to see Tomas de Torquemada open the door. At first he, too, was taken aback saying that he was surprised to see me, but he extended his hands to both of us welcoming us into his office.

"I was told you were here, Carlos," Torquemada said, "and I expected you would visit me, but I did not think you would bring him."

I had never been so close to Torquemada, although I had seen him many times on public occasions. From a distance, he always appeared tall, austere. Standing in front of him, I saw for the first time that he was only of medium height, thin as a reed. His eyes were a deceptively soft brown; his hair white as snow; his clean-shaven face stern and unsmiling. He was well into his seventies but looked much younger. He certainly moved with a young man's agility.

Don Carlos began an apology bringing me and for coming at such an early hour, but Torquemada put him at ease saying he was always rises before daybreak.

"You might be interested in what my judges told me about the boy," he said pointing to me.

He opened a door to an adjacent room, introduced the three

men seated at a table, and asked one of them to repeat his report.

"We knew that the Abrabanel boy had not left Spain with the exiles," one judge said speaking as though I were not present. "We also knew that a month earlier he had taken up residence in the Caldera with the other apprentices. He then vanished, leaving no trace. But we expected him, like other Jews who remained in Spain, to seek baptism in a church. Every church was alerted to report his presence and special guards were set up at Don Alfonso's clinic. When Alfonso delivered him to us, the boy pleaded immunity from the Edict of Expulsion. We decided to seek clarification of his status."

Torquemada told Don Carlos he would personally make the presentation to the queen on behalf of the Inquisition.

"By tomorrow, the boy will be stripped of his self-declared immunity," he said. "May God have mercy on him."

I fell to his feet pleading for mercy. Don Carlos ordered me to rise and when I did, he asked the Inquisitor General to speak with him privately. Torquemada obliged, instructing the three judges to wait in the chapel adjoining his office. I started to leave, too, but Don Carlos told me to stay since my future was to be discussed. Torquemada did not object but told Don Carlos it would be futile to intercede in my behalf since it would be to no avail. Don Carlos admitted that was his purpose, but said he also would use this opportunity to reach an agreement about their mutual interests in the newly conquered territories.

"I have just returned from Granada where I reorganized my troops," Don Carlos began, "and I was told the Inquisition is sending its agents into the occupied territories. I suggest that we reach an understanding of each other's mission so there will be no clashes between the agents and the soldiers."

"My agents are not fighters," Torquemada replied. "They will not interfere with your work."

"Why must your agents be there?" Don Carlos asked.

Torquemada replied that the Inquisition must be on the alert, against contamination of faith in those areas which had for so long been under the Moslem rule.

"Contamination?" Don Carlos asked.

"Most assuredly. Contamination and perversion of Christian faith," Torquemada replied and, pausing to sit down at his desk, he asked, "General, I want to ask you a question of a military nature. Five hundred years ago the Arabs invaded Spain. How could the invaders have taken over an entire country so rapidly and subjugate it so completely and for so long?"

"Brilliant military maneuvers and superbly efficient civil administration," Don Carlos replied. "We teach it in our military academies."

"Your teachings are wrong," Torquemada replied. "Our defeat was caused by the Jews. They welcomed the Arabs as liberators, giving them an easy victory."

"Nonsense, unsubstantiated fantasy," Don Carlos replied.

Torquemada said he did not wish to argue military policy but he stressed the utter defeat of Catholicism under the Arab occupation. He pointed out that churches were converted to mosques; that there were mass conversions to Islam; that Arab influences had infiltrated into, and totally dominated, Spanish culture. "And that, too, was facilitated by the Jews," Torquemada concluded, "They established the precedent of discrediting the Catholic faith."

"No, Father, that is sheer nonsense," Don Carlos replied.

"The Jews were in league with the Arabs," Torquemada continued speaking slowly, accentuating every phrase, "polluting our faith because Judaism and Christianity are natural enemies."

Don Carlos repeated that all this was false and began a defence of the Jews but Torquemada cut him off.

"Do you know how many Christian families are married to Jews?" Torquemada asked rhetorically. "I do not know of a single family that is without Jewish blood. This Jewish blood is in the conversos. They must be watched as well trained to be faithful to their new religion. That, Carlos, is the function of the Inquisition."

Don Carlos asked, "Is this not function of the priests in churches? After all, the priests minister to us from birth to death."

"The priests!" Torquemada grumbled. "They have all become bell ringers, interested only in fashionable services, gaudy churches, outward appearances. Our concern is with the inner soul. My agents are the cleansers of the soul of Spain. And, that is why they are coming to Granada."

Don Carlos said, "As long as the Inquisition does not interfere with the army, my troops will not hinder your agents."

The Inquisitor General reminded Don Carlos that the agents of the Inquisition are dedicated and disciplined. "General, do not be concerned about them interfering with your army. My agents follow orders," Torquemada said.

"Father, your organizational talents are admirable. Had you selected the battle field as your arena, you would have been a great military leader," Don Carlos said and smiled.

"I know you mean that as a compliment," Torquemada said. "But I also know that you are really alluding to what people say about my agents. That they are spies, ruthless, blood-thirsty."

"No, I was not alluding to that," Don Carlos said, "I was referring to the exceptional leadership you've demonstrated in maintaining a tight control and a strict code of discipline within your ranks."

"In your army," Torquemada replied, "discipline is a matter of life and death. With us, it is a matter of eternal life or eternal death."

"Why, then, the public floggings? Why the autos-da-fe?" Don Carlos asked.

"You should read the Bible," Torquemada said. "'If a man abideth not with Me, cast him into a fire and he is burned.' That is what Christ said."

"I always looked on Christ as a shepherd guiding his flock," Don Carlos said.

"Not as a butcher who leads them to slaughter," Torquemada

Sacred Sword

interrupted. "Is that what you mean?"

"It's not what I say," Don Carlos said. "It's what the people say. To them, 'Inquisition' is synonymous with 'brutality'".

"You are not the first to question the use of force in the safeguarding of faith," Torquemada replied. "You must read Saint Augustine on the meaning of love of God which requires one to use any measure, even death, to demonstrate that love. We therefore teach that tolerating heresy is, itself, heretical."

Torquemada praised Queen Isabel as the only ruler who recognized the spread of heresy in Spain and empowered him to take all measures to expunge it. "We all know about the queen's zeal," Don Carlos said, "but let me ask you another question: What about the non-Catholics, the Moors and the Jews. How can you punish them for rejecting what they never accepted?"

"The Jew is the personification of Satan and the source of all heresy," Torquemada replied and then turning to me, he added, "For eight years I pressed for the expulsion of this evil from Spain and for eight years one person stood in my way: your father. Don Isaac! He and he alone frustrated my plan. And, Carlos, by defending him you are doing Satan's work."

I was petrified. How could Don Carlos possibly save me from a man so infected with hate?

Don Carlos quietly said that he had spent eight years with Don Isaac and he had never heard him challenge catholic faith.

"Furthermore, in the campaign for Granada," Don Carlos said, "it was Don Isaac Abrabanel, Sami's father, who helped establish our faith in the conquered territories."

"Nonsense!" Torquemada shouted.

"Don Isaac, your 'Satan'," Don Carlos said calmly, "provided the financing for the rebuilding of the churches there. Don Isaac helped to put up the silver cross atop the Alahambra. Don Isaac supervised the disposition of all the mosques converting them into churches."

"Be careful, Carlos," Torquemada said menacingly, "your

Sacred Sword

defense of Don Isaac may be another act of heresy."

"Another act of heresy?" Don Carlos asked.

Torquemada then accused him of blatant heresy in having helped the Moriscos to escape during the reconquest of Granada.

"The Moriscos, like the Jewish conversos, were catholics. They were converted and taken into the church. Letting them return to Africa, as you did, is worse than heresy. It is promoting heresy," Torquemada said and then added menacingly, "Even though you are a hero of Spain, I may bring you before the Holy Tribunal."

"Tomas de Torquemada, don't threaten me!" Don Carlos retorted, grasping his sword's handle. "You and your agents may strike terror in the heart of every Spaniard, but don't underestimate the power of the army. It's the army that keeps Spain united. Without it, we will again be divided into hundreds of splinter groups, easy prey to another invader. If you or your agents threaten my men, I will run you off the land as I did the Moors."

Torquemada warned Don Carlos of the consequences of such talk and reminded him that the Inquisition must cleanse the faith no matter who pollutes it.

"Cleanse the faith?" Don Carlos taunted, "How many times has the Inquisition confiscated a land only at the behest of the throne? How many times have you personally ordered an auto-defe when the Crown's property was involved? Is this the religious cleansing you were so anxious to achieve?"

Torquemada winced. He clenched his fists, obviously stung by Don Carlos words. The two men stared silently at each other. I knew that my presence embarrassed Torquemada and that this would worsen my plight.

"Father, forgive me," Don Carlos said, suddenly cringing and bowing before the Inquisitor General. "I did not come here to quarrel with you. I came to ask you a personal favor."

"What is it Carlos," Torquemada replied, chastising him for his arrogance but adding that he now welcomed the humility he was showing. "It's about this boy," Don Carlos said, placing his arm over my shoulder.

"The queen will decide," he said. "She will preside at the hearing."

"She will rule in your favor," Don Carlos interrupted. "He will be denied immunity."

"Then it is no longer a matter for the Inquisition. He will be turned over to the secular officials and they will decide the fate of the Abrabanel boy."

"Abrabanel no longer exists," Don Carlos said producing the baptismal certificate. "He was baptized this morning."

Torquemada scanned the certificate and replied that the perfunctory conversion by the old priest did not change the status of the case.

"His name is now Alberto," Don Carlos pressed, "Alberto di Cadiz. I helped him. The boy is now a converso and I can no longer help him. I beg you, as a favor to me, give him a chance to live."

Torquemada's anger subsided especially when he looked at Don Carlos who was still standing with his head bowed and his hands reaching over to touch Torquemada's robe.

"As a favor to you, I grant your request," Torquemada said. "He will be treated as any other converso. But, I will never forget that he is an Abrabanel and he will be watched."

"He is in your hands, Father," Don Carlos said thanking Torquemada.

Don Carlos quickly took me back to the Judicial chambers. Before leaving me in that small room, he warned, "Never forget Torquemada's threat. My beloved Sami, you would be inviting your own death."

I thanked him for saving me, asking him whether he could help me get out of Spain.

He shook his head violently explaining that I was now Torquemada's ward.

"Don't ever forget, you're in his hands." Don Carlos said as he bent down hugging and kissing me, saying softly, "Alberto di Cadiz, you are entirely on your own."

My trial at Madrasa Fortress was brief. The judges asked me no further questions. I felt like someone else was on trial. When they called my name, I did not respond.

"Alberto di Cadiz," a judge called out again and again until I realized that he was summoning me.

I stood and faced the Holy Tribunal.

"For the moment, you are free to go," the judge announced.

I walked out into the courtyard clutching the baptismal certificate, feeling revolted. I sat down beside the pool.

An eerie silence filled the courtyard; the only the sound was the fountain splashing into the pool. My head began to ache and the ache spread to my eyes, my neck, my chest, unbearable pain. I was free but I felt trapped, imprisoned.

I dipped my head into the pool and toyed with the possibility of lowering my head deeper into the water beyond my nose, ending my life. The thought was oddly comforting.

"How strange," I thought, "only moments before I fought for life. Now that I am saved, I prefer death."

I withdrew my head from the cold water, letting it cascade down my shoulders. My head still throbbed but I could accurately account for my plight. I had become a convert. I had not only rebelled against my father but I had now totally cut myself from him.

My stomach muscles tensed, sending a wrenching pain to my abdomen. I looked up and saw the gilded letters of the church sparkling in the moonlight, "Church of Christ the Redeemer".

I vomited bile into the pool.

The judge's words, "For the moment you are free," resounded in my ears when I stepped onto the cobblestone road outside the Fort of Madrasa and started to run. It felt good to run away from the Holy Tribunal, from the dungeons, from the church. I had no idea where I was running, but I ran wildly, laughing and crying at the same time.

When I reached Toledo's familiar streets, I knew no matter how far I ran, no matter how much distance I put between me and the Fort of Madrasa, my freedom would only be, "for the moment".

I passed Alfonso's clinic. I did not stop. I did not want to return to Alfonso. I did not want to be his apprentice. I did not want to be a physician. I wanted to run away from Alfonso, the cause of all my suffering. If not for him, I thought, I would have been safe with father in Naples not a hunted converso in Toledo.

I stopped by the dry well where I had earlier hidden from the wrath of the mob. Sliding down the well I felt at ease, sheltered from the hostile world. Feeling safe and secure, I was able to think.

In retrospect, everything I had endured was predictable. Father forewarned me. How could I have been so blind, so stupid? Father was correct about everything. I had to admit that his was the "voice of Sinai".

I asked myself over and over again, "What would father say to me, now?"

I smiled as I conjured up his image. Strange! There I was, at the bottom of a hole in the ground, smiling as I imagined father talking to me, inimitably lecturing, "To be prepared for any eventuality, is the surest means of surviving any crisis."

The crisis was the Inquisition. My goal was to survive, to be reunited with my parents in Naples. How? Don Alfonso's clinic was obviously the first step. There, at least, I could live, eat, and plan my eventual escape.

My decision to return to Alfonso had nothing to do with the prestige of being his apprentice or even with becoming a physician. It was, in my father's words, "the surest means to survive the crisis". I was certain Don Alfonso would take me as an apprentice now that I had been converted, cleared at the trial, and permitted to remain in Spain.

I came out of the dry well feeling fresh, confident, and ready to take my first steps toward my escape. I entered Don Alfonso's office and told him about my conversion and my release.

"I don't want you," Don Alfonso stated boldly.

I was stunned.

"You promised to take me on as an apprentice if I was cleared by the Inquisition," I said.

"I don't want you around the clinic," he repeated, "but I am ordered to take you on as an apprentice."

"Who ordered you?" I asked.

"The Inquisition," he replied.

He explained that he would have to report my comings and goings, and would then become daily involved with the Inquisitors.

"They swarmed around here like in a nest of bees when they searched for you. Now, they'll continue camping on my doorstep," he grumbled.

I was going to tell him I was no longer interested in being an apprentice, but I thought it best to say nothing.

"The less I see of you, the better," he said. "You may lodge in the Caldera with the other apprentices, come to classes, but under no circumstances are you to approach me privately."

He also ordered me to pay fifty marvedis monthly for my apprenticeship. I quickly realized that he would thereby keep me away from the dispensary since I would have to work somewhere else to earn money for lodging.

When I left Alfonso I also realized that I no longer could count on the dispensary as a base from which to plan my escape.

My first reaction to Alfonso's rejection was keen disappointment. Yet, when I reconsidered his conditions I realized that being known as his apprentice but not tied down to his schedule or to the dispensary would serve me well. I could freely move about and have time to effectuate my escape.

Finding work, however, was difficult. People avoided me even though every one knew of my reprieve from the Holy Tribunal. "You're a marked man," a former neighbor said. "If anyone sees me talking to you, I'll have to account to the Suprema."

Everywhere I went, I was chased away, ridiculed, even spat upon. The stigma of the Inquisition stuck to me like a festering sore. In the street children ran after me, taunting, "You're a converso."

I soon learned that all conversos suffered the same ridicule. At every public occasion, especially at church services, priests warned the populace to be on guard against "converso-backsliders" suspected of judaizing innocent Christians. Now, that there were no Jews in Spain to vent its hostility upon, the Inquisition transferred its venom to the conversos. The queen proclaimed a stringent 'Edict of Faith' alerting the masses how to detect conversos' heresy. The Edict encouraged spying, even by deception, to entrap a suspected heretic. Spying on one's neighbors for the Inquisition became a way of life. What amazed me was that this overt hatred was now considered proper behavior even for the cultured Spaniard, not just for the riff-raff.

With this attitude rampant, I could not find employment in the city where, only one month earlier, I was well known and well regarded. Since no one would hire me in Toledo, I went to the farmers across the Tajo River; they were no different than Toledo's gentry. Fortunately, an aged woman whose husband was deathly ill hired me to look after their small farm. Desperate, she paid me a few marvedis a week plus a meal each day. The pay was not enough to meet Alfonso's tuition but, more important, the job could provide the essentials I would eventually need to escape; I was allowed to use their horse to get to and from the farm.

Before I could start working on the farm, I had to get permission from the local Inquisition to leave the city. I realized I would perpetually be under its surveillance. Even that did not dim my hopes of outwitting them later. I went about my work in the dispensary and on the farm thinking only of ways to escape.

As an apprentice, I stayed at the Caldera but the other apprentices distanced themselves from me, afraid that showing any friendship would put them under suspicion. This fear was the direct result of the Edict of Faith which obligated every Spaniard, on pain of death, to report any heresies. Suspicion of an informer's presence was so prevalent that even I, a victim of the Inquisition, was suspected of being its spy.

Twelve of us shared the cramped Caldera. The daily routine of living together brought us face to face. They never greeted me; their attempts to avoid me were embarrassing. Therefore, I would wake up very early, leave the Caldera before any of them awoke, and not return until they were asleep. In the clinic, too, my duties were arranged so that I worked in complete isolation, which pleased them and Don Alfonso. These unbearable conditions made me dream of the day when I could flee.

But, escape grew more difficult because new restrictions were placed on my movement. First, I had to report every Friday to a special agent in the Hermandad, the Inquisition's office, to account for my week's activities. Second, travel restrictions applied to me and not to other apprentices. They were allowed to visit outlying villages as part of their duties, but not I. Third, and most difficult, I was required to attend all church services. Absenting myself or even being late just once would put me under suspicion of heresy.

Escape was virtually impossible.

I decided to win the trust of my agent at the Inquisition, so that I would be freer to move about. I became the perfect eager converso; the first to arrive at church service, the last to leave. Also, my weekly reports at the Hermandad were so detailed, no suspicion could fall on my behavior. When I gave these reports, I found other conversos but spoke to none, even though I hungered for companionship, for someone to talk to.

After the first two months, I thought I had won my agents' trust because they told me to report every other week. I soon learned trust was not the reason. Spying had become so prevalent that the Inquisition knew every move I made without my reports. My chances for escape, I realized, were nil.

With the passing of summer and fall and the onset of winter, the sleeping regimen I had established at the Caldera became progressively more difficult. The winter was particularly cold. The weather turned bitter and the rains came down with annoying regularity. Staying out of doors as I did much of the night was unbearable. Alfonso and his patients also complained about conditions in the dispensary's dormitory. The large room, with its tile floor and huge cathedral windows, was always colder than anywhere else in the building.

One morning while we sat there waiting for Don Alfonso to start his visitation, an apprentice, Gaspar de Pamplona, came up with a solution.

"We'll have to keep that furnace lit all night," Gaspar said. "One of us should sleep in store room off this hall and tend the furnace. We can take turns."

"I'll be glad to move in right now for the rest of the winter," I volunteered.

They agreed and that day I moved out of the Caldera. For the next few months, I rose in the middle of the night to stoke the furnace. My new room was a tiny niche, a small storage area filled with firewood during the winter. I made it more spacious by piling the wood to the ceiling, thereby gaining more living space. It became my regular quarters for as long as I remained in Toledo. I was grateful to Gaspar not only for suggesting this new arrangement but for the way he brought up the idea. It seemed to me that he did so intentionally, to enable me to move out of the Caldera.

Gaspar, the oldest apprentice in our group, was an arrogant, ruddy-faced, fat man in his late twenties with long flowing hair. He constantly combed his hair and groomed his beard. The others disliked him for this annoying quirk and for strutting about like a peacock bragging about his noble birth. But, since he made it possible for me to leave the Caldera, I overlooked these annoying traits.

For the first six months, I was forced to live like a hermit, or worse, a pariah. Alfonso never called upon me to answer a question. When we examined patients, I could only trail the apprentices, never participating in hospital procedures or speaking to patients. The apprentices continued to distance themselves from me.

Only Gaspar paid any attention to me. He did not openly befriend me, to be sure, but in many simple ways he made me feel like a person again.

He would make room for me in the wagon or would walk alongside me when we trailed behind Don Alfonso. These little things were important to me at the time. He seemed to go out of his way to recognize my presence.

When I first met Gaspar, I disliked him, as did the other apprentices, not only for his pomposity but also for his crudeness. But, lonely and hurt, I valued his friendly acts.

About two months after I had moved into the storage room, Gaspar surprised me by visiting in the middle of the night.

"I'm sorry I woke you. I couldn't sleep," Gaspar said. "I came to help you. I'll tend the furnace tonight. You can sleep."

Without waiting for my reply, he began stacking cords of wood into the furnace. When he had the fire ablaze, he heated up some water in the kettle and handed me a cup of hot cocoa. He offered to relieve me of my duties for the rest of the week.

"I wouldn't trade places with anyone," I said sipping the hot drink. "This is a perfect arrangement. I'm glad I can finally thank you for setting it up."

"It made sense to everybody," Gaspar said, "except to Alfonso."

"Alfonso! Unhappy over it?" I asked.

"When I first suggested it, he cursed so much, I thought he'd kick me out of the dispensary altogether," Gaspar said.

"Well I guess he has his reasons," I said to Gaspar.

Gaspar replied, "You like medicine so much, you even defend the bastard."

I knew why Don Alfonso was displeased with my living so close to him, but I did not want to share that with Gaspar.

"You don't like medicine?" I asked changing the subject.

"Hell, no," Gaspar replied violently combing his hair. "I'm a Pamplonan. What am I doing here? I don't want to be a physician. Where I come from, the doctors can't even afford a pair of shoes. I came to Toledo hoping to become apprenticed to the Santandors or the Biscayas so maybe, one day, I could be knighted. But Ferdinand gives nothing away. Knighthood costs money, which I have very little of."

"So you're here only for food and lodging?" I asked.

"But not for long," Gaspar said. "I'm getting out of here. I hate them all, including Alfonso." I listened sympathetically to his ranting and smiled when he said he was putting up with the Caldera and the dispensary because he preferred the glamor of Toledo to the barrenness of his mountains. We talked all night but never once did I mention my dreams of escape. Near dawn, I reminded him it was almost time for the apprentices to report for morning duty and he was not safe being seen with me.

"We have a saying among the mountain people," Gaspar said, "'The heart get lighter when the words get heavier'. Thanks for letting me talk. I'll be better in the morning."

The trust between Gaspar and me was firmly established one day about three weeks later. That day, Alfonso took us to the Fort of Madrassa to witness the flogging of a condemned heretic, as part of our training. When we arrived, the prisoner, Jose Bahia, was already tied to a post in the Fort's quadrangle facing the huge cross which dominated the area.

When the townspeople, who were ordered to be present at the flogging, assembled in the quadrangle, an official announced that the prisoner was a converso found guilty of attempting to leave Spain without permission. Ordinarily the penalty would have been death, the official said, but since the prisoner confessed and gave the Inquisition the names of his accomplices, a lighter penalty, one hundred lashes, would be imposed as a penance.

The burly jailer, stripped to the waist like the victim, administered the lashes with deadly accuracy. As the whip cracked against the body, Jose Bahia emitted a shrill cry, and the official's voice counted the stroke. This litany, the crack, the cry, the count, stopped on the nineteenth stroke when Bahia's screaming ceased. His body hung limp, supported only by the rope which tied his wrists to the pole. Don Alfonso examined the prisoner to determine if the Limit of Safety had been breached.

Don Alfonso could call a halt to the flogging if he thought the victim would die or order it continued. Don Alfonso ordered us to revive Jose Bahia by dousing him with water and then certified that the flogging could continue. This pattern, flogging — fainting — revival, continued until the hundred lashes were completed.

"That was cruel," Gaspar confronted Alfonso when we were all in the wagon heading back to the dispensary. "How could you let those officials continue the flogging after he fainted so many times?"

"Applying the full punishment is more merciful," Don Alfonso replied. "Otherwise, the victim must return a second, third, or fourth time, as often as necessary to complete the entire sentence. And each time the flogging begins all over again. That's how the Inquisition interprets of the Limit of Safety procedure."

"You're as cruel as the Inquisition," Gaspar shot back.

"Shut up, you fool," Don Alfonso snorted.

We were amazed by Gaspar's candor. Criticizing the Inquisition was either a sign of courage or a mark of stupidity. Despite Alfonso's annoyance, I admired Gaspar for his compassion and courage.

He completely won me over. We continued meeting several times in the middle of the night, talking until the early morning.

During one such secret session, Gaspar spoke of his high Spanish birth and of his family, a Pamplona nobility whose land bordered the Pyrenees. I knew about his aristocratic lineage because he would not let us forget it. But he told no one, except me, that all the Pamplonas were poverty-stricken. He explained that during the Reconquista, the Spanish Monarchs also had to cope with a civil war. It often happened that after the Arabs were driven from an area, a local baron would occupy land that had once belonged to the king. The Monarchs would turn their militia against such a recalcitrant baron, forcing him to submit rather than face a full scale war.

"Only the Pamplonas refused to yield their property," Gaspar said. "We fought Ferdinand's militia a long time and when our leaders finally sued for peace, the king extracted a high price. He took most of our holdings. We retained only the "ricos hombres" title, the highest rank in Spanish nobility, but not much more."

Like me, Gaspar felt trapped in Toledo. His fondest dream was to return and reclaim his ancestral land. I encouraged him to come to my room and talk about it any time he desired.

One night Gaspar came to my room and found it empty. That night, he waited and was surprised when I returned at dawn.

"What did you do all night?" he asked.

I told him I worked as a cemetery watchman to help pay for my apprenticeship. Sometimes a corpse would be held overnight in a little hut to await burial. I called it the 'dead room'. I would be paid to spend the night there cleaning the body and making sure no one molested it. Oftimes, in cases of violent deaths, families paid me quite well for restoring facial injuries so the body could be viewed at the wake.

I did not tell Gaspar that working in the Dead Room gave me an opportunity to study the human body. It became my private laboratory.

I spoke to no one about my working on cadavers. I knew the church considered tampering with dead bodies a desecration. To me, it became a regular, completely secret, learning procedure.

Once, Jose Bahia's body was my companion in the Dead Room. I recalled that, after his flogging, Bahia became ill complaining of pains in the chest. An apprentice was sent to attend to him at his home.

After his report to Don Alfonso, Bahia's condition was diagnosed as the winter fever, which had raged all winter. Two days later, Bahia died.

Watching over his body, I noticed that the welts from the flogging had left deep scars. I wanted to know if injured tissue differed from healthy flesh, so I made a semi-circular incision along one scar, separating the severed flesh by prying it up from the rib cage. In so doing, I felt a jagged piece of a bone. Moving my lantern closer, I discovered that the rib was fractured. It had punctured the lung which still contained a pool of blood.

A few days later, while scrubbing the floor in the clinic, another chore I had undertaken to earn money for my maintenance, I looked up at Don Alfonso and quietly said, "A lung can be punctured from within the body."

"Where did you see a punctured lung?" Don Alfonso asked.

"Jose Bahia died from a punctured lung, not from the winter fever," I stated not answering his question.

"I asked you, where did you see a punctured lung?"

"In the hut next to the cemetery," I replied, "Bahia's lung was punctured." He said nothing, so I then described in detail the fractured rib, the splinter perforating the lung, and the pool of blood in the lung.

"You are doing autopsies?" Don Alfonso asked.

"Yes," I answered with pride.

He warned me that the church considered dissection a serious offense punishable by death. Many papal edicts against dissection were aimed at physicians because of the tenet that cutting into any part of a dead body denied that person salvation in Christ. Those edicts also proclaimed that surgery was looked down upon as a desecration of "God's finest creation: man" and doctors were ordered to desist from incisions beyond the skin level.

Don Alfonso considered it sheer nonsense.

"I can get away with surgery," Alfonso said with a chuckle, "because the patients I heal can defend me if the need ever comes up. But you don't cure anyone with an autopsy. The dead don't come back to life. And if you're caught, there's no one to sing your praises."

"But, there's so much to be learned from the dead body," I pleaded. "You're a great teacher, but I understand you only when I see it before my eyes. Autopsy can make us better doctors..."

Don Alfonso interrupted, "Don't tell anybody what you've done."

"Then will you teach me to be a surgeon?" I persisted.

From that day, Don Alfonso's attitude towards me changed. He called on me to assist him in most medical cases and took a personal interest in my progress. Although I continued to be an outcast with the other apprentices, except for Gaspar, and although Don Alfonso still kept his distance from me, in public, I soon became known as Alfonso's protege.

Don Alfonso made it a point, however, never to discuss the Inquisition with me. For example, he never asked about the reports I was still submitting to the Inquisition and he never even mentioned the name 'Torquemada'— except once.

That was on the night we were called to treat the injured at a fire which had destroyed several buildings in the crowded Zocodover Plaza. About a hundred died in the flame. The seared bodies of the dead were placed in the foyer of a near-by church where we treated the survivors. The smell of burned flesh was overwhelming, yet, as we worked on the survivors, their relatives stood near, oblivious to the ghastly surroundings and to the sickening odor of charred bodies.

"The stench of burning human flesh has become routine," Alfonso whispered, "because of Torquemada."

Later that night, when we finished our work, he invited me to his home. His housekeeper served us a light meal and we talked about the medical problems we faced that day. As I was about to leave, I asked him to explain his remark about Torquemada.

"Tomas de Torquemada came from good stock," Don Alfonso said. "His paternal great grandfather, Lopez, was knighted by the King of Castile about a century before Tomas' birth. His grandfather, Alvar, added wealth to the family's rank working as a builder and an architect. Tomas' father, Pedro, was a leading financial figure in the town of Torquemada which, by that time, was totally owned by the family. Juan de Torquemada, Tomas' uncle, a renowned theologian, was the cardinal of the district of Valladolid. With his elevation in the church hierarchy, the family fortune and rank grew. As Pedro's only son, Tomas was one of the richest young aristocrats in Spain. Nothing was spared to prepare young Tomas to assume his wealth and title.

"But Tomas chose otherwise. At age nineteen he began spending his days in the village church as a minor functionary. A year later he decided to enter the Dominican Monastic Order. His father was despondent since Tomas' celibacy would end the Torquemada nobility. But neither his father's pleading nor the intercession of his uncle, the cardinal, could deter young Tomas' resolve.

"Even before his acceptance into the Order, he demonstrated his abhorrence of luxury by refusing to participate in the sumptuous family dinners. He would not display the coat of arms due his rank nor even wear his elegant clothes. He walked barefooted and lived on a meager diet. His behavior was an enigma to his parents."

"What made him chose that kind of a life?" I asked.

"Everyone asked 'why?' Why should a young man, brought up in luxury, reject his wealth? Why should a man who had received the finest training in science and mathematics seek the confining strictures of a Dominican monastery? Why spurn noble rank for monastic anonymity?"

"Did anyone ask him why?" I asked.

"Everyone did, but he never explained," Don Alfonso said. "But, I knew why!"

"You knew?" I asked.

"Yes," he replied, "It's because Tomas de Torquemada had a Jewish grandmother."

"Torquemada had a Jewish grandmother!" I called out in disbelief.

"His grandfather, Alvar, married a Jewish woman," Don Alfonso said. "No one faulted him for marrying her. Christians marrying Jews was a common practice. But when Tomas learned about his Jewish grandmother, he considered her a stain he would try to wipe clean for the rest of his life. Amazingly, he did just that."

"What do you mean," I asked.

"She vanished," Don Alfonso said. "Her name appears nowhere. The present church records contain the names of Tomas' entire family: his father, Pedro; his mother, Francesca; his uncle, Juan; his grandfather, Alvar; and so on, going back several generations. Only Alvar's wife, the Jewish grandmother, is missing. The fact that her name appears nowhere must have been Tomas' work."

"You're asking me to believe that Torquemada expunged his grandmother's name from history?" I asked.

"Remember," Don Alfonso replied, "Tomas first served as a minor functionary in the village church where his family records were kept. Tomas must have destroyed her records."

Without intending to question Don Alfonso's veracity, I asked if he had actually seen those records.

"Many times," he replied. "and they are still there for anyone to see."

"Is there any evidence that omitting the grandmother's name was the work of young Torquemada?" I asked.

"No, it's only my theory," he said, "but a good doctor is a student of the mind as well as of the body."

I asked him to explain how he understood Torquemada's mind. Don Alfonso thought a moment and then replied, "If what we remember or what we try to forget is said to mirror one's character, then Torquemada's relentless purging of the Jews can only be explained by his violent reaction to having a Jewish grandmother."

As I was about to leave, Don Alfonso informed me that Abram Senor had suffered a heart attack in Barcelona while waiting to board a boat to Italy. To save him from prosecution, one of the king's clergy converted him and for about a half a year, Don Abram was on the brink of death. Only a month ago, he was well enough to return to Toledo and resume his duties at the court.

"Ever since his recovery," Don Alfonso said, "he's been hounded by Torquemada, ordering him to appear before the Holy Tribunal for the slightest infraction."

When representations were made to the king on behalf of Abram Senor, the king ordered that any act of heresy against the

Treasurer should be tried only in the presence of the Monarchs. This infuriated Torquemada. Don Alfonso said that Torquemada enigmatically warned the king, "Very soon this will come to an end. Abram will either prove himself a faithful Catholic and we shall embrace him as a brother, or he will be exposed a Jew and shall be destroyed as a relapsed converso."

Don Alfonso therefore prohibited me from visiting Abram Senor because my presence would only play into the hands of the Inquisition. At my insistence, Alfonso solemnly promised to arrange for me to meet the aged Abram when it would be considered safe.

Two days after my meeting with Don Alfonso, Gaspar burst into my room announcing that he had been called to testify before a Royal Committee about certain lands in the Pamplona Region. He described how Don Abram Senor conducted the hearings of the committee. I asked Gaspar to tell me how the old man appeared and how I could get to see him.

"When I told him that I'm apprenticed at the Alfonso clinic and that I knew you, the old man gave me these," Gaspar said throwing three gold escudos on my bed. Then he added, "Oh yes, he said you should come to see him because he has word from your father."

In my excitement, I disregarded Don Alfonso's admonition not to visit Don Abram and rushed out to his casa.

To me, that day was a magnificent one. The early spring weather was pleasant and, for the first time in months, a burst of happiness was rekindled within me. I felt alive. I walked into Abram Senor's casa kissing his hand and embracing him with tears of joy flowing down my face. Though he was frail and weak, I felt strengthened by his embrace and remained in his arms for a long, precious moment.

He held on to me tightly and breathing heavily, he whispered.

"Sami, Sami, it's been so very long." I stood, holding his hand close to my face, unable to let go. Then we sat in his room talking about all that had happened to us since that fateful day in August.

I haltingly confessed my conversion but he waved me off with a sweep of his frail hand saying, "That should be the least of your concerns."

He had no direct message from father, only a report from a visitor from Naples who said my family was doing well. Abram Senor then said there was a slim possibility that he could send a letter to father when the visitor returned to Naples.

We spoke so long that day, we did not realize how late it was and how hungry we were. Don Abram tinkled his little bell and a servant brought in some refreshments. For me, eating at Abram Senor's table was like a festive dinner. He poured two glasses of wine from a decanter which, he said, he reserved only for special occasions.

Raising his glass he called out, "This was your father's favorite wine. I pray that soon you will toast each other."

I sipped the wine but immediately put down the glass. I could not drink. My throat tightened and I was on the verge of tears, imagining my father's anguish at losing a son. Don Abram urged me not to despair, to look forward to the day when I will be reunited with my family. He promised to do everything to bring about our reunion. I then drank the wine toasting his good health. When I left, I promised to visit him at least once a week.

That was the first of many visits. True to his word, Don Abram transmitted the letters which I brought each visit. I read each letter several times before sending it because I knew it would be read by the Inquisition. At one time I rewrote an entire letter in Abram Senor's presence because its reference to the holiday of Passover could have been used against me as evidence of a relapse. Abram Senor was puzzled by the extreme caution I displayed in writing my letter. I explained that I wanted to avoid possible peril to either of us.

"How can you possibly live that way?" he asked

"I have learned to live with it as one learns to live with a physical disability," I replied. "I'm always on guard. I always take this sort of safety measures."

"How can one guard against the unseen?" Don Abram asked.

"By living in isolation," I replied.

"Impossible!" Don Abram said. "You see patients. You work with Alfonso. You talk to Gaspar, don't you? He told me he is your friend."

"Yes. He's the only one I trust," I said. "And even to him, I don't tell everything."

"I'm too old for that sort of vigilance," Don Abram said, "my security is with God. When He summons me, I shall go."

That was the last conversation I had with Don Abram.

Like everyone in Toledo, I was aware that spies were everywhere. I knew that agents of the Inquisition had penetrated every segment of Spanish society. It enlisted spies by promising a share of the condemned heretic's property to the informant. Neighbor spied on neighbor; worker on land owner; husband on wife; wife on husband; parent on child; child on parent; the rich on the poor; the poor on the rich. I suspected the workers with whom I worked on the farm, the traders in the market, the patients in the dispensary, and the apprentices in the Caldera. At times, I even suspected Don Alfonso.

But, I did not suspect Gaspar.

One day Gaspar also went to visit the aged Abram Senor, but he did so without telling me. When he arrived at his home, he saw through the window that the old man was sitting alone in his library. The servant announced Gaspar to Don Abram who profusely thanked him for bringing us together. He offered him some refreshments but Gaspar politely refused.

"I can't," he said, feigning excitement, "Alberto sent me to fetch you. Some Jewish scrolls were found in one of our rooms and he thought you might tell him how to dispose of them."

Without asking any further questions, the aged Abram instantly rose from his chair and called for his coachman. He turned back only to take a woolen shawl which he wrapped around his shoulders.

"There is no danger, Sir," Gaspar said entering the carriage and helping cover the old man with the shawl.

Gaspar directed the coachman along the narrow streets and soon the carriage stopped in front of the *Sinagoga*. The magnificent but simple red-brick structure was erected more than a century earlier when Toledo was home to Spain's most celebrated Jewish poets, philosophers, and scientists. It stood high above the banks of the Tajo river surrounded by a lush glen of trees. The simple exterior walls sharply contrasted with the artistic interior walls elaborately decorated with the lace-like, filigreed Hebrew letters forming many Biblical verses. The entire building had a distinct beauty and, although it lacked the characteristic horseshoe arches of Moorish architecture, it was one of the city's most striking structures. When the Jews of Toledo were exiled, the synagogue was closed by official decree. It remained closed pending conversion to the Church of Transicion. The synagogue's main features, however, the *bimah* in the center of the hall and the holy ark on the east wall, were still untouched by the carpenters.

"I will open the door for you and I will bring Alberto right away," Gaspar said, leading Abram Senor into the synagogue through the rear door.

Abram Senor whispered, "Thank you," as he stepped into the synagogue.

"Here," Gaspar showed him to a seat beside the *bimah* and, lighting a lamp, repeated, "I will bring Alberto to you."

Don Abram Senor was overwhelmed the moment he walked

in. He had not visited his synagogue since the exiles left the city. Carried away by memories, he moved about the large room. He could not merely sit and wait for me. He felt drawn to the raised, elaborately decorated *bimah*. Lamp in hand, he mounted the three steps, pleased that little had changed. Even the names of the elders of the community remained on the wood-carved railing.

"Rodrigo Nahmias, Samuel Zarazal, David Lopez, Abram Senor, Isaac Abrabanel" he read the names embossed artistically on the sides of the maple-wood lectern. For twenty-five years he had been the *Nasi*, the leader, of the Synagogue, presiding over religious and communal meetings.

He walked to the heavy bronze menorahs and noticed that the cups still contained wicks and oil. Don Abram stretched his trembling hand up to the seven-branched candelabra and, using the flame in his lamp, lit each of the seven wicks. He gazed on the exquisitely decorated walls where bas relief biblical quotations formed a decorative gold and green panel near the ceiling.

The words of the Psalms of David seemed to leap at him as he read his favorite verse, one which he so often chanted, "I love the habitation of Thy House, the place where Thy Glory dwelleth."

Humming aloud the hymn, "I love the habitation of thy house," he stepped down from the *bimah* and walked to the seats along the eastern wall, which had been reserved for the *chacham*, the rabbi, and the dignitaries of the congregation. He sat in the first chair next to the Holy Ark. It was his chair. Here he had prayed for more than a quarter of a century. He felt elated sitting there once again as he looked about the great hall, recalling the many family ceremonies that had taken place there. He remembered how often he had participated in those sacred moments — marriages, births, funerals — calling names of the families whose joys and sorrows he had shared. Standing at the lectern where the cantor once stood, he imagined hearing the congregation singing the well-known melodies. He began to hum, his body swaying rhythmically to those time-hallowed tunes which once filled the synagogue.

Then he faced the Holy Ark.

He approached it, his head bowed in reverence, fingering the richly embroidered velvet curtain over its doors. He pulled at the tasseled cords and slowly opened first the curtain and then the massive mahogany doors of the Holy Ark. He stepped back staring at its stark emptiness. Gone were the *Torahs*, gone were their richly decorated silver cases, gone were the ornamented crowns. The shadow of his body, cast by the light of the menorah, grotesquely danced in the emptied ark. He closed his eyes and remained standing in sad and reverent silence.

He fell upon his knees, as he would on Yom Kippur and, lying prostrate before the ark, cried out, "*Shma Yisrael adonai elohenu adonai ehad.* Hear O Israel the Lord our God the Lord is one."

He was a peace with himself and with his God.

Suddenly, he felt a hand helping him to his feet. Thinking it was me, he stood up to embrace me. Instead, he saw Gaspar's smirking face.

"Come, Jew, it's time to go," Gaspar said leading him out of the synagogue to the Hermandad.

The trial of Abram Senor, as stipulated by royal decree, was held in the presence of King Ferdinand and Queen Isabel. Tomas de Torquemada was his prosecutor. Torquemada demanded the death sentence as for any converso convicted of heresy. The Inquisition's witness was Gaspar de Pamplona, who testified to the Holy Tribunal all that he saw in the synagogue. He was introduced not as an informant but as an agent of the Inquisition. The aged Abram offered no defense and even firmly corroborated Gaspar's testimony describing, in detail, his actions and feelings when he remained alone in the *sinagoga*. In a gentle voice, he told to his judges he knew what they had to do. He was resigned to the inevitable but calmly told them he was at peace because he also knew he was right in what he had done. He refused to recant even though he was promised a less severe death than the auto-da-fe demanded by the Inquisition.

The Holy Tribunal's deliberation was brief and their sentencing short: death by fire.

While the trial was going on, I was kept in total ignorance. I accidentally learned about Don Abram's fate two weeks after he was arrested when I came by his home to visit. Because of my added duties at the clinic and my studies with Don Alfonso, I had missed my weekly visits with Don Abram. This time, I was only passing by to apologize for my absence. The moment I came to his door, I sensed something was wrong. The militia man guarding the house stopped me from mounting the few steps to the patio. He said he did not know any details, but when he mentioned the words 'trial' and 'confiscation', I realized the worst had happened.

With trepidation, I went to his office in the palace asking for Don Abram's whereabouts but no one would talk to me. When I asked Don Alfonso if he knew anything about Abram Senor, he was reluctant to tell me much except that Gaspar had testified against him. I confronted Gaspar. He readily confessed to everything, telling me all that had transpired before and after the trial. As Gaspar was telling me the gruesome details, I immediately recognized my role in Don Abram's entrapment. I was crushed, realizing that I was the tool bringing death to my beloved Abram Senor.

I was overwhelmed by feelings of guilt. I lost interest in the study of medicine and totally cut myself off from Alfonso.

When Gaspar told me Abram was imprisoned at the Fort of Madrassa, I tried desperately to get in to speak with him. I even approached the dreaded Inquisition headquarters in the Fort, but I could not get past the monk in the foyer.

I pleaded with Gaspar to help but, though he tried, he could not get me into the prison.

I was obsessed with hostility for everyone, repelled by anything associated with Toledo, including Alfonso and his dispensary. I suspected that he had collaborated with Gaspar because he had prohibited me from visiting Abram Senor.

Strange as it may seem, Gaspar retained his friendship with me and I did not reject him. His role in Abram's incarceration meant that he would be able to return to Pamplona, where he would become the area director of the Inquisition and would probably be able to reclaim some of his land. I wanted to use his connection with the Inquisition to get to Abram Senor. I considered him the devil incarnate, the source of all evil, yet I kept close to him because he was the only one who spoke freely of the trial and because he could vividly describe his last day with Don Abram. I asked him to repeat over and over those precious moments in the *sinagoga*. He obliged me, even recalling some of the hymns Abram Senor sang. Gaspar also proved useful as a messenger through whom I managed to pass a long letter to Don Abram.

I left my quarters at the dispensary and went to work full time at the old woman's farm. Several days later, a neighboring farmer told me about the announcement ordering the populace to the auto-da-fe of Abram Senor. That day, Alfonso sent an apprentice to the farm to tell me that he had to talk to me. At first, I refused, but when he said that there was a message from Abram Senor, I rushed to the clinic. When I entered his room, Alfonso placed his hand over my shoulder.

"Berto," he said, calling me by that name for the first time, "You can be a great physician."

I twisted out of his grasp saying angrily, "I don't want to be a physician."

"Listen. Very soon you will be on the way to Cordoba," Alfonso pleaded with me. I turned away from him.

"Here is your letter of introduction to Don Jimenez, the

Sacred Sword

physician to the Court of Cordoba."

"I'm not interested." I said, refusing to take the letter from his extended hand. "I want to see Don Abram,"

"Alberto, I can no longer help you here. No one can. Believe me, I knew nothing about Gaspar. But I know all about you. You can be an outstanding physician. And this is my only interest in you. Good physicians are rare in Spain. You can be the best. The best surgeon if you want."

I turned my back to him.

"Your presence here in Toledo is a constant peril to you; your name is synonymous with Toledo," he said speaking slowly, stressing every word. "I managed to have you transferred out of Toledo to Cordoba where you can be anonymous. Right after the trial, I protested to the Inquisition that your presence in my dispensary places severe impositions on our medical work. I even appealed to Their Majesties about this. The Inquisition finally agreed to allow you to leave Toledo. I did not select Cordoba or Jimenez. Remember, the Inquisition chose Cordoba for you, not I." He said that the first he heard about Abram Senor's plight was when he was summoned to attend to Don Abram during the trial.

"Why didn't you tell me about the trial?" I cried out.

"I feared for your own entrapment," Don Alfonso said, "I knew your feelings and I was afraid you'd do something rash."

"I want to see him," I shouted.

"You can not," he replied. "As his doctor, I visit him every day and all we do is talk about you. All day long, he reads your letter."

"Thank God I sent that letter!" I said.

"And, he agrees with me," Alfonso said.

"He agrees with you? On what?" I asked.

"That you must leave Toledo," Alfonso replied. "Although that is a great loss to me."

Don Alfonso was almost in tears. He said something at that moment that made me cry. "I love you almost as much as Abram

Senor," he said and then he could speak no longer.

I apologized for my rudeness. He took my hand, squeezed it tightly, and gave me the letter to Don Jimenez.

"Go with God," he whispered hoarsely, "and don't forget me."

"When you see Abram Senor," I said leaving his office, "please tell him how sorry I feel."

"I saw him this morning and I told him," Alfonso said. "He gave me a message for you."

"What did he say?" I asked.

"He said to tell you: 'I have lived a long life. So must you.'"

4

I decided to leave Toledo immediately. I could not get out fast enough. Like a man running from a burning building, I took no personal belongings with me nor did I look back. I detested the city, its people, and its memories. The anguish I felt over the imminent death of Abram Senor was the most intense feeling that I had ever experienced, stronger than the guilt at deserting father, stronger than the dread of being locked in the Inquisition's dungeon. I could not rid myself of the thought that I brought on the death of this beloved man.

I could not forgive myself nor the Inquisition.

I distinctly remember the dreary day I left Toledo. It was raining and it never rained at that time of the year. As the rain pelted me, I prayed that it could somehow wash away my guilt about Abram Senor's death.

As ordered by the agent in Toledo, I presented myself to every Inquisition office on my three weeks route to Cordoba. I met hundreds of its agents and was interviewed by many of its priests. They all seemed exactly alike: self-righteous, pious, inhuman. When I looked at the green and gold banner of the Inquisition I understood it was no mere coincidence that the Inquisition's insignia was a sword juxtaposed with a cross. They were shaped alike.

I have no clear recollection of the three weeks that I walked the road to Cordoba. I recall neither where I stayed nor how I even subsisted. Those three weeks simply vanished from my memory. I only remember that when I finally reached the outskirts of Cordoba, Don Alfonso's words, "The Inquisition chose Cordoba for you," echoed in my mind, making the name Cordoba synonymous with the Inquisition. If the name "Toledo" had become an anathema to me, "Cordoba" now became an abomination. I kept asking myself, "What is to be my special 'mission' here? What does the Inquisition have in store for me? How will I be manipulated here?"

I stayed on the outskirts of the city, sleeping two nights in the cemetery which had a "dead room," just like the one in Toledo. When I finally made my way into the city, I learned that Jimenez, to whom I was to be apprenticed, was a well-known figure and everyone knew the Casa Lombardia, Jimenez's dispensary.

The small, two story house stood in a clearing outside the city walls near the Puerta de Sevilla on a hillside sloping towards the Quadalquivir River. The Casa Lombardia was set at the edge of an orchard and enclosed by a low brick wall. Even from a distance, I saw that it was run down, with a caved-in roof and a fallen gate. When I entered the patio, I realized the entire area was in total disorder. Bits of glass from broken windows and pieces of furniture were strewn all around. I had to watch out for the loosened guard railings on the stairs and for chunks of plaster falling off the ceiling.

"Welcome to Casa Lombardia," Jimenez greeted me, "I've been expecting you."

I shall never forget my surprise when I saw Jimenez standing at the door of his dilapidated casa. He looked exactly like Gaspar, older, but the same chubby face with thick lips, the same reddish brown hair but streaked with gray, and the same pudgy hands. I am sure he noticed my reaction but he did not mention it. I handed him the letter from Don Alfonso and told him nothing about my background. He told me nothing about his work.

When he showed me to my room across the patio, I noticed medicine bottles and hospital equipment strewn all about like the pieces of broken glass. The two patients in the hospital lay unattended on dirty beds amidst filthy surroundings.

Thanks to Jimenez's indolent nature, I was not disturbed by

him and by the patients. If not for orders to attend special sessions of "Instruction of Faith" in the nearby San Miguel Chapel each Tuesday afternoon, I could have remained secluded indefinitely. For several weeks, I stayed in my room or lay outside in the groves, unconcerned with my appearance or my duties in the nonexistent dispensary. Two months passed this way. I could not work up an interest in medicine or in Jimenez. His resemblance to Gaspar was certainly no help. Even the coming of the Lombardia's new caretaker made no impression on me.

"This place stinks," were his first words when he walked into my room.

I did not reply.

"My name is Andres and you're probably the apprentice, Alberto di Cadiz from Toledo," Andres said and, smiling broadly, he added, "You're the apprentice that hasn't apprenticed and I'm the caretaker that doesn't care."

He waited for my response to his jest, but receiving none, he shrugged and began preparing his cot.

"I do care, though, about where I sleep," he said. "Jimenez tells me we are to share this room and I can't tolerate disorder around my bed."

"I'm sorry, that's your problem," I mumbled.

He solved it by moving his bed out of my room, allowing me to remain in my self-imposed isolation. I was grateful to him but said nothing. I was more grateful to him for not pestering me to explain my moodiness or my apparent madness. Although he began immediately to make order in the Casa Lombardia, he did not hound me to get to work. During the first two weeks, he came to my room often to report on his progress or to entertain me with his jokes.

Andres, a year older than I, was a friendly and talkative person. He constantly told stories of life in Cordoba, sharing tidbits about its citizens. I showed no interest in his chatter. But when he told me about Jimenez, I listened because I knew the

Inquisition chose him to be my master physician. Andres related that Jimenez once worked on a farm for a local baron. Although the land was good soil, Jimenez could not make it produce enough to support his wife and two sons, much less to pay the fiefdom due to the landlord. When he was evicted from the farm, Jimenez moved his family to the *juderia*, where he set up a carpentry shop.

"Was he Jewish," I asked, thinking perhaps that was the reason I had been assigned to Jimenez.

"No, of course not," Andres replied, "I guess he figured he'd get more work there, because the Jews were mostly artisans. But, he fared worse as a carpenter than he did as a farmer."

Jimenez was reduced to utter poverty, relying on charity from the church and handouts from his neighbors. It was rumored that his sons, Rodriguez and the dull-witted Diaz, left their father's home when their mother died because they were ashamed of his disrepute.

Despite his pock-marked face, Andres was attractive, with curly flaxen hair and bluish eyes always sparkling with laughter. His effervescence and wit made him seem flippant and careless, but I soon realized he was an able administrator. In about a month, he cleaned up the mess at Casa Lombardia, bringing in Jimenez's son, Diaz, to help repair the building.

Andres jolted me out of my lethargy, too. He arranged our schedules, assigned patients' beds and established viable medical procedures in the dispensary. In time, he organized several women's groups from local churches to cater to the sick and wounded. In less than a year, under Andres' expert management, the Casa Lombardia became a bustling clinic and, at last, well regarded throughout the city.

Under normal circumstances, Andres and I would have been good friends. I liked his warm, easy-going manner. I would have enjoyed getting close to him; he was much like the person I used to be. But during my first year in Cordoba, I deliberately changed my behavior to create the impression that I was a dolt. I shunned all personal contacts and resisted all overtures of friendship, including Andres'.

I behaved like that only to avoid any involvement with the Inquisition. In Toledo, I learned the bitter lesson that any person, patient or colleague, nobleman or worker, vendor or farmer could turn out to be the spy, the Gaspar.

At the Casa Lombardia and even in the city, my self-imposed isolation gained me the title *el mudo*, the silent one, for I could go for days without saying a word to anyone. Even while attending the sick, I rarely spoke and when I did, it was only to discern the patient's need. The name I gained was an apt description of my assumed character and when people called me, *el mudo*, they meant not just the silent one, but the dumb one.

I was quite satisfied with the image I created because I succeeded in avoiding the Inquisition's attention.

I did attract the attention of Don Luis, the knight who served Count Juan de Trastamara, the ruling lord of Andalusia. Officially, the dispensary and its groves belonged to the count, and his knight, Don Luis, came to inspect our work. While he was interviewing me, someone called out, "You won't get much out of him, Don Luis. He's our el mudo."

Don Luis replied, "I prefer a physician who can heal to one who can only howl."

The count's daughter, Maria, who accompanied Don Luis, whispered to the knight, "But he should be more cleanly dressed."

In her presence, I became aware of my shabby appearance and quickly walked away.

Despite the outward dissimilarities between Andres and me, we developed an excellent working relationship. Under his gentle prodding, I overcame my despair but not my suspicion of everyone around me. If Andres or anyone else proved to be a Gaspar, I made certain that they would find me difficult to manipulate.

Andres paid no attention to me or to my strange mannerisms but on the one occasion, when he and I celebrated our birthdays, he hinted that my behavior was not natural. On another occasion, when I imitated Diaz's guffawing laughter, Andres accused me of wearing a mask to hide my real personality. Despite these observations, he never probed my past. I had no reason to suspect him yet I scrupulously kept my distance. Much to his annoyance, I persisted in my isolation although we now had to share a room due to the dispensary's growth. Even when he demonstrated his trustworthiness, which should have dispelled any doubts I had about him, I did not change my behavior.

For example, one evening about a year after I arrived in Cordoba, Andres burst into our room. He pulled me from my bed ordering me to follow him.

"You have to go to the Morales home," he said when were outside the Casa Lombardia.

"Jimenez has been treating her. Why me?" I protested.

"It's not Beatriz," Andres replied. "It's Alonso."

"Who's Alonso?" I asked.

"The new baby," Andres said.

"Still," I claimed, "it's Jimenez's patient."

"This one's not for Jimenez," Andres insisted, "It's for you alone."

I followed Andres who was running ahead of me through the narrow lanes of the *juderia*. I had trouble keeping up with him because he was darting in and out of twisting alleyways. When we entered the patio of the Morales home, Andres leaped up the stairs to the second floor and entered the Morales apartment. In the tiny home, Beatriz was hovering over the crib where her two-week-old son lay near death.

The tiny infant was almost completely hidden, buried under a mountain of blankets. When I peeled off his swaddling clothes, I found his fever-wracked body covered with red blotches. He had difficulty breathing and his mother said he had refused to suckle the entire day. The baby's penis was infected; and I immediately recognized that he had been circumcised. I washed the wound, applying some ointment to it, and said nothing about the circumcision. I stayed with the baby much of the night, continually bathing his wound and applying Jimenez's ointment to it and to the red spots on his body. Just before morning, the infant let out a healthy squeal and began nursing ravenously at his mother's breast.

While we headed back to the Lombardia, Andres asked, "Will he live?"

"Can't tell with a baby," I replied.

"I'm not asking about the baby," Andres said, "What about the father who had him circumcised? Will Felipe live?"

I did not reply nor did I comment on the circumcision. As a matter of fact, I was annoyed that Andres had questioned me. We both knew what it meant. If the Inquisition's agents learned about the circumcision, the baby, the parents, and the one who did the circumcision would be hauled before the Holy Tribunal. Andres even recalled that the Edict of Faith dictated that anyone withholding such information from the Inquisition could be put to death.

Andres and I were duty-bound to report this incident to the authorities.

"Felipe has to get himself and his family out of Cordoba," Andres said. "Sooner or later the Inquisition will find out about the circumcision. Then we'll all pay the price."

I said nothing although I knew he was right; Morales had to get out of Cordoba. But, several days later, while accompanying Jimenez to attend a sick nobleman from Alicante, I heard the patient ask Jimenez whether we knew anyone who could manage a pottery factory. He described the artistic quality of the Formentera glazed pottery which was famous throughout Europe. Realizing this was an opportunity to whisk Morales out of Cordoba, I told the nobleman that I knew someone who might qualify and would bring him in a few days.

When we left the nobleman's house, Jimenez asked me

whom I had in mind. "Felipe Morales," I casually replied.

"What do you know about Morales?" Jimenez asked in what seemed an accusing tone.

"He once mentioned that he had family in Formentera," I replied.

Jimenez countered that Morales would not be permitted to leave Cordoba so I wondered whether Jimenez knew about the circumcision. Fearing further questioning, I quickly left him and sought Andres.

"Can you teach Felipe how to manage a pottery factory in Formentera," I asked Andres.

"Felipe works in the tile factory," Andres replied. "That doesn't qualify him as a craftsman. They make fine white-glazed pottery in Formentera."

"Can you teach him, at least, to appear like a factory manager."

"Whether I can teach him is not the point," Andres quipped, "Formentera is far enough from Cordoba."

During the next two days, Andres spent almost all his time preparing Morales for the interview with the nobleman from Alicante. At first, Morales resisted going to Formentera because he knew so little about the pottery manufacture. But, after Andres' instruction, Morales made a good impression on the nobleman who arranged for him and his family to move immediately to Formentera.

Andres and I were relieved that the episode was behind us. That night, however, Jimenez came into our room inquiring about our interest in Morales. He did not explain why he came to question us, and I immediately suspected he would involve us with the Inquisition. Andres quickly allayed my fears telling Jimenez the clinic received a very handsome fee by introducing Morales to the nobleman. Jimenez seemed satisfied.

When he left, I told Andres that I suspected Jimenez knew more than he was willing to admit. Andres disregarded my remarks.

Despite the work Andres had done for Morales, I still could not get myself to trust him, although we often talked openly about the Inquisition. My obsession that the Inquisition would involve me with another "Abram Senor" episode was still so strong that I continued to shun Andres' friendship. His behavior was so much like Gaspar's — befriending me and overtly opposing the Inquisition — that I decided to stay on guard, watching his every move.

Even when I attended his sick mother, I treated her like any other patient, never speaking about my work with her son.

She seemed much younger than his step-father, Don Gutierrez, who told me Andres was twelve when he married the young widow. Andres' mother boasted about her husband's former military career and bragged that he was now a member of the Cortes of Cordoba, in charge of licensing guilds and trades.

Don Gutierrez interrupted and, embracing his wife, he said, "When I was given the Medal of the Crown honoring my military service, I publicly announced that my real reward for my years in the army was my new wife and my wonderful son."

It was Don Gutierrez who arranged for Andres' appointment as caretaker of the Casa Lombardia. When the *cortes* announced the appointment, people sneered. Andres was young, they said, inexperienced and ribald, more a court jester than a court appointee.

"To the surprise of everyone," Don Gutierrez said, beaming with pride, "Andres demonstrated exceptional talent in reorganizing the run-down Casa. His ability to work with tradesmen and shipping agents accounted for his success."

I agreed with their boasting about Andres but I sat impassively, listened courteously, careful not to become personally involved with them.

Like everyone else, I was impressed with Andres' astounding accomplishment. Secretly, though, I saw in him a potential for my own salvation. I never gave up my hope of escaping from Spain, so I plotted to use Andres' wide contacts with shipping agents transporting goods and passengers in and out of Spain. I worked closely with him to get to know them so when my time for escape would come, I could contact them without his knowledge.

I was amazed that after two and a half years of this close relationship, Andres never questioned me about my behavior, never imposed himself on me, never even attempted to sway me from my set pattern which must have been enigmatic and bothersome to him.

One cold Tuesday afternoon, I was on my way to the Instruction of Faith session at the San Miguel Chapel that I had attended every Tuesday for the past three years. I passed through the busy market place in my characteristic abnormal gait, taking long strides and bobbing up and down with each step. In the chapel, I sat apart from the other conversos, waiting for Father Pedro to begin the usual three-hour harangue. I suddenly realized that my security was nearing its end because my apprenticeship with Jimenez would soon be over.

I was apprehensive about leaving the safety of the dispensary: I knew that I could not survive on the outside. Very few conversos did.

"Maybe I could prevail on Master Jimenez," I thought, "to allow me to remain his apprentice indefinitely."

The elderly Jimenez often complimented me on my knowledge of medicine. But he kept me at arm's length. He would be foolhardy to jeopardize his own safety by becoming too closely identified with me. At best, conversos were considered a liability.

While I was sitting in the church, preparing my arguments to Jimenez, Father Pedro walked in and began his weekly discourse. He quoted lengthy Biblical passages describing heresy and warning us of the dire consequences of relapsing into sin. The melancholy, and abnormally short, rotund Father Pedro, believing that good theology did not require good delivery, droned endlessly. I struggled to stay awake because even slight disinterest on my part could be considered heresy.

Late in the afternoon, when I returned to the dispensary, I was eager to speak to Jimenez. Andres was perched in a wagon outside the Casa Lombardia, waiting for me.

"Jimenez wants you come to the San Sebastian right away," Andres called out.

I climbed up on the wagon and Andres immediately began racing towards the San Sebastian. As always, I remained impassive. I did not utter a word. He probably expected me to show some interest, at the mention of "San Sebastian", a monastery outside Cordoba used as a hospital during civil disasters such as a plague or a hurricane.

When we reached the monastery's vineyards, I saw a crowd surrounding an overturned cart. I directed Andres to cut across the vineyards so we would reach the group more quickly. When we arrived I saw a person lying under the overturned cart and I barked out orders to Andres to clear away the people hovering around the victim. Jimenez was attending the stricken man who was clutching his bleeding leg, alternately cursing and crying, unable to withstand the pain.

"Get a bucket of hot water!" I shouted. "Bring a bed to the vineyard! Go pray further away!"

"Bad fracture," Jimenez whispered. "We have to set the bone right now. Get Andres and both of you hold tight."

Andres and I pinned down the victim, holding his arms and good leg while Jimenez, despite his obesity and his pudgy hands, swiftly pulled on the fractured leg, expertly jerking it into position. At that instant, the injured man let out a blood-curdling cry and, fortunately, fainted. He would have felt greater pain when Jimenez treated the raw wound, washed it, applied his *hierba* ointment, and placed a splint on the injured leg.

The bed I ordered was brought to the field by several monks who were directed by Father Hernandez, the elderly abbot. He told us he had his office converted to a bedroom for the injured man. Jimenez, Andres and I lifted him, placed him on the bed and, with the monks' help, we carefully carried the bed back to the abbot's room. We stayed with the injured man only briefly because there was little more to be done for him. We retired to a corner of the dining room where Jimenez introduced me to Father Hernandez.

The abbot looked at me quizzically and asked whether we had met before. I said nothing. He then asked, "Are you the Abrabanel boy?."

Astounded and overcome with suspicion, I could only manage to nod.

"I knew your father," Father Hernandez said. "And, I met you twelve years ago in the Cathedral of Toledo."

He remembered me from the time of his session with father, discussing the role of Inquisition. He even described the way I looked when I was nine. I did not want to get involved with the abbot, so I lied that I could not recall the incident, hoping that would end our conversation. He said he knew of my hardships in Toledo and about the role in Abram Senor's trial. I detected a deep compassion in his voice but I was too frightened by his disclosures to thank him for his concern.

"Years tend to take their toll," Father Hernandez said. "You have grown up and I have grown old."

A wisp of a man, he had scrawny hands that seemed too long for his body. He was almost bald except for a few strands of white hair, which blew about in the wind. Despite his old age, he had an air of authority. Andres said he ran the monastery with just his piercing eyes which issued commands and commanded respect.

Jimenez taught Father Hernandez to treat the wound with the special *hierba* ointment and said he would return the following day. I was impressed with the abbot but, true to my assumed character, I decided to steer clear of him, lest he involve me with the Inquisition.

Andres' wagon took us back to the Lombardia, racing down

the rutted roads. It was a long and tiring ride. I sat opposite Jimenez comparing the two master physicians under whom I had served. Jimenez set the leg masterfully. His *hierba* ointment served us well in so many instances. But, where Don Alfonso always shared his diagnosis, Jimenez never gave any explanation. During years as his apprentice, I learned simply by observing and asking.

"The bone will probably set well," I said, "but what about the crushed toes? Can you prevent the tissue from blackening?"

"If that should develop," Jimenez replied, "I shall attend to it then."

"Is there a way to lessen the pain by some potion, or by inducing sleep?" I asked recalling how the injured man fainted from the pain.

Jimenez dismissed my question as irrelevant. When I tried to explain Don Alfonso's use of narcotics to deaden a patient's pain, he said that he was not interested in Alfonso's experiments.

"Alfonso is a butcher," Jimenez said. "Butchers need potions. Doctors don't."

I immediately changed the subject to avoid a debate on the merits of surgery by saying, "Poor man, he must have suffered the tortures of hell."

"Now that son of a bitch knows how others feel," Andres said.

Jimenez instantly reprimanded Andres for his remark and threatened to denounce him to the authorities. I was amazed at Jimenez's quick reaction, so I asked, "Who is the injured man?"

"Don't you know?" Andres replied, "He's Manuel."

The name made no impression on me and I asked again, "Who's Manuel?"

This time, Andres turned around saying, "He was Torquemada's Chief Administrator in Toledo and now he's the Director of the Inquisition of Andalusia. He's the hangman."

Jimenez grabbed Andres by the scruff of his neck and,

holding him tightly with his pudgy hands, shouted, "I'm reporting you to the Suprema."

Andres twisted out of Jimenez's grasp, laughing off his threat.

But I did not. I was perturbed because only two weeks earlier, Jimenez and I were called to stand by during the flogging of a patient whose only crime was crying out in a moment of pain, "It feels like the Inquisition's torture chamber." Someone reported it to the Holy Tribunal and he was tried as a heretic.

When we arrived at the Lombardia, I was still deeply troubled. I wanted to ask Jimenez if he would really report Andres. But, again, I chose to remain silent. Yet, lying on my cot, a radical change was taking place within me. During the past three years, my only concern was to remain alive and to make certain that I would not manipulated. Now, I was no longer worried about myself only. I was deeply concerned about Andres' safety. I turned and tossed as I imagined Andres' punishment at the hands of the Inquisitors.

After a sleepless night, I made a very important decision: I would confide in Andres to warn him of the danger facing him if Jiménez reported him to the Inquisition.

I finally fell asleep, but when I awoke, I learned that Andres had already gone to the San Sebastian with Jimenez. I waited impatiently for his return, thinking only of Andres' safety. I could not concentrate on my work in the dispensary. In the late afternoon, he rode in with Jimenez who went straight to his room to rest from the long journey. Andres was in his usual jovial mood. He carried a large crate of grapes from the San Sebastian's vineyards.

"I don't know how well you set the leg yesterday, my dear doctor," Andres said, dangling a cluster of grapes in front of my eyes, "but we already received a very handsome fee for your services."

"Andres," I said, throwing a grape in the air and catching it in my mouth, "how would you like a trip up the River?"

Andres was startled by my light-heartedness as well as by my response. Ever since my arrival, he had repeatedly invited me to take a boat trip up the River which I had repeatedly refused. After so many refusals, the expression, "boat trip up the River", took on the meaning of "never". In a moment of dismay, for example, Andres would call out "we'll get that fence fixed when you take that boat trip up the River."

The River was Andres' window to the outside world through which he could escape from the narrow confines of Cordoba. He and his boat were a common sight along the River. Ship captains greeted him as he rowed out to meet them and city officials considered Andres and his boat as a natural part of the city's port. He was very proud of his small boat on which he had painted bright green and yellow stripes. It was the only one of its kind along the Guadalquivir.

"Don't be so shocked," I repeated, "How about a trip up the River?"

"When?" Andres asked suspiciously testing my sincerity.

"Right now! This minute!"

Andres dropped the box of grapes and shouted, "Let's go! I'm free. You're free. And the River's full of life."

As we raced toward the river, he asked why I had suddenly changed my mind.

"It's nothing," I answered casually, "I just want to talk to you." It was early April and, although summer was still far off, its signs were everywhere. Fields were turning green, displacing the rust brown stalks of winter. Red poppies and purple asters burst in a splash of color, as though hailing summer's early arrival. Cool evening breezes drove away the day's heat and whispered through the huge sycamore and eucalyptus trees. The trees also showed signs of shedding their winter grays: tiny green buds which were about to burst forth with their summer brilliance.

When we got to the River's edge, Andres led me to the wharf where his boat was tied alongside one of the ocean-going caravels.

"The Guadalquivir is Spain's deepest river," Andres proudly explained as though it were his river. "Ships from all over, from as far away as Cadiz and even the Canarias, drop anchor here. This is one of the busiest ports in Spain."

As we were sailing out of the port, Andres spoke glowingly about the River pointing to interesting sights. Here the water was shallow because of the outflow of one of many estuaries; there it was deep. Here an old castle was being repaired; there a new one being constructed.

I interrupted him.

"Andres, I have little interest in sight-seeing. My only reason for the 'trip up the River' is to get out of sight of everyone so that I could tell you about myself and all that had happened to me before coming to Cordoba," I said to his astonishment.

I began by telling about father's experience in the palace when he tried to avoid the Edict of Expulsion. I related, in detail, my experience with the Inquisition when I attempted to acquire my right to remain in Spain. As I continued, Andres stopped rowing, his eyes riveted on me and his body leaning forward so as not to miss a single word of my story.

I described meeting Torquemada when Don Carlos saved me from the Holy Tribunal. Then I told Andres about Gaspar's perfidy stressing my role in bringing about Don Abram's death. I reminisced about the aged Abram recalling many pleasant incidents with him.

Then, I stopped talking because I choked up. Tears welled in my eyes and I turned my head away from Andres.

Andres pulled the oars into the boat, allowing her to glide with the current. He moved to my side of the boat and, putting his hands over my shoulders, whispered, "I know how you feel and I now understand why you wore your mask."

I apologized for breaking down; but he merely asked, "Why didn't you tell me all this before?"

"Because I didn't trust you," I answered.

"Even after I helped you with Morales?" he asked.

"So did Gaspar," I said.

"Then what convinced you to trust me?"

"What you said about Manuel," I replied.

"I don't remember anything, except his broken leg," he replied.

"When we were riding back from the San Sebastian," I said, trying to jog his memory.

"What did I say about that son of a bitch?" he asked.

"That he was a son of a bitch, a hangman," I replied. "And that can get you in a lot of trouble."

Andres laughed and, ridiculing my fears, he said, "You could be in trouble. I could've been acting the part just to trap you. Like Gaspar."

I leaned over to Andres, grasped him by the arm, and said, "I'm not worried about myself. I'm worried about you."

"Worried about me! What the hell are you talking about?"

"Jimenez. He threatened to report you to the Inquisition."

"Jimenez is as harmless as a puppy dog," Andres replied.

"I suspected him of being my Gaspar," I said.

"He's no spy, I tell you," Andres said.

"So, if it's not you and it's not Jimenez," I asked, "who is the agent manipulating me here in Cordoba?"

"You're overly concerned with the Inquisition," he said.

I would not be put off.

"Maybe Father Hernandez was the person responsible for my coming to Cordoba," I said.

Andres again scoffed at me, telling me that if I would only allow myself to befriend people, I would find Father Hernandez to be a most a gentle person, a lovable priest. I violently shook my head asserting that as long as there was still a possibility of another devilish atrocity in the making, I would not change the image I had created of myself. I would trust no one.

"Berto, let's take a different approach," Andres said. "The

Inquisition did use you in Toledo. They used you to get rid of Abram Senor. But now, they're finished with you. You're just like any other converso. Why must there be an agent spying on you more than on anyone else?"

"Don Alfonso told me so," I replied. "He specifically said that they selected both Cordoba and Jimenez."

Andres challenged me again, "If so, why hasn't the Inquisition already made its move? Why have they waited almost three years?"

"I don't know," I replied. "But remember, since coming to Cordoba, I've kept out of sight. I've become *el mudo*."

"They're not interested in you," Andres flatly stated.

When I insisted the Inquisition had targeted me for some special mission, Andres picked up the oars and bluntly replied, "I'm sure you're exaggerating."

He began rowing back to the wharf. We sat in silence listening to the cadence of his oars swishing through the water. Then, taking hold of the oars and stopping his rowing, I asked, "Andres, do you really believe that? Do you really believe I'm exaggerating. Even after I told you everything that happened in Toledo?"

Andres again pulled in the oars and, after a long pensive moment, he said, "No, I only wanted to make you feel better. I do believe that you're going to be used by the Inquisition. And, I'm as eager as you to find the special agent, the Gaspar, in Cordoba." We both sat silently as the boat drifted into a clump of reeds at the shore.

"What about Manuel?" he asked. "Have you ever met him before?"

When I said I had never met the man, he told me Manuel was transferred from Toledo to Cordoba at about the same time I had arrived at the Casa Lombardia. As the Area Director of the Inquisition, Manuel was the most inaccessible person in Cordoba, so he could not personally be the spy watching over me. He might be the one ordering someone else to do it.

I named every person with whom I had contact over the past years and concluded that Jimenez was the only one who was ever close enough to observe me.

"Could he be the agent?" I asked despite Andres' previous assurances. "After all, Don Alfonso also told me that the Inquisition assigned me to Jimenez's clinic."

"Anyone can be an agent of the Inquisition," Andres replied. "Anyone but Jimenez."

"What makes you so sure," I asked.

Andres then related the fascinating saga of Jimenez's evolution as a physician:

When Jimenez worked as a carpenter in the *juderia*, he fell off a roof he was supposed to repair. He suffered multiple fractures in his arms and legs and was hospitalized for several years in a charity institution. To assure better care for him, his wife worked at the hospital as a cleaning woman. When Jimenez recovered enough to be able to limp along, he was given simple assignments to help the doctors with easy chores. It was his wife who first noticed Jimenez's unique talent in dealing with patients and it was she who encouraged him to stay at the hospital even after his total recovery. Through her intercession, one of the doctors took him on as a permanent helper.

For ten long years, Jimenez did all kinds of menial work, slaving for the doctor and the hospital. But, to Jimenez's everlasting credit, he managed to learn enough of the art of medicine to receive his certification from the Royal Medical Commission in Toledo. He was a poverty stricken doctor serving farmers and peasants as far away as Seville. He subsisted on their gifts of food staples which he brought home to his hungry family. But, he also proved himself to be a likeable doctor, helpful to many people in need. Several years later, when the Inquisition moved against the

Cortes of Cordoba, civil turmoil swept the city. Jimenez was enlisted by the *cortes* to rally the peasants and his former patients against the Inquisition. Jimenez was quite popular with the poor farmers and he succeeded in rallying quite a number of them to oppose the Inquisition. The *cortes* repaid him by appointing him their physician and administrator of the Casa Lombardia with the stipulation that it was to be a public clinic.

This success came too late to help Jimenez. The following year, the Inquisition toppled the *cortes* and he narrowly escaped being its first victim.

His wife was not as fortunate.

"Jimenez's wife died in the Inquisition's dungeons when she was brought in for interrogation," Andres said. "And that's why he can't be an agent of the Inquisition."

When we reached the wharf, the sun had already set and the crescent moon could be seen sliding out of its cloud cover. We walked slowly back to the Casa Lombardia.

"You see, Berto, Jimenez is certainly not your spy," Andres said. "And he wouldn't report me to the Inquisition because he can't run this dispensary without me."

"Then why did he threaten to report you when you spoke against Manuel?" I asked.

"Probably because he suspects you of being an informer," Andres replied.

"Me? A spy for the Inquisition!"

"We're no different than you. Around here, nobody trusts anybody. Everyone considers everyone else to be a spy," Andres replied. "Jimenez probably threatened me for his own defense. He wanted to make sure you would not report him to the Inquisition for not reacting to my outburst."

"Tell me about Jimenez's children," I asked.

Andres said he and Rodriguez had served together in the

same militia. Through his step-father, Gutierrez, Andres helped Rodriguez attain the rank of captain and they remained close friends even after Andres had left the militia. As for Diaz, Andres shrugged his shoulders saying, "Diaz is a poor soul, an idiot who can do nothing right. I bring him to work at the Lombardia only to satisfy Jimenez's desire to have his son close."

"So, why is it that every time Diaz comes around the dispensary, he's always angry, always hostile towards me," I asked.

"Well," Andres explained, "first he's an idiot and you're a converso. So, there's no telling what goes on in his demented mind. Also, the talk around the city is that you are better than Jimenez and patients are asking for you when they come to the clinic. Diaz may be dim-witted, but he's smart enough to realize that from the first day you came to the Lombardia, you were a threat to his father."

"I have done nothing to offend Jimenez," I said. "In fact, I'm eager to stay on as his assistant."

"Diaz can't forget the years his father was held up to public ridicule. He probably feels that your mere presence is a threat," Andres said.

"So," again I asked, "if it's not Jimenez, who is the agent watching me?"

"Berto, let's think this out together. Tell me about everyone you met, I mean, anyone with whom you established any kind of close relationship, since you left Toledo."

We named patients, traders, church officials, even Andres' parents. We both decided there was absolutely no one who even came close to me. Jimenez was the only one. And he was eliminated as a suspect.

My immediate worry about Andres allayed, life returned to normal again.

Three weeks later, I encountered the Count of Trastamara and met his beautiful daughter, Maria.

5

During the Easter Festival, the city of Cordoba celebrates its annual *Gran Fiesta*. Ordinarily, the *Fiesta* begins right after Easter and continues for a week with unbridled revelry and tumultuous merry making. In preparation for the *Gran Fiesta*, we converted every space in the Casa Lombardia, even the groves, into a hospital facility in order to accommodate the many people who would be injured in the drunken brawls and general hysteria that would grip the city for the week.

The start of the *Gran Fiesta* was always signaled by an extravagant parade over the San Rafael Bridge led by the Count of Trastamara astride his white stallion. The populace, young and old, would follow the parade as it entered the city and proceeded to the sprawling gardens of the Alcazar, where the count would give money to his troops and distribute food and drink to all.

This year, due to his illness, the count did not lead the parade nor did he attend the *Gran Fiesta*. Don Luis de Teruel, the count's ranking knight, represented him. He supervised the affairs of the House of Trastamara and was the overseer of the count's wide-ranging interests. Don Luis was about thirty-five, exceptionally tall, and swarthy. As the count's *hidalgo*, ranking nobleman, Don Luis was a familiar figure in Cordoba. He was well-liked by the count's entourage and by the townspeople.

On the two occasions I met Don Luis, I found him to be charming, efficient, and very bright. We first met when he inspected the hospital grounds soon after Andres' appointment as caretaker of the Casa Lombardia. At that time, he instructed Andres to make proper use of the irrigation canal for the groves surrounding the Lombardia. He also interviewed me, as the new apprentice, and was gracious to me despite my uncooperative behavior. Maria, the count's daughter accompanied Don Luis on the visit. She was the one who commented about my unclean appearance. My second meeting with Don Luis occurred about a year later, when he came to reinspect our improved medical facilities. Although he criticized Andres for not keeping adequate supplies on hand, I was impressed that, in so doing, he was careful not to hurt Andres' feelings. And, when he questioned me about my work, I was still uncooperative yet he was compassionate and seemed to understand my feelings.

At sunrise on the *Gran Fiesta*'s fourth day, Don Luis suddenly galloped into the grounds of the Lombardia on his stallion. He summoned me to urgently call Jimenez. I explained that the old doctor had worked through the night and had gone to the *cantina* to rest. Don Luis asked Andres, who was just waking up, to find the doctor. While he was gone, Don Luis explained that Jimenez had been treating the count for a shoulder wound and that the count suffered great pain all night. Andres returned dragging Jimenez who was too drunk to be of help. Don Luis then ordered me to ride back to the castle with him. As we left, he instructed Andres to sober up Jimenez, so that he could look after the sick at the Lombardia.

Trastamara Castle overlooked La Campina region, south of Cordoba, from a low hilltop. We rode through a valley of green meadows and lush vineyards criss-crossed by rivulets of the Guadalquivir River. We arrived early in the morning. The distressed countess met us at the gate and was obviously surprised to see me. She neither greeted me nor even acknowledged my presence.

When Don Luis explained Jimenez's condition, she demanded, "Why did you not summon the doctor from Seville?"

To make matters worse, my slovenly appearance — unkempt hair, unshaven, grimy clothing — made a very bad impression on her: And, when she asked me if I knew how to treat a wound, I just nodded, saying nothing to assure her.

"Jiminez knows the count's condition," she reprimanded Don Luis. "This coarse apprentice knows nothing of the illness."

After a whispered conversation with Don Luis, she reluctantly led me to the count's bedchamber. I felt no distress at her hostile reception nor did I take notice of the castle's elegant furnishings. My one concern was to treat a sick patient. The moment I walked into the count's chamber, I did not even wait for a formal introduction but immediately approached his bedside to examine the wound. At first touch, I realized his body was exceptionally warm.

"How long have you had this fever?" I asked.

"It's not the fever," the countess snapped, "it's the wound, the pain."

"How long did you have this fever?" I repeated, disregarding her.

"About a week," the count answered.

When I reached over to remove his bandages, the count told me not bother with a full examination, saying that he only wanted Jimenez's *hierba* ointment.

"I will decide whether to use the ointment," I stated ordering his servant to undress the bandage. Don Luis stepped forward reminding me that it was the Count Luis de Trastamara whom I was attending and that I was to treat him with deference. I gently pushed Don Luis aside and undressed the bandage myself.

"I'm going to apply pressure around the wound," I said to the count. "Tell me when you feel pain."

I pressed my finger near his shoulder blade, working slowly over to his back. He winced when I pressed on the reddened area below his nape and cried out when I pressed a bit lower.

"Now to move your hand and arm. Tell me which movement causes you pain," I said.

He indicated slight pain bending the elbow and much sharper pain raising his hand. I immediately recognized the nature of the wound and knew that it had to be excised by a relatively simple surgical procedure.

"You have an inflamation not a superficial wound," I said, "and that is why you have a fever. Your wound is deep. It reaches your muscle which accounts for the pain you feel when you raise your hand."

I explained that Jimenez's *hierba* ointment would give only temporary relief from the pain but it would not cure the inflamation.

"What do you recommend? " the count asked.

"Surgery," I answered.

I heard a gasp in the room. They were surprised and frightened.

"I am not here to debate the merits of surgery with you," I said, "but I know that if the wound is allowed to grow further into the muscle tissue, you may expect far greater pain than merely the small cut of a knife."

Since they were reluctant to decide, I offered to return to the city so that Jimenez could come and treat the count with the *hierba* ointment. I assured them I was a good horseman and could quickly get back to Cordoba so Jimenez could return to the castle in ample time. I stood off to the side as the count and countess huddled with Don Luis debating whether to allow me to cut into his body. As they continued talking in hushed tones, I picked up my pack making ready to leave.

"Please do it," the countess said.

Those three words, "please do it," signalled a flurry of activity in the count's bedroom. I washed my hands in the basin and ordered their strongest wine poured it into a large cup. I insisted that the count drink it all. Then, I had his bed moved beside the window so I could better see the wound during surgery. As soon as the count showed signs of becoming disoriented, I asked Don Luis and two servants to hold his body tightly, pinning him face-down on his bed. I reached in my pack and took out my small knife with the stubby handle. I knew exactly what incision to make, deep into the wound, and I knew what to expect when the tightened skin burst open. Before proceeding with the surgery, I asked the countess to leave the room but she disregarded me and remained watching from the far corner. When I cut into the count's shoulder, she cried out, causing the count to turn his head towards her. I signalled Don Luis to escort her from the room.

By the time I finished cleaning and dressing the wound, the count had fallen asleep. Don Luis and I tiptoed out and he led me down to the sitting room where the countess and her two children huddled together, deeply concerned about the count. I told them that everything went well. The countess introduced me to her daughter, Maria, and her young son, Enrique. I explained the procedure I had used, assuring them that the count would be completely cured in a few days. They asked many questions about the surgery, in general, and about the count's condition in particular. I responded to each question as Don Alfonso would. They were relieved by my repeated assurances and encouraged that the count would fully recover and would no longer have any pain.

Maria then asked about the procedure for becoming a doctor. I explained that my apprenticeship with Jimenez was coming to an end. If I chose to be a doctor, however, I would have to be examined by a Royal Commission and then be certified as a physician by a medical board from Toledo.

"Do you want to be a doctor?" the countess asked.

"Of course," I replied telling them about my success as apprentice to Don Alfonso in Toledo.

"You are a very strange man," the countess said. "At first, you were shy, hardly saying a word. Even when I asked if you knew how to treat sores, you just nodded your head. You said nothing. But when you approached the count, you ordered us about as though we were your servants."

I apologized but she immediately said she liked me better when I displayed confidence. Suddenly, my confidence dissolved. Awkwardly, I kept tugging at the buttons of my dirty

Sacred Sword

jacket; straightened out my filthy, unbecoming peasant garb, and tried to wipe the blood stains off my hands and clothing. I realized my shabby appearance. I knew that this was strange; in the past three years, I had not cared how I looked. Now, I was apologizing for my appearance saying how uncomfortable I felt in those rags.

The countess ridiculed me for my behavior but Maria said, "If you're so uncomfortable, take off your jacket."

I thanked her but kept my jacket on. I could not admit that I had no shirt underneath.

"The jacket fits you so well," Maria said teasingly. "How can you be so handsome and yet be a physician?"

"Maria!" the countess rebuked, "you are embarrassing our guest."

"Mother, if someone told me that I was pretty, I wouldn't feel embarrassed," Maria said.

I wanted to return the compliment by telling her that it was her beauty that was causing my discomfort but, instead, I mumbled an apology for my appearance. I reminded her that she embarrassed me about my shabby clothing when she first visited the Casa Lombardia.

"I remember," Maria said softly, "and I'm really sorry."

"No," I said, "You were right. I should always be neat."

"But I should not have embarrassed you," she said.

"Stop talking about his clothing," the countess said good naturedly, "and bring some refreshments."

Ordinarily, after attending to a patient, I would leave immediately in order not to get involved with non-medical matters but, this time, I agreed to stay, thanking her for inviting me.

Enrique, the nine year-old, asked, "Will my father recover in time for the ceremonies at the end of the *Gran Fiesta*?"

The countess explained that in past years, Enrique rode behind his father and took part in the elaborate closing ceremonies. I told him the count would not be well enough to return to Cordoba that soon, explaining that although he would be cured, he would need at least a week to recuperate.

Maria returned with a tray of fruit and candy and while serving us, she surprised me by saying that she was annoyed that I paid no attention to her when she visited the Casa Lombardia.

"You weren't sick," I said jokingly, "and I pay no attention to healthy people, even very pretty ones like you."

She laughed, "Well, at last. Thanks for the long overdue compliment."

We chatted in the salon most of the morning. Ever so often, I caught myself staring at Maria and once when she served me some fruit our hands touched. We smiled but said nothing. I wanted to tell her that was the first time I had smiled in three years.

I told them about my many accomplishments as an apprentice, even boasting how I, at one time, swam half way across the Guadllquivir in a driving rain to save a drowning child. My desire to make a good impression was a strange phenomenon. I was bragging and I enjoyed it.

Enrique provided me with yet another opportunity to brag about my medical accomplishments when he said, "If my father recovers, we shall be very thankful to you."

"Don't say 'if'," I snapped. "Your father has already recovered. Before the surgery, he had a diseased wound that was painful and dangerous. But now, after my surgery, he has only a flesh wound that will soon heal."

The countess said she was impressed with my confidence and that she, too, was beginning share it. She then turned to Enrique telling him that his tutor had been waiting all morning so he must return to his lessons. Before leaving, Enrique, as pompous as a nine-year-old can be, expressed, "the gratitude of the House of Trastamara" for my services. We all laughed at the child's obvious attempts to carry on the noble traditions of his family.

I enjoyed every moment in the salon with Maria. We were alone several times, when her mother went to speak to Enrique's tutor and, later, when she left us to watch over her husband. We ate lunch together and, despite my shabby appearance, I felt no discomfort. I told her so.

"It's not what you wear that makes the man," Maria said. "What's inside of you is more important."

When I said Don Carlos had told me the same thing about a soldier's uniform, she brightened up saying that when she was little, Don Carlos had served in her father's militia. She described his character so well that I complimented her ability to judge a person, especially someone she met when she was so young.

She came up to me and gazed into my eyes for some time. Then she said, "I can tell a person's character by looking into his eyes."

I felt exhilarated having her so close. I kept asking her all sorts of questions about my character but not really listening to her answers. I just wanted to keep her there, close to me. She soon realized what I was doing and, gingerly, pushed me aside and glided away from me.

Maria was beautiful, a warm unassuming woman with exquisitely delicate features. She had a radiant, magic glow. Sitting in that salon, we said things to each other that strangers do not speak about the first time they meet. We revealed our likes and dislikes, our good and bad habits, our quirks, our whims.

Her mother passed by the salon to tell us she had some chores to attend to, she instructed Maria, "Entertain our doctor while I'm gone."

"Now, tell me dear doctor," Maria saiod when her mother left, "how can I entertain you?"

"Tell me that you're real, not a vision," I said.

"I'll pinch you so you know you're not dreaming," she said, squeezing my hand.

We touched for only a brief moment but my heart thumped so violently I thought it could be heard throughout the castle. She asked me how long would I be able to stay. When I told her that I might have to return to Cordoba to help Jiminez, she stomped her feet and crimped her pretty face, unable to hide her disappointment. I was thrilled. She expressed my feelings.

The countess and Enrique returned. She again asked for reassurances about the count's condition because she had passed his room and it seemed that his face was contorted with pain.

"Is he sleeping," I asked.

"Yes."

"When you sleep, do you feel pain?"

"No, of course not," she said.

"Neither does he," I replied.

With this assurance, the countess said she would return to the count and instructed Maria, "Tell Teresa to prepare the Portico Room. Our physician will stay with us for a few days.

"There's really no need for me to stay here," I said to the countess. "It's the *Gran Fiesta* and I'm sure Don Jimenez will need me at the Lombardia."

"The count needs you, here," the countess replied. "Jimenez will be informed. You will remain here to attend to my husband."

I was glad she ordered me to stay and even happier when she took Enrique with her, leaving me alone with Maria.

When he mother was out of sight, Maria mimmicked me, "'There's really no need for me to stay here."

"I only said that to tease you," I said.

"I know," she replied. "And what would you do if my mother had said 'Good, go back to Cordoba'?"

"I would have said, 'without me the count cannot be healed,'" I replied.

She sat down next to me on the divan, held my arm and thanked me.

When she fingered my filthy clothing, I again fumbled with my dirty jacket.

"Maria, you're so beautiful. Wearing these rags, I feel unworthy."

She playfully slapped my wrist and kissed me lightly on each cheek saying, "One is for telling me I'm beautiful and one is to make you feel worthy."

"So, I'll keep saying you're beautiful," I said puckering up my lips.

She danced away from me, leaving me alone on the divan.

"I'm going to get Teresa to prepare your room, then, like mother said, I will entertain you."

When she returned, she led me down to the gardens where we sat on a marble bench facing a delicate statue of a man and a woman in a loving embrace.

She pointed out the flowing lines formed by the woman's hair, her breasts and her body.

"See how her soft curved lines contrast with the sharp angular lines of the male figure," she said.

Then she continued describing other features of the statue.

"I'm amazed at your fine perception of art," I said encouraging her to continue.

"Do you know what makes this a work of art?" she asked. "It's made of stone, lifeless, hard, inert marble. Yet, it captures the feeling, the love, the warmth of life itself."

We sat there for the rest of the afternoon talking about life, our lives, and our feelings. I shall never forget her comparison of human life to the statue.

"Through this sculpture, the artist, suceeded in doing something we can probably never hope to accomplish," she said. "He captured the moment of love and made it permanent, unchanging. It will withstand the onslaught of time and weather. Do you think we, frail human beings, can do that in real life?"

I was about to comment on her intimate and challenging observation when a short, fat, energetic woman suddenly burst into our garden.

"Alberto," Maria said, "this is Teresa. Without her, the entire castle would fall apart and with it the House of Trastamara."

"Alberto," Teresa called out, her voice cackling and circling me several times. "Alberto di Cadiz! So, you're the butcher they were telling me about."

Maria left me in Teresa's care saying, "I have to dress for dinner. Now, go with Teresa and you be on time."

Teresa poked me in the ribs with her elbow, motioning to me to follow her as she waddled ahead of me. She went up a flight of stairs along a tiled portico stopping in front of a room overlooking a magnificent rose garden.

"I don't know what Maria sees in you, but she said to get you the best room in the castle," she snickered. "Get in there, your highness, I'll be right back."

I sat at the edge of the bed enjoying an unfamiliar feeling of well being. For the first time in years, I was totally unaware of the Inquisition. I thought about Maria's olive-skinned, beautiful face, her large soft brown eyes, her long dark brown wavy hair and her lovely graceful body. I put my fingers to my face, recalling her soft, velvet lips when she kissed me. Only Maria could, with just a smile, dissolve all the torment that had burned in me for so long.

The sun was about to set. Only then did I realize that Maria and I had been together from the early morning to twilight. I could not remember ever spending so much time with any one person, not since my boyhood with Asher.

Teresa soon returned, handing me a suit with a matching silk shirt and an elegant pair of riding boots. "And now, my Lord," she said, grotesquely curtseying, "after you've had your bath, the countess would be honored if you would join her at the banquet hall where a special dinner will be served in your honor."

As she walked out, she winked at me whispering, "Maria will be there too."

I was about to get undressed when the count's knight, Don Luis, knocked at my door inviting me to the castle's bath house.

"I congratulate you, young man," he said leading me there. "You did a masterful bit of surgery."

"Have you witnessed surgery before?" I asked.

Sacred Sword

"Not too often in this part of the country," he said, "but I could easily tell, just by watching, that you are a master surgeon."

In the steaming bath house, luxuriating in its warm baths, Don Luis told me about himself.

Don Luis was King Ferdinand's illegitimate son, born before the king's marriage to Queen Isabel. King Ferdinand assigned him as *hidalgo* to the Count Juan de Trastamara, a *ricos hombre de natura*, the highest rank of nobility awarded only to direct descendents of the original conquerers of Aragon. In ten years as the ranking *hidalgo* of the House of Trastamara, Don Luis played an important role in administering the count's estates and maintaining the unity of the realm.

He was certainly a charming, pleasant person.

"You impress me very much," Don Luis said while walking with me back to my room, "I'm certain that when the count recovers he will be equally impressed with you."

I appreciated Don Luis' encouragement and, even more, I was flattered by his friendliness towards me. He treated me as an equal, telling me of plans for Andalusia and his various duties as the count's *hidalgo*.

Refreshed and cleaned, I returned to my room where I quickly dressed in the suit of clothing Teresa had brought me: a dark green velvet jacket braided with gold stripes, elegant epaulets and satin pants with matching gold stripes. Although it did not fit too well I was not uncomfortable because I enjoyed wearing clean clothes and soft leather shoes instead of my course jacket and heavy boots.

When I stepped out of the room, Don Luis was at my door ready to escort me to the dining room.

"You are wearing the uniform of a famous general," Don

Luis said, "It belonged to General Carlos de Santa Fe who for many years was the commander of the Trastamara militia."

"I knew the general," I said.

"Yes I know you did," Don Luis said without explaining how he knew about my relationship with Don Carlos. "At one time, he and I served the count together, until Carlos was transferred to command the palace guard for Ferdinand and Isabel. The Trastamara militia he trained is still the realm's most powerful military force."

"Don Carlos left the service of the count and you remained?" I asked.

"Don Carlos did not leave. The Monarchs summoned him. They paid the count dearly in land and gold for Don Carlos' transfer. Personally, I prefer to be with the count than with the Royal Council of Ministers in Toledo where intrigue and deception is the order of the day."

"How do you know about my relationship with Don Carlos?" I asked.

He replied, "Don Carlos and I have maintained personal contact through the years. I know everything about Carlos and Carlos knows everything about me."

"Where is Don Carlos now?" I asked explaining that I had not seen him since I left Toledo.

"He is still in Granada with the army of occupation," Don Luis said. "The defeated Moors, thousands of them, opted to return to Africa rather than live under Spanish rule. Carlos has been negotiating their transfer, although the church has prohibited their leaving Spain. I know that he has a great love for you. I hope we, too, can be friends."

I was amazed and flattered by his friendship, treating me like a member of the noble family. I was further drawn to him because of his relationship to Don Carlos.

Maria met us in the corridor, just outside the dining hall. She said her mother would not join us for dinner because she preferred to watch over her husband. Don Luis excused himself hurrying to the bedroom to relieve the countess so that she could dine with us.

"What kept you so long?" Maria asked as soon Don Luis disappeared. "I was waiting for you."

I told her that Don Luis and I were talking while taking our baths.

"Who is more important, Luis or me?"

I took her hand, kissed it, and said, "You are not only more important, but much prettier."

She feigned annoyance and led me into the dining room where Enrique was already at the table.

"You look refreshed," Maria said taking her seat next to me, "and that uniform is exquisite."

"She really means to say that you're still handsome," Enrique teased.

"Well, she's right," I said. "Put a monkey into a velvet jacket with gold epaulets and even the monkey will look handsome."

The three of us burst out laughing.

"And such a beautiful jacket," Maria teased.

"And such a beautiful monkey," Enrique added, causing a even greater volley of laughter.

Teresa came in, watched our behavior for a while and then left throwing up her hands and shouting, "Crazy *ninos*!"

I had not laughed so heartily in so long that for a fleeting moment I wondered whether I was laughing because the danger had passed or was I allowing laughter to mask my fears? I quickly dismissed the entire issue, refusing to let it interfere with my joy.

When the countess walked into the dining room we stopped laughing and stood up to greet her. She sat down at the table, asking what made us laugh so. When Enrique pointed to me repeating the phrase, "such a beautiful monkey", the three of us again dissolved in laughter.

"I am happy to hear laughter again around the castle," she said, "but I fail to see the humor in mocking our guest."

The more she protested, the more we laughed. Finally, even the countess joined in the merriment repeating, "such a beautiful monkey".

Teresa supervised the servants who served the meal. We all ate heartily, except the countess. She only picked at her food, still apprehensive about the count's condition.

"Why is he is breathing so heavily?" she asked.

"Madam," I said, "we have an expression which says: 'When wine goes to the head, the body should go to bed'."

The countess repeated the phrase and smiled.

"And while he's sleeping, his body is curing itself," I said assuring her of his recovery.

She looked at Maria and said, "He's not only handsome, he's also a very good doctor."

After the meal, I followed the countess to the bedroom to look in on the count. Don Luis said he had awakened just moments before and that he was still groggy from the wine he drank before the surgery. But, he did not complain about any pain. Examining the incision, I detected no complications, so I left the bedroom and returned to Maria.

Enrique was anxious to show me around the castle. Maria tagged along, intimating that I was in for a special treat. He led us first to the the Armorial Room where he described the various trophies on display and then sat upright and erect in one of the richly upholstered chairs, declaring, "This chair was used for the coronation of James the First. My great uncle Ricared served as the *Justicia* of the Realm during his reign."

Maria explained, "The *Justicia* title was awarded to the ranking nobleman, empowering him to arbitrate disputes between the monarch and aggrieved noblemen."

"My father, Count Juan de Trastamara," Enrique proudly announced, "is now the *Justicia* of the Realm.

Sacred Sword

Then Maria and I trailed Enrique from room to room where he showed us bejeweled crowns, precious gifts, scrolls of ancient treaties, and special medalions, each of which he meticulously described. He never seemed to tire nor falter on a single date or a name in his narration. Enrique made the old relics, which he gingerly fingered, come alive. Don Luis joined us as Enrique was describing a little-known historical event. He looked to Don Luis as though asking him to corroborate some of the outlandish incidents he brought up. Don Luis smiled, silently applauding Enrique, and congratulating him on his knowledge of history.

Enrique pointed to the opposite wall, high above our head, asking me to reach for a sword resting on brackets. I tried but it was too high for my reach. I looked about for a bench or a chair so that I could grasp the sword. Don Luis, who was exceptionally tall, towered over me and brought the sword to Enrique. The youngster fondled the sword's handle and solemnly said, "This is the sword of El Cid. It's over 300 years old."

Maria called on Don Luis, whom she described as, "the best swordsman in Andalusia," to tell me its quality. Don Luis took the sword out of its scabbard, swished it expertly several times and said it compared favorably with the best of Cordoban swords.

Enrique was most proud of the official chart tracing the lineage of the Trastamara nobility from the dawn of Spanish history to the present *ricos hombre de natura*, his father. Enrique recalled the venerated names of kings and princes who shaped the empire. It was already late at night when he announced that he would take us to the Tower Room.

"That's enough," Maria said, "Alberto will be here for the entire week and you'll have ample time to show him around."

"I know what you want," Enrique said as he left, trailing his sister to his room, "you two want to be alone."

While Don Luis and I waited for Maria to return, he told me that my mere presence in the castle was making history. I looked at him quizzically as though challenging his remark, so he pointed out that only members of the nobility were allowed entry to these rooms or even to view some of the relics Enrique showed us.

"Also, you are the first commoner permitted to be alone with Maria," he said, explaining the strict social protocol established by the nobility. "However, I assured the countess that this will in no way detract from the status of the House of Trastamara."

When Maria returned, I asked Don Luis to repeat what he had just told me. He did and she teasingly mocked him saying, "Luis, you keep to your protocol. I'll keep to my doctor."

Don Luis began to leave but, at the door, he turned back explaining somberly that his function was to protect the well being and the honor of the House of Trastamara.

"I hope he's right," I said when he was gone.

"Right about what?" she asked.

"Your being alone with me 'will in no way detract from the status of the House of Trastamara'," I said imitating his solemn tones.

Maria laughed saying, "come, I'll show you the Trastamara status. We not only have royal blood but also gypsy blood."

She led me across the patio into the Map Room where she stopped in front of an artistic woven map of Spain showing the coats-of-arms of every major province in bright color.

"We love to travel," Maria said, her finger pointing to a route on the map. "Last year, we sailed along the Guadalquivir to Cadiz, up the Atlantic Ocean and over to the Bay of Vizcaya. Summers are magnificent there. The heat is not oppressive and the entire region is like a lush garden in full bloom. This year, because of my father's illness, we made no vacation plans yet."

"In less than a week, your father will be well enough to travel," I said. "You can start making plans."

"You make it sound like you're sorry he's recovering," she said.

"As a physician, I'm delighted the surgery went well. If Jimenez were here instead of me, you'd be here all summer."

She clasped my hand and was about to say something but then changed her mind. She let her hands drop to her sides saying, "Here, I'm doing all the talking and I know nothing about you."

"There's so little to tell," I said.

"What about your sailing experiences?" she asked.

"My whole sailing experience is limited to one attempt in a fishing vessel," I said. "I was a little boy, six or seven-years-old. I talked our boatsman into taking me on one of his trips. A storm blew up and the ship foundered in the rough seas. A Portuguese navy ship was sent to 'rescue' me. My parents met me at the dock and my mother told me, 'If it's fish you want, get it from the fishmongers'."

Maria laughed heartily then she teasingly said, "You'll have to learn to sail if you want me to love you."

"In that case, I'll sail to the colonies and back," I replied without a smile.

We sat for a long blissful moment enchanted by the bright moon shining through the huge bay window until Teresa walked in and startled us with her booming voice.

"So there you are!" she bellowed at me. "Your eminence, before you plan your next voyage, will you plan an immediate trip to the count's room where you are urgently needed."

I ran down the corridor and up the stairs, taking them three and four at a time, my heart pounding. Maria and Teresa were far behind. Arriving, breathless, I found the countess holding the count's hand.

"What's wrong?" I asked her.

"Nothing," she whispered. "He just fell asleep again but Teresa wants me to wake him up to give him something to eat."

I waited until I saw Teresa. When she came into the room, I said, "No food. Not even Teresa's broth. Right now, sleep is the only thing he needs."

Teresa insisted that her food would cure him more quickly than my care and, saying that, she lifted the soup bowl from a

Sacred Sword

nearby table and was about to walk past me.

"Sleep, that's what he needs," I said, blocking her way.

Unhappy with my decision, Teresa marched back, thumped her bowl on the table, and muttered under her breath, "Great physician! How can anybody get well on an empty stomach?"

I pecked Teresa on the cheek and said, "If everybody ate your broth, they'd all be healthy and I'd be out of work."

I then turned to the countess and suggested that since they were all up the night before, they, too, needed sleep. I volunteered to stay with the count through the night.

"Come, *contesa*," Teresa muttered. "If he does that, at least he'll be doing something useful around here."

The countess hesitated but Maria assured her she, too, would stay with her father promising, "If he wakes up, mother, we will call you."

The countess and Teresa kissed Maria, and before leaving, she kissed me and whispered, "Berto, thank you for everything."

Maria and I sat on a divan facing the count. In quiet whispers, we shared our thoughts and dreams through most of the night until we fell finally asleep in each other's arms. Neither of us heard Don Luis come in, waking us just before dawn and sending us off to our beds.

I walked Maria to her room where she put her arms around me saying, "If my mother can kiss you, so can I."

We kissed and she quickly turned away, closing the door behind her. Back in my room, I fell asleep with my clothes on happy and content. When I awoke the glaring sun was already high in the sky. Enrique stood outside the open window throwing pebbles into my room.

"Good afternoon," he shouted.

"How's your father?" I asked. "Is he awake?"

"No, but everyone else is." he said and, handing me some clothes, he added, "Here, Teresa, sent these for you."

I took off the green uniform and quickly dressed in the white trousers and blue *camisa*. Then I followed Enrique to the Tea Room overlooking the garden. The room and its adjoining garden were a beautiful masterpiece of architecture. A sprawling arched lilac tree in one corner cast its shade over a bed of delphiniums and other colorful flowers, which splashed the entire area with bright blue, purple, green, and yellow hues. The hollyhocks stood tall and gaunt against the log fence entwined with red rambler rose vines. In the center of the garden, the sun's rays glittered around the pink water lilies.

"Well, well, good afternoon, doctor," Maria greeted me. "It seems that the physician slept as well as his patient."

"Not quite, dear," the countess said. "The count woke up early, ate a good meal, worked with Don Luis for a while and then went to sleep again."

I sat next to Maria, who looked radiantly beautiful in the bright sunlight. Enrique teased me saying that if he had not thrown pebbles in my window, I would still be sleeping. I ruffled his hair, thanking him for waking me up.

I turned to the countess and said, "I'm delighted the count is feeling better and I apologize for not being there when he awakened."

"He said that he heard you and Maria talking through most of night," the countess replied.

Maria twittered and I blushed, but the countess assured us that her husband could not recall anything we said. Teresa served a delicious breakfast and before I had a chance to finish my bun, Don Luis came in informing us the count had just gotten up and insisted on coming down to the Tea Room.

We hurried to his room. He was sitting up, trying to dress himself. I rushed to him and got him back into bed. Then I tied his hand in a sling saying, "Sir, the incision in your shoulder has not yet healed. You must not move your hand for a day or two."

He held his other hand to his head and jokingly rebuked me for giving him all that wine.

"My grogginess is worse than my shoulder pain," he said with a grin.

"Just consider that a toast," I said applying Jimenez's *hierba* ointment to the scar, "a toast to the end of the wound."

For the rest of the day, the countess stayed in his room. We all took turns making his recuperation a bit more pleasant. I described some of my medical experiences in Cordoba. Enrique brought his art work and demonstrated some of the acrobatic tricks he had mastered. From time to time, Don Luis would come in for a conference with the count on commercial matters or affairs of the realm making me realize the extent of his power. In the evening when I examined his wound, I told him he could walk around the castle and take his meals with his family on the following day.

Maria and I shared lovely moments together in the library, paging through some of the illuminated manuscripts. We walked through the various chambers of the castle, viewing the paintings and statues in each room. Later, we strolled in the gardens, enjoying their magnificent landscaping and the intoxicating fragrance of exotic flowers.

The count was already in the Tea Room the next morning when I came in for breakfast.

I noticed that despite his recent illness, the stout, short man in his early fifties looked well and youthful. His blond hair, combed straight back, was sprinkled with gray and his round cherubic face was somewhat fleshy. When I began to unlace his shirt to examine his wound, he smiled, telling me he forgot which shoulder had hurt him.

Later, Maria came down and we spent the morning with her father, taking him for short walks around the portico.

During the next two days, Maria and I were constantly together, walking, riding through the forest surrounding the castle, lounging in the courtyard, taking our meals alone in the valley. Teresa provided me with clothing that reminded me of home: soft lace shirts, silk pants with matching jackets and a fine riding habit.

On one occasion, Enrique stealthily followed Maria and me when we went walking in the forest. Suddenly we heard his voice behind us, "Hey, look, the Lovers!"

I thought he was teasing us because we were sitting beside a brook holding hands. But, he was pointing to the horizon where two huge boulders on a nearby mountain ridge resembled two people in an embrace. I did not know what he had in mind but, I enjoyed his enthusiastic shout, "the lovers," as if he were telling the whole world Maria and I were lovers. By then, everyone at the castle knew about my relationship with Maria. Don Luis even arranged for me to leave the dispensary for a month so that I could accept the count's invitation to join them on their sailing vacation.

That evening, a festive dinner took place in the castle's dining room where several dignitaries, including Father Hernandez, were present. The countess wore regal attire which included a bejeweled pendant. Maria told me it was a family heirloom worn only on special occasions. The count, also resplendent in noble garb, announced that this was a special dinner to honor me. Don Luis raised his glass, toasting me and boasting that it was he who first brought me to the castle. At that moment, the countess leaned over to me whispering behind her fan that she almost kicked me out of the castle when I first arrived. We laughed when I asked whether she preferred me in my dirty clothes or in the embroidered suit I was wearing.

"I know you have all suffered with me," the count said after dinner, "and it's too bad that you missed the *Gran Fiesta*, but Don Luis arranged for you to see the entertainment."

"We're going to Cordoba?" Enrique asked.

"No Cordoba is coming to us," the count replied. "Father Hernandez will say mass in the chapel and then we will meet in the Music Room for the *Gran Fiesta* entertainers."

On our way from the chapel to the Music Room, Maria and

I passed the little pond in the courtyard's garden where I threw a pebble into the water. We stopped to watch the ripples spreading through the pond.

"That's us, " I said. "We met by chance and its effect will encircle our life."

We walked slowly into the Music Room where someone was introducing a group of gypsy singers. Maria and I nestled close to each other on a small divan listening and swaying to haunting love songs. We felt the singing was directed to us, especially the old Moorish ballad,

Love is power, love is life.
Love is nourished by tears and strife.

Then the singers announced that they would sing the same ballad but they would change the lyrics to reflect modern life in Spain. Instead of singing about the Moslem prince pining for his beloved, the new lyrics were about a Castilian knight whose beloved left him for another man when the knight went off to war. The song ended with the chorus:

If the Inquisition had known
How much I loved you
And the bad coin in which you paid me
They would have burned you as a Jew.

The singer kept repeating the phrase, raising her voice with each repetition:

They would have burned you, burned you
They would have burned you as a Jew.

My muscles tensed. My head was spinning. I gasped for air and bolted away from Maria. I began to tremble. Shaking my fists at the singers, I shouted, "Stop it! Stop it!"

When they finally stopped, I shouted in a mad-like shriek, "burn me as a Jew, Jew, Jew!"

I stormed out of the Music Room.

Maria ran after me, calling my name in the dark, beseeching me to return. I heard her but I could not stop. Don Luis suddenly seized me by the arm near the pond and sternly ordered me to return to the Music Room.

He reminded me that out of deference to the count, I must go back to the Music Room and apologize to him. The dignitaries had left and the entertainers had been dismissed by the time I slowly entered the room. Only the count and countess were there. Maria sat far off to the side.

Teresa appeared with a damp towel to apply to my perspiring forehead. I waved her off. The count motioned to me to come forward.

"I'm sorry, Your Grace," I said, bowing as I approached him. "I am the Jew of the ballad. I sent an innocent old man to his death, to be burned by the Inquisition. I am the one who should have been at that auto-da-fe."

Out of the shadows, Father Hernandez appeared. He placed his hand on my shoulder saying softly, "You are now one of us, son. No one is going to burn you."

He told the count I was the son of Don Isaac Abrabanel and revealed my part in the celebrated trial of Don Abram Senor. As Father Hernandez spoke about my past, I felt oddly relieved for I was no longer parading under false colors as I had been in the past few days. I could now retreat into my isolation.

Standing before the count, it occurred to me that coming to the castle, meeting the count and countess, becoming involved with Maria, even the gypsy's singing, could all have been part of a plan to entrap me or someone else through me. I tried to recall those who were in the Music room; which dignitary was the informant, which entertainer was the spy? I looked around wondering, who would be the next victim, Don Luis? Maria? The count?

"Your Grace, I ask your permission to leave."

"You will have my permission, soon," the count replied.

He told me how well he had known my father whom he often met at the Royal Council of Ministers. Then, he severely reprimanded me for my outburst which, he stressed, betrayed a lack of self-control. The countess interrupted his rebuke, reminding him that I had cured him. He thanked me for attending him so expertly which, he said, indicated to him that I would be a great physician. He ordered Don Luis to prepare an "adequate compensation" for my medical service.

"But, for your own safety," he concluded, "I caution you to exercise prudence in the face of the authorities so that you may live to become a great doctor."

The count and Don Luis left. Father Hernandez trailed behind them, but the countess remained. She asked me to sit beside her and said she admired me for helping her husband and for all I had done these past few days with her family. She then took off the pendant she was wearing and pressed it into my hand.

"I give it to you, not as a fee. But, as my way of showing you that you have become very dear to us."

I placed the pendant on the count's empty chair.

"It's a family heirloom," I said. "I can not take it."

She was deeply hurt by my rejection, saying that every piece of jewelry she possessed was an heirloom. I picked up the pendant promising that one day I would find a way of repaying her.

"You must find a way of repaying her," she replied pointing to Maria sitting in the far corner. "You healed my husband but you also hurt my child."

I did not know if Maria heard her mother's parting words. I saw her sobbing. I wanted to embrace her, to dry her tears, but I stood there unable or unwilling to approach her.

When I finally came by to stand at her side, she wept and,

through bitter tears, whimpered, "And only moments ago, you said we would last forever."

"Maria," I said, "you don't understand."

"I don't want to understand," she said stamping her foot. "I want to know what happened to our dreams?"

"We were in heaven then," I said. "Now we're back on earth. And the earth is Spain."

"Berto, I don't now what you're talking about," she said with tears now streaming freely, "but I do know that you love me and I love you even more."

She ran away from me, vanishing down the darkened corridor.

I remained alone, sitting on the divan Maria and I had shared earlier in the evening. I welcomed the solitude and the darkness, waiting for daybreak so that I could return to Cordoba without having to see or to speak to anyone. Suddenly, I felt a tap on my arm. I was startled and looked up. It was Father Hernandez. For a long while he sat beside me.

"Come," he finally said, "your heart is heavy. It is time to commune with the stars."

He led me out of the castle, down a path along the castle wall. The full moon lit our way. We walked, neither of us saying a word, until he turned off the path and sat on the trunk of a fallen tree.

"Many years ago," Father Hernandez said, "your father asked me who would help the Jews if the Inquisition turned against them. At that time I told him that he, through the monarchs and I, through the church, would resist the Inquisition. But I was wrong. Neither of us, neither monarch nor church, could stop the avalanche. You are now its victim."

I said, "Father, I'm a victim. But it's no longer the fear of death but the absurdity of life that disturbs me. I am torn between a world of love that seems a fantasy and a world of hate that is real. I can live in neither. ."

The abbot did not reply immediately. He sat transfixed,

alternately looking up at the stars then staring down at his feet.

"No one can help you decide which world to choose," he said. "The struggle will be long and agonizing. But after the struggle, you will come out either as a victim or a victor."

I did not understand.

"Father help me find my real world."

"No, my son, I can not help you. Only you can help yourself. You have all that it takes, wisdom and courage, to solve your problem. But I want to help you with something else."

"What is that?" I asked.

"I want to help you live," he replied stressing every word.

"Are you also going to lecture me 'to be prudent with the authorities,' as the count did?" I retorted.

He stood up and looked straight at me, "In a way you and I are alike. I am a Dominican priest and have taken an oath of silence. And you, you are known as *el mudo*, the silent one."

He walked away from me to his perch by the tree trunk and talked as though to himself, "I, too, faced a dilemma of love and hate. Too often have I seen that those who cry 'peace' were more than likely seeking blood. They who professed belief in the Holy Trinity, understood only the trinity of power, lust, and greed. They invoked the love of Jesus but meant the love of self. They draped themselves in the mantle of Christ only to hide their own stains. If Jesus walked into their midst tomorrow, they would serve him a more gruesome death than did Pontius Pilot."

"You mean, the Inquisition?" I asked.

"The Inquisition is a religious scandal. It makes a mockery of faith, substituting despair for hope, suffering for charity."

"The Inquisition is a religious scandal," I repeated his words slowly and distinctly. "Then why is it permitted to scandalize? Why the silence? Is it not true that he who tolerates Torquemada makes himself an accomplice!"

"It is not for me to defend the Church," he replied. "The Inquisition and the Church are not one and the same. Certainly not in Spain. I have personally known Torquemada. He certainly does not speak in the name of the Holy Father. Tomas de Torquemada entered into an unholy alliance with Isabel. It is her power that sustains him, not the Church of Rome. "

"Has the Pope lost his voice?" I asked.

"Papal appeals have been issued by Pope Sixtus, calling for a more humane treatment of all accused sinners," Father Hernandez replied.

"Is that all the Pope could do?" I asked, "Appeal for humane treatment! What about exposing the 'scandal'?"

Father Hernandez replied, apologetically, "Without Isabel's support, there is little the Holy Father can do."

He stood up and clasped his hands over his chest. I looked at his frame silhouetted, erect and motionless, in the moonlight.

"As I say, it is not for me to defend the Church," he said slowly after a long silence. "Perhaps in time she will act so that there will be no need for her to be defended."

Again, I did not understand him but, trailing him back to the castle, I refrained from further challenging him or the church.

"I found my world," he said when he stopped to rest. "It is with Christ. I do not expect you to understand that. But I know you will understand when I tell you that I have found my peace in total isolation."

He stopped talking. Gathering up the skirts of his robe, he walked ahead of me into the Main Gate, heading to the chapel.

I went to my room and, although exhausted, I could not sleep. My two worlds collided. I could not forget that I was a target of the Inquisition; I could not forget Maria. I was deeply in love with her; deeply grateful that the countess allowed me, a commoner, a converso, to shower my love upon her daughter. As the long sleepless night wore on, I recalled every moment I spent with her, every word we spoke, every dress she wore, every kiss we shared. I still felt unworthy of her.

She was a resplendent flower set in a beautiful garden and I a severed branch about to become a smoldering log.

I thought about the past three days. I had expunged from my mind all that had happened to me; my break with father, my dread of the Inquisition, my dream of escaping Spain. I now realized that during those three days, I was deceptive and dishonest with myself and with Maria. How could I have blotted everything out of my memory?

I was the monkey draped in a silk suit.

At the break of dawn I dressed in my old tattered clothing, casting away the elegant dress on the bed. I took only the countess' pendant so I would not hurt her feelings. But I was determined that, somehow, I would return it to the House of Trastamara where it belonged.

When I got to the Main Gate, the stable hand had my horse saddled. Don Luis suddenly appeared.

"This is from Teresa," he said, handing me the green uniform I had worn the first night. "I also have three messages for you. The first is from the countess, who said you will always be welcome here. The second is from Father Hernandez, who bids you to come to the San Sebastian Monastery should you encounter any trouble with the Inquisition. And, this is from Maria."

He handed me a folded paper sealed with wax and wished me well. I mumbled an inaudible "thank you" and rode toward Cordoba.

When I was a good distance from the castle, I cracked the wax seal and opened Maria's letter. It contained only the unsigned words of the gypsy's song:

Love is power, love is life
Love is nurtured by tears and strife.

I rode slowly to Cordoba. I was in no hurry to return to my isolation, my fate. I rode aimlessly, letting the horse wander without direction from me. I do not know how I reached the city.

Cordova, just recovering from its bout with the *Gran Fiesta*, was deserted even at mid-morning. It was so quiet, I thought the hoof beats of my horse would awaken the city. However, when I arrived at the Casa Lombardia, Jimenez waited at the gate.

"Welcome from your vacation," he sneered. "Did it take all this time to cut up the count?"

To avoid a confrontation, I told him I had applied his *hierba* ointment to the wound and the count was feeling better.

"But you didn't tell him that my ointment cured him, not your surgery," Jimenez said in anger.

I replied, apologetically, that I was tired and needed some sleep. He ordered me into dispensary to attend the many patients who were in need of immediate care. Although I was tired, I was glad to get away from Jimenez to work alone in the clinic.

When at last I returned to my room at night having been on my feet all day, I lay on my cot thoroughly worn out, emotionally and physically. I was determined to put the castle and all that happened there out of my mind. But I could not. I could neither sleep nor forget any part of those three days in Trastamara Castle. When Andres awoke and saw me sitting up in bed, he quizzed me about my experience with the count. I told him everything — about the surgery, about the outburst in the Music Room, even about my talk with Father Hernandez — but not about Maria. He said he knew about Maria. I imagined either one of the gypsies or one of the dignitaries told him.

"Will you be seeing her again?" Andres asked. "I know you're holding back something important."

"No," I replied, "and do me a favor; don't talk about that any more."

"So, what are you going to do now?" he said with scorn, "Lock yourself in that clinic of yours again?"

"Have you forgotten?" I replied, "My isolation is my security."

"You're crazy," Andres said. "I can understand your reaction to the gypsy's song, but not to see Maria again, that makes no sense."

"To me, it makes a lot of sense," I snapped, "I can never forget that I am an Abrabanel and neither can Torquemada,"

"Are you mad? You have the Count of Trastamara on your side and you're afraid of the Inquisition? You are mad!" Andres said, then walked out of our room slamming the door in disgust.

In a way, he was right. I was becoming mad, suffering the agony of longing. It was tearing my heart. Everything I did reminded me of Maria. Each morning while dressing in my shabby clothing, I remembered our first meeting when I fumbled with my jacket. When I attended a patient in the clinic, I recalled her questions about becoming a physician. When I walked alone in the fields of Cordoba I remembered the long walks Maria and I took in the Campina forest. When I passed by the river, I thought of the words of love we exchanged by the pond. When I looked at the stars, I saw her sparkling beauty.

It was hopeless. I was deeply in love. I could not be with her and I could not live without her.

A few days after I returned to Cordoba, Don Luis summoned me to the castle to remove the count's bandage and to advise them whether the count was well enough to travel. I went in the morning and returned almost immediately. Andres eagerly waited for me and pounded me with questions about Maria.

"I spent only a few moments with her. Nothing has changed," I said reminding him I still feared the Inquisition.

Andres pleaded. "Everyone is afraid of the Inquisition but you have the protection of the Count of Trastamara."

I pointed out even Father Hernandez anticipated I would have problems with the Inquisition and that was why he invited me to visit him. Andres ridiculed my tears, throwing up his hands and turning his back on me.

"Andres, when we were on your boat, you agreed that the Inquisition was manipulating me."

"That was before you had the support of the most powerful count in all of Spain," he replied. "You're rejecting him and spurning Maria."

"Stop it," I pleaded with him. "Stop arguing with me and leave me alone."

"I can't stop," he said. "Someone has to knock some sense into you."

I again pleaded for him not to pursue it any further, insisting my mind was made up and I knew what I was doing. He would not stop. He questioned my sanity saying that I was inflicting needless anguish on myself. I refused to reply.

"Why don't you accept Father Hernandez invitation to visit him," he said defiantly. Then he added, "unless you still suspect he's the agent of the Inquisition."

To stop his badgering, I agreed to speak to Father Hernandez. We decided that the next time Andres drove Jimenez to the San Sebastian, I would offer to accompany him. But the next day, Jimenez bluntly rejected my offer, stating only he would attend to Manuel. Andres, who overheard, told Jimenez's there was so much work in the dispensary's groves that he could not spend the time to drive to the San Sebastian. Jimenez reluctantly agreed to have me drive but ordered me not to come near Manuel.

I did not. I went straight to Father Hernandez.

The old priest embraced me warmly, welcoming me into his small office. He immediately asked if I had any trouble with the Inquisition.

"You know, I sent the message with Don Luis because I feared the Inquisition would move against you."

When I said that no action had been taken yet, he smiled, thanking God for my safety.

"I asked Don Luis to invite you here, but not to mention it to anyone," Hernandez said, "because if anyone knew of my invitation to you, that, in itself, might arouse suspicion against you."

"Father," I said, "I dread the Inquisition."

"You are not alone," Father Hernandez replied.

"No, Father, it's not like everyone else's fear," I said. "I feel that I am being used by the Inquisition."

Father Hernandez shook his head telling me that we were all being used by Inquisition and stressing that my role in the death of Abram Senor was not unique.

"I must know if the Inquisition is planning any other "Abram Senor" for me."

"I do not know, my son," Father Hernandez replied. "I have little to do with the Inquisition."

"But when we talked at the castle," I reminded him, "you said that you knew Tomas de Torquemada?"

"I did," he replied. "Many years ago."

"Would you know if he had any special interest in me?"

"Why do you ask?" Father Hernandez said.

I told him that Don Carlos, who had intervened in my behalf with Torquemada, warned that I would always be under the Inquisitor General's surveillance. Father Hernandez said he knew nothing of Torquemada's plans for me, but that he knew much about Torquemada.

"When I was seven years old," Father Hernandez related, "my parents committed me to the Santa Cruz Monastery as an oblate. They took the monastic vows for me. Thirteen years later, because I had not personally taken the obligatory vows, it was technically possible for me to withdraw from the monastic order. That is what I wanted. I was unhappy. But then, Torquemada became the prior of the monastery.

"One of his first duties was to rule on the technicality which would allow me to resign. He ruled that it would require papal dispensation to renounce my parents' vows, but assured me he would initiate such a request and would even add his approval to it. However, he asked me to delay my resignation for one month suggesting that I should engage in prayer to seek God's guidance before making a final decision.

"I did as he requested and during that month Torquemada drew me close to him, taking me everywhere he went. For me, who had never been outside the Santa Cruz Monastery, those thirty days with Torquemada were a fantasy. I was caught up in a veritable whirlwind of secular and religious functions which encompassed the entire scope of church activity. I spent long sessions with renowned sculptures and artists planning the building of the Cathedral of Segovia. I took several trips to Majorca where Torquemada supervised the construction of the Monastery of St. Tomas. I met with papal nuncios on religious issues of ordination of priests. Despite all these preoccupations, Torquemada meticulously supervised every detail of the sprawling Santa Cruz Monastery. I stood in awe before Torquemada, for I learned to admire his brilliance."

Jimenez interrupted Father Hernandez, asking him to send someone to help lift Manuel off the bed so he could be dressed. Father Hernandez called a young monk to assist Jimenez. When Jimenez left, I wondered aloud whether Jimenez had eavesdropped on our conversation. Father Hernandez shrugged his shoulders saying, "I am not concerned either way."

He then continued.
"After those thirty days, there was no further talk of my withdrawing from the Order. Instead, I became Torquemada's disciple. I remained at his side for the next twenty years. I rose in the Church hierarchy through his sponsorship."

"What is it in de Torquemada's character that makes him succeed in all he undertakes?" I asked.

"Torquemada is not as naive as he projects himself," Father

Hernandez replied. "His methodical mind, which enabled him to grasp complex mathematical problems and to design intricate architectural structures, was applied to every decision he made regarding his own status within the Church. He left nothing to chance. He would allow no interference. His refusal to accept any honors, for example, was not because of humility, but an adroit decision aimed at retaining his independence which he would have lost if he became Bishop of Toledo. Single-mindedly he maneuvered to get the only position he ever really wanted: Inquisitor General of Spain.

"How did he accomplish that? When Isabel of Castile visited Avila, Torquemada made certain that he personally accompanied the impressionable sixteen-year-old Queen through his Monastery. He remained with her day and night. She was profoundly impressed with him and deeply moved when he refused her monetary gift stating, 'I prefer your soul rather than your purse.'

She chose him as her confessor. This position he accepted, not for the honor entering the Royal Court, but for the pledge he made her take in return: to appoint him Inquisitor General. And that was fifteen years before such a position ever existed."

"Why was he so eager to become the Inquisitor General over any other position in the church," I asked. "Did he foresee what he could control?"

"He schemed for that position for only one reason," Father Hernandez said, "to cleanse Catholic Spain from what he termed the 'historical blemish of the Judaizers and the Moors'. He believed that since the dawn of Spanish history, the Jews have had an undue influence on Spain. He attributed every evil aspect of Spanish culture to that influence.

"Torquemada faulted the Jews with being anti-Christian and anti-Spain because, after the invasion by the Moors, Jews sided with the Arab emirs. In turn, they used the Jews to rule the conquered Spaniards."

"Did you believe he was right to blame the Jews for Spain's

collapse in the face of the Arabs invaders?" I asked.

"Of course I believed," Father Hernandez replied. "We all believed. For us, following Tomas' teachings was an act of faith."

"And his campaign to oust the Jews from Spain?" I asked quietly. "Was that also an act of faith?"

"Remember, by then, Queen Isabel had made him the most powerful man in Spain. No one dared question his decision or her edicts."

When I asked him if he still believed in Torquemada's plans, Father Hernandez explained that since he was sent to Rome as papal legate, he was able to free himself from the inordinate influence that Torquemada had exerted on him.

"I was surprised that you knew about my role in the death of Abram Senor," I said. "You told the count about it after my outburst in the Music Room. Do you know if the Inquisition is planning any other "Abram Senors" for me in the future?"

"I have little to do with the Inquisition," he replied, "but, as I told you before, using you against Abram Senor is typical of the Inquisition's operations. I urge you to trust God and abide by your Christian faith so you never give the Inquisition cause to suspect you of heresy."

Two weeks after my meeting with Father Hernandez, Don Luis came to the dispensary to summon me to the Casa del Rio, the count's mansion in Cordoba. The count and his family would stay overnight in Cordoba and would leave on the following day for their annual summer trip. I knew that being with Maria would open old wounds so I tactfully refused, making some lame excuse about important medical work.

Don Luis smiled good-naturedly and said, "A 'request' from the Count of Trastamara is an 'order'."

I had no choice but to accept the invitation.

"Actually," Don Luis said, "it was Maria who asked that you

be invited to join them for dinner tonight."

"Then the request is not an order," I replied.

Just then Jimenez came in to give me a special assignment for that evening. Don Luis explained to him that the count had invited me to dine with the noble family and apologized for my not being able to do Jimenez's bidding.

When Don Luis left, Jimenez was impressed that he had personally come to my room.

"Do you know Don Luis that well?" he asked. "He could have sent a servant to deliver the invitation."

I told him that we spent many hours together at the castle in friendly conversation. Jimenez then asked me to enlist Don Luis to help his son, Diaz, get some work in the castle or at the count's local mansion.

"Diaz is a sexton in a run down church," Jimenez explained. "If I could help him find better employment, I think that would help improve my relationship with my son."

I promised to intercede with Don Luis.

I left early for the Casa del Rio situated on the banks of the Guadalquivir. After I was ushered into the palatial home, the count greeted me in the foyer. We sat in his library and he asked me about my work in the dispensary, about Andres' effectiveness, and about Jimenez's reaction to my attending to the wound. I responded only by nodding or speaking half sentences. He was obviously irked by this and was about to walk out of the room. When I helped him get up from his chair, I noticed his firm grasp.

"I see that your wound is healed," I remarked, asking him to allow me to examine the scar.

"Excellent scab," I said running my finger over his bared shoulder, "fine healing."

"You are an amazing fellow," the count said lacing up his shirt. "You only come alive at the sight of disease."

"I'm sorry, Sir," I apologized, "you have correctly summed up my predicament but, under the circumstances, I have no choice." He seemed more vexed by my answer and began to lecture me about my behavior but at that moment, Maria walked into the library. I greeted her awkwardly. Her father apparently recognized the tense situation and graciously left us alone.

"I asked Don Luis to call you," Maria calmly said noticing my anxiety.

"I know. He told me," I said. "I'm glad you did. I needed an excuse to come."

"You need an excuse?" she asked.

I did not, could not, respond. She looked at me, at my dirty jacket, at my slovenly grooming.

"I see that you no longer care about your appearance in my presence," she said.

"Maria, when I left you three weeks ago, I knew it would not be easy. But I never imagined it would be this painful."

"Then, why?" she implored. "Tell me, why all this pain? Why do you make it difficult? We talked about love, about life together. What happened?"

"I'm a hounded man," I said.

"You are what?" she cried out, "A hounded man? You are a thief? A scoundrel?"

"No, I am a converso," I said.

She burst out laughing hysterically. Tears streaming down her face; she flung herself at me.

"I knew you would say that," she cried out. " Do you know how many conversos there are, right her in Cordoba? I asked Don Luis. He tells me there are hundreds! Hundreds of families. Why are you any different from them?"

"I don't know any of them," I replied. "But that's not the problem. It's me. I'm not an ordinary converso. I'm the son of Don Isaac Abrabanel."

"What are you talking about? What difference does that make?"

I told her about my father, recalling that Torquemada threatened me that he would never forget I was an Abrabanel. I explained how I had been manipulated to bring about the death of Don Abram Senor and why I chose isolation as a way of life.

"Maria, the only satisfaction I have is that in the past three years I haven't caused any of the autos-da-fe," I said.

"What autos-da-fe?" Maria asked.

"Come," I replied, "let me show you the sights of Cordoba."

I led her through the streets passing first through the *juderia*. We stopped to talk to several conversos but the moment I approached them, they scurried away like frightened animals. From there, I took Maria to the Plaza de la Corredera in the center of the city.

"What do you smell," I asked her.

"Roast meat," she replied.

"Roast flesh," I corrected her, "roast human flesh. Four weeks ago the ceremonies of the *Gran Fiesta* started here with the *Gran*d spectacle of burning human beings, all conversos. I scooped a handful of sand from the center of the plaza and asked her to smell it. She pushed my hand away.

"This is the *quemaban*, the burning place," I said.

"Take me away," she begged.

Quickly we walked in silence back to the Casa del Rio. We sat on the back porch, which extended on stilts over the Guadlquivir. Maria was very quiet.

"Maria, try to understand," I said, "I can bring only pain to those I love. Love means to keep, to hold. I can never keep you; you can never possess me. Even as a Trastamara princess, you must share me with the Inquisition."

"What are you talking about?" Maria protested.

"Ask Don Luis or ask your father. Ask them about Queen Isabel's new Edict of Faith, giving the Inquisition lifelong control not only over the converso but over his children."

Maria did not argue, did not challenge. She asked with resignation, "Is there any place the Inquisition cannot reach you?"

"The Inquisition has already reached me and anyone close to

me," I said speaking very slowly. "I am trapped in its snare and anyone I get close to will become entrapped as well."

Maria was silent, pensive. I was convinced she finally understood. I wanted to embrace her, to tell her I love her. I resisted. I walked to the very edge of the porch staring at the river. She held on to my arm.

"I'm relieved because, now, I can share your pain," Maria said. "Remember that gypsy song, 'Love is power love is life: Love is nourished by tears and strife'."

As that moment, Don Luis called to us saying the countess would like us to come in for dinner. Before going in, Maria took out a an embroidered shirt she had tucked in the porch cupboard. I put it on and joked lamely, "It's almost as elegant as the monkey suit."

I was genuinely glad to join the family because of the warm reception I received from everyone, especially the countess. She hovered over me asking whether I was eating properly and getting enough rest. I knew she saw through my malaise despite my assumed contentment. During the meal, I asked Don Luis to get me appointed as Jimenez's permanent assistant.

"When you receive your certification," Don Luis said, "you will be offered a more important appointment in Cordoba. That will be the count's compensation for your services."

"Thank you, sire," I said to the count, "but I don't want to compete with Jimenez."

"The count will build a hospital in Seville where you could practice and teach medicine," Don Luis explained stressing the need for such a facility in Andalusia.

Once again, I thanked the count but I declined his offer, stating I would then attract the attention of the Inquisition.

"If I am to survive, I must remain the *el mudo*," I said reminding Don Luis that I would rather heal than howl.

He ridiculed my fear of the Inquisition suggesting that I was overly sensitive only because of my sad experiences in Toledo.

"This is Cordoba," Don Luis said, "the domain of the House of Trastamara!"

The count lifted his cup of wine saying, "You have my protection. And, rest assured, as long as you remain here, the Inquisition can do you no harm."

Echoes of the assurances Don Alfonso once gave me, about his dispensary being a safe haven rang in my mind, but I did not have the temerity to question the count's well-intentioned promises. I merely lifted my cup to the count and sipped my wine. Fortunately, Enrique interrupted, describing their plans for the summer vacation, thus bringing an end to further discussion of my own plans.

When the evening was over, Don Luis informed me that the count would return to the castle in six weeks for the Conference of the Trastamara Nobles. He said he would remain in Cordoba and invited me come to him if I should need anything. Maria saw me to the door asking that I come by the port to see her the next day before she embarked on their summer cruise. I responded that I would try. I did not have the courage to tell her I considered that evening to be our farewell dinner. I resolved that I must protect not only myself but her, as well, from the Inquisition. She again asked me to come to the port and I assured her I would try to be there.

Don Luis then ordered his coachman to drive me to the Casa Lombardia. While waiting for the carriage, I intervened on behalf of Jimenez's son, Diaz. Don Luis listened compassionately but categorically stated that Diaz was a hopeless case and that he was much better off now where he was.

"In that church he's in isolation," Don Luis said, "and can do no harm to himself or to others."

Andres was waiting up for me when I returned to the Lombardia. I told him all about my evening and asked him to go down to the port the next day to tell Maria I could not to meet her because of some medical emergency. I explained that I would end my relationship with Maria because I must control my destiny to avoid any entanglements that might endanger me or her.

"You are a coward not a man," Andres shouted angrily. "You are breaking away from Maria and for no reason. Fear dictates your actions. You're hurting her and yourself."

"I know," I replied, "but I'd rather live with fear than than jeopardize myself or others."

"Then, it's back to becoming *el mudo*," he sneered, then he beseeched me, "You're throwing away something precious. Berto, you have a beautiful future with the count, Don Luis and of course, with Maria."

"I wish you were right," I said with sad resignation. "The count and Don Luis live in a dream world. The Inquisition has not reached them because they, too, have isolated themselves from it. But sooner or later, the Trastamaras will have their share of victims."

Astounded, Andres snorted, "And we consider Diaz an idiot. You could be his twin!"

"I've made up my mind," I said. "Don't argue with me. I'm going to sleep. Just do me a favor; go to the port tomorrow and make up some excuse to Maria."

6

Very early in the morning, Jimenez surprised me. He ordered me to go to Posadas, a small town about half way to Seville, where a plague was scourging the town. According to the excited messenger, the innkeeper Pablo Duenas, the townspeople were in panic. He reported that almost all the townspeople were stricken with stomach pains. Jimenez could not go because he had to attend to the ailing Manuel so I was to ride back with Pablo. I was glad to get away from Cordoba, especially from Andres. When I was about to leave, I woke him up, told him about the emergency in Posadas, and demanded he meet Maria at the port.

"At least I won't have to lie," said Andres.

I followed Pablo. We rode our horses along the valley of the winding Guadalquivir River, arriving at Pablo's inn in the late afternoon. I immediately started attending to the stricken people. After treating a few patients, it became clear to me that contaminated food caused their stomach pains. I set up an apothecary to produce more of my purgative, which I brought along with me. Pablo helped me make it and distribute it to all the town's residents. Working together through the day, we became good friends.

That night, I stayed at Pablo's inn where his wife invited me to have dinner with them. I barely touched her food, explaining my suspicions regarding the contaminated food. She assured me that no one in her family was affected by the plague and casually mentioned that she bakes her own bread and does not use the town's baker. That gave me the clue about the source of the contamination.

In the morning, I asked Pablo to take me to the baker's wheat bins. We found an inordinate amount of mold and rat droppings mixed in his wheat. The baker, also infected with the stomach ailment, pleaded his innocence but promised to destroy the infected wheat. We produced more of my purgative and before the day was over, the 'plague' vanished. Since we had worked all day, I decided to remain another night in Pablo's inn.

Late that night, someone knocked on my door. When I opened it, a man stealthily walked in. Furtively he looked around the room and closed the door behind him, making certain no one saw him enter. He introduced himself as, Diego de la Fuente, the town's judge, and explained that he had heard of me during his visits to Cordoba.

"Please do not light the lamp," he whispered. "You do not know me, but you stayed in my home many, many years ago."

Fearing some cabal against me, I got up, opened the door, and asked him to leave. The stranger closed the door, sat down on my bed, and desperately pleaded with me to hear him out. He was elegant, well-dressed, and handsomely groomed.

"Does the town, Segura de la Orden mean anything to you?" he asked.

I repeated the name, Segura de la Orden, several times but failed to recognize the place or the person facing me. I grew impatient with the stranger, broadly hinting for him to leave but he was not to be put off.

"Your father stayed in Segura de la Orden when he fled from King Juan of Portugal. Segura de la Orden," Diego repeated in an effort to recall the name.

"Yes," I responded hesitatingly, but still suspicious.

"My name is Diego de la Fuente," he said, "I was in your father's employ, serving as his agent for his transactions in Castile. I helped to transport your family to Segura de la Orden."

Still wary, I acted detached, unimpressed. Diego described

the home where we stayed, recalling many insignificant details of my boyhood days in Segura de la Orden. He then handed me father's book, called "The Forms of the Elements".

"Look at the inscription," he said. "It will tell you who I am and maybe you will overcome your fears."

"'To Diego, friend and colleague — from Isaac'" I read the inscription and seeing father's handwriting made my heart race.

I fondled the book and leafing through its pages, I felt a peculiar attachment to Diego.

"All right," I said. "I am pleased to meet you."

"I am a converso," Diego de la Fuente said, "I've been considered a converso since my father converted more than forty years ago. I served your father for more than two decades in Portugal and in Spain. Now, I need your help."

"What can I do for you, *Senor*?" I asked.

"Can you get me a certificate of *Limpieza de Sangre*?" he asked." I need to be certified that I am of pure Christian blood."

"But," I said, "you just told me you were a converso?"

Diego explained that there were two categories of citizens in Posadas: the Old Christian and the New Christian. All conversos were called "New Christians". Since the Posadas town council recently prohibited New Christians from holding public office, there was a maddened rush by everyone to produce limpiezas.

Diego spoke in a cool and deliberate manner as though addressing a panel of judges. He stated, as far as the local people were concerned, to be a converso was as bad as being a Jew. The Council of Attorneys following the ruling by the town council, went further than the edict, stipulating that only "Old Christian" attorneys can represent a client in court.

"I have reason to fear for my life because I lived secretly as a Jew and there are those who would report me," he said. "So, I must leave Spain either for the colonies or the Netherlands."

He went on to explain only Old Christians were allowed to travel out of Spain. A special commission of the Inquisition screened all passengers in every port to make certain that anyone leaving Spain must show a *Limpieza de Sangre*.

"Are there others like you," I asked.

"Thousands throughout Spain," Diego said. "They would now leave everything behind if they could produce the limpieza certificate."

"Why come to me?" I asked. "I am certainly not involved with any agency issuing the limpiezas."

"You are my last resort," Diego replied. "I've tried everything. Now I come to you, the son of Don Isaac Abrabanel."

Diego pressed my father's book into my hand and, before he vanished into the dark streets of Posadas, we embraced.

"Come to see me next week at the Lombardia," I told him not knowing what I could do for him or why I agreed to help.

An amazing transformation overcame me. Only the day before, because of my consummate fear of the Inquisition, I decided to break with Maria, whom I loved so dearly. Yet today, one day later, ready to help a total stranger, I threw all caution to the wind. Was it clutching father's book? Was it my sudden emancipation from the Inquisition? I did not know then and I do not know now. What I do know is that I firmly decided to help Diego, knowing full well that, if discovered, I would bring the full wrath of the Inquisition on myself.

When I returned to Cordoba, I first reported to Jimenez about the Posadas plague and then I sought out Andres to begin my quest for Diego's *limpieza*. He was not at the Casa Lombardia and Jimenez could not tell me where he had gone. He seemed to have vanished. When he did not return that night, I again asked Jimenez about Andres. This time he raged at me for annoying him. He wanted to know why I was so anxious to find him. I made some excuse but I knew I aroused his suspicion.

Andres returned the following evening. He told Jimenez the *Cortes* of Cordoba sent him to the surrounding towns to inspect their clinics. Back in our room, Andres pelted me with questions about Posadas, telling me that everyone in the area was singing my praises. I shrugged my shoulders saying that I had much more important things to talk about than the cure of a stomach ache.

"What's more important than being the most talked about doctor in town!" Andres responded.

"How do you get a *Limpieza de Sangre*?" I asked, disregarding his compliment.

"Well the first thing you do," Andres burst out laughing, "is to get yourself de-circumcised. "

"How do you get a *Limpieza de Sangre*?" I asked, stating that I wasn't impressed with his humor.

"What's so important about a limpieza?" Andres replied. "I want to hear about your work at Posadas. "

"I'll tell you all about Posadas later," I said. "First tell me, how do you go about getting a limpieza?"

"Simple," he said. "Just get an affidavit from a church attesting that your parents were Christians and then you get that document authenticated by a notary."

"You mean, it's not the Inquisition that issues it?" I asked.

"Not at all," Andres replied, "What do you have in mind?"

"Never mind," I said. "Do you have a *Limpieza de Sangre*?"

"No," he replied. "I never needed one. Why do you ask?"

"Let's get you one," I said.

"'Let's get you one'," Andres protested, mimicking me, "With all the work I have to do, here and at the other clinics, you want me to take off just get that useless document?"

"Andres, I never asked you for a favor before," I said, "I'm asking for one now. I want you to process your limpieza and I want to go with you when you do it."

"Fine. We'll go next week," he said.

"No, tomorrow. First thing in the morning," I insisted.

"What's happened in Posadas?" he asked.

"Nothing," I said, "I just want to know how a limpieza is processed."

"Whom are you fooling?" Andres said, "For the past three years your only interest was the patients in the dispensary. Suddenly you're interested in a *limpieza*, which is only important to Old Christians. "

"Exactly," I answered.

"Exactly, what?"

"I want to know how a New Christian can become an Old Christian."

"Berto! You're playing with fire!"

I rather enjoyed watching Andres assume an unfamiliar role. He now lectured me that tampering with a limpieza would invite swift retribution from the Inquisition.

"I can't understand your sudden interest in a limpieza," he said "unless you want to escape from Spain."

"Not me, someone else," I said.

"Who?" Andres asked.

At first I did not want to tell him, but when he threatened not to help, I related Diego de la Fuente's plight, stating that I wanted to help because Diego helped my family. I assured him that neither of us would be involved with the authorities because Diego would handle it by himself. "But first, I have to learn the legal procedure," I said. "That's all I want from you."

Andres promised nothing, instead he suddenly asked, "Would you like to know Maria's reaction when you didn't show up at the port before she sailed?" Andres asked.

"Maria is not the issue," I said. "Anyway, there's no solution to my problem with Maria. "

"That's exactly what I told her," Andres said.

"You did what?" I asked.

"I told her that you were incapable of solving your own

problem," Andres said. "And, that she would have to pull you out of your own quagmire."

I raged at Andres. It was the first time in three years that I shouted at him. I accused him of interfering in my private life. I stormed at him that it was my problem, not his.

"With a beautiful woman like Maria, I wish I had your problem," he said not fazed at all by my anger.

"Andres," I yelled. "There is no problem! For my protection, for her protection, I am not going to see her! And, that's it!"

"You have the Count of Trastamara," Andres shouted back, "What more protection do you want?"

"Andres, my mind is made up, and I don't need your advice," I retorted, storming out of the room in anger.

He followed me out to the groves where he apologized and to assuage my anger, he said, "Tomorrow we'll go to the San Miguel Church to process my limpieza."

We went to the church early the next morning.

There, Andres stated his name and his parents' names to a minor functionary who asked us to follow him to the records room in the rear of the church.

The sexton searched several ledgers looking for Andres' birth and baptism registry. We waited impatiently while he leafed through several musty journals, apparently unable to trace Andres' name.

"Your father's name was Xavier and your mother's Angelina?" the official repeated, pacing around the room looking for other journals.

"Yes, yes, I told you," Andres replied, begging him to hurry.

"Well you didn't have to come here if you're in that big of a hurry," the sexton said. "You could have had anyone come down for the limpieza. All we do is certify that the person is registered with the church."

After a lengthy search, he found the information and wrote Andres' name and his parents' names on a sheet of paper which he signed and gave to Andres, reminding him to have it countersigned at a notary.

I asked Andres to go to a notary who did not know him because I wanted to learn what a notary would do under ordinary circumstances. Andres agreed even though we had to go to a distant part of the city, the Plaza de San Agostino, where the goldsmiths had their shops. Andres approached a *notario* who asked no questions and who, for a few *marvedis*, notarized the paper, affixing the city's seal which made it an official-looking document.

"Well," Andres asked as we bustled through the crowded streets making our way back to the Lombardia, "did you learn anything from my limpieza."

"Much," I answered.

"Tell me," Andres said, "because I learned nothing."

"Three things," I said. "First, neither the official in the church nor the notary knew you, yet they processed the document. Second, your father's been dead almost ten years, yet from the church's registry of births which the sexton looked at, your father could be assumed to be still living."

"You said that you learned three things. What's the third?" Andres asked.

"That's the most important detail," I replied. "The man in the church said that you didn't have to come to the church in person to get the limpieza. Anyone could request it for you from the church and get it on your behalf."

"So," Andres asked, "what does that mean to Diego."

"That means, if we find a name of a bona fide Old Christian, who may have died fifty years ago, Diego could assume his name. Then, it would be simple for him to acquire the limpieza. Just like you got yours."

"Are you planning to raid the church records for the name of a bona fide Old Christian?" Andres asked.

"Of course not," I answered, "that would be dangerous."

"Then where will you get the name you need?" Andres asked.

"What better place is there than the cemetery!" I announced to a startled Andres. "We can find the name of a fine Christian whose pure Christian ancestry can be then substantiated through official church records!"

Andres whistled. "Berto, you're a genius," he said. Let's go."

"No. Not you," I said. "That's my task."

I told him that I would go alone to the cemetery because I did not want him involved in this scheme. He stubbornly insisted on going with me, warning me that there may be pitfalls in the process which only he could avoid.

"Anyway," Andres added mockingly, "I wouldn't trust you to do anything right that wasn't connected with medicine. Your behavior since you got involved with Diego is very suspicious. Even Jimenez noticed a change in you. With such a careless attitude, you could endanger yourself, Diego and me. You need me around!"

I had no choice. Andres came with me that evening to the San Rafael Cemetery on the outskirts of the city. We waited until nightfall to enter the cemetery where, with lamp in hand, we began searching for an appropriate Christian name, hopping over old gravestones.

Suddenly we saw two militia men calling us from the cemetery's fence and asking what we were doing there. I told them we were going to haul a body into the dead room inviting them to help. They refused and went on their way. Andres congratulated me on my quick response.

We continued stepping gingerly over the old markers looking for an name Diego could use.

Andres said he felt uncomfortable walking around the graves.

"It's a desecration of the dead," he said.

"Someone once said," I replied, "'If it could save our people from disaster, vulgarity may well be a virtue.'"

"Who said that," he asked.

"My father," I replied, "when he compared the Jews to horses."

Andres repeated the phrase, 'vulgarity may be a virtue'. Then he quipped, "The dead help the living to survive. That's certainly a virtue."

Andres hurried among the gravestones saying he would be relieved when our chore was over. He made sure not to chose the name of a well-known Cordoban personality whose family would be recognized by any church official. He cautiously picked a name from a medium-sized gravestone and we hurried out of the cemetery. The following morning, we visited a church far from the clinic where, without difficulty, we procured the limpieza and then had it notarized.

When I met with Diego he looked worried, as frightened as he was when he first came to my room in Posadas. He told me he was being watched by the Inquisition, which suspected he was trying to escape. I gave him the *Limpieza de Sangre* and, while thanking me, he warned me not to be seen with him. He quickly left the clinic without telling me his plans. I never saw him again.

About two weeks later, Jimenez summoned Andres and me to accompany him to the San Sebastian Monastery to assist him in removing the splint from Manuel's leg. As we rode to the monastery, Jimenez asked if I had spoken to Don Luis about Diaz. The truth, that Don Luis considered Diaz to be an idiot, would pain him deeply. So, I lied. I said that I had not seen Don Luis, but would ask about Diaz as soon as Don Luis returned from the castle. Jimenez was so anxious to help his son that he even suggested that I could go to the castle anytime to meet with Don Luis.

Jimenez then turned to Andres and asked if he could take

over management of the monastery

"Since Father Hernandez left the monastery, it's never been the same," Jimenez said. "The place is in shambles."

"Father Hernandez was transferred?" I asked.

"Big mystery," Jimenez replied. "Everyone there seems to know why, but no one's talking. You'll be there until a replacement can be found for Father Hernandez."

The moment we arrived at the monastery, we saw that Jimenez was right. The place was in shambles; harvested fruits and vegetables rotted in the fields; barns and storage rooms reeked from heaps of garbage; workers walked about aimless, doing nothing. It had been less than a month since Father Hernandez left, but it was obvious that all work had come to a standstill.

When we helped Jimenez remove Manuel's splint, I noticed the toes were dark red, almost black, but said nothing fearing another confrontation with Jimenez. Manuel was concerned that although the fracture set well, he still could not move his leg. Manuel decided to remain in the monastery to recuperate and continued to run the Inquisition from his room.

While Jimenez and I were busy with Manuel, Andres took charge, assigning the brothers and workers to specific tasks and preparing a full work schedule for the monastery. At Manuel's request, he stayed several days after we left to manage its affairs. Andres met with each monk, selecting several individuals for special duties. He hired teamsters to transport the undamaged fruits and vegetables to the market of Cordoba.

In less than a week, the San Sebastian Monastery was again functioning smoothly. He met frequently with the ailing Manuel and with his assistant, Father Lopez, who carried on most of the work of the Inquisition and found time to help Andres manage the monastery.

Andres was impressed with the young aggressive assistant. Father Lopez was very bright; he always displayed strong leadership. Andres suggested to Manuel that Lopez could easily run the affairs of the San Sebastian, especially since all administrative functions were now running smoothly. Manuel refused. On another occasion, Andres complained to Manuel that he could not work in both places and innocently asked whether Father Hernandez would be returning.

"Father Hernandez's whereabouts is none your business," Manuel stormed at Andres, "and I prohibit you from delving into the Inquisition's affairs."

Andres was about to ask if Father Hernandez was therefore working for the Inquisition but, in view of Manuel's outburst, Andres wisely decidedly not probe any further.

I was glad when Andres returned to the Casa Lombardia and Andres was glad to be back because Manuel was becoming progressively more irritable. I ascribed it to the pain in his foot. However, when Andres described Manuel's grim reaction to his question about Father Hernandez, we surmised that the Inquisition transferred Father Hernandez from the monastery. We knew that Hernandez ranked high in the church hierarchy and so it seemed strange that he could be disciplined by the Inquisition.

It was a mystery that intrigued Andres.

He began a systematic investigation to uncover what had happened to Father Hernandez.

He asked me to recall the exact conversation I had with the old priest at Trastamara Castle. When I replied in generalities about our talk, he badgered me for details. I then recalled verbatim some points in our conversation saying that he called the Inquisition a "scandal".

"That's it," Andres said. "If he called the Inquisition a 'scandal', someone must have overheard and probably reported him."

I ridiculed his suggestion because I recalled that we were outside the gates of the castle in total isolation.

"Anyway," I said, "even the Inquisition would not dare place a spy in the Trastamara Castle."

Andres was convinced that Father Hernandez was disciplined by the Inquisition. He was certain of that because the same monks who normally worked so closely with him would suddenly withdraw the moment he asked about Father Hernandez.

"If we could get one of them to open up, I bet we would find the answer to the mystery," Andres said.

Andres went to the monastery several times just for that purpose; to "open up" one of the monks. One day he rode into the Casa Lombardia in the monastery's wagon driven by an elderly monk, Nicolas de Gascogne. While Nicolas was being fed in the clinic's kitchen, Andres told me he had selected the old monk to accompany him to the market of Cordoba to help sell the monastery's produce, because Nicolas had shared a room with Father Hernandez. Once he got Nicolas away from the monastery, Andres questioned him at length about Father Hernandez's disappearance. At first, Nicolas refused to admit to anything. Finally, he promised he would tell all, if Andres would promise to reunite him with Father Hernandez.

When telling me this story, Andres quipped that he would have promised Nicolas anything, "even the Royal Palace."

After Nicolas finished eating, he came to our room and first told us how he had joined the Dominican Order:

Nicolas was of French noble birth and, as a young man, had led a garrison of French troops who were stationed near the Santa Cruz Monastery, where he met Father Hernandez. Nicolas and Hernandez became friends and when the battle was over and the French troops were to be recalled to France, Nicolas opted to remain in Spain. He joined the Dominican Order at the Santa Cruz Monastery so that he could be near Hernandez. For three decades they were together, during which time Nicolas served as an aide to Hernandez, traveling together all over the Catholic world and ending their careers in the San Sebastian Monastery.

When Father Hernandez was suddenly transferred from the San Sebastian, Nicolas said he felt lost. He realized that as long as Hernandez was with him, he could tolerate the confining life at the monastery but with Hernandez gone, Nicolas took a dislike to the monastic regimen and sought ways of leaving it. When Andres took charge of the monastery, Nicolas convinced himself that he could be reunited with Hernandez only through Andres, who was seen frequently with Manuel and with Father Lopez. Nicolas turned to Andres for assurance.

Nicolas then related the following:

On the fifth day of the *Gran Fiesta*, Father Hernandez returned from the Trastamara Castle. He was summoned to Manuel's room accompanied by Nicolas, but Manuel asked Nicolas to leave. Nicolas waited outside the door where he could hear everything that was going on in the room.

Manuel asked Father Hernandez whether Alberto di Cadiz blasphemed the church or demonstrated acts of heresy while at the Trastamara Castle. Father Hernandez replied that there was no heresy expressed. Manuel pressed for details asking specifically about events in the Music Room and what conversations took place between Alberto and the priest. Father Hernandez simply repeated there was no heresy at any time and as to his conversation with me, he flatly stated he does not intend to report to the Inquisition about any of his activities.

Manuel threateningly accused him of withholding information. Father Hernandez reminded Manuel that his ecclesiastical status puts him beyond the authority the local agent of the Inquisition. Manuel then apologized for using threatening words, explaining that this investigation was initiated at the specific request of the Inquisitor General. Manuel further indicated that the Inquisition had information that Alberto's behavior might be considered heretical.

Father Hernandez stated that the information was false, repeating that Alberto neither blasphemed the church nor showed any act of heresy. Manuel then concluded by saying the matter would be turned over to a Court of Inquiry to decide the issue of heresy.

A few days later, Father Hernandez was called to Court of Inquiry, which was held in secret in the vestry of the San Sebastian Chapel. It did not last long. When he returned to his room, Nicolas noticed that Father Hernandez was quite perturbed, sat down and hurriedly scribbled a few pages.

While writing, he told Nicolas he would be transferred but assured him he would soon send for him. Suddenly, they a heard a carriage stop at the door. Father Hernandez quickly gathered up the pages he had written, wrapped them in an old shirt, and secretly handed them over to Nicolas. He glanced at the figure walking up the path and furtively whispered to Nicolas to guard the papers until he reclaimed them.

Father Lopez entered the room, helped Father Hernandez with his belongings, and escorted him to the waiting carriage.

After relating these events to us, Nicolas handed the Hernandez papers to Andres reminding him of his promise to reunite him with Father Hernandez. Andres took the papers, solemnly assuring Nicolas to do all he could to find Father Hernandez. He then escorted the old monk to the wagon sending him back to the monastery. As soon as Andres returned, we began deciphering the Hernandez papers which were obviously written in haste, with most of the words abbreviated.

Sacred Sword

"Court of Inquiry at the San Sebastian"

I repeated the events in the Music Room after which the Presiding Judge asked whether I considered them heretical. When I replied in the negative, the judge asked whether Alberto bemoaned his fate as a Christian.

I replied, he bemoaned his part in the auto-da-fe in which Abram Senor perished. The judge countered stating that Alberto referred to himself as a Jew. I replied that the lad was only quoting the conto hondo, the song the gypsies sang.

Judge: Yet, you anticipated that as a result of the episode in the Music Room, he would be in trouble?

Hernandez: I don't follow your question.

The judge paged through the folios Manuel handed to him and said, "Did you not send a message inviting Alberto to visit you should he encounter any trouble with the Inquisition?"

I was shaken to the core by the judge's question. In anger, I glared at Manuel and said, 'Tell your spy at the castle, whose identity you need not betray, that the message I sent Alberto was nothing more than an act of friendship.'

Manuel: A heretic does not need friends. He needs to be watched.

Hernandez: A converso needs to be encouraged in his faith.

Manuel: That is the work of the Inquisition.

I accused him of not doing his work well.

The judge asked whether I was opposed to the Inquisition, I replied:

I am not opposed to defending the faith. I am not even opposed to punishing heresy. But I am opposed, unalterably opposed, to agents who spread fear and hate, terror and violence. Must Christianity thrive, as a parasite, on the destruction of others? Is our Mother Church so weak that she cannot nurse the faithful with her own breasts, but must resort to feeding her children with severed limbs from the Inquisition torture cham-

bers? Does our Church have no warmth for the faithful except from the fires of smoldering flesh? Does the blood of Jesus arouse our lust for more blood? You do not propagate faith. You promote hate. Is that what we will bequeath to our future generations?

Manuel was incensed at my words and, after a whispered conversation with the judge, the judge called out: "This Court of Inquiry agrees with Hernandez's evaluation; to wit, that no heresy was evidenced by the suspect. In my capacity as head of the Dominican Order, however, we feel that you have placed yourself in a difficult position with the director of Inquisition. We therefore have no choice but to transfer you to another area where you will continue to do work in the vineyard of the Lord."

"So, it's obvious that someone in the Trastamara Castle reported my behavior in the music room to the Inquisition," I said when we finished reading the Hernandez papers.

"The Inquisition has placed an informant in the castle," Andres said.

"And, all the questions related to me," I added. "Does this confirm that the Inquisition had a special interest in me?" I asked, recalling Nicholas' testimony that the investigation was at the behest of the Inquisitor General.

Andres agreed, but he could not get over the fact that the Inquisition would spy on the count.

"You must warn the count," he said.

I theorized that there may not be an agent in the castle, that anyone, one of the gypsies or any of the guests may have reported the incident in the Music Room. I also wondered why Father Hernandez wrote the report. Why did he tell Nicolas to save it until he reclaimed it? What could he possibly have had in mind when he wrote it?

We came up with a possible explanation when we pored over the notes and found, in tiny script, the letters, 'SPQR' written on the reverse side of the papers.

"Father Hernandez undoubtedly intended to send this report to Rome," I suggested. "That's what SPQR stands for."

We debated at length whether there was an informant at the castle and whether I should immediately report this incident to Don Luis so that he might warn the count.

At about midnight, Andres came up with the first clue when he asked, "Why should this mild-mannered, compassionate priest, suddenly lose his temper, when the judge read from Manuel's report?"

"Read that part to me again," I asked.

Andres read: "The judge paged through the folios Manuel handed to him and said, 'Did you not send a message inviting Alberto to visit you should he encounter any trouble with the Inquisition?'"

"Father Hernandez reacted strangely to this simple question," Andres said and continued reading from Hernandez's notes, "'I was shaken to the core. In anger, I glared at Manuel' and so on.
"

We both found it strange that Father Hernandez should react so strongly to a seemingly meaningless statement.

"Read the judge's question again," I asked.

Andres read, "'Did you not send a message inviting Alberto to visit you at the monastery.'"

"Read Father Hernandez's response," I asked Andres.

"'Tell your spy at the castle,'" Andres read hurriedly, "'whose identity you need not betray...'"

"'Did you not send a message inviting Alberto to visit you at the monastery?' 'Did you not send a message to Alberto to visit you at the monastery,'" I repeated the judge's question several times, until Andres plugged up his ears, begging made me stop, saying he knew it by heart.

Andres began reading the entire Hernandez papers when I said, "Stop, I know who the informant is."

"You know?" Andres asked. "Who told you?"

"The Presiding Judge and Father Hernandez," I replied.

"I see nothing," Andres said.

"Follow my reasoning," I said testing my theory. "The night I left the castle, Don Luis gave me the message from Hernandez who later told me that he gave it directly to Don Luis asking him to tell no one."

"What does that prove?" Andres asked.

"Only one person could have known about this message and only one person could have informed Manuel about it," I replied, trying to contain my shock and dismay. "That can only be Don Luis."

"Don Luis, an agent of the Inquisition spying on the Count of Trastamara! That's incredible," Andres called out. "He's the count's *hidalgo*. He's sworn allegiance to the count; he's vowed to protect the count with his own life. He can't be the spy."

"Father Hernandez discovered it, during the interrogation by the judge. And, that's why he was 'shaken to the core'."

"You make no sense," Andres scorned me.

"First of all, Father Hernandez knew that he personally and in secret gave Don Luis that message for me. Second, he hears the Presiding Judge mention the message. Third, Hernandez realizes that someone gave that message to Manuel. It can only be Don Luis and he tells as much to Manuel. That was Father Hernandez's mistake."

"What does he tell Manuel?" Andres asked.

"That he knows that Don Luis is the informant," I said.

"What the hell are you talking about?" Andres asked. "Where do you see that he tells that to Manuel?"

"Read the part where Father Hernandez glares at Manuel and says something, but read it slow," I told Andres.

Andres read, "Tell your spy at the castle, whose identity you need not betray, that the message I sent..."

"'Whose identity you need not betray,'" I interrupted his

reading and repeated the phrase over and over again. "'whose identity you need not betray'. It's as though Father Hernandez was saying to Manuel, 'Hey, you don't have to tell me who the informant is. I know.' Father Hernandez was telling Manuel that he knew. And, Manuel realized it."

"By God!" Andres said, "Berto, you're right! That's why at the very end of the Hernandez papers, the Judge says that Father Hernandez would find it difficult to work with Manuel. So, Hernandez was removed from San Sebastian, to protect Don Luis."

"I wonder if Don Luis is also the agent assigned to manipulate me." I thought aloud.

"If he is," Andres said, "then we have a powerful adversary."

"No ifs," I corrected Andres. "It's Don Luis for sure. And I must inform the count"

"That won't help you," Andres said. "What evidence do you have? Hernandez is not here. His paper is unsigned and Nicholas' testimony, in and of itself, does not incriminate Don Luis."

Andres was correct because there were many other people who could have reported the incident in the Music Room. And, the unsigned Hernandez Papers could not be proof unless interpreted by my private discussions with Father Hernandez. If the count was called upon to chose between me and Don Luis, I would stand no chance.

"Well, we have three or four weeks before the count returns to Cordoba," I said. "We can use the time to get some evidence to back up our discovery."

"So, we're going to investigate the Inquisition!" Andres laughed at the new and dangerous venture we were about to undertake.

7

Andres began to systematically "investigate the Inquisition", a term he became very fond of using during the next few weeks. His search was unwittingly facilitated by Manuel. His leg was still ailing, so he remained in the monastery and converted his chamber into the local headquarters of the Inquisition. Andres found all sorts of excuses to visit the San Sebastian while he pursued his investigation.

His main source of information was the monastery's rubbish heap where he would sift through discarded papers looking for any evidence linking Don Luis to Manuel or any plan involving me in some scheme. Whenever he would return from the monastery, he would quip, "Bad news, Berto, no mention of Don Luis. Good news, Berto, no mention of you."

One day, he found a list of conversos near Manuel's office. The scrap of paper caught his eye because it bore Diaz's signature.

Was it possible that Diaz, Jimenez's idiot son, was working for Manuel?

Andres recalled that Jimenez had mentioned that his son was the sexton at Our Lady of Grace Church in the old juderia section of the city. He decided to go there. When he asked for directions to the out-of-the-way church, he learned that, because it served so many conversos, the townspeople called it, "The Jewish Church". The small building was tucked in the back of a two-storied edifice with a cornerstone that still bore the Hebrew inscription, '*bet din*', court of justice. Layers of dust and grime on the windows allowed little daylight into the shabby building. Walking through the empty central hall, Andres tried a side doors adjacent to the altar. It lead to a small dark room, bare except for cot and a table with a flickering oil lamp. The smell of oil from the sputtering wick and the room's putrid odor were overbearing. When his eyes became accustomed to the dark, Andres recognized Diaz with his large head lying on the cot. Diaz made no effort to get up.

"Are you ill?" Andres asked.

"No, just resting," Diaz replied. "Who's this."

Andres introduced himself explaining that he was in the vicinity to purchase some equipment for the monastery and decided to visit. He apologized for disturbing Diaz and offered to leave, but Diaz sprang up begging him to remain, saying how grateful he was for the chance to talk because his life as sexton of the church was lonely. He shuffled to the table to rekindle the lamp but his hands fumbled so badly that Andres had to help him. Diaz murmured that he always had trouble with his clumsy hands and often relied on neighbors to help him around the church. Andres sat on the edge of the bed to chat.

He reminded Diaz that it had been almost a year since he visited his father at the dispensary. Diaz replied that it was difficult for him to get around and that he preferred lying in his dungeon-like room and avoiding the difficulties of getting to the Casa Lombardia.

Diaz said his work in the church primarily involved being a messenger for the priest.

He asked Andres how he managed his work in the Casa Lombardia. Andres informed him he was also managing the San Sebastian Monastery.

Diaz stammered, "How can you manage a monastery? What do you know about religion?"

"To supervise a monastery," Andres quipped, "one has to be a paymaster as well as a preacher."

Diaz asked Andres to explain the joke and when Andres did, Diaz chortled slapping his knee, repeating the two words 'preacher' and 'paymaster'. When Andres offered him work in the monastery to get him out of the depressing, run-down church, Diaz replied with the same moronic laugh that the Dominican Order would not employ him.

"But, I saw your name on a list I found while Manuel's room was being cleaned," Andres said.

"Means nothing," Diaz replied.

"Well, as long as you're working for Manuel" Andres said casually, with an eye on Diaz's reaction, "you stand a good chance of getting work in the monastery."

"Sending lists doesn't mean nothing," Diaz stammered in half sentences pausing between each phrase, "Every church must send lists...to Manuel. Every week we send lists. Lists of conversos at services. Don't know what they do with lists. And don't care. I wish I didn't have to do it. Takes me the whole day... just to write those names."

Diaz lay on his cot, sighing and rubbing his eyes. Andres sympathized with Diaz for being locked up in the small church. Andres again offered to train him for some work that would get him out of the Church and into the monastery.

Diaz replied haltingly. "It's best for me. It's my work. Only work I know. This church gives me this room. And plenty food."

Andres was surprised that Diaz accepted his disability so calmly but pitied him, telling him that if there was anything he wanted from the Casa Lombardia, food or clothing, Andres would be glad to help.

Diaz thanked him, saying he had everything he needed and added, "But, there's something I can do for you."

"For me?" Andres asked.

"Well, for your friend, Alberto," Diaz replied. "Tell him his uncle is here. Alfredo. He's part of this church. A tanner. Works not far from here. Down by the river."

Andres replied he had done business with Alfredo in the past but did not know that he was my uncle.

"Alberto should visit his uncle," Diaz said.

"I doubt if he'll go," Andres replied. "He's very careful."

Diaz came to life, running up to Andres, clasping his arm, and insisting that I visit Alfredo.

"It's so cruel of Alberto that he doesn't visit his uncle," Diaz suddenly spoke clearly and distinctly. "Alberto has cut himself, totally and completely, away from his people for all these years. He must not do so."

Andres tried not to show his surprise at Diaz's abrupt change in mood and mannerism. Walking out of the church, Diaz kept in step with Andres pleading, "Alberto owes it to his uncle to come and help him out of his misery, especially when Alfredo has complained about him to me many times."

When Andres got into the wagon, Diaz shouted, "He must come to his uncle, like you told me to come visit my father. At least once in a while."

Andres agreed to tell me, but his suspicion was aroused. Diaz speech was clear; his gait erect. He was not merely offering information; he was persuading Andres to get me to visit. Therefore, instead of returning to the clinic, Andres headed to the river bank on the outskirts of the city to seek out Alfredo.

He saw the tanner crouched on his knees scraping the bristles off a fresh piece of hide while singing to himself.

"Watch out, young man," Alfredo chuckled. "I would invite you to examine this beautiful piece of Cordoban leather, but you'd have to wait several months before you could even handle it. So, right now, I suggest you wait outside before you get yourself splattered with this filth."

Andres instantly liked the tall tanner with the winsome smile who went on with his work, singing to himself. Andres watched him and when Alfredo finished, he rinsed his hands and walked over to Andres.

"Well, what can I do for you," Alfredo asked, wiping his sullied hands on a slightly less sullied rag.

"I just came here to talk," Andres replied.

"I always like to talk," Alfredo replied, "but I don't believe we've met."

"We did," Andres said, "I bought harness straps from you last year. My name is Andres."

"Ah yes," Alfredo said extending his hand, "Andres, the caretaker of the Casa Lombardia, Jimenez's dispensary. How is the old doctor?"

"He's fine," Andres replied, "I also bring you greetings from Alberto."

"Alberto?" Alfredo mused stroking his chin. "So many Albertos around here, it's hard to keep up with them."

"Alberto, the apprentice to Jimenez," Andres replied.

"Heard of him, but never met him," Alfredo said, adding with a twinkle in his eyes, "and, if he's a physician, I'd just as soon wait till I really need one."

Andres remembered that 'Alberto' was my converso name.

"The son of Don Isaac Abrabanel," Andres said.

"The son of Don Isaac," Alfredo whispered the name with awe, repeating it several time.

His smile vanished. He no longer stood tall and erect but cringed before Andres. His eyes darted in every direction as though seeking escape. He immediately began protesting, "I'm a good Christian."

Andres was amazed by the man's changed behavior. The more he tried to pacify Alfredo, the more frightened the tanner became. He went back to scraping the hide with short hard strokes, staring furtively at Andres.

Alfredo then stood up from his crouched position, paced nervously, then came up to Andres. Bowing before him, Alfredo loudly protested, "I committed no heresy."

Andres suddenly realized Alfredo probably suspected him of being an agent of the Inquisition. Andres, therefore, swore by his mother's life that he had nothing to do with the Inquisition. But,

Alfredo was too alarmed to heed him. The more Andres' tried to assure him, the more terrified Alfredo became.

At last, Andres held Alfredo by the arm and said with quiet firmness, "I came here because I want protect Alberto."

"Protect Sami?" Alfredo said dropping his scraper.

"From the Inquisition." Andres said.

Alfredo responded, "How can I possibly protect him."

"First, did you ever tell Diaz that you wanted Alberto to come here to see you?" Andres asked.

"No, never," Alfredo answered calming down somewhat.

"Did you ever speak to Diaz at all about your nephew?" Andres asked again.

"No, never," Alfredo answered.

"Did Diaz ever talk to you about Alberto," Andres asked.

"No, never," Alfredo replied.

Andres whispered, "Diaz is a spy."

"Diaz!" Alfredo laughed loudly, "Diaz is the town idiot."

"That's what he wants you to believe and I think Diaz wants to use you to trap Alberto," Andres said.

"I tell you Diaz is an idiot," Alfredo repeated

"And, I tell you Diaz is the Inquisition," Andres insisted.

"Diaz? Inquisition?" Alfredo gasped, holding his scarred fingers to his lips. "If that's true, Diaz is the angel of death."

Alfredo explained that because Diaz was considered an innocent simpleton, he was permitted to attend all the conversos' weddings, funerals, and other functions where certain prohibited Jewish rites were clandestinely observed. Andres cautioned Alfredo to be careful in any future dealings with Diaz.

"It may be too late," Alfredo replied with a tremor, recalling the names of conversos burned in an auto-da-fe and those still in the Inquisition's prisons. In each case, Diaz had been present when the victim had celebrated some ritual.

Andres could find no words to console Alfredo, except to promise he would arrange for him to meet me. Andres then bought some leather goods from Alfredo, explaining that if anyone was observing their conversation, he could thus account for Andres presence.

Andres hurried back to the Casa Lombardia and described his meetings with Diaz and with Alfredo. I wanted him to take me immediately to see Alfredo, but Andres convinced me not to rush off to the *juderia* in view of Diaz's expressed interest in such a visit. He suggested that we should first approach Rodriguez, Diaz's brother, to determine whether his father, Jimenez, was in any way in league with his not-so-idiot son.

"If Jimenez is with the Inquisition, he's more dangerous to us than Diaz," Andres said.

I taunted Andres that only three weeks earlier, he was certain that Jimenez could not be with the Inquisition.

Andres replied he was wrong about Diaz and might also be wrong about Jimenez, but he could not be wrong about Rodriguez.

"Rodriguez and I are like brothers and I know that he's the only person Diaz trusts," Andres said.

I knew that Andres and Rodriguez were close friends, so I suggested that perhaps it would be better if Andres went to speak to Rodriguez alone. Andres insisted that I go with him because I might be able to detect any connection between Diaz and Don Luis. I agreed, but only because I thought that we would then go together to see Alfredo.

When we rode up to his military encampment, a walled-in military compound on the outskirts of Cordoba, Rodriguez welcomed Andres with an embrace and invited us to his quarters. Andres was surprised when Rodriguez asked him why he was talking to Maria the day the count's family left the port of Cordoba. Andres told him about the message he was to deliver and, in turn, he asked Rodriguez what he was doing at the port at that time.

"When the Count of Trastamara is in the city, my company is his honor guard," Rodriguez explained. "And, when the Council of Nobles convenes at the La Campina Castle this fall, my troops will participate in the ceremonies."

After drinking several cups of wine, Rodriguez castigated Andres for staying away so long. I replied for Andres explaining that his additional work at the monastery kept him busy and left him no free time. Rodriguez said he knew about the havoc caused by the departure of Father Hernandez.

"I just saw Diaz in the church and offered him work at the monastery," Andres said. "I thought I'd get him out of that miserable place but he refused."

"I know. He doesn't want to move out of there," Rodriguez said.

"Diaz told me that it's the work he does best," Andres said, "What do you think he meant by that?"

Rodriguez hesitated, obviously reluctant to answer but Andres pressed him, telling him that he saw Diaz's name in one of the papers addressed to Manuel.

"I don't know if he's working for Manuel," Rodriguez said.

"What do you know?" Andres asked, but Rodriguez refused to say anything else.

"If it's me," I said, "I can leave you two alone."

"No," Rodriguez said, "I only know that Diaz is not as dumb as he wants people to think he is."

From earliest childhood, Rodriguez explained, Diaz was self-conscious about his deformed head. He often spoke about it to Rodriguez. At one time, Diaz even confessed he exaggerated his indolent behavior to avoid being with people. But there was much more to Diaz's mental agility than was apparent on the surface. Diaz was very close to his energetic mother and was repelled by his father's failures. He held him responsible for his mother's death, because of his inability to intercede with the Inquisition. When Rodriguez left for the army, Diaz felt even more forsaken. At the age of fourteen, Diaz opted for the priesthood, enrolling in a seminary of the Dominican Order.

"When I asked him why he wanted to become a seminarian, Diaz replied that it would lead him into the Inquisition," Rodriguez said. "I reminded him what they had done to our mother, but he countered that by working for them, he could discover who caused mother's death."

Rodriguez did not agree with Diaz's plan and tried to dissuade him, but Diaz's mind was made up. He began to study for the priesthood and, at the same time, made himself known to the Inquisition authorities. Rodriguez guessed that Diaz's superiors probably recognized the unique role he could play for the Inquisition, disguised as a simpleton. They put him to work in the 'Jewish Church' where he has been ever since.

Rodriguez emphasized that this was conjecture on his part. But he was certain of one thing, Diaz was living a secret life which he refused to share with anyone. Andres asked if Jimenez knew anything about the secret life.

"Absolutely not," Rodriguez replied. "My father is constantly enlisting everyone's help to find better employment for him and is still desperately trying to ingratiate himself to Diaz. This seems to be his life's ambition."

When we returned to the Casa Lombardia, I again wanted to put everything aside and run to see Alfredo. However, Andres argued it would be wiser to plan my meeting with Alfredo so that Diaz would not know about it. I ridiculed Andres for being so cautious, claiming that I intended nothing more than a family reunion with Alfredo.

"I'm not concerned about your intentions," Andres said, "but, to visit Rodriguez now would play into Diaz's hand. If Alfredo is correct, if Diaz was put in the *juderia* as an informant, then the entire converso colony is in serious danger. Your presence there can only hasten the Inquisition's action against them."

Andres even surmised that Diaz probably had enough information to proceed against Alfredo but that he had not done so because he wants to use Alfredo to entrap me.

"Then, it's back to the River, again," I said.

"What are you talking about?" Andres asked.

I reminded him that our first secret meeting was on the river and that, under the circumstances, it was the safest place for me to meet Alfredo. I proposed to take Andres' boat up stream near Alfredo's hut and paddle into a tributary where Alfredo would meet me. Andres agreed and undertook to make the necessary arrangements. When Andres left to prepare the rendezvous, I started working on getting Alfredo a limpieza certificate.

Several days later, Andres reported that the Inquisition surveillance at the port was so strict, it would be unwise for me to take his boat since it was so well known. Instead, he arranged for Alfredo to await me in a boat at a secluded spot along the River.

Andres took me to the pre-arranged place, where I plunged in and swam to a small islet where dense foliage hid Alfredo's boat. Although it was late spring, the weather was cold and the water even colder. I rolled into the boat drying myself with the towels and covering myself with the blanket Alfredo handed me. The moment we touched each other, we burst into tears, crying and laughing at the same time.

I first told him all that had happened to me during the past three years, beginning with my confrontation with father. He said that everyone in Cordoba's Jewish community had been caught up in the same debate about the wisdom of the exile.

"Even the *Cortes*," Alfredo said, "urged us to remain, to disregard the Edict, promising to defend us."

Alfredo remained in Spain because his Christian wife was assured her family would protect him and their four children. He cried when he related how she became the first victim, killed in the first day's of rioting instigated by the Inquisition. Like me,

Alfredo had become a converso to save his life but, since he was considered an unworthy Christian, his children were seized by the Inquisition and, to this day, he had been unable to discover their whereabouts.

"What happened to your mother, Benevita?" I asked.

"She's gone," he replied.

"Gone?" I cried out.

"Gone out of Spain," Alfredo quickly corrected himself.

He related that before the Edict of Expulsion was issued, Asher passed through Cordoba on his way to Turkey where he was sent to arrange for the exiles' resettlement. Benevita insisted on going with Asher because he was unmarried and "needed someone to look after him". Alfredo told me that he had received a message from Benevita that she was well. We shed tears of joy, thanking God that she got away from the storm raging in our accursed land.

"Everyone of us is caught up in this storm," Alfredo said. "At the *Gran Fiesta* this year, eighteen conversos were burned to death in the auto-da-fe. The waters have reached our noses. We're all drowning. We're all in mourning. Mourning for the living and mourning for the dead. Now that we know who Diaz is, very few of us will survive."

"No one will remain once Diaz really gets started," I said. "You must leave Spain as soon as possible."

I handed him the limpieza which I had rolled up in an oil skin, informing him that the name on the certificate is of a bona fide Old Christian so he could use it to safely get out of Spain. He refused to take it, saying that he could not leave his friends behind. When I insisted that he must leave, he argued that his disappearance would certainly bring on swift action by the Inquisition and those who remained would suffer even greater punishment. I asked how many conversos lived in his colony, especially those in mortal danger.

"We all are. One hundred and fifty six of us," he replied emphasizing each of the numbers. "Why do you want to know how

Sacred Sword

many of us there are?" Before I could respond, I heard Andres whistle from the nearby shore. I quickly embraced Alfredo, telling him that Andres was alerting us to some danger and that we had to part immediately.

"Get away from here," I said, "but prepare an adequate excuse for being on the river just in case someone saw you."

I plunged into the water and returned to Andres.

As I climbed, dripping and tired, up the river bank, Andres told me troops were patrolling the opposite bank heading towards the islet. I prayed Alfredo got away in time and we quickly made our way back to the Casa Lombardia. I told Andres everything Alfredo said, stressing the danger facing the converso community.

"Andres, there's only one way out," I said. "We must get limpiezas for every one of them."

"How many are there?" Andres asked.

"According to Alfredo there are 156," I replied.

"No problem. We can resurrect 156 dead Spaniards to save 156 live conversos," he said.

"But even if we succeed in providing the limpiezas, how do we get them out of the *juderia* and out of Spain?" I wondered aloud.

"Since they'll all have pure Christian blood, we'll dress them up as priests and nuns," Andres jestingly.

"You may be joking," I said, "but there's something to what you say."

"What do you mean?" he asked.

"We'll dress them up as special workers like nurses, soldiers, and whatever other professionals we can think up."

"And you think we can get them out of Spain, just like that?" he said snapping his fingers.

"We got Morales out, just like that." I said snapping back.

"Moving the Morales family was relatively easy, because it involved a series of fortunate accidents," Andres said.

"Well, we'll have to create a few more 'fortunate accidents'," I replied.

"And the first 'accident' will have to be Diaz!" Andres countered. "We'll have to get him out of the *juderia* because, as long as he's around, there's no way we could move even one person."

We stayed up most of the night going over our plans, the limpiezas, the notaries, the transportation, but always ending up with the one obstacle for which we had no solution: getting Diaz out of the juderia. Andres doubted that we could accomplish that.

"I got it," I said as we were about ready to go to sleep.

"You can get Diaz to leave?" Andres asked.

"Not me," I responded, "Jimenez."

"Diaz won't even talk to his father," Andres said scoffing at my suggestion.

"Let's analyze everything we know about Diaz," I said. "First, you offered Diaz work in the monastery and he refused. Second, we now know why he refused. He's not an idiot and he's not lazy. He's working there for the Inquisition. Third, Manuel is seriously ill and cannot be moved out of the monastery. Fourth, and most important, we know that because Jimenez does not know about Diaz's involvement with the Inquisition, he still would like to get better work for him. Jimenez believes doing that favor for Diaz will bring about a reconciliation between them. Remember what Rodriguez said, 'it's Jimenez's life's ambition'. So, this is all we have to do: convince Jimenez to persuade Manuel to bring Diaz into the monastery to care for him."

"Jimenez will probably do it, but why should Manuel agree to transfer Diaz?" Andres asked.

"Rodriguez told you that Diaz started working for the Inquisition when he entered the seminary," I said. "That's at least seven years ago. If you were in the army seven years, you'd get some upgrading in rank. I imagine it's no different in the Inquisition. And, I also imagine that Manuel not only knows of Diaz's work but probably communicates secretly with him. Therefore, Jimenez's suggestion to bring Diaz into the San Sebastian will give Manuel and his staff an opportunity to work with Diaz without resorting to secret meetings."

Andres was still skeptical, but he finally said, "If you can accomplish that, if you can remove Diaz from the *juderia*, I'll find some way to get them all out."

The prospect of helping conversos escape gave new meaning to my life. I felt as though I had stayed in Spain against my father's wishes just so that I would be in a position to rescue not only Alfredo but the entire colony. Without verbalizing it, I had rid myself of the guilt which had plagued me since I separated myself from my father. It was as though Providence had entrusted me with the lives of my uncle and the other conversos.

This was my motivation. But I could not understand what motivated Andres to undertake this peril. I am certain of one thing: it was not mere adventurism.

There was much more to Andres than was apparent on the surface. Outwardly, he projected a devil-may-care attitude, a constant free and easy manner, always playful, even brash. For some unfathomable reason, he wanted to give the impression that he was flippant. He once accused me of wearing a mask to hide my true nature. These same words, would best characterize him. But, I knew why I wore my mask. Why did he hide his sincerity and goodness?

To me, he was a saint.

We began the first stage of our plan the very next morning. I offered to drive Jimenez to the San Sebastian. As before, Andres claimed he could not drive because of special dispensary work. Jimenez agreed and we were soon underway. I told him about

Andres' meeting with Diaz, describing the dismal conditions of the church. Jimenez was visibly upset but his face lit up when I told him Andres would employ Diaz as his assistant at the monastery.

"I would be grateful to Andres," Jimenez replied.

"It's not Andres. It's you, who can help Diaz?" I said.

"Me?" Jimenez asked.

"Only Manuel can get Diaz into the San Sebastian," I said. "And only you can persuade Manuel to do it."

"What about Don Luis," he asked. "You know him well."

"This is out of Don Luis' realm," I said then repeated, "Only Manuel can authorize Diaz to work in the monastery. And, only you can get Manuel to act."

"How?" Jimenez said. "I'll do anything."

"Simple," I replied. "Tell Manuel that he must have a constant attendant to bathe his leg. Then recommend Diaz be brought in for this work."

"Working as a nurse!" Jimenez said dejectedly, "That's not going to do much good for Diaz."

"It doesn't really matter how he gets there," I explained. "Once Diaz begins to work at the monastery, Andres could train him for more important tasks."

Jimenez interest was aroused. He allowed his imagination to wander, conjuring up scenes of Diaz as manager of the great monastery and how grateful he would be to his father for making it possible. I noticed his excitement and stressed that he must make the request immediately, before Manuel's leg heals. I volunteered to be in the room to support his suggestion to Manuel. Fortunately, he agreed.

At the monastery, we found Manuel writhing in pain. I was astounded by the deterioration of his leg as Jimenez unwound the bandage and began to bathe the reddened leg and apply the *hierba* ointment.

"It's not healing," Manuel complained. "It feels good only when you massage it but as soon as you stop, the pain starts all over again." Jimenez could have seized the opportunity to suggest bringing in Diaz but he simply continued massaging the injury showing that the fracture was completely healed.

"The break may be mended, but the pain is worse than it was," Manuel shouted. "It subsides only when you massage it with your ointment."

"In that case," Jimenez said, "I suggest bringing in someone to massage you whenever the pain sets in."

He waited for Manuel's reaction but I quickly said, "How about Diaz? He once worked in our clinic."

Jimenez added, "I will instruct Diaz how to treat your leg."

Manuel thought a while, then calling Father Lopez, he sent us outside to wait. After their brief conversation, Father Lopez came out and informed Jimenez that a messenger would be immediately dispatched to bring Diaz to the San Sebastian. While we waited for his son, Jimenez attended Manuel. I could hardly wait to tell Andres our accomplishment. When Diaz arrived late that afternoon, he said nothing to his father who instructed him how to properly care for the injured foot.

On our way back to the clinic, Jimenez was overjoyed despite Diaz's silence. He profusely thanked me for my help and I assured him that Andres would stand by his word to train Diaz.

While Jimenez was still in a happy mood, I asked, "Doesn't the purple coloration on Manuel's toes look like the beginning of the blackening disease? Can we treat that?"

"I have cured it before," Jimenez said.

"Do you use your *hierba* treatment alone?" I asked

"I suppose you would recommend cutting off the toes," Jimenez said tauntingly.

"The sooner it's done, the more of the leg he will have," I replied recognizing, too late, that suggesting surgery was a mistake.

"Your operation on the count has made you quite an expert," Jimenez said in anger. "Don't be carried away by your pride. The count's wound would have been cured by my treatment, too. Remember, Manuel is my patient. Don't try to ingratiate yourself with him and don't give him any of your advice. What he needs now is a physician not a butcher."

Even under normal conditions, I would not have argued with Jimenez. At this time, when our objective was to keep Diaz out of the *juderia*, neither Manuel's leg nor my ideas of surgery mattered to me. Therefore, I not only agreed with Jimenez, but apologized for my remarks. I changed the subject back to Diaz; urging Jimenez to teach him well so that Diaz could stay at the San Sebastian long enough to work for Andres. Jimenez calmed down enough to repeat his thanks to me and Andres.

When we arrived at the Casa Lombardia, Jimenez went to his quarters totally exhausted from the long day at the monastery. I found Andres in our room waiting for my report.

"Diaz is out of the *juderia*!" I said trying very hard to contain my excitement." And, will probably stay there for a long time."

Andres shared my feelings, reporting that while I was at the San Sebastian, he prepared the rescue project which he divided into two parts: getting limpiezas and providing transport. He would process the limpiezas and I would coordinate transporting the people.

"What do I know about ships?" I asked.

"I solved that problem, too," he said but preferred to tell me about the limpiezas, first.

He would avoid local churches but would travel to other towns to garner names of Christian families. He would have the certificates notarized by several notaries in outlying districts. This way he would not arouse suspicion processing the 156 limpiezas. While he arranged for the limpiezas, I was to find someone in Seville with whom I would negotiate the cost and method of transporting the colonists.

I asked him why Seville and repeated that I knew nothing about ships. He replied that since we were well known in the city, it would be dangerous to use Cordoba's port. Our presence at the port would certainly attract too much attention. But, he said, his father gave him the name of a shipping agent, Orlando Franco, who handled passage for colonizing companies and for travellers to Africa. Andres also explained that if we transported the conversos to the colonies, we would not have to resort to subterfuge, such as dressing them in various uniforms, because colonizing companies are eager to get as many immigrants as possible.

To help me negotiate the transportation needs with Orlando Franco, Andres taught me about colonizing companies, port procedures, and passage costs.

As for the money, Andres volunteered to borrow from his merchants, allegedly for the dispensary. He knew it might get him in trouble with the *cortes* but he was willing to chance it. I then remembered the *contessa's* pendant which I hid in the bundle of clothing Teresa gave me when I left the castle. I pulled it out of the pocket of the green uniform and asked Andres if it would suffice. He had no idea what it was worth but advised me to take it along.

Next, we needed an excuse for me to leave Cordoba. I went to Jimenez with Andres and suggested that I go to Posadas to check on the plague that had raged there. Jimenez was not amenable to my leaving. Andres declared that I found a lady there, urging Jimenez to allow me to go. At the same time, he mentioned the favor he was doing for Diaz. Jimenez agreed.

In the morning, I left for Seville just before dawn, pushing my horse to the limit as though I were running a race. Thanks to Andres' instructions, I travelled a shorter route than the usual road along the winding river and arrived in Seville just before nightfall.

Finding Orlando Franco was easy. He was well-known around the port area, not as a shipping agent but as the owner of a waterfront inn where he jovially greeted me. A robust man with a thick mustache, he wore a sweaty red bandana around his thick neck, constantly using it to dry his gleaming face. He was so busy serving customers that it was impossible to approach him. Only later that night when he sat down to have his own meal, could I introduce myself.

"Andres from Cordoba sent me," I said.

"Who's Andres?" Franco asked in a booming voice, biting into a leg of lamb, letting its juices drip down his chin.

"Don Gutierrez's son," I replied.

"Ah, if the old general sent you, you must be in trouble," Franco shouted.

I said I needed passage to the colonies for 156 persons. He asked two questions: Who was the group? Which colonizing company I was representing?

Andres had not prepared me for either of these questions, so I tried to conceal the group's true nature stating they were all healthy-bodied people, anxious to get to the colonies. Orlando Franco continued questioning me about them. The more I skirted around the subject, the more he pressed me to identify the group.

He wanted to know why they were not being organized by a legitimate colonizing company. His persistent probing and his reaction to my answers made me wonder if Andres had been mistaken about him.

I got up, slung my belongings over my shoulder, and said, "My friend, you and I can't do business. I have the money and I have the people. They have limpiezas. And that's all you need to know. The rest is none of your business. Good night."

Orlando Franco grabbed me by the hand pulling me down next to him.

He lowered his voice, saying it was fortunate that I had come to him and not to anyone else. Without any further explanation, he shook my hand and said, "We have a deal."

I could not understand his change of heart but I asked him about the advisability of sending my passengers to Africa.

"Why Africa?" he asked. I replied that time was of the essence and, if there were no ships leaving for the colonies, we would consider transporting them to Africa.

"Africa is not safe for them," Orlando Franco said.

He told me of fleeing Spaniards tortured by Moorish officials who disemboweled the forced emigres searching for jewels. He said some ship captains sold their passengers into African slavery.

Orlando Franco never mention the word, "conversos", but I was convinced that his references to "fleeing Spaniards" and "forced emigres" were his allusions to the Jews escaping Spain.

Orlando Franco assured me of two things: First, heavy traffic of "fleeing Spaniards" was already underway to Spain's new colonies, so that when our group arrived in Seville, they would not have long to wait for transport. Second, that he would select only trustworthy ship captains who would treat our passengers with compassion and would guarantee their safe passage. I realized that Andres was right: Orlando Franco was no ordinary shipping agent.

Grateful for his assurances, I handed him the *contessa*'s pendant as payment for the entire group asking him if it was sufficient to cover all costs including his commission.

"With this, you can buy passage for another thousand persons," he said, removing his red bandana and knotting the pendant in its folds.

When we ended our talks, it was too late for me to return to Cordoba. Franco's Inn was full but he allowed me to sleep on a bench in the restaurant. Despite the noise of regaling sailors, I slept well because of my accomplishment in Seville. In the morning, Orlando Franco introduced me to a captain whose ship was leaving for the colonies in three days. His caravel had space for five passengers. Franco set the price with the captain and I assured them that my passengers would arrive on time.

When Andres met me outside the Casa Lombardia, I was exhilarated describing my success in Seville. He was just as excited about his accomplishments with the limpiezas. Jovially we argued who would speak first and it was obvious that he could not contain his exuberance, so I sat back and listened.

When he made the rounds of churches to get the limpiezas, he noticed several clerics were suspicious because he came with a list of names of persons he could not identify. At one church, however, the priest questioned one of the names to be certified as a Christian, saying the man had been dead for several years. Yet, the priest signed the certificate.

"My son, avoid using the churches," the priest said handing the signed document. "Any five persons can sign a statement attesting to the Christian ancestry of any individual. Such a written statement, properly notarized, constitutes a bona fide limpieza."

Andres had the distinct impression the priest knew what Andres was doing with the limpiezas but when he thanked him for his advice, the man simply said, "Go on about your business. The church is far too busy to be involved in all this paper work."

Andres easily got former patients, tradespeople, and clinic workers to sign, especially since most of them did not know how to read and therefore knew nothing about the contents of the documents they were signing. Andres showed me his first batch of notarized limpiezas, waving them aloft as though waving a flag. I jestingly clapped my hands applauding his success.

He sat back as I related in detail how I met Orlando Franco and that we had five places aboard a caravel leaving in two days.

"Berto," he announced with pride, "We're now ready to ship out our first group."

Andres and I were delighted when we met with Alfredo, with no risk since Diaz was away, to share our accomplishments and to plan our next steps. He would prepare a list of persons to be processed for resettlement, based on a need. Persons who already had been found guilty of heresy but had been "reconciled" — that is, they served a prison term or had their property confiscated _ had top priority. If found guilty a second time, they would face an auto-da-fe as "relapsed" heretics. They had to get out first.

"We must plan an orderly departure," Alfredo said, handing

us the first list of five names.

"It's ironic," I told him, "when my father used the term, 'orderly exile', I recoiled with anger. Now I know better."

In reviewing the list Alfredo gave me, I noticed that Alfredo's name was not on it. I insisted he must go first. He refused explaining that he had to supervise the 'orderly departure' of all the others.

"If Diaz returns early and learns of this scheme, you would be his first victim," I argued.

"I would be his second, you would be first," Alfredo argued. "You should be on this list as well."

I could not tell him about the spy in Trastamara Castle, so I said that my contacts in Seville assured me of safe passage any time I desired. Only when I promised to supervise the escape of the entire colony did Alfredo accept his limpieza. The very next day, I escorted the first group. The happiest hour of my life was when Alfredo's ship sailed away.

While I was in Seville supervising the departure of the first group and arranging for future departures, Andres spent an entire day training Diaz in the San Sebastian. Jimenez was happy with the reports of Diaz's success and, far more important, we were happy with Diaz's absence from the *juderia* so we could do our work there.

During the next three weeks, Andres produced the limpiezas; I arranged the transport. We meticulously scheduled every move in advance, making certain no one would know the exact nature of our work. Even the conversos themselves knew none of the details about their escape. Working in tandem, Andres and I got all the conversos out of Cordoba. As far as Jimenez was concerned, Andres was busy at the monastery working with his son. That satisfied Jimenez so much that he did not mind my prolonged absences from the Lombardia.

I would have taken advantage of this "orderly departure" for my own escape. I did not do so because I felt duty-bound to warn the count about Don Luis and I had to tell Maria why I must leave Spain despite my love for her. I did not even provide a limpieza for myself because Andres had unlimited sources for the documents and because I had maintained such good contacts with Orlando Franco. I knew I could safely leave whenever I wished.

With the conversos gone, Andres and I turned our attention to substantiating our suspicion about Don Luis. We had only Nicolas' word and the unsigned document by Father Hernandez. If I were to accuse Don Luis of spying, I would need more substantial evidence than that. In addition to his continuing "investigation of the Inquisition," Andres suggested that when the count returned, I should urge him to trace Father Hernandez in order to confront Don Luis.

I had to learn when the count would be back from his travels. According to what Maria told me before, the family had planned a six week voyage but eight weeks already elapsed. Therefore, I called on Don Luis at the Casa del Rio to discuss with him an alleged problem at the Lombardia. I hoped, in my conversation, I would learn of the county's arrival, but would also detect something to link Don Luis to Manuel.

Don Luis was a gracious host; he invited me for supper where we talked about the clinic. When I asked about the count's return, he said, "Did you mean Maria or do you have any business with the count?"

I was startled and did my best to hide my shock fearing that Don Luis had an inkling of our discovery about his being the Inquisition's spy. When I stammered a reply, he said I should not be embarrassed in his presence; that I could speak freely about my love for Maria. To avoid any suspicion, I did just that. I waxed poetic about her and thus regained my composure.

We spent the rest of the evening in interesting conversation. Don Luis told me the count was delayed by an important meeting of the Royal Council of Ministers which was considering the Inquisition's request to place its agents in military units. The count decided to attend the meeting personally rather than being represented by his hidalgo.

His mentioning the Inquisition gave me the opportunity to broach that subject hoping to learn something of his involvement with it. I therefore asked, "Why would the Inquisition want its agents in the military and what does it matter to the count?"

"Three organized groups wield power in Spain today: the church, the nobility and the military," Don Luis explained. "The Inquisition penetrated and now controls the church and the nobility. No ecclesiastical appointment can be made without Torquemada and, since Queen Isabel is subjugated to him, the Royal House is also under the Inquisition's control. Only the army is still independent."

Don Luis pointed out that the Spanish army actually consists of several militias belonging to key noblemen which are the main support of the royal army.

"Today, the army is more powerful than the other two groups combined," Don Luis said. "It wields real power in every part of Spain. It has its own treasury. It is its own authority. And, he who controls the army, controls Spain. Through the years, the House of Trastamara succeeded as the dominant force in Spain because its militia was always the strongest and the best financed in the realm. The best example is Don Carlos' superb success with the count's militia. Torquemada realizes that if the Inquisition is to accomplish its avowed mission, directing Spain's destiny, it must control that army. The count is the key to that control. At the meeting of the Royal Council of Ministers, the queen empowered the Inquisition to assign agents to all military units and the count was authorized to negotiate with Torquemada on behalf of Spain's armies."

Throughout our discussions, I detected no clue that Don Luis was anything but supremely loyal to the House of Trastamara.

Even when I asked his opinion about the Inquisition agents within the army, he replied, "The count must preserve his power by preserving his control over the army, because wherever the Inquisition has established its operations so far, it ultimately has asserted total control."

Subsequently Don Luis and I met several times. We talked about many issues and I freely shared my opinion on various subjects; my evaluation of Jimenez as a physician, the merits of surgery, my feelings towards Maria, even my fears of the Inquisition. He was always friendly, always hospitable. I never discovered anything that might, even remotely, link him with the Inquisition.

Andres and I pored over Father Hernandez's report of the Court of Inquiry to make certain that we were correct in our suspicions. Even Andres who was originally dubious about my discovery agreed, "It's all there, Berto, black on white, Don Luis is the spy."

Don Luis was brilliant. I knew that he would be a tough adversary if I ever had to confront him.

One morning he surprised me by visiting the dispensary. He came to tell me the count's ship was in Seville making its way slowly up the Guadalquivir. He invited me to meet the ship midway along the river and join them in a leisurely sail back to Cordoba. I readily accepted because that would be my chance to warn the count about Don Luis but when I learned the count was not aboard ship because he remained in Toledo, I searched for an excuse not to go because I did not want to have to face Maria. Don Luis reminded me that a request of the House of Trastamara was an order to be obeyed.

"And I represent the House of Trastamara," Don Luis said patting me on the shoulder.

Before leaving I informed Jimenez that I would be gone for about three days. I also told Don Luis to stop at the Hermandad to report to the Inquisition that I would miss the Instruction of Faith session. Surprised that I still had to report my whereabouts to the

Inquisition, Don Luis reminded me I was under the protection of the count and promised to look into the strictures still hanging over me.

Don Luis and I rode along the river bank, escorted by soldiers from the count's militia. Late in the afternoon, we sighted the count's caravel. After a soldier shouted to attract the crew's attention, sailors immediately lowered a boat into the river and brought us aboard.

The moment I saw Maria, I felt the same thrill as I did seeing her the first time. My determination to leave her dissolved. She was stunningly beautiful, dressed in white lace, her hair fluttering in the gentle breeze. We embraced, whispering how much we had missed each other. I greeted the countess and Enrique, asking them about their voyage. The countess complained that the count was in Toledo at the Council of Ministers. Without him, she said, it was no vacation. But, Enrique described the trip in glowing terms. Teresa, too, was delighted to see me but still teased me about cutting people up.

"I don't know why I went on this trip," Maria said, reaching for my hand, "when everything I want is right here in Cordoba."

Our three days of sailing along the river were relaxing. Ordinarily such a slow-paced existence would not suit me but I became a totally different person in Maria's presence. Don Luis had arranged special sleeping accommodations in the towns we passed. He even engaged entertainers who boarded our ship along the way. He had left us on the first day explaining he had to return to prepare for the Council of Nobles' meeting at the castle. The Council, comprised of the six ranking noblemen allied through family or historic ties to the House of Trastamara, normally met every two years to analyze mutual problems. But, this year, because of the urgent matter affecting the future of the House of Trastamara, the count convened this special meeting.

During those three days, I felt as though I had known Maria all my life. I was amazed no one brought up the episode in the Music

Room nor did Maria even ask me about my fear of the Inquisition. The only twinge of conscience I felt was in not telling Maria my plan to leave Spain. I could not do so for that would entail exposing Orlando Franco. She asked about my work in Posadas, recalling that Andres met her at the port. I boasted of my success there, mentioning nothing about the conversos, about my uncle or about our discovery of Don Luis' duplicity.

When we docked in Cordoba, Don Luis met the boat, informing the countess that the count, who was already at the castle, requested she come immediately rather than stay overnight at their River House. Some of the noblemen had arrived, he said, so that her presence was needed there. As she hastened to the awaiting carriage, I thanked the countess for the three splendid days.

"Thank him," she said pointing to Don Luis. "It was his idea."

Entering the carriage with Maria, the countess invited me to ride along with them to the castle. I readily accepted, hoping to see the count before his council meeting. But, as we were about to leave, Andres rode up.

Don Luis introduced him to the countess. He was about to introduce Maria, when she said she remembered Andres meeting her at the port before they departed.

"Princess, you might as well forget him," Andres said, pointing to me. "Now that you know me, you must admit I'm far more desirable. I'm perfectly harmless and I don't even have a cutting knife."

We all laughed at his antics as he emptied his pockets protesting his innocence. But, I noticed it was all an act so I asked him what brought him to the port. He replied that I was urgently needed at the dispensary and apologized to the countess for taking me away.

When they drove off, I climbed into Andres' wagon asking him what was the urgency. He told me Don Luis had hurried back to Cordoba not only to meet the countess, but also to meet with Manuel.

"Yesterday, I helped Diaz carry Manuel from the monastery back into his *casa* in Cordoba. I heard that Don Luis will come here today, right now, to meet with Manuel." Andres said.

Andres quickly drove his wagon along the river where we passed Manuel's house not far from the count's Casa de Rio. We walked back along the river where a crew of carpenters had been working to fix Manuel's porch. Andres and I sat under on one of the interior supports of the porch where, hidden from view, we could hear all that was going on inside the house. We expected to hear secret conversation definitely linking Don Luis to Manuel.

"This is the kind of evidence we need," Andres whispered.

Soon, Don Luis came into the room, where Father Lopez sat by the sick man's bed, and announced, "I come to you officially, dispatched by Count Juan de Trastamara, to express his deep concern for your welfare. The count wishes to assure you that he would have been here himself had he not been so occupied with the meeting of the Council of Nobles."

"So his grace has returned," Manuel replied, welcoming Don Luis. "Please convey to him my gratitude for his felicitations. I hope that immediately after the Council of Nobles' meeting we can negotiate placing of our agents in the count's militia."

"That is why I am here," Don Luis said, suggesting a day for their meeting. He repeated the count's concern for Manuel's illness and left immediately.

Andres and I left when Don Luis rode off. We recognized that this had been only a required courtesy call to establish a meeting date. Andres was embarrassed and upset that he had treated it so urgently, taking me away from the count's family. I assured him that nothing was lost.

"I can reach the castle quicker riding my horse than his carriage can lumbering up the mountain side." I said.

We discussed our dilemma: knowing that Don Luis was a spy

but having totally inadequate evidence. During the three days I spent on the count's ship, Andres had explored every avenue to find some incriminating evidence. He came up with nothing. He mentioned that although Manuel had been transferred out of the monastery, the two cabinets containing the Inquisition's official documents were still there.

"Have you searched those cabinets?" I asked Andres.

"Of course not," Andres replied, "with Manuel there, I couldn't even go near them."

I suggested that we go to the monastery to search those cabinets since Father Lopez was still with Manuel. But Andres said he would go to the monastery and I should get to the count before the meeting to tell him about Don Luis. Even though the count might not believe me, he would at least be alerted to the possible danger Don Luis posed. Andres reminded me to urge the count to trace the whereabouts of Father Hernandez.

"Father Hernandez will be our best evidence," Andres said.

"Can you get to the cabinets with Diaz there?" I asked.

"No problem," Andres replied.

I immediately left for the castle and Andres set out for the monastery.

When Andres arrived at the San Sebastian, he went directly to Manuel's former room. Two men stopped him at the door and asked him to wait. They went inside. Moments later, he was ushered in, surprised to find Diaz sitting at Manuel's table and Nicolas sitting across from him. Diaz told the men to take Nicolas away.

"Sit down," Diaz ordered Andres. "I am now Chief Investigator for the Inquisition in Andalusia. Father Lopez will continue as Assistant Director to Manuel. Now, to business:

"Nicolas tells me that you promised to get him transferred from here in exchange for information about Father Hernandez."

Diaz was no longer the shy, dim witted, fumbling fool. He spoke to Andres sharply in a threatening tone, demanding to know what we learned from Nicolas.

Andres remained silent. Diaz summoned Nicolas, ordering him to recount everything that had transpired between him and Andres. When Nicolas related his dealings with us, he was again sent out.

Diaz upbraided Andres for interfering with the affairs of the Holy Inquisition. When he asked about me, Andres said that the countess invited me to the castle.

Diaz snorted, "I suppose he went there to tell the count what you learned from Nicolas."

Andres nodded.

"You have compromised our confidential information. I am having you imprisoned and turned over to the Holy Tribunal," Diaz shouted at Andres, then turning to his guards he said, "Lock him up."

8

I arrived in the castle but could not get into the count's private chambers because Don Luis was meeting with him and forbade interruptions. Rodriguez and his troops stood as guards of honor, under strict instructions to keep everyone out of the count's office.

I asked Rodriguez if he had seen Maria. He told me that she and the countess were showing the visiting ladies around the castle grounds. I strolled around the courtyard hoping to find the countess to help me get in to see the count, but she was nowhere to be seen.

At noon, a messenger whom I recognized from the monastery entered the castle grounds asking for Don Luis, but he, too, was forbidden to disturb the meeting. The messenger handed Rodriguez a note asking him to transmit it to Don Luis. He immediately emerged from the count's chambers and spoke briefly to the messenger. Don Luis summoned me and ordered me to return immediately to Cordoba to attend Manuel whose condition had worsened.

It seemed strange that Jimenez would call for me to attend Manuel. Nonetheless, I followed Don Luis's order but before leaving the castle grounds, I asked Rodriguez to find the countess for me because I had to consult with her on an important matter. When he did not return, I followed the messenger down the mountain path toward Cordoba. About half way down, Rodriguez caught up to me saying the countess was waiting for me. I turned my horse around, shouting to the messenger that I would catch up with him as soon I said 'good-bye' to Maria and the countess. He said continued on his way to Cordoba, urging me to hurry.

The countess was alone in the Tea Room and asked why I

sent Rodriguez for her. I begged her to arrange for me to talk to the count, explaining I had an urgent message for him. She asked me to explain the urgency but, since I could not disclose the truth, I said in a hushed tone that it had to do with the episode in the Music Room. The countess was distraught, recalling my behavior that evening. She beseeched me to be calm saying the Council of Nobles meeting was under way and the count could not be disturbed, but she allowed me to sit in the count's private chambers, adjacent to the Grand Salon, so that I could talk to him as soon as the meeting adjourned. With the door slightly open, I could hear the discussions and could even see Don Luis sitting at the count's right helping to coordinate the meeting.

The count explained that the purpose of the conference was to guide him in his forthcoming negotiations with Torquemada on the issue of placing Inquisition agents in military units. He reported that Torquemada had appealed to Their Majesties to allow his agents to work within the army's ranks to stamp out heresy from the military. Isabel agreed; Ferdinand did not. He withheld approval pending direct negotiation between Torquemada and the Count of Trastamara. The count reminded his guests that the army of Spain, although nominally under the crown, was really an extension of the Trastamara power.

"In essence, each of us still retains control over our own troops by providing their clothing, their housing, their food, and their pay. In return, the crown compensates us by assignation of conquered lands, conferring or increasing our noble rank, and by outright grants of money. In other words, Their Majesties pay us for the use of our troops but, in principle, we retain authority over them.

"The Inquisition now wants to share that authority with us by stationing their agents in every military unit. We could find no reason to oppose such a move if it were only to provide religious guidance. But experience has proven that the Inquisition assumes full authority wherever it establishes itself. Therefore, the question is: how can we limit its power?"

None of the six noblemen expressed any opposition to control by the Inquisition. Despite the count's assurances that their opinions would remain secret and that no informer was present, no one spoke against the Inquisition.

Pedro of Cadiz gave a typical response. "For the past two years, I have not convened the Cortes of Cadiz except for ceremonial functions. The work of the city is carried on by the magistrates, tax officials, and other departments. Our ports and ship building activities are functioning well. As for my militia, I will abide by whatever agreements the Count of Trastamara, as my liege lord, enters into with the Holy Inquisition."

Other noblemen voiced similar sentiments. Each expressed satisfaction with the status quo deferring to the count's final decision. Vincente, Duke of Cordoba, went even further in his remarks about the Inquisition, praising their agents and recommending complete cooperation.

"No one can question my initial opposition to the Inquisition," he began. "My cortes held out the longest when I opposed its establishment. I now find that more can be done by cooperating with their agents than by opposing them. I did not agree to expulsion of the Jews from the realm, for example, but in working with the Inquisition, we managed quite well in the final disposition of Jewish properties and especially in the reassignment of their liens. In all matters of confiscation, the Inquisition maintains exact records of all property. Their agents display fair-mindedness and, because we respect their authority, they respect ours."

Ramon de Monterey, the lowest ranking nobleman, said he saw no problem with Torquemada's request. Although he pledged full support to the count's decisions, he said that trying to rein in the power of the Inquisition was beyond the scope of the Council.

The count graciously acknowledged his noblemen's remarks but rebuked them because no one addressed his immediate question: limiting the power of the Inquisition within the Trastamara militias.

Despite the count's exhortation, everyone remained silent on the issue, except the old and venerated duke, Don Gonzales di Alicante.

He was more than eighty-years-old and was loved by his peers and by the populace at large. His humor and affability were legendary. Despite his years, he stood tall and erect, with his bushy snow-white hair falling regally to his shoulders.

"Juan, I tell you it's useless," he said, calling the count by his first name. "You can get more milk out of a bull than bravery out of these frightened cows. They like their titles but won't lift a finger to defend them. The Inquisition doesn't have to go far to diminish their authority. They have none. Their courts are under the thumb of the Holy Tribunals and their militias would cringe before Torquemada's agents if you allowed them access. My dear Pedro, you say your magistrates function well in Cadiz. How many of your ships have been confiscated by the Inquisition merely at the whim of its agents? And, you, my noble Vincente, how many times have your courts ordered property seizures only at the behest of the Suprema with no legal evidence of wrongdoing.

At first the noblemen laughed when old Don Gonzales — for all his years, a maverick among them — began his tirade. But when he called out individuals' names, they shouted and asked the count to silence him. The count allowed him to continue.

"There's more wealth in confiscation than in honest taxation," Don Gonzales said. "With a promise of a 30 to 50 percent share of a confiscation, the search for heresy has become the most treasured prize in Spain today. Wealth has become a peril to its owner. The Inquisition has more gold in its coffers than we have in all our combined treasuries. But, your nobles sit on their noble asses, wallowing like pigs in the mud slung in their faces."

Several of the noblemen pounded on the table, There was but, again, the count said nothing.

"Ramon," Don Gonzales continued, "your title doesn't entitle you to sleep with every woman in your mountain hideaway. Get out of bed and see what's happening to your district. Your women are being burned as whores and you are impotent when it comes to the Inquisition. So are all of you."

At last the count tried to halt him by thanking him for his opinion, but the aged Gonzales stood up to the count saying, "I'm not through. My word of advice is, if you give the Inquisition a free hand in the militia, it won't be long before their Holy Tribunals replace our military courts and their agents assume power over your commanders. I say to you, our militia is the only good thing left in Spain. Keep it."

The other five noblemen criticized Don Gonzales, bitterly complaining and asking why the count did not silence him. The count deferred to Don Luis who humored them, quieting their anger. Don Luis restored peace with his wit and charm. He then reminded the group that the Royal Council of Ministers had already agreed to Torquemada's request, and what they needed to discuss was the logistical agreement to be reached with the Inquisition. He suggested several methods to guard against excesses avowing that the Inquisition still respects agreements reached with the House of Trastamara. As an example, he cited the requirement that before any member of the Council of Nobles could be brought to trial for heresy the Count of Trastamara must be notified. He urged the group to show its strength by establishing a set of principles to guide the count in his negotiations with the Inquisition.

Even now that I knew Don Luis was a spy, I could not help but admire his talents.

The count adjourned the meeting thanking Don Luis, referring to him as, "the highest *hidalgo* in Spain". Physically, he towered over everyone in that room. When Don Luis announced the luncheon recess, the countess walked in to the Grand Salon, took her husband by his arm, and led him into the library. She whispered something to him and then left me alone with him.

"What is the urgency?" the count asked. "Speak quickly because I must return to my guests."

I planned to take him step-by-step leading to our discovery of Don Louis' treachery, but the count's abruptness frightened me and I blurted out, "Don Luis is a spy. He's put here by the Inquisition."

"What are you saying!" the count gasped.

I rapidly related everything we knew about Don Luis: Nicolas' disclosures; Father Hernandez's papers; and my interpretation of his revelations at the Board of Inquiry.

The count said nothing. He sat for an interminably long time, his face buried in his hands, looking down at the floor, not saying a word. I had never seen him act so strangely. Gone was his stern, sharp, austere demeanor. He looked worried, beaten. Was he questioning my veracity? Was it fear of the Inquisition? I could not tell if he believed me.

Finally, he stood up, told me to remain in his chambers, and said, "I must confer with Don Luis."

I was stunned and frightened. What I feared most was about to happen: confronting Don Luis with no evidence. Could I stand up to Don Luis without it?

The count soon returned saying he mentioned nothing to Don Luis about my accusations, but asked him to prepare charts showing the numerical strength, present locations, and lists of the commanding officers of all the Trastamara militias.

"That will keep him busy all afternoon and will give me a chance to pursue this further," the count said.

"Do you believe me?" I asked.

"You leave me no choice," he replied. "I must go on the assumption that if your information is correct, Luis can seek his revenge on me."

"Revenge? The count is afraid of Don Luis!" I said and then, apologizing for my outburst, I added, "It's hardly conceivable that the Inquisition could threaten the House of Trastamara."

"Twenty years ago," the count replied, "we all would have scoffed at the idea that an erratic monk could challenge the power of Spanish nobility."

"Was that your main concern? The challenge to Spanish nobility?" I asked.

"It's too late for excuses," the count said. "The fact is that we did not oppose the Inquisition as long as it did not challenge our authority. As a matter of fact, we considered the Inquisition our ally, serving to unite our warring factions. At least we were being united on one issue, our faith."

"Did you believe that the Inquisition would bring unity to Spain's people?" I asked.

"Yes, of course," the count said. "You see, the curse of disunity has plagued us since the beginning of time. Every principality, every noble family, battled each other. Even our national hero, El Cid was jailed, tortured by his own people. Until recently, we were battling still. But, the frenzy of the mobs, directed by the Inquisition against the heretics, or the Moors, or the Jews, created an image of Spanish unity."

"Unity of hate." I said.

"It didn't really matter," the count answered with candor. "We were willing to believe that it was unity of faith. So we supported the Inquisition's program of *limpieza*, purity of Christian blood, in the hope of creating some kind of harmony among our warring clans."

"And the moral issues," I protested, "spilling innocent blood, burning human beings?"

"Morality is subject to change," the count said. "Violence, at times, may even be viewed as an act of pacification. So, the Inquisition was welcome by all."

"Why?" I asked.

"To each his own," the count answered. "To Torquemada, a

cleansing of faith; to Ferdinand, funds for the treasury; to Isabel an act of obedience; to me, a hope for a united people."

"Were you concerned about Torquemada's growing power?"

"Not at all," the count replied. "To us, he was a hero of Spain who brought us true independence, as great as any military hero."

"Torquemada, a hero?" I asked.

"He freed Spain from subservience to the Pope," the count replied. "When Torquemada denied Pope Alexander the right to name the five inquisitors to direct the Spanish Inquisition, it marked the first triumph of Spain's quest for independence from Rome."

I again asked if Torquemada's power continues to grow, would he not one day be more powerful than the Spanish Monarchs.

"Right now, Torquemada's power is not my concern," he said. "I am concerned about my family."

"Because of the Inquisition?"

"Because of Luis," the count said.

"How can Don Luis be a threat to you?" I asked.

The count signaled for his servant, sending word that he would not join the noblemen for lunch, but would return for the afternoon session.

"I married the countess five years before Ferdinand's marriage to Isabel," the count said, his hand propped on his ornate writing desk.

"For twenty years, we were childless. We were resigned to the fact that our *ricos hombres* title would end with us, but we could not resign ourselves to a life without children. So, we decided to adopt a child.

"The church brought us Maria, and Maria brought us happiness."

The count reached into his desk, unlocked a concealed secret drawer, and drew forth an official-looking document.

"This is Maria's baptismal certificate," he said handing me

the document. "Look at the date, 'the twenty-fifth day of June in the year of our Lord 1480'."

"That's only sixteen years ago," I remarked, "Maria is almost twenty-years-old."

"That's right," the count said. "The Inquisition brought her to us as an infant. She was taken from her parents, convicted conversos who were declared unfit to bring up a Christian child."

"Does Maria know any of this?" I asked.

"Neither she nor Enrique, who was born to us eight years after we adopted Maria, know anything," the count said. "And, that is why I am concerned about what Don Luis might do."

I asked him to explain.

"When I confront him with your accusations, his only weapon will be to disclose to Maria that she was adopted," the count said fingering the baptismal certificate. "She will be devastated."

The count surmised that Don Luis would assuredly find some way to communicate this fact to Maria. He might use it to avoid punishment or to wreak vengeance on the count.

"I am now asking you to stay in the castle to watch over her," the count said. "Your responsibility is to make certain Don Luis does not approach her."

I accepted his bidding and also told him Don Luis had instructed me to attend to Manuel.

"Manuel can wait," he replied. "We cannot."

I assured the count that I would do everything in my power to protect Maria and would see to it that no harm came to her.

"Don Luis must not see that you are still in the castle," the count said. "He is exceptionally bright and would suspect that something has gone awry."

I told the count that Don Luis saw me leave for Cordoba with the messenger but did not seen me return with Rodriguez.

"I hope you said nothing to the countess about Don Luis when you asked her to intervene in your behalf?" he asked.

"No, I thought it best to disclose it only to you," I replied.
He stood up, thanked me profusely, and left.

I doubt if he had any idea how I felt when he shared those secrets with me, especially charging me to protect Maria. From that moment, I was no longer an intruder in her life. I had become her protector; all obstacles to my loving her vanished.

I remained in his room eagerly waiting for the second meeting of the Council of Nobles to start. When it finally did, I stealthily bolted out of the room searching for Maria and making certain to stay out of Don Luis's sight.

Maria was neither in her room nor anywhere I searched. Teresa told me that the countess was entertaining the ladies outside the castle and Maria might be with them. When I finally caught up with the countess, she told me Maria was with he art tutor, Master de Silva. I found the art teacher instructing Enrique and apologized to Master de Silva for interrupting.

"Where's your sister?" I asked the boy.

De Silva answered that Maria was modeling clay in the studio behind the north patio. I darted over to the studio where, from afar, I saw her standing over a work table, her back to me, trying to shape a man's head. She wore a loose gray smock and a scarf around her forehead. Her face and hands were covered with blotches of dried clay. I stealthily moved in closer, admiring her beauty, thinking that most woman need to dress up and apply cosmetics to be attractive. Not Maria. She was absolutely stunning, despite her ill-fitting smock, her unkempt hair, and her grimy hands. She was struggling with the unfinished bust muttering in disgust.

"'Art is slavery'," I said, quoting Master de Silva's famous adage.

Startled, she reached up to remove the soiled scarf from her head. I grasped her hand, stopped her, and told her to go on with her work.

"But I look so terrible," she complained.

"You look so terribly pretty," I said, rubbing a smudge of clay off her forehead.

She said she had seen me earlier, riding up to the castle, and wondered why it took me so long to find her. I told her I had to speak privately with the count. She asked what we talked about and I made up an excuse, telling her that we discussed my imminent certification as a physician.

"Now, back to work on that clay," I said.

"Work!" she repeated, "That's all it is, work. There's no art in this. And don't lecture me about art is slavery. I want to draw, to paint, but old de Silva keeps me in this shed, forcing me to sculpt."

"If you want to paint, you must learn to sculpt," I said. "The trouble with most artists is that their work is flat, has no depth. Look, the cheek on this model is not on the same level with either the eye or the mouth. When you take a piece of clay and actually build the cheek higher than the eye, lower than the nose, slightly curved away from the mouth, you then learn the first lesson of art: proportion. The cheek has its own dimension."

I kissed her cheek. She was about to embrace me but I continued my 'lecture'. "Now look at the mouth. The lips are not just a smudge of red paint on a canvas. They, too, have their own dimension yet they're related to the cheek, the nose, and the chin. Only when you form lips of clay with your hands do you get the feel of what the dimension of a mouth should be."

I kissed her mouth and felt her hands grasp me around my neck. I sat her down on the bench and, brushing her lips with my finger, I said, "Lips are not a smudge on a canvas. They are sculpted in beauty. And when yours quiver as a rose on the bush, they speak of love."

"That's like the poem you wrote for me when were sailing on the Guadalquivir," Maria said, squirming out of my embrace.

"But the real thing is better than the written word," I said, kissing her again.

"I read it to myself so many times, I know it by heart," she said.

Your lips are delicate
As the petal in full bloom
When they part in laughter
They bring joy to my heart
When they frown in anguish
They bring sorrow to my soul.

"No more anguish and no more sorrow," she said taking me by the hand and leading me to her room, saying she had to get ready for the Council banquet that evening. "This will be my first banquet with you as my escort."

"I'm not taking you to the banquet tonight," I said, recalling to myself the count's admonition that Don Luis must not see me or get close to Maria. "I was not invited and even if I was, I would feel out of place with all those dignitaries."

"As the physician to my father, you would be a welcome and prominent guest," she assured me. "As a matter of fact, my father already sang your praises, so many of the dignitaries are anxious to meet you."

"But it will rob us of the precious little time we have to be together," I argued, reminding her that I would soon have to leave for Toledo for my certification. "So, I already asked Teresa to serve us a private dinner anywhere but in the Grand Ballroom."

Maria would have none of it. She insisted on going to the banquet with me.

"I'll tell you the real truth," I said sternly. "The reason why I want to keep you away from the banquet is that your father might decide to contract a suitable marriage for you with some titled nobleman."

Maria ridiculed the idea. But, I reminded her that marriages among noble families were arranged for political power and a banquet of this kind was a natural mating ground.

"Maria, if you love me, don't go to the banquet tonight," I pleaded.

Maria flung herself at me saying although she thought the idea silly, she would do anything to please me, even miss the banquet.

"Which is the most secluded part of the castle?" I asked.

"The Throne Room," she replied.

"Lead the way, little one," I said, extending my arm.

"Don't call me that," she said taking my arm and clinging closely to me, "Only my father calls me that. You're certainly not my father. You're my lover."

"You belong to me as much as to your father," I said.

She laughed and tightened her grip on my arm as she lead me along the garden walk which skirted the inner turret of the castle. We climbed the steep stairway to its highest tower. When we reached an elevated terrace, I unbolted the latch on the ornamental gate and we continued up another steep flight of stairs coming to another terrace overlooking the entire La Campina valley. The view was breathtaking, enhanced by the rays of the setting sun which emblazoned the castle gardens, the hills and farmlands with golden splendor.

I held Maria in my arms whispering, "This beauty is but a reflection of you."

We were interrupted by Teresa who was struggling up the steep incline carrying a tray of food. She opened the door of the Throne Room where she set up a special table for our dinner. Teresa was surprised the countess had allowed us to even visit the room, much less to eat in there.

"It's used only for the king and queen," Teresa said. Then, feigning annoyance, she curtseyed before me asking to be excused. As she walked past me she shouted, "and if there's anything else you want, get it yourself, Senor. I'm not climbing those steps again."

The Throne Room was truly fit for a king, with exquisite and tastefully decorated furnishings and artistic masterpieces adorning its walls. As Enrique had done previously, Maria now described the many historic events which took place in the secluded apartment. We sat down to eat the sumptuous meal Teresa had prepared, but we barely touched any of the food. We could not part from one another.

In the adjoining bedroom, a huge gilded crown bearing the monarch's coat of arms towered above the bed canopy. With childlike glee, Maria jumped up on the bed, sinking into its soft bedding. She patted the coverlet, inviting me to join her.

"This is Ferdinand's private room and there were more than just military affairs taking place here," she said impishly.

I lay next to her in a loving embrace, unconcerned with the passage of time. At about midnight, Maria flitted about the room lighting all the lamps to show me the crystal chandeliers throughout the Throne Room. I thought it would attract too much attention and quickly blew out the lights.

Before Maria could get annoyed, I asked her, "If you could have any wish, what would you want most right now?"

"To marry you tonight," she whispered.

"Seriously, where would you like to go, now that we have each other," I said, hoping to take her away from the castle.

"You really mean it. You'll go anywhere I want?" she said.

"Anywhere," I responded. "Ask, and it shall be granted."

"Take me to La Caverna," she said.

"Where?"

"La Caverna. It's the Trastamara hunting lodge, one of the most beautiful resorts in Andalusia," she said, "and it's less than half a day's ride from here."

"Your wish is my command," I said. "We start at dawn so that we can have a full day at La Caverna."

When we returned to her room, I could still hear the musicians playing in the Grand Ballroom which meant that Don Luis was probably busy with the guests. I made her promise to go to sleep immediately so that we could leave early for La Caverna.

"I promise to go bed, but I can't promise that I'll sleep," she said. "I have to get you out of my mind and that's impossible."

Before going back to my room, I sent word through Rodriguez to the count that Maria and I would leave the castle. In the morning, when I came to Maria's room to awaken her, she was already up and dressed, ready to leave. She said this was the first time she would venture out of the castle unaccompanied by guards or chaperons. She said she did not know how I accomplished her 'escape', as she called it, but while racing out of the castle she called out, "I love you for this."

The castle was situated atop the La Campina hilltop and the southern descent was steep and precarious. I was amazed at Maria's horsemanship, as she galloped through the narrow decline with reckless abandon. At one time, when she took a perilous high jump with her horse, she looked back shouting, "That's what you do when you're free and in love!"

At the foothills of the mountain, almost without notice, the skies darkened and the rain started. I found a cave-like formation in a hill below us. When I jumped down to the cave, I scraped my leg and realized Maria would fare no better on the jagged rock. To help her, I placed myself against the boulder and she stepped down on my shoulders. From there I let her gently down on the ground where we remained in an embrace. Claps of thunder and bolts of lightning raged about us. We held on to each other oblivious to the storm.

Not until our wet horses neighed did we realized that the rain had stopped. We quickly gathered our few belongings and continued our ride to La Caverna. When we reached the steep sloping roadway leading to the entrance of the hunting lodge, my horse lost his footing and I had to jump off to avoid injury. Emilio, the stable hand who saw the fall, rushed over to help. Maria apologized, saying that she should have warned me about the sudden steep decline. Emilio reported that the horse's foot was in good condition and also explained that the steep decline which caused his fall was built during the war as a precaution against a sudden attack on the La Caverna.

"Before a rider gets into La Caverna," Emilio explained, "a horse or wagon must stop and slow down."

When Maria introduced Emilio as Teresa's son, he said his mother already told him all the nice things about me.

"Teresa talks too much," Maria said leading me to the gardens of La Caverna.

We rested in the fabled gardens much of the afternoon. Maria suddenly announced that we would go climbing on a nearby mountain. She rigged leather straps to my shoulders and tied on a cloth bag filled with food for our picnic.

Emilio handed me a small machete to cut down the underbrush on our climb. He then drove us to the mountain in the carriage and when we arrived, Maria dismissed him saying we would walk back to La Caverna.

Climbing the mountain was an exhilarating experience. I led the way up, cutting vines and branches blocking our path. But I struggled because of the heavy food pack hitched to me. When we reached the middle level, La Mesa, Maria finally untied the leather straps from my shoulders. La Mesa, a flat terrain area within the moun-tain range, served as our picnic ground. There was no one around. I had the mountain and Maria to myself.

Immediately after the banquet, the count called in Don Luis, in the presence of his guards, accused him of being an agent of the Inquisition, spying on the House of Trastamara. Don Luis was startled, but said nothing in his defense.

"Why, Luis, why the disloyalty?" the count asked. "You were under oath to me."

"Even before you accepted me as your *hidalgo*, I had taken an oath to serve the Inquisition," Don Luis replied.

"Then your betrayal began the day you came into this castle," the count said.

Don Luis retained his regal demeanor as he unfolded the events that brought him to the House of Trastamara:

Luis was the illegitimate son of Ferdinand, king of Aragon. His birth became known at a most critical political moment when Spain's ranking noblemen were engaged in delicate negotiations to bring about the marriage of Ferdinand and Isabel, Queen of Castile. With this union, the warring kingdoms of Aragon and Castile would unite, paving the way for the peaceful consolidation of the two hostile kingdoms which had plagued Spain for centuries.

Count Juan de Trastamara, the chief architect of this marriage, faced almost insurmountable difficulties. At any juncture the entire plan could have been aborted. Aside from the personality clash between the arrogant, flamboyant seventeen-year-old Ferdinand, and the shy, contemplative eighteen-year-old Isabel, there were other serious obstacles. First, the Pope objected because the projected bride and groom were first cousins. Second, the bride's relative poverty required substantial financial maneuvering by the Count of Trastamara to make the marrying couple economically compatible. Third, the hostility between the Castilians and the Aragonese was unrelenting.

After many months of delicate negotiations, the birth of Ferdinand's illegitimate son came to light. Isabel fumed that a bastard son might one day contest her future children's claim to the throne of the new kingdom. The Castilian noblemen supported their queen, demanding assurances that only children born to Isabel would be recognized as claimants to the throne. To save the marriage, the Count of Trastamara worked out an agreement signed by all the nobles of the realm denying royalty to the bastard son, Luis. His mother, Elvira, was forced to agree to lay no claims to the throne in behalf of her son. Luis was thus brought into the world as an unwanted son: castoff by his father and denied noble blood. In his early years, Luis would repeat his mother's assuring words that he was born of love, while Isabel's children were born of contention. As a result, young Luis developed a keen resentment for Isabel, who prohibited his entry to the palace, and for Ferdinand, who disowned him. Luis, therefore, took an immediate liking to Torquemada for he was the only one in the realm who would publicly reprimand Ferdinand and Isabel, imposing severe religious penance on them.

Manuel, King Ferdinand's second cousin, was appointed Administrator of the Inquisition and was also charged with young Luis' education. Knowing of the boy's affection for Torquemada, Manuel forged an early bond between the two, inviting Torquemada to assign tutors to the young, sensitive lad.

On Luis' twentieth birthday, Manuel brought him to the Santa Cruz Monastery where Torquemada personally indoctrinated him in the religious and political aims of the Inquisition. Receptive to and influenced by Torquemada's mission, Luis emulated his mentor's enthusiasm. When, at last, Luis took an oath to work for the Inquisition, he did so with incredible fervor.

Torquemada laid upon Luis the mission of delivering the power of the House of Trastamara into the hands of the Inquisition. Torquemada impressed upon him the importance of that mission, comparing it to his subjugation of Queen Isabel. Luis was told that it might take years and that he would be serving two masters but in the end, when the army would come under the Inquisition's control, the purification of Spain would be assured.

Upon the recommendation of Manuel, King Ferdinand commissioned Luis to be the *hidalgo*, the ranking knight, to the Count of Trastamara.

"Why are you telling me all this?" the count asked.

"For two reasons," Don Luis replied, no longer aloof. "First, I realize that my life is now in your hands and telling you the entire truth is my way of pleading for mercy. Second, although I have loyally served the Inquisition, I hold you in high regard and I hope to compensate for my dishonor by relaying this information to you."

"Dishonor cannot be rectified," the count replied. "You have done irreparable damage to the House of Trastamara. You are no better than a common spy."

Don Luis said nothing in his defense except to repeat his plea for clemency.

"I have several options," the count said. "I can refer you to the Royal Magistrate and demand the death penalty or I can convene my own court and put you to death here."

He reminded Don Luis that under the feudal system, death was the punishment for breaching one's oath to a lord. Don Luis said he recognized the seriousness of his offense and was also aware of its consequence. And that was why he asked for mercy.

"There is yet a third alternative," the count said.

"Another alternative?" Don Luis asked.

"Banishment," the count replied. "I grant you the choice, death or exile?"

"To which country?" Don Luis asked.

The count did not reply. Don Luis bowed his head and thought for a long time.

"Banishment," Don Luis finally said, looking submissively to the count. "It is better to remain alive, even in exile, than to be dead in one's native land."

Summoning the guards to take Don Luis, the count said, "You will be banished to Africa."

"Africa!" Don Luis called out dejectedly.

"To Africa," the count replied, turning his back on Don Luis who pleaded, asking to be sent anywhere but to Africa.

The count dispatched a messenger to Don Carlos with a

report of Don Luis' perfidy and ordered the general to arrange Don Luis' banishment to the Moors.

Although it was very late at night, the count summoned his Council of Nobles. Grimly, he told them of Don Luis' disloyalty, announcing his banishment from Spain. They were aghast. Several expressed surprise that the count had not put him to death. The count explained neither compassion nor mercy made him spare Don Luis' life. He meant to avoid complications with King Ferdinand, Don Luis' father, who was initially responsible for assigning Don Luis as the *hidalgo* to the House of Trastamara.

The elderly Don Gonzales asked if it was safe to send Don Luis so far. The count replied that three armed soldiers would deliver the prisoner to Don Carlos in Granada.

"Luis is probably the best swordsman in Spain," Don Gonzales reminded the count. "Better keep him shackled."

The following morning, the noblemen stood at the castle gates when Rodriguez rode out with two soldiers, escorting Don Luis to Granada. The prisoner's hands were shackled in irons; he rode between the soldiers. He stared ahead, looking to neither side, while the group jeered him, shouting their contempt. Rodriguez saluted the count, then ordered his men to a fast gallop.

"How far do we ride?" a soldier asked Rodriguez when they reached level terrain, leaving the castle far behind.

"All the way to Granada, but we'll stop off at several places along the way," Rodriguez replied. "Right now we head to La Caverna.

"That's a long way off," the soldier grumbled.

"Shut up and keep riding," Rodriguez barked out.

"So the *hidalgo* was finally trapped in his own *hilado*, web," one of the soldiers jeered Don Luis.

"The *hidalgo* has a heart of *hielo*, ice," the second sneered.

Rodriguez reprimanded his men for taunting the prisoner. But, Don Luis, who had commissioned Rodriguez captain of the castle guard, called out that the soldiers were fine men and their aversion to him only proved their good training. Rodriguez alerted his soldiers to be on guard for Don Luis' attempts to escape, explaining that his flattery was typical of his manipulation and deception. He knew that Don Luis was really stung by the soldier's jeers and complimented them only to gain their trust.

They had ridden almost half the day, when Don Luis slowed down his horse and tested his irons, trying to free his shackled hands.

"They're secure," Rodriguez said, noticing Don Luis tampering with the irons.

"They're cutting into my skin," Don Luis complained.

"You should have your hands cut off," one of the soldiers called out.

The soldiers kept cursing and taunting him. Rodriguez again silenced his men, ordering them to ride ahead while he rode beside Don Luis to protect the prisoner. Don Luis whispered a request to Rodriguez, to have the church say prayers for him if he died.

"You're being banished not executed," Rodriguez sneered, suspecting him of another deception.

"I chose banishment because I knew that in any other country, my honor would sooner or later be restored."

"You honor restored!" Rodriguez retorted. "After what you've done?"

"My contribution to the Church," Don Luis said. "would be recognized anywhere."

Rodriguez scorned him for being ungrateful to the count, reminding him that the count spared his life.

"If not for the count," Don Luis sneered, "I would have become one of the most prominent figures in all of Spain, second only to Torquemada. I never considered myself an informer."

At that, the soldiers cursed him and Rodriguez, appalled, called him a despicable traitor. A soldier rode up and punched him so hard he fell off his horse. Rodriguez did not scold the soldier; he only ordered his men to lift Don Luis back on his horse.

Don Luis lost his temper, shouting at them that they were allied with 'the Jew Alberto' and grew progressively more violent, fuming at the soldiers, deriding their defense of the count. The more they taunted him, the more abusive he became, repeating invectives against the count, against me, against Maria, whom he cursed as having "Jewish blood in her veins".

The soldiers hurled obscenities at their prisoner, drawing their swords, urging him to escape so that they could kill him. Rodriguez intervened, telling them not to pay attention to Don Luis because he was crazy, ranting hysterically.

"It'll be a miracle if we don't kill him before getting to Granada," a soldier called out.

"Hey, there's La Caverna," Rodriguez shouted, speeding up his horse and then leading them down the steep decline into the gates.

Before eating their noon meal, the men tied up Don Luis securely and walked over to the nearby lake, cooling their feet in the shallow water. Don Luis lay down to rest, covering himself with his cloak. Emilio, the stable boy, came by and saw Don Luis but did not notice the shackles. He welcomed Don Luis telling him that Maria and I were up on the mountain.

When Rodriguez and the soldiers returned from the lake, they drove Emilio off. Don Luis pleaded with them to loosen his irons so that he could wash the blood off his bruised hands. Rodriguez reluctantly agreed, ordering his soldiers to draw their swords while he unlocked the irons and untied Luis. They escorted him to the lake. Don Luis emerged from the water calm and composed.

"I'm grateful for letting me wash and I am sorry for my anger," he said. "Captain, I will give you no more trouble."

They were stunned, but suspicious of his changed attitude.

"I must accept my punishment," he said. "I'm no longer a *hidalgo* to be respected. I'm just Luis, a criminal."

To prove it, he helped the soldiers with their packs, served them their food, and cleaned the mud off their boots. He showed his bleeding wounds to Rodriguez who allowed him to eat without putting on the irons.

During the meal, Don Luis entertained them with intriguing accounts of life in the castle, lauding the count's chivalry and brilliance. He continued praising the count, repeating several times how grateful he was that his life was spared. He agreed with Rodriguez that banishment was not death and asked him to express his gratitude to the count for not killing him. He also asked Rodriguez to apologize to the count in his behalf for the shame he brought on the House of Trastamara.

Rodriguez did not know what to make of Don Luis' change of heart. Candidly he asked Don Luis what caused it, still suspecting a deception.

He said. "All my life I was brought up to respect authority but was never prepared for this. You are quite correct in being suspicious of me but I assure you I have now accepted my fate. I guess the cold water restored my sanity,'"

He remained subservient, rinsing their plates, cleaning up the area, returning their utensils to the stable and grooming their horses. The soldiers, impressed with his servility, helped bandage his wounded wrists and even apologized for taunting him. Rodriguez said to his soldiers that Don Luis' changed attitude would make the rest of the trip easier. Don Luis mildly chastised the soldiers for their behavior, instructing them what should be done with an uncooperative prisoner. He congratulated Rodriguez for protecting him from the soldiers ire and also suggested better ways of handling such a situation. Rodriguez allowed Don Luis to stretch out on the ground without replacing the iron shackles. Don Luis thanked them all profusely saying that he needed to sleep because he had not slept the previous night.

They believed him.

Rodriguez and the soldiers unbuckled their sword belts and sat down to rest. When they thought Don Luis was asleep,

Rodriguez posted a guard and sauntered off with the other soldier to see the fabled La Caverna's gardens. Moments later, Don Luis saw the guard turn his back to urinate. He took one of the swords and plunged it into the soldier's back, killing him immediately. He stealthily led his horse out of the stable and raced to the mountain.

At that moment, Maria and I were enjoying a picnic on the mountain's second plateau where I had made a clearing with my small machete. La Mesa, the popular picnic area, was accessible only on foot either from the west side through a thick overgrowth or from the east by a very steep and slippery path skirting a water fall. Maria and I vied to see who would climb atop La Mesa quicker, using each side several times. Despite the pack tied to my back, she beat me only once, when she skidded down the water path. We were delighted at being alone on the mountain, our private playground. After our meal we prepared to climb higher. Maria once again buckled the leather straps to my back and was about to tie the empty food basket to them.

Suddenly we saw a horseman approaching in the valley below. While he was tying up his horse to a branch, Maria recognized Don Luis and waved to attract his attention. I quickly told her that the day before I had exposed him to her father. She could not believe what I was telling her but, when I warned her that he was probably coming to kill me, she became frantic. I quickly quieted her, hurried her to the waterfall path, and ordered her to slide down the wet smooth rock as she had done before.

"Take Don Luis' horse; ride fast to La Caverna for help," I said.

I watched her as she started her slide. Then, to protect her, I attracted Don Luis' attention by revealing myself at the opposite end of the Mesa, allowing Maria to escape undetected.

Don Luis had already reached the first level just below the Mesa. I could clearly see him with sword in hand and hear his boast that he was coming to kill me. I was unarmed, except for the small path-clearing machete. To fight him would be fatal. My only chance to survive was to delay the confrontation long enough to give Maria time to bring help.

I slowed his climb by creating rock slides in his path, and when he disappeared from sight, I knew he was right below me under the extended lip of La Mesa. I waited until I saw his head bobbing up over the knoll on the western approach, then I ran to the other end, sliding down the slippery rock to the lower plateau where Maria had just fled. I made certain to stay close to the wall of the towering cliff to avoid being seen by him.

At first, I considered dashing down the mountain and running to La Caverna, but I was certain Don Luis would see me from above and, because of his superior physical condition, overtake me in a long foot race.

I gave up the idea of trying to escape and continued to play for time.

Don Luis suddenly appeared on the Mesa. I stayed hidden, watching him climb further up the mountain, probably thinking that I was hiding in the ridges above. I quickly made my way back to the first level, searching for a hiding place. There was none. I was exposed and saw him running to the east end to slide down the rock at the waterfall to reach my level. I speedily scampered up the western path back to the Mesa and, again, was out of his sight. Panting, terrified, I had to sit down to rest while he searched for me on the first level below. From my perch atop La Mesa, I saw Maria galloping off. I prayed she could bring help before it was too late.

I hid in the bushes as best as I could, but Don Luis spotted me. He assaulted the heights in record time, climbing up the slick wet rock on the eastern side! I quickly bolted down to the first level, eluding him again.

This maneuver, shifting from the lower to the upper levels, worked to my advantage for a while. I successfully repeated this tactic three or four times in the hope of gaining the time I needed until Maria could return with help.

However, when I tried the same maneuver a fourth time, it was apparent that Don Luis realized that my delaying tactic was my only defense. Ever crafty, he reversed the procedure by hiding from me. I had no way of knowing where he was, but I dreaded the inevitable moment when he would pounce on me. I quickly tied the machete to the leather strap which had been tied to my shoulders. In my other hand, I held a rock.

I suddenly heard a bellowing roar from Don Luis, whose towering figure swooped down from the rocks above, landing less than twenty steps from me. For an instant, we stared at each other. Then he lunged at me with his sword pointing to my stomach. At that moment, I hurled my rock, which glanced off the sword, deflecting its thrust.

"What would you do if you were in my place?" I said, hoping to gain time by talking to him.

He lowered his sword, saying vehemently that were it not for me, he would be the hero of Spain. Even now, he said, he could escape but preferred to do away with me before fleeing from his soldiers. I asked, quite civilly, why his loyalty to Torquemada outweighed his fidelity to the count. He told me the count had spared his life but spoke with fervor about the Inquisition's plans for the salvation of Spain. To keep him talking, I asked what was the salvation of Spain. He began to answer, stating the need to purify the faith, but then he stopped.

"Oh no, I will not fall for another of your delaying tactics," he yelled. "You are the culprit, not the count. Without you he would never know. You're devil's emissary and you deserve to die."

I pleaded with him not to kill me, just as the count spared his life. That seemed to enrage him even more.

"You black-hearted son of a whore," he snarled, "some die in bed, some on the high seas, but you, Jew devil, you will die here, now, high in the mountain so that God will see you perish. I will slaughter you like a pig."

When he lifted his sword, preparing for the fatal lunge. I immediately grabbed the machete, which was tied to the leather strap, and began to circle it over my head. The machete whistled as it passed very close to him. For a while, he kept his distance, prancing on his feet, careful not to be ensnared by the flying knife. He climbed up on a boulder to get out of my range. I took advantage of his position and stopped twirling the machete; my hand was tiring. I knew I could not keep it up for long. The moment he jumped down, however, I started the machete flying again. He picked up a large stone and threw it at me, missing me by a hair's breadth, but I did not stop twirling the machete as he probably expected I would.

In measured steps, he crouched down, edging closer to my spinning machete and holding the sword perpendicular to the ground. Before I could adjust to his new tactic, he lunged beneath the arc of the flying knife; his sword cut the strap, sending the machete hurtling away. As it cut loose, it tore deeply into his right upper arm. Blood spurted but he quickly switched the sword to his left hand and once again lunged at me. I showered him with gravel and dirt, deflecting his aim. His entire body was now covered with blood flowing freely from his injured right arm.

"Luis," I shouted, "you're going to die losing all that blood. Give me your sword. I can still save you."

"I'll give you the sword," he cried out, "right in your belly."

He lunged wildly at me but I ran to the far end of the Mesa hiding in a bramblewood bush. He ran after me but I could see that he was weaving and wobbling, his feet scraping the ground as he neared.

When he began hacking away at the bramblewood branches, he became entangled in them and fell to the ground.

I quickly stepped on his wrist, forcing him to release the sword which tumbled down the ravine. He was lying in a pool of blood but managed to stand up, trying once more to jump me. He staggered and fell face down and did not stir. I cautiously approached his still body and succeeded in stopping the blood gushing from his wounded arm. For just a brief moment, Don Luis lifted his head staring at me.

"We'll get you ... both ... you and Maria...are...," he mumbled and died.

By the time Maria returned galloping into the valley with Rodriguez, I was already back in the valley. She ran into my arms crying and laughing with barely contained hysteria. I did my best to calm her and then asked her to wait so that Rodriguez and I could dispose of the body. As I was walking up the mountain with Rodriguez, he apologized to me, saying that allowing Don Luis to escape was his fault. He asked me not to tell anyone of his negligence for that would ruin his military career. He said they would report they had killed Don Luis as he attempted to escape. Of course, I promised him it would remain our secret.

While burying the body, he told me about Don Luis' ranting during the long ride from the castle. Rodriguez specifically recalled Don Luis cursing Maria, saying Jewish blood flowed in her veins. He conjectured that Don Luis was simply out of his mind and I agreed with him that their prisoner was hysterical at the time and that simply calling her a Jew was probably his way of cursing her. However, I asked Rodriguez not to disclose any of this to Maria.

I rested briefly at La Caverna, then Maria and I decided to return immediately to the castle. After Rodriguez and his men left, carrying the dead soldier with them, we started to ride back to the castle. I was amazed at her stamina, riding without a stop. It was almost dark when we finally arrived. Maria went to her room and immediately fell asleep.

I told the count and countess of our harrowing experience relating every detail of my struggle with Don Luis at La Caverna. We tried to figure out what he meant by his last words: "We'll get you, both, you and Maria are..."

"It doesn't signify anything," said the count. "Probably the ranting of a dying, angry man."

"No," I said, apologizing for disagreeing with him, "Don Luis was telling me what I always suspected: I am a threat to Maria's safety. It would be wise for us to part."

The countess asked me not to make rash decisions but to allow a full investigation before taking any action. The count not only ridiculed my fears about Maria's safety but was annoyed at my suggestion that he could not protect his own daughter. I was amazed by his rebuke in view of the fears he had expressed earlier. It then occurred to me that the count had probably not shared his fears with the countess and that he was now protecting her from alarm. I therefore mentioned nothing further about Don Luis and asked about the meeting of the Council of Nobles.

He replied that in view of the tense situation created by Don Luis' exposure as a spy, he would now reject out of hand the Inquisition's plan to place its agents within the military. He was certain that his Council of Nobles had gained time since neither Torquemada nor the queen would press the issue.

When the countess asked about my immediate plans I said I was leaving for Toledo in the morning to meet with the Royal Council of Medicine for my certification as a physician.

After a moment of thought, the count said, "While you are in Toledo, it would be wise for you to try to secure the queen's permission to visit your parents in Naples."

He added that if I encountered any difficulty, I should contact him. I thanked him for his advice and for his offer to help. Walking with me to my room, he reminded me of his promise to build a special hospital for me in Seville and said he would begin working on the plans as soon as I returned from Toledo.

Early the next morning Maria greeted me in the Tea Room where we had breakfast and discussed my examination by the Royal Medical Commission. We walked together, hand in hand, to the gate. I told her that while in Toledo, I would try to have the queen grant me permission to visit my parents in Italy. She said that she would go with me to Italy. As I was about to mount my horse, she wished me well on my examination.

Riding to Cordoba, I thought over the events of the past two days. It suddenly occurred to me that the count's suggestion about visiting my parents was not accidental. I thought it was his way of sending me a subtle message that he agreed with my fears, that my presence at the castle would endanger Maria.

I did not know a greater tragedy awaited me in Cordoba.

9

I was about to enter the gate of the Casa Lombardia, when two men on horseback came up on either side of my mount. I recognized the Inquisition agents to whom I regularly reported.

"Follow us to the Hermandad," one of the agents commanded abruptly, "You are to appear before the Preliminary Judgment of the Holy Tribunal on the charge of heresy. You will await trial in prison."

Shocked and frightened, recalling my first experience with an Inquisition dungeon, I pleaded with him to inform the Count of Trastamara. He gave me no assurance nor did he disclose any details of the charges against me as he lead me to a cell and locked its door. I was both appalled and relieved to see Andres sitting at its far end calling out, "Welcome to this luxurious inn."

Despite his attempt at humor, he, too, was frightened. He described his confrontation with Diaz and his two days in jail. He was not allowed to contact anyone, not even his father. He whispered that Diaz, now elevated as Chief Investigator, ordered his arrest after ferreting out the truth from Nicolas. Sitting by him in a corner of the cell, I told Andres everything that happened in the castle, describing my narrow escape from Don Luis. I mentioned the count's advice to me that in Toledo that I should seek permission to leave Spain, Andres agreed that the count, too, was concerned for his daughter's welfare if I were to continue my association with her.

What concerned us most, however, was that the charges against us may have stemmed from rescuing the conversos. If so, Orlando Franco, his ship captains, and everyone who signed the limpiezas for Andres would be implicated. We decided, come what may, we would not betray them. We did not understand how the Inquisition could have uncovered our tracks unless someone with whom we dealt was an informant. As we were trying to figure out who that person was, the cell door opened and we were immediately taken to our trial.

The secret hearings were held in a small courtroom where Father Pedro, my instructor at the Instruction of Faith sessions, presided. He announced that this court would determine if there was sufficient evidence to pass sentence on us thereby avoiding a lengthy trial at the Holy Tribunal. He energetically took charge of the proceedings ordering us and the other two judges about with a firm hand. He was more animated on the judicial bench than in the pulpit.

Father Pedro opened the hearings by calling out, "Andres Alvarez, adopted son of Gutierrez Delgado, residing in and caretaker of the Casa Lombardia: You are accused of encouraging conversos in their practice of heresy. In the home of Alfredo the tanner you participated in a religious ceremony. You have been observed going into the home of several conversos where heretical rites were performed which you have not reported to the Inquisition."

Andres and I breathed a sigh of relief when the accusations mentioned nothing about helping conversos escape.

"How do you plead to these charges", Father Pedro asked.

Andres denied the charges, adding, "I visited the home of Alfredo and even befriended him only on the advice of Diaz, an agent of the Inquisition."

The officials with Father Pedro whispered amongst themselves then reprimanded Andres on his attempts to implicate Diaz in these accusations. In reply, Andres recalled the exact date he visited Diaz even quoting Diaz's exact words. Father Pedro silenced him ignoring his protests.

"Alberto de Cadiz, son of Isaac Abrabanel," Father Pedro intoned: "You are accused of guiding the accused Andres leading him to commit acts of heresy. You are charged with backsliding, observing Jewish rituals. You are further accused of tutoring the daughter of the count of Trastamara in the faith of Judaism. How do you plead?"

I had difficulty suppressing my sense of relief because, again, the charges mentioned nothing about the false limpiezas or about the circumcision of the Morales infant.

I called out, "Not guilty," taunting the judges that none of the accusations could be proved at a full trial of the Holy Tribunal.

Father Pedro cut me short stating, "Here we are not concerned with your arguments, only with confessions."

"How can I confess?" I said, "Andres and I are innocent. I'm sure that count's daughter would testify before the Holy Tribunal that I never even spoke to her about Judaism. The Count of Trastamara would also testify to my innocence."

At the mention of the count's name, Father Pedro again conferred with his colleagues and then he called out, "I remind you that you are here as an accused heretic not as a witness. Alberto de Cadiz, do you still refuse to confess?"

"I confess to no heresy," I replied, "because I committed none."

"Andres Alvarez, do you still refuse to confess?" Father Pedro asked.

"If it'll make you happy, Father, I would confess," Andres replied, "But I got nothing to confess to."

Father Pedro stood up, his face reddened with anger as he banged his hand on the table to quiet Andres.

"Guilty! Guilty! Guilty! You will be held at the Betazar Compound until your trial," he shouted.

I asked that the count be informed about my trial but no one paid any attention. We were led out of the chapel and taken to the dreaded Betazar Compound at the far end of the city. Two burly guards ordered us to walk through one of the gates and when Andres halted a moment to look around the compound, the guard heaved himself at Andres sending him sprawling to the ground.

"You pig! You're not here on a tour," the guard growled. "When I say move, I mean move!"

I sensed Andres' pain and clenched my fist in anger. From behind, I felt a powerful smash on my head which knocked me out. When I got up, I heard a maniacal shout, "Don't ever make a fist at me."

We were led through an arched stairway opening into a small foyer where the guard left us in the charge of our jailer, Mango. He was a brute whose grotesque bald head seemed attached to his shoulders with no neck at all. He had two holes beneath his eyes for a nose and his high pitched voice sounded like the snorting of an animal.

He led us through a maze of corridors passing several locked doors with narrow window slits. He stopped in front of one door, unlocked it, and shoved us inside the cell. The windowless cell stunk of putrid odors. I heard the voices of other prisoners but I could not see them. It was pitch black. When my eyes grew accustomed to the dark surroundings, I noticed two narrow slits near the ceiling, the only source of light. With increasing horror, I counted forty six human forms lying about or leaning against the wall.

Soon, someone called out, "feeding time," and most of them rushed to the door where guards deposited two pots, one containing thin stew and one coarse bread. The inmates fought over the food like starving animals. Those fortunate to get at the pots stalked off with their bit of stew in their cups and a slice of bread clenched in their hands. Others retreated empty-handed wandering about the cell begging for food.

"When is the next feeding time?" Andres whispered to a skeletal man who was gasping for breath.

"Next food?" he wheezed. "Next day."

Andres and I walked around the room, careful not to step on anyone, discussing ways of improving conditions in the cell. I pried loose a floor tile saying that a toilet facility could be provided by digging into the dirt under it and instructing the inmates to use only that area. I also began to suggest a plan for distributing food to avoid fighting and starvation.

"Look at these wretched souls," Andres interrupted me, saying, "How long will it be before we become just like them?"

That was the first time I had ever heard a note of pessimism from Andres and I told him so. "It's neither pessimism nor optimism," Andres replied. "It's being a realist. When the Inquisition sets out to get someone, no one can stop them."

"The charges against us are false. Who can possibly testify to them?" I said trying to buoy up Andres' spirit. "Anyway, when the count gets word of our arrest, we'll be out of here right away."

We looked about the room trying to recognize any of the inmates. I saw only one who looked familiar. I asked him where we met. He reminded me that we were introduced in Franco's Inn in Seville and said that he was charged with taking a passenger without a limpieza on his ship. The captain had been in the cell for more than a month and was not called for his trial. But, his property was already confiscated and his family had to pay for his food during his imprisonment. He was allowed no visitors nor did his family know of his whereabouts. He pointed to several inmates who were in the prison more than a year still awaiting trial.

Towards evening, I noticed one prisoner, lying next to the wall, had not stirred since we were brought into the cell. Even when the food was brought in, he did not scurry about for his share. I touched the motionless figure and called out to Andres that the man was dead. From all around the cell, I heard hissing and grumbling:

"Mind your own business," one shouted.

"Leave it be," another voice pleaded.

Andres asked the skeletal creature next to him for the meaning of this.

"This way, they don't reduce the rations," the man replied.

"The body count remains the same."

I then looked around the cell and realized with horror that there were other dead bodies lying around us with a few who would be dead by morning.

Neither Andres nor I slept at all that night. It was not the hunger nor the putrid odor that kept us awake but the fact that we might be here, waiting for our trial, without anyone knowing of our presence. We canvassed our cell mates to learn if anyone would be leaving, having served his term, in hopes of getting word to the count. We found no one.

But, we were fortunate. In the morning, our names were called to appear for trial.

We were led to a court room dominated by the green-embroidered banner of the Inquisition draped across the judges' table. It bore the image of a monk holding a sword in one hand and an olive branch in the other. In the foreground, a reclining dog chewed on the handle of a whip whose lash formed the banner's border. The Latin words: "Misercordia et Justitia", Mercy and Justice, were emblazoned in gold letters around a cross of Jesus.

While waiting for the judges, I tried to encourage Andres, assuring him, since there would be no witnesses to the charges of heresy, no sentence could be passed on us. The judges walked in.

Our trial began with a stern announcement by the presiding judge, "The accused are herewith warned that the charges against them are grievous; that they carry the penalty of death by fire; that the evidence is conclusive; and that by confessing their guilt their souls will be restored to grace of God."

The judge first read the charges against me. I was stricken with fear because they now included many items not mentioned at the preliminary hearing. They listed circumcising the Morales son; defaming the Inquisition in the Music Room of the Trastamara Castle; helping conversos to escape; and, again, "judaizing" the daughter of the count of Trastamara.

The judge did not bother to ask me how I pleaded to the

charges. He put down the document from which he was reading and solemnly stated that each charge was substantiated by reputable witnesses before duly constituted authorities. I thought of Morales, wondering what happened to his family.

When the same charges were read to Andres, he explained his help to the conversos as a "good deed that one human being can do for another."

"To the list of charges, we should add that of being an arrogant heretic, an impenitent sinner," the judge said. "You show no contrition, you seek no forgiveness. To the contrary, you seem to take pride in your sinfulness."

The judge then turned to me asking if I had anything to say before the court handed down its sentence. I said nothing.

"I consider your silence not an admission of guilt but the scorning of our authority," the judge said. "The church took you into her bosom to offer her love and protection and you have betrayed that love, spurned her protection."

After a brief conference with his colleagues, he passed sentence on us: death by fire: auto-da-fe.

We were brought back to the cell where Mango greeted us with a powerful blow.

"You're now mine, all mine now," Mango bellowed gleefully.

I could not accept that this was to be our end. I kept assuring Andres that the count would learn of our condition and we would be released from these dungeons.

"What was the last thing you told the count?" Andres asked.

"That I was leaving for Toledo for my medical certification," I replied.

"So, as far as the count is concerned, you're now enroute to Toledo," Andres replied.

Our fate was sealed.

Very soon we learned that one of the main functions of terror and torture in the dungeon was to make the prisoner confess. This accomplished two things. First, theologically — the heretic's soul would be saved from eternal damnation. Second, practically — the dossiers of the Inquisition increased tenfold with names of those incriminated by the confessions.

Mango was the master of terror. For us, he decreed the 'witness treatment', which provided for one victim to be present while the other was being tortured. Generally, it was used for close relatives, a husband and wife, a child and parent, or a grandparent and a grandchild. Mango guessed right. Andres and I did have a special relationship.

We were brought into a room with an arched ceiling curving down on stuccoed pillars. Like our cell, the room was windowless. Black smudges of soot from its two torches blackened the walls leading to the roof where a small opening allowed the smoke to escape. At doleful-looking monk sat at the entrance to the torture chamber holding a missal in one hand and a crucifix in the other.

"Confess, my beloved children," he said to us. "Confess and you will be spared the torture."

Andres patted the monk's bald pate saying, "Would you have me confess to committing a righteous deed?"

Mango shoved us into the chamber selecting me as the first victim. Announcing that it was called the hanging treatment, he tied my hands behind my back with a long rope the end of which was looped through a hook in the ceiling. Without warning, two guards who were standing behind me hoisted me up higher and higher until I reached the ceiling. I cried out as the rope cut deeply into my flesh. My hands were about to break and I felt as though my arms were being torn out of their sockets. I let out a piercing cry begging them to let me down.

Just then, I heard two voices; the monk asking me to confess and Andres shouting a comforting word. For that, Mango clouted him a crushing blow. While Andres reeled from the blow, they tied his hands at his back, ready to hoist him up. I shouted, "Brace yourself to counter the pressure on your arms."

But the damage I most dreaded was done. At the sudden upward pull of the rope, I heard the crack. The bone in his forearm broke in two. He let out a chilling cry but they continued hoisting him to the ceiling. I saw blood dripping from the fractured bone which pierced his flesh. I tried to scream to the jailers that his arm was broken but I could utter no sound. I felt as though life was being drained from me. We dangled there, alternately crying and fainting.

I do not know how long we were hanging, probably the entire day because it was almost dark when they lowered us. We both fell with a thud to the floor only to be jarred by a sharp kick from the jailers who ordered us to stand and march.

Mango returned us to a cell where the stench and putrid conditions were bearable because we savored our reprieve from the torture. Although in pain, I examined Andres' broken arm. The rope had torn deeply into his flesh. In the semi-darkness, I could feel the jagged edges of the bone protruding from the skin. I wanted to reset it but the pain would have been unbearable.

I felt more anguish than pain.

If only I had continued with my self-imposed isolation. If only I had not told Andres about Abram Senor. If only I had not involved him in the inquiry of Father Hernandez. If only I had not sought his help in getting the limpiezas.

"Even at death, life is worthless," I thought, "when it is reduced to brooding over 'if only'."

I blamed myself for everything that was happening to him. I could tolerate my pain. I could even live with the expectation of my own gruesome end. But I could not live with my feelings of guilt. I, and I alone, had inflicted this suffering on innocent Andres. I stayed up most of the night, soothing him, fanning his wound and trying to ease his suffering.

In the morning, the distribution of food was announced by the guard but this time, it was different than in the first cell. The two pots were brought in but no one struggled over them. The inmates were in tortured pain and could not even move to get to the pots. The guards walked around, distributing portions of food to wobbly feet and shaky hands. When they reached Andres, he could not extend his hand, so I took two slices of bread from the first pot. The guard hit me with a ferocious blow on my arm.

"Only one slice for each prisoner," he shouted. "If he's too lazy to get it himself, let him starve."

"But his hand is broken," I said. "I beg you, give him a piece of bread."

"No talking in this cell," the guard again shouted and again hit me, almost cracking my cheek.

I took only one bite from the bread and barely wetted my lips with the water. I slithered over to Andres who apologized that I got hurt on his account. He mistakenly reached for the water with his broken arm and spilled half on the floor. Again he apologized and refused to drink the remaining water.

"What do you think?" Andres asked cradling his hand.

"I think your arm is broken. Hold it still. It will heal by itself," I replied.

"Nature heals, but the doctor takes the fee," Andres quipped and even managed to smile.

Lying in any position caused even more pain. I helped Andres move about trying to alleviate the ache in his broken arm. We finally fell asleep and were abruptly awakened by Mango standing over us. He bellowed, "Follow me!"

When I helped Andres to his feet, Mango dealt me a blow and shouted, "Each prisoner must obey orders without assistance from the other."

I began to explain that his arm was broken and, for that, got another jabbing fist into my stomach.

"So, the Holy Tribunal has abandoned you to everlasting hell," Mango snorted. "Come! I'll give you a taste of it."

He led us to the torture chamber where, again, we were greeted by the same monk who pleaded with us to confess. This time, however, Andres paused to listen to him and even asked, quite seriously, which heresy would interest him.

Thinking that Andres was ridiculing him, the Monk replied, "Confession is not only good for the soul. It's also good for the body."

Mango ordered us to strip and to lie down on our backs on narrow tables, set in front of an oven. A kettle of boiling water hung over it. The guards first tied my hands and my legs so that I was unable to move. They then did the same to Andres who let out a blood curdling cry because his fractured hand was being crushed by the straps.

"Wait," the guard mocked him. "We haven't even begun."

I saw them pour the hot water in a pot with a long, narrow snout.

"From the tip of your toes to the top of your head you will feel the burning arrows of hell," Mango trumpeted ordering the men to pour the boiling water over me slowly.

They started pouring the water in a small but steady stream. They began with my toes, slowly and mercilessly continuing up my legs. I screamed in agony. When they reached my genitals, my whole body convulsed.

"You circumcised Jew bastard," Mango shouted with glee emptying a bucket of steaming water on them.

I fainted.

They revived me with cold water and in my agony I heard Andres' shriek. For a moment, I forgot my own pain. I felt as though it was I who was pouring the boiling water over him. I was tormented inside as well as outside.

My entire body was inflamed as scalding water burned my stomach and chest. I screamed, begging for mercy, when they emptied another whole bucket of boiling water on me. I was delirious when I saw a guard hold a funnel over my head. He forced its short end into my mouth. Suddenly the monk appeared, pleading with me to confess and promising that if I would, the torture would immediately stop. I tried to turn my head away from him but a vise-like instrument held me tight with the snout of the funnel pressing my tongue.

With the first spurt of boiling water flushed my throat, I tried to scream but only a hissing, gurgling roar came out. I begged God for death; for the water to go down my wind pipe.

Finally, they untied my hands and threw me back in the cell. I did not see Andres when they carried me out of the torture chamber, nor was he in the cell. I sprawled out on the cold wet floor, feeling a momentary relief. I lay motionless, crazed by the intense pain wracking my body. I remembered Alfonso's words: "It is amazing how much pain the body can tolerate; the body not the brain."

When my mind cleared, I groped along the floor, searching for Andres. He was nowhere. A feeling of relief swept over me when I thought that Andres must have confessed to the monk, and was now out of pain.

Suddenly I felt Andres' body flung on top of me. Carefully, I slid away from under him, trying to avoid any jarring movement which would increase his pain. Neither of us could talk. The torture we felt at the slightest touch of our blistered skin had drained us of our energy. We could neither move nor speak. We just lay for the rest of the day.

When I heard Andres' heavy, rhythmic breathing, I was thankful that, at least, he was sleeping peacefully. Then, I too fell asleep. I suddenly awoke feeling Andres' head on my arm. He whispered that he went through the same burning torture I did but, when he fainted and could not be revived, Mango thought he was dead. He ordered his men to cast Andres into a chamber with dead bodies. Later, when a monk heard Andres moaning, he called the guard who dumped Andres' body over me.

"It won't be long," I comforted him.

When the guards came around with the water and bread, we took our rations and I bathed his bruised body with our allotted water. We ate our bread in silence, surprised that we could still chew and swallow the hard bread despite our burned mouths.

"I'm sorry, Andres," I said watching him stroke his limp hand.

"Sorry for what?" he asked.

"For causing you so much pain," I said. "It's because I got you involved with the conversos."

Andres smiled, "Don't be silly. You didn't get me involved. It was me. I first got you involved. With the Morales baby."

He recalled how he, as a boy, decided to oppose the Inquisition and grabbed at the opportunity when he discovered the Morales case.

"Doesn't matter anymore," he said haltingly. "I made peace with death. Only, I have lots of questions."

I did not encourage him to talk, knowing how painful it was, especially since I had no answers for him.

"How should I die?" Andres asked pulling at my arm to get my attention. "That's my first question. Dying will end it. But, Berto, how? How should I die?"

"Go with the monk," I replied. "Confess to whatever he wants. And, no further torture."

"And you?" he asked.

"I don't know, Andres, I don't know," I said. "I became a converso and the only decent thing I did was help conversos. It doesn't seem right to confess, to agree with these evil men that helping my brothers was heresy. It would make a greater mockery of my meaningless martyrdom."

"Martyrdom! You're crazy!" Andres said. "I think the hot water burned your brains."

"You're right," I said, "I'm confused."

"What's there to be confused about?" Andres said again groping for my hand, "It's not a matter of right or wrong. It's not martyrdom."

"You're not a martyr?" I asked.

"Of course not," Andres replied. "A martyr is given a choice:

'do this and live; do that and die'. When he chooses death he becomes a martyr. You and me will die without being given a choice."

"And you weren't given a choice," I whispered.

"No, I wasn't," he stated emphatically.

"You had a choice, Andres," I said, "You had a choice."

Andres tried to change his position and in so doing, scraped his fractured arm against the floor. A pain shot through his body and he let out a scream that rang through the cell. I did my best to relieve his pain. When it subsided, I urged him to try and sleep before Mango came for us again. He refused.

"No. Tell me what choice did I have?" he asked.

"You could have joined with the howling mob. You could have turned your back on Morales. You could have turned me in a dozen times," I said.

"You call that a choice?" Andres replied. "Those just came natural..."

"And what's more important," I said not letting him continue, "You were chosen by them. That makes you a martyr."

For a while we were silent. His wound began to bleed again. I tried to bandage his arm with bits of my clothing. Although in pain, Andres seemed unconcerned with my treatment or with his bleeding wound.

"Tell me why," Andres asked edging closer. "Why is God so unrighteous. So uncaring."

"A long time ago, I asked my father the same question," I said, "and he then replied that this protest against God is justified. It's even in the Bible, 'O God my God, why has thou forsaken me!'"

"That's it, Berto," Andres said sitting up, "'O God my God why has thou forsaken me!' That's exactly how I feel. He has forsaken me. I want to know why."

"There is no answer." I replied almost apologetically.

"No answer!" Andres protested. "There's got to be an answer."

"My father only said that asking the question doesn't make

it a fact," I replied. "I didn't understand him then and I don't understand him now."

After a lengthy silence, when I thought he had fallen asleep, Andres said in a hushed tone, "Berto, your father was right."

I said nothing. I did not want to debate theological dogma with him. But, Andres nudged closer to me.

"We were forsaken by men, not by God," Andres said excitedly, "Don't you see? Blaming God removes the guilt from man. Just asking the question, 'why has God forsaken us, makes the killers God's messengers."

He was so caught up in his own discovery that, for a moment, he forgot his broken arm and, trying to lift it, he once again fell on it. He shuddered as the sharp pain streaked through his body. He grasped my thigh with his other hand, digging his nails into my flesh. His contorted face turned white. Cold sweat covered his body. I helplessly held him, feeling his tears streaming down his cheeks. When the pain finally subsided, he stated that if we were to go to another torture routine he would see the monk first.

His color returned; his face no longer contorted. He repeated, "O God, my God why has thou forsaken" and then grew silent. He would welcome death as a reprieve from pain, he said.

"But, when I go to my death, I will not blame God," he said with almost unbridled enthusiasm. "I will blame everyone else, the people, the church, the monarchs, even the count, but not God."

When I did not share his enthusiasm, he repeated his belief that God wants us to point the finger at the guilty rather than ask Him why they flourish.

"Don't ask 'where was God?' Instead ask 'Where were you?'" Andres stated with an air of finality.

"You've discovered something brilliant," I said.

"Not so brilliant," he replied smiling, "You can learn more about God in Torquemada's torture chambers than in all the seminaries in the world."

Andres said that he could now sleep, so I helped him lie

down, making certain he would not chafe his wounded arm. I assured him I would watch over his arm as he slept. But, despite my good intentions, I, too, fell asleep.

Andres soon awakened me, saying "Berto, this is the last night of our lives. We ought to treasure every moment, not sleep it away."

He told me how much he admired his step father, proud that he was an officer in the militia, describing all he had done for him. He spoke lovingly of his mother. We reminisced about our past experiences, our first days in Cordoba, the boat trip, his meeting with Alfredo. He asked me about Maria, about the count, even about Enrique, the count's son. He asked me to tell him again how I fought Don Luis up on the mountain. He recalled the accusations at our trial asking me if I judaized Maria. When I said I did not, he replied that may signify Maria was in real danger.

Andres was so decent that on this, his last day of life, suffering in that dungeon, he tried to think of ways to send a message to Maria to warn her of the danger facing her. I teasingly dubbed him a saint and he ridiculed me for calling him that. But, getting serious, he did agree that he could be a martyr.

"You know, Berto," he quipped, "I never was a martyr before. What am I supposed to do when I go to my death?"

"Well," I said, "you pray that your soul goes to heaven."

"What's the soul?" Andres asked.

"It's what makes you good, moral, kind," I replied. "The soul tells you what's right and what's wrong."

"Pray for me, Berto. I did so little praying in my life, God wouldn't recognize my voice."

"Try it yourself, Andres. Make believe that heaven is the Casa Lombardia and you're in charge."

"Dear God," Andres said softly, "there's nothing much left to this body of mine. It'll soon be destroyed. But my soul is in pretty good shape. So, after I'm gone, let my soul live on. I want to welcome my friend Berto when he comes up."

Tears welled in my eyes as I whispered "amen" to his prayer.

Neither he nor I spoke again. I bent over to look at Andres and saw him sleeping, his face serene, his body relaxed. I wept silently, then moved closer and kissed his forehead. I knew this was my farewell to my beloved Andres.

In the morning, Mango awakened us with his usual kick in the ribs. We dutifully staggered behind him to the torture chamber, greeted by the solemn monk. With a nod of our heads, Andres and I said good bye to each other. He followed the monk.

I cannot understand now, why I refused to do the same. Perhaps I could not make peace with the thought of confessing, for then I would die as a redeemed heretic. I did not want their redemption. I guess that by suffering I was atoning my own heresy: separating from my father.

I was contemplating these thoughts when Mango strapped me into an especially-constructed chair. His henchman tied my arms to the arm rests and my feet — still blistered from the boiling water — to a bench-like extension protruding from the chair. Mango produced a small knife, much like my surgical knife except narrower and longer. He poked its sharp end under my toenail. The moment the blade pierced below my nail, I let out a scream that resounded through the outer courtyard. He pushed the knife deeper and deeper and with every twisting motion, I convulsed in agonizing torment. Every thrust of the blade was ever so slow, only to cause greater pain. My nails were ripped off; my feet were covered with the blood that spurted from every toe. I cried, shouted, pleaded, but the more I cried, the more I shouted, the more I pleaded, the more did my executioners howl with glee, pushing the blade further into my bleeding toes. At one time, as a result of my twisting and writhing, I freed my hand and inadvertently slapped Mango's head. He reacted with unbridled rage pounding me so hard, stabbing me so much, piercing me with his blade all over my body, I was certain I would die from the multiple wounds. I fainted several times, but was revived.

Sacred Sword

When I looked at the empty chair next to mine, I whispered a silent prayer, thanking God that Andres had escaped this hideous torture. The brutality lasted most of the morning, ending abruptly when church bells began to ring through the compound.

I was taken past the almost empty cell, when Mango shouted, "It's time for the auto-da-fe. Get out there and join the marchers."

I then realized that the church bells were summoning the populace to the supreme spectacle, the burning of heretics at the stake. The bells were clanging, tinkling as they would normally during a church festival. The monk who had stood watch at the door of the torture chamber now helped me dress in a *sanbenito*, a sleeveless tunic identifying me in public as a condemned sinner. I could not join in with the other marchers, my swollen feet were bleeding. When the monk released me, I fell helpless on the road.

The procession of heretics was already a good distance away when a donkey cart was brought out from the compound. I was lifted into it and lashed to the side of the cart so that I could be displayed to the jeering crowd. I did not know any of the marchers who were to die with me. I did, however, recognize many of the spectators. I was astounded by the vast number of former patients who, at one time, had blessed me, thanked me, even kissed me for healing them. Now they were cursing and vilifying me as my cart slowly passed, each jolt sending spurts of pain through my wounds.

We were marched into the Plaza de la Corredera, which had been converted to the *quemaban*. I was amazed at the sight of thousands of spectators crowded into the huge quadrangle. A thundering roar rumbled through the square when we were brought in the south entrance.

The plaza was an enormous rectangle where porticoed galleries supported the upper balconies. Every available space was filled to capacity. I counted twenty-eight stakes in the center, each with a pile of firewood at its base. A carnival-like spirit pervaded the plaza: vendors selling sweets; banners, representing the church and the nobility strung along the galleries; church bells ringing; children romping. Many parents carried children on their shoulders to afford them a better view of the mass auto-de-fe.

Sporadic hooting and jeering rang out as each heretic's name of us was called out and dragged to a stake atop a pile of fire logs. But, when one man struggled while being bound, the crowd roared and cheered as though watching a bull putting up a good fight in the ring.

Few of us put up any resistance. We were all in tortured agony. The fortunate ones fainted before they were even tied. Some cried, others weakly protested their innocence. Most of the condemned were totally passive, submitting silently. When my turn came to be tied to the stake, I put up no resistance. I was too weak to struggle and too pained to shout.

On a given signal, the spectators grew silent. The Bishop of Cordoba, probably the one who presided over the Board of Inquiry that Nicholas had described, began his long harangue. He scorned us for our heresy, condemning our souls to everlasting hell. He then ordered the bodies of the "reconciled" heretics, those who had confessed their heresies, to be brought in. He called out their names and recited a special prayer granting them the full pardon of the church.

I strained to see the bodies piled in a wagon, hoping to catch sight of Andres. Their pyre was quite far from me but I got a glimpse of a mop of blonde hair, which I knew to be his. For a moment I felt no pain, recalling only his smiling face and his gentle soul.

The Bishop of Cordoba exhorted the spectators: "Let the death of these heretics serve as a warning to each of you. Heresy will not be tolerated. Let the death of these heretics serve as a reminder to each of you that the Holy Inquisition, which is entrusted to preserve the faith, will not tolerate the faithless. Never forget: Redemption in Christ means the destruction of the heretic."

Then, on a signal from the Bishop, the torch was applied to

the first stake. As the fire leaped up from the oil-soaked logs, a deafening cheer burst forth from the approving spectators.

I was still sufficiently alert to wonder about this display of hate. I could understand Mango and his henchmen, insensitive, inhuman, trained to hate. But ordinary people, the mothers, the shopkeepers, the farmers and, above all, the little children, who were decent human beings. Why were they so full of hate?

I tried not to look at the victims who were being burned, one at a time, probably to prolong the entertainment for the spectators, but I could not drown out their screams as the fire began to singe their bodies. I tried to shout words of comfort to them but my voice was drowned out by the mob's cheering. Before long, I was sickened beyond terror by the stench of burning human flesh. The smoke around me became dense. I felt I would not be able to hold out much longer, so I decided to recite my final prayer. The only words that came to my mind were: "O God, my God why hast thou forsaken me!"

More than twenty were already burned. The fire was beginning to close in on me. The smoke grew thick and I began gasping for air. The heat was intense. The scorching flames blistered my body and I struggled like a trapped animal, trying to free my bound hands. My stomach retched and I began to vomit over my chest. Then I fainted.

At the same moment that I was being carted from the dungeons to the auto-da-fe, the Count of Trastamara summoned Manuel to the mansion in Cordoba to transmit the Council of Nobles' rejection of any negotiation with Torquemada. Father Lopez came to the mansion to explain that Manuel could not travel because of his leg injury.

The count stated that the House of Trastamara would conduct no business with the Inquisition until the matter of Don Luis was thoroughly investigated. He notified Father Lopez of the

Sacred Sword

formal rejection, stating that a meeting with Manuel was no longer required. But, when Father Lopez described Manuel's condition, saying it was progressively worsening, the count volunteered to visit the ailing man immediately.

Manuel struggled to get up to properly greet the count but could not even to sit up in his bed.

"I had not realized how sick you were," the count said. "I will not stay long so you can rest."

Manuel pleaded with the count to remain, saying that talking to him would take his mind off his injured leg. Manuel began to read a lengthy explanation of the Don Luis' episode but when he could no longer stand the pain, he asked Father Lopez to read the rest of the document.

The count interrupted Father Lopez's reading by getting up and saying, "We can discuss this when your health improves."

Manuel implored the count to stay and, to prove that he was well, he sprang out of bed exposing his injured leg.

"It's only a minor injury," Manuel said. "The matter of placing the Inquisition agents in the army is vital."

The count was appalled.

"You have the blackening disease," the count said. "That's not a minor injury. Forget the Inquisition. Forget the Don Luis document. You will lose your life. Get Alberto to do something about your leg."

"You mean, cut it off?"

"I've seen people die from the blackening disease and I've seen many live after a good amputation," the count said. "It seems to me you have little choice and little time."

"Jimenez assures me, it will heal by itself," Manuel said.

"Jimenez!" the count stated, "He's of no use to you, now. You have Alberto, the best surgeon in all of Spain. That is, if he has not yet left Cordoba to get his certification in Toledo."

Manuel trembled, actually quaked in his bed.

Looking at Father Lopez, he asked, "How far have we gone with him? "

"He's part of the twenty-eight," Lopez replied, "The auto-da-fe is in progress right now."

"Get Alberto!" Manuel barked slumping back in his bed turning his head away from the count.

Father Lopez left immediately.

The count was stunned. He stared at Manuel with disbelief, and, without saying a word, stormed out of the room.

Father Lopez galloped into the Plaza de la Corredera plowing his horse through the crowd. He ordered the official in charge to free me, but the Bishop intervened, questioning Lopez's authority to rescind a sentence of the Holy Tribunal. Lopez was tough, unrelenting. He shouted that he had no use for delicate negotiations or tactful debate. He threatened the Bishop with severe reprisals if he continued to question Manuel's orders. The Bishop backed off. However, his underlings claimed the smoke was too thick to attempt to save me. Father Lopez shrieked at two of his agents, ordering them to plunge into the smoke and take me out. They looped a rope around my stake, dragging it out, and pulling me through the burning logs.

At that moment, the huge crowd was awed into silence when the count's ornate carriage rattled into the plaza. Father Lopez approached the carriage and, after a brief discussion, I was placed, more dead than alive, in the count's carriage and taken to the River House.

I lay in agonizing pain. Jimenez proved his worth, tending to my wounds. Had it not been for his care I doubt if I would have survived the first day. He cleared the ash from my nostrils and wrapped me in cold compresses to heal my seared body. He bathed my toes, cleaned my stab wounds, and swathed my entire body with his *hierba* ointment.

From the moment I was brought to the River House, Maria

did not leave my bedside. Even in my delirium, the mere sight of her soothed me. Jimenez taught Maria how to care for the wounds, how to apply the compresses, even how to feed me without causing pain to my inflamed throat. I often begged her to leave, to get outdoors and not to be chained to my room. She refused, always smiling, always pleasant.

I spoke very little either to Maria or to the count. I was in deep mourning for Andres. When the count asked me to describe my experience at the Holy Tribunal so he could investigate the Inquisition, I burst into tears at the very mention of Andres' name. Maria was deeply affected by my wounds and by the tragedy of Andres' death. She recalled how she met him at the port and both times he was so full of life, so caring, so concerned. Often her eyes would well up with tears and, without mentioning his name, we would both be united in mourning.

One day, while Jimenez was attending me, I told him how grateful I was for his care. He replied that he was ordered by Manuel to forego all other duties at the clinic and to stay at my side until I recovered. Several days later, Jimenez told me he informed Manuel that I would be ready to see him the following day. I was not ready. I could not step on my feet, nor could I move my body.

But, when Jimenez described the condition of Manuel's foot, admitting that the disease had entered the dangerous stage, I decided to go immediately to Manuel. I asked to be lifted onto a cart, not much different than the one used to transport me to the *quemaban*, and be driven to Manuel's home to examine the leg. As I lay in the cart, the count arrived highly agitated and angry. He told me that his investigation proved Manuel had ordered my arrest and directed my torture so that I would confess and incriminate Maria. I suspected it all along. He questioned whether I should bother saving Manuel's life. I replied that my sole concern was the diseased leg, not the man.

When his servants carried Manuel out for me to examine the leg, I was not surprised how badly it deteriorated for I had anticipated this condition the first time I saw the injury at San Sebastian. The toes were jet black and red streaks extended above the ankle. He was writhing in pain. I decided immediate amputation was necessary. I would have preferred to postpone the surgery for a week to regain my strength, but I could not. Any further delay would cause death. I instructed Father Lopez to bring Cordoba's best sword maker to the count's mansion.

"As soon as I can manipulate my hands," I told Lopez, "I will return for the surgery."

"Remember," Manuel shouted, "if you fail, you will forfeit your life."

"Tell the executioner," I said to Father Lopez, refusing to talk to or even to look at the ogre, "my life has already been forfeited. I hope I can save his."

At the count's mansion, I described to the craftsman the type of blade I needed. While the blade was being manufactured, I prepared myself for the amputation by sawing pieces of wood while sitting in a specially built chair. Gradually, I felt strength returning to my hand.

Two days later, the craftsman came by to show me an unfinished blade on which I made several corrections. The following day, when he delivered the saw, I still could not stand on my blistered feet. I ordered the servants to attach poles to a chair with which they carried me to Manuel's house.

Jimenez came with me to do the amputation. I asked Father Lopez to summon someone strong enough to hold the patient. He called his servant, Reinaldo, a towering muscular figure. I whispered my instructions to him and then explained the surgery to Lopez and Jimenez.

On my signal, Reinaldo administered a sharp blow to the base of the patients's head, rendering him unconscious. He then pinned him down while Father Lopez and Jimenez held the leg in place.

I swiftly sawed through the bone in precision-like motion.

Jimenez cauterized the wound with boiling oil, stopping the bleeding.

Reinaldo picked up the severed leg from the floor and asked, "What do I do with this?"

"Take it to the Plaza de la Corredera, the *quemaban* is probably still hot," I replied.

During the next two months, I checked the leg regularly without saying a word to Manuel. In time, the wound completely healed. When he tried to engage me in conversation, I refused to reply and when he offered to pay for my services, I refused to accept. The more I refused, the more money he offered. He did not give up trying to befriend me or pay me, sending money through various messengers. I finally sent him a message: "If I would save a dog's leg, I could not take a fee from the beast."

News of my successful operation on Manuel's leg travelled fast throughout the Andalusia. But, for me, although the pain gradually diminished, those days were a period of aimless drifting and constant torment from bitter memories of Andres' death. I was incapable of resuming normal life. With the exception of my regular follow up on the amputation, I remained secluded in my room at the Lombardia unable to undertake any medical assignments in the dispensary.

I was drawn to anything that reminded me of Andres: his clothing, his family, even his boat. I rummaged through our room fondling anything that was his. I put all his belongings in a wooden crate and placed it in one corner which became his memorial niche. I would sit there and brood all day long, day after day.

My first venture out of the Casa Lombardia was to the home of Andres' parents in an alley not far from the Plaza de la Corredera. I hesitated outside and, timidly, knocked on the door. When his mother opened it, she embraced me, crying bitterly while holding on to me. I followed her and Don Gutierrez into the house, mumbling through tears how close Andres was to me. They responded that Andres spoke of me constantly. She sat down weeping softly asking why God allowed this to happen. I repeated Andres' reply to this, but I shall never forget Don Gutierrez' response. He dried his reddened eyes saying, "When anyone claims he's representing God, he usually becomes God to himself."

He told me that until they were summoned to the auto-da-fe of the twenty-eight persons, they knew nothing about Andres' sentencing or even that he had been brought to trial by the Holy Tribunal.

They described their shock when they heard Andres' name called out as the bodies of the six reconciled heretics were carted into the *quemaban*.

Don Gutierrez asked me to tell them everything that happened to Andres, especially during his last days. I told them everything, his suffering, his profound insights, and his heroism. Throughout my telling, we wept together. I spoke especially, about Andres' abiding love for them. For the rest of the afternoon, I reminisced about Andres and the work we had done together at the Lombardia, mentioning nothing about the limpiezas or the conversos.

To my utter surprise, Don Gutierrez asked, "Was he accused of helping conversos to escape?"

I was stunned by his question and asked him how he knew about it.

"Andres came to me once and asked for names of ship captains in Seville," his step-father said.

"When he said he wanted someone who knew about the colonies, I surmised Andres was involved with the conversos and recommended Orlando Franco."

He said no more and I thought it best not to ask him about Franco. After I shared their evening meal, Don Gutierrez walked me back to the Casa Lombardia. We wandered through the grove sitting at the edge of the stream. Then I asked about Orlando Franco.

"When we were young, Franco and I served in the army together," he said. "He was a tough, uncompromising, hard-headed soldier who won many battles and received many decorations for bravery. He was known for barbaric treatment of the Moors and for harsh punishment of the troops he commanded. Because of this, Orlando Franco rose in the ranks, assuming command of the militia's toughest unit which scored phenomenal successes on the battlefield. Throughout that time, we were very close. Then, at the height of his military career, I heard he suddenly resigned his commission. For many years I lost contact with him."

Before continuing his story, Andres' father made me swear that I would never reveal what he was about to tell me.

"About six years ago," he continued, "I met Orlando Franco again, quite by accident, in the San Sebastian Monastery and I noticed that he tried to avoid me. I was hurt and offended by his abrupt behavior. I confronted him and told him of my hurt feelings. He apologized. Then, in confidence, he related that he had resigned from the army at the request of the Inquisition which placed him in charge of the Betazar prison compound. He was told that the Inquisition recognized his ruthlessness. After two years, he asked to be relieved from his duties. He entered the monastery, ostensibly to work as an assistant to Father Hernandez, but he admitted to me, he actually came there to pray for his sins.

"One time, he confessed to Father Hernandez the dreadful work he had done in the Betazar Compound. The aged priest replied that penance by prayer alone was not enough. He had to do something undo the hurt he had done to others. At the time, he was pondering Hernandez's advice wondering what he could do. I later learned that Franco asked to leave San Sebastian and became a ship captain in Seville, apparently helping people in trouble to get to the colonies."

I asked Don Gutierrez why he had made me take an oath not to reveal any of this to anyone.

"Because Orlando Franco warned me that no one is to know his past relationship with the Inquisition," he replied.

My visit to Andres' parents was a soothing balm. Yet, I did not visit them again. I was still apprehensive about the Inquisition and would not chance making them its victims because of contact with me. Instead, I would go out to the wharf, untie Andres' boat, and aimlessly row along the river recalling how much he loved a "trip up the river".

Drifting along the water, I began writing this journal. Putting my recollections of Andres into words, describing his agonies and his joys, was my way of erecting a monument to his life. Writing helped me in my bereavement because laughter and pain are ephemeral but the written word gives them an eternal quality.

I did not return to work.

Jimenez pleaded with me to come back because patients were flocking to seek my services. He told me I was famous and acknowledged the importance of surgery. He beseeched me to teach him but I could not get myself to work at the Casa Lombardia.

The river, the boat, the journal, these were my obsessions.

In the next month, however, I swung to the other extreme, plunging into the work in the clinic without concern for time. When work was done at the Casa Lombardia, I would look for patients outside the dispensary riding to outlying villages attending to farmers and families who could not come to the clinic. I travelled extensively, as far as Seville, for people were calling on me to do all sorts of surgery. Often I would not return to my room for days but would lie down to sleep in some building or even in an open field. Jimenez was right, my fame had spread. I have become a known personality in the towns and villages along the river.

But neither fame nor dedication to surgery drove me. I was like a horse running without a rider. I had no direction, no control over my actions.

The person who suffered most from my eccentric behavior was Maria. She was at my side, caring for me, looking after me. More important, she tolerated me. She urged me to talk about Andres, about our torture, about my guilt. She encouraged me to write this journal and listened when I read what I had written. The reading became a ritual which had occupied much of our time. I would often implore her to return to the castle assuring her that I could work out my own problem.

"You feel responsible for Andres' death. I feel responsible for your life," she replied telling me never to ask her to leave.

One evening, while dining in the River House, the count suggested that I leave Cordoba, get away from the city's bitter memories. Both he and the countess invited me to live in the castle. Enrique and Maria urged me to accept. I courteously declined because I did not want to burden Maria and the family with my suffering. The count jokingly reminded me that his wish was a command. Then, he quickly said, "Berto, don't treat me as you did Manuel. You could not accept a favor from him. Please accept our invitation as a favor to us."

Of course, I relented and began living at the castle where my life centered about Maria. Under her care, the nightmares came less frequently and I felt some surcease in my torment. I gradually began to take advantage of the luxury of the castle with Maria at my side. We never tired of each other. Several times we rode to La Caverna, strolling in its gardens, galloping across meadows, even hiking up La Mesa. For six weeks Maria and I were rarely separated. I became part of the family. I could not imagine life without her. That was why I kept postponing my to return to the

Casa Lombardia. I simply could not leave Maria.

On day, I met privately with the count and countess. I told them how much I loved their daughter and said I wanted to propose to Maria. I would first ask for their approval but confessed that I was concerned about my being a commoner. I repeated Don Luis' statement that my mere presence would stain the honor of the House of Trastamara.

Would marrying me, I asked, completely destroy her titled status?

The count said nothing but called for Maria. When she walked into the library, the count, in a rare display of humor, told her I was talking about her behind her back.

"Now, young man," the count said, "ask her your question."

I proposed to her.

She flung herself at me and, crying joyously, she said quietly, "Yes, Berto, yes."

"Would your marrying me stain your honor as a Trastamara princess?" I asked when she calmed down somewhat.

"My honor," she said dabbing her eyes, "is to be your wife."

Unabashedly, we embraced as Maria and I were choked up, unable to say anymore.

She ran over to her parents, hugging and kissing them, and thanking them for their approval. Shaking my hand, the count asked why I had suddenly become quiet. I replied that I was thinking about my mother and father who were being denied this joyous moment. The count reassured me that he would leave no stone unturned to help unite me with them.

Maria, still in a state of bliss, repeatedly called out, "Dona Maria di Cadiz."

The countess, also dabbing her eyes with her lace handkerchief, burst out laughing. "Well," she said to her husband, "there goes our honor."

When we told Enrique, he said he was happiest of all because I would be near all the time and would not leave so often.

Even Teresa finally approved of me, teasing that it took me so long to do "one thing right."

The family began to plan a wedding befitting the Trastamara Nobility.

Maria and I returned to Cordoba. She set up a special room for me in the River House. I resumed my regular duties in the Casa Lombardia. I was no longer the *el mudo,* nor was I obsessed with mourning. My return delighted Jimenez for the Casa Lombardia was becoming a renowned medical dispensary. In view of its success, I advised the count to postpone plans to construct a hospital in Seville. He agreed to finance the expansion of the Casa Lombardia.

My fears vanished. My laughter returned. For a while, it seemed my only problem was setting a wedding date.

One morning, about two months after my return to Cordoba, the count urgently summoned me to the Casa del Rio, the Trastamara mansion. When I arrived, he told me Manuel would soon be coming for an audience. He explained Manuel had repeatedly asked for it, but the count had repeatedly refused.

"This morning, Manuel sent me this message," the count said reading Manuel's note, "'Today, I leave Spain and will not return. I beg you to grant me an audience. I wish to speak with you, Excellency, and to Alberto, the physician'."

The count sent word to Manuel to meet him aboard his ship anchored in the port. The count did not wish anyone present during the talk with Manuel. We rode to the port and, at the appointed time, Manuel arrived, climbing up the ramp with little effort. He limped only slightly thanks to an expertly fitted artificial leg. He said he was fully recovered and was healthier today than he was before the injury. I had the urge to examine the leg but resisted. I could not get myself even to touch him.

The count was even more disdainful. He scolded Manuel for my torture and for his attempt a incriminating Maria. He warned Manuel that he would be given only a few moments for this audience. Manuel pointed to the ship anchored next to the count's caravel which will take him to England, never again to return to Spain. He then paused, overcome with emotion at the prospect of leaving his beloved land. The count was not moved. He ridiculed his behavior.

"Now get to the point," the count ordered.

"Well, I'm a lucky man," Manuel said apologizing for his outburst. "I am alive and for that I thank you, Alberto, for your surgery and you, Eminence, for bringing him to me. I tried to express my thanks many times, but neither of you would even talk me. As far as you are concerned, I don't exist. Alberto, you sent word with Jimenez that you consider me an animal, not a human being, and to acknowledge my thanks would restore my humanity. That is why I am here, now."

The count sneered warning Manuel he would call off the audience.

"I'm a man of honor, your Eminence," Manuel said briefly tracing his lineage to the Aragonese nobility. "I have now found the only way to express my gratitude to you, Sire, a way which could insure the very safety of the House of Trastamara."

"The House of Trastamara requires no help from you," the count angrily said. He stood up, indicating that the audience was over.

Manuel made no move to get up.

"The Trastamaras, Sire, do not need my help," Manuel replied and, in a soft almost inaudible whisper, he added, "but the daughter of Rosita and Nehemia Rahim, the adopted daughter of Count Juan de Trastamara may one day be utterly dependent upon the Inquisition."

The effect on the count was immediate. He sat down, demanding an explanation.

"Maria was brought to you by the Inquisition to be used as a wedge to pry open the Trastamara power," Manuel said.

From his coat pocket he produced a scroll from which he

read, "'The Holy Inquisition shall have the power to claim any child or children born to conversos who are deemed to be unworthy Christians.'"

"I know what the queen's Edict of Faith says," the count said raising his hand to stop Manuel from reading any further.

"This decree, which is retroactive to all children born of converso parents, could someday be used to claim Maria," Manuel said and, pleadingly, added, "What is even worse, this edict gives the Inquisition power over any child born to Maria."

Manuel hastened to explain that this could never occur in the count's lifetime but he stressed there would be no guarantee for her safety in the future.

"The House of Trastamara has, in fact, become exposed," Manuel said.

The count was silent.

Manuel went on to explain that bringing me to Maria assured the vulnerability of the House of Trastamara. Both Maria and I would, throughout our lives, be entirely under the Inquisition's scrutiny.

The count listened to Manuel's explanation, glaring at him but still made no comment.

"The idea of controlling power through an arranged marriage should not come as a surprise to your Excellency," Manuel said reminding the count that he had arranged Ferdinand's marriage to Isabel, a pairing which change the course of Spanish history uniting Aragon and Castile. "A marriage between Maria and Alberto could unite the power of the Inquisition with the power of Trastamara."

The count's face contorted. He stared at Manuel with disbelief.

"Why are you telling me all this?" he asked.

"For only one reason. I want to establish my own sense of humanity," Manuel replied and, turning to me, added, "I am not a dog. I am a human being with deep human feelings. I am a man of honor and I want my honor restored. The only way I can do that is to repay you for giving me my life."

"Is that the only reason?" the count asked.

"Yes," Manuel replied after some hesitation.

"Might there be some other motive?" the count asked. "Are you trying to enlist my support for your stay in Spain?"

"Not at all," Manuel replied with a smirk, "but what I told you will settle my accounts with Ferdinand who hatched up this scheme."

"The king? What has Ferdinand to do with this?" the count asked.

"You are an avid follower of chess, the game made popular by the Moors," Manuel said. "In chess only, one piece is important, the king. Every piece may be sacrificed to save the king. But not only in chess. Here, too, we're all expendable. We exist only to preserve Ferdinand."

Manuel looked first to me then to the count and added, "I have now been sacrificed. Nothing can be done to save me. Can't bring a checked pawn back to the playing board. But, I can, at least, expose Ferdinand. I am gratified to thus settle my accounts with him before I leave my country."

The count again asked Manuel how was King Ferdinand involved in the scheme of the Inquisition to wrest his power.

Manuel replied that while it was common knowledge that he had served as the Chief Administrator to Torquemada, what no one knew was that Ferdinand appointed Manuel to that position.

"The king appointed you?" the count asked. "Were you not an official of the church at the time of your appointment?"

"No, Sire, it had nothing to do with the church or with church doctrine," Manuel replied. "I was placed in Torquemada's inner circle to protect Ferdinand's interests. Mine was a two-fold mission. First, to insure that the confiscated property of a condemned heretic would accrue to the Royal Treasury and second, to use the Inquisition to expand the king's suzerainty over the nobility. The House of Trastamara, the most powerful force in Spain, thus became our principle target. Our first move was to plant Maria in your heart and home. When we learned that Abrabanel's son remained in Spain, we made our next move, laying the groundwork for a possible marriage between Alberto, the converso and Maria, the daughter of a converso."

Manuel spoke in a matter-of-fact tone, as though testifying in a court of law naming Ferdinand as approving the marriage plan when it was first proposed by the Inquisition.

"Ferdinand and Torquemada both decided to wrest power from the House of Trastamara," Manuel said. "And, the path to seizing that power was through Maria."

Determined to prove his point, Manuel traced his two-decades of service to Torquemada and King Ferdinand, recalling that he had been charged with Don Luis' upbringing; that he united Don Luis and Torquemada; that he arranged with Ferdinand to appoint Don Luis as the count's *hidalgo*. Manuel also candidly stated that he also arranged for Gaspar to spy on me in Toledo for the sole purpose of bringing about my transfer to Cordoba.

"Why Cordoba?" Manuel asked rhetorically, "because Maria was in Cordoba."

He dismissed the death of Abram Senor as a minor skirmish in a well-laid stratagem designed to curtail the power of the House of Trastamara. He knew about the Morales infant and about Diego for whom I provided the first limpieza. He even had evidence implicating me in the escape of the conversos. Yet, he took no action against me. His sole interest in me was to nurture a romance between me and Maria. And, that was Don Luis's assignment.

"Alberto, who brought you to the castle to tend to the count?" Manuel asked, turning to me, "Who brought you to the Casa del Rio after you left the castle following the incident in the Music Room? Who brought you to the count's ship to sail for three days with Maria? Don Luis. Always Don Luis."

I nodded and then asked, "Why then was I brought up on charges at the Holy Tribunal?"

"That was an act of desperation by Luis when he learned that you and Andres discovered his treason," Manuel replied. "To save himself, Luis deceived me, convincing me that we could accomplish our goal by having you confess to the charges of judaizing Maria."

Manuel paused, again sighing and shaking his head, he apologetically explained that it was only because of his illness he allowed himself to be duped by Luis and then to lose control over events that were unfolding in the Betazar compound.

"And that was the beginning of my downfall," Manuel said ruefully. "It ruptured my relations with you, Eminence, and that terminated my worth to Ferdinand. So, in reality they are doing to me what you did to Don Luis."

"Are you not here to seek my help in your struggle with the king?" the count asked.

"Forgive me, Excellency," Manuel said avoiding the count's glare, "even the Count of Trastamara can do little in matters pertaining to the Inquisition. Sooner or later, the entire Spanish nobility will bend to the will of the Inquisition. In the case of the House of Trastamara, it may not be in your lifetime or in Torquemada's lifetime, but any future Inquisitor General will certainly wield power over Maria."

The count argued no longer. He simply shook his head in disbelief.

"It would be wise not to overlook my revelations now that you are planning your daughter's marriage," Manuel said. "For, then, you would be playing into the hands of those who have set the trap."

The count rose and extending his hand to Manuel, he said. "I thank you for your disclosures."

"And, I thank you, Sire, for this audience," Manuel said holding the count's hands perhaps longer than considered proper.

He then faced me, taking my extended hand, he relished in my words of gratitude to him.

"Thank you for giving me my life," Manuel countered, "I now consider my debt paid in full both to you and to King Ferdinand. Now, I can leave Spain in peace."

He closed the cabin door behind him.

When Manuel left, the count was thunderstruck. He kept repeating, "Amazing, amazing."

I asked him what he made of these revelations. He replied that he believed Manuel. However, the count also believed that threatening Ferdinand and Torquemada with Trastamara military power would deter them from making any move against the House of Trastamara. He rationalized that Manuel's exile clearly indicated the end of Ferdinand's assault on the House of Trastamara . I knew he was trying to assure me, or himself, of our safety but I insisted that the threat to Maria had not minimized and that a plot pursued for so long, since her infancy, should not be taken lightly. The count dismissed my warning, probably unwilling to admit his own vulnerability. Yet, after I repeated Manuel's advice that my marriage to Maria would play into their hands, the count suggested postponing the wedding until he confronted the king in the presence of Torquemada.

We agreed to say nothing to Maria or to the countess about Manuel's visit or his disclosures. As for the marriage, the count would tell them protocol demanded that he apprise Ferdinand first before any public announcement could be made.

I had no faith in his confrontations with Torquemada and Ferdinand because whatever the outcome, Maria would remain a victim. I kept my opinion to myself; to argue this point with the count would be futile.

Manuel's disclosures made a profound impression on me. While he was divulging the plot involving Maria and me, I realized that I must think of leaving Spain if only to protect Maria. After Manuel departed, I did not share this with the count for I had no clear plan how to pursue my objective.

I left the count's ship for the Casa Lombardia where I thought over Manuel's confessions. All the pieces of the four-year mystery now fell into place. My first resolve was to contact Orlando Franco in Seville to arrange my passage to Naples. But, in the morning, after mulling over the problem and analyzing all the known facts, I realized it would be dangerous for me to travel under a false limpieza since I was already well known throughout Andalusia and beyond. I also decided to delay my escape plans because, according to Manuel, the Inquisition's plan involving me and Maria was still active. So, I would still be under their scrutiny and attempting to leave Spain would be both dangerous and impossible.

In truth, the real reason for my decision not to leave Spain was that it meant leaving Maria. I was not willing to make that sacrifice. I shuddered at the thought of losing her. She had become intrinsically part of my very being; I could not bear the thought of life without her. Therefore, I hatched an alternate plan and, the following day, relayed it to the count.

We sat alone on his porch at the River House. He reviewed his military options describing several avenues to confront the king. I told him he might succeed in protecting the House of Trastamara but Maria would end up a victim.

"When I returned from my fight with Don Luis," I said, "you suggested that I appeal to the queen to allow me to leave Spain and visit my parents in Naples. If she grants me that permission, then at some future time, you could visit Naples with Maria."

"That's not realistic. Isabel will not approve your request," he said. "If Manuel is right, you are still a key player in their design."

"However," I replied, "if you officially inform the Monarchs that you oppose my marriage to Maria, I am of no further use to them."

Before he had a chance to reply, I reminded him that, sooner or later, I would leave for Toledo for my medical certification. At that time, I would get an audience with the queen. He did not object to my plan but he was determined to face Ferdinand with Manuel's disclosures and, if necessary, to threaten military force.

At the noonday meal, I told Maria of my plans, suggesting that she and her family could come to visit me in Naples. The countess agreed and wished me success with the queen. Maria was saddened by my imminent departure, saying it would be months before we could be together again. We went out to the porch, sitting silently for a long time. I told her that, to save my life, I could have left Spain with the conversos but I loved her so much I could not stand the thought of parting from her.

"This will be only temporary," I said. "I leave for Toledo, not for the medical certification, but for enabling us to be together for the rest of our life."

Maria held on tightly to me saying she would count the days until we were once again united.

When I bid farewell to the family, the count took me aside privately and said, "Your plan is bold but also dangerous. After all, Toledo is not only the Royal Capitol of Spain. It is also the headquarters of Torquemada's Inquisition — and no one can forecast its action."

10

Four years earlier, I left Toledo, with remorse, full of hate for everything and everyone in that city. I felt none of that now. On the contrary, a burst of enthusiasm bordering on ecstasy overwhelmed me when I saw the city from a distance. I was only sorry Maria was not with me to share the splendid sight. Bathed in the afternoon sunlight, the masses of red-tiled roofs and the rust-colored buildings adorned with flowers and green foliage looked like a painted masterpiece. My heart kept cadence with the horse's gallop as we crossed the San Martin bridge into the beautiful city.

I headed directly to my former home, the Casa Floridiana, jumping out of my carriage, walking slowly to the open outer gate. I looked around me. Nothing had changed. It was the same as on the fateful day I left after my confrontation with father.

"Welcome, my house is your house," a man greeted me at the gate, "My name is Angelo de Orgaz. I recognized you the moment you jumped off the carriage."

I told him I had just come from Cordoba and, greeting me once again with the traditional greeting, *mi casa es su casa,* my house is your house, he invited me to wash up and rest. I said I only wanted to look around the house and then I would be on my way. He obliged, leading me through the rooms, telling me that he had changed very little in the house since he bought it from father because the original furnishings were so beautiful. As I passed the large reception hall, bitter-sweet memories crowded my mind. Soon I was lost in reveries of the past.

I recalled the phrase *mi casa es su casa,* anguished at the thought that it could well mean, 'my house is his house'.

He asked how long I would stay in town. When I told him

I would probably remain several weeks, he invited me to stay in the house until I found lodgings in Toledo. Deeply touched by the impact of being in my home, I readily and gratefully accepted.

A servant took my bag and led me to my old bedroom at the top of the stairs on the second floor. So little had changed. My cane-backed chair and my writing table, even my large basin and water pitcher remained. The water pitcher was still on the small ledge father had built into the wall. I noticed only one difference: the knobs on the chifforobe were new. The old ones were always falling off.

I left my room to walk through the corridors, peeking into the other rooms. I wanted to ask permission to wander but Don Angelo was nowhere to be seen. I suspected he knew my feelings and graciously absented himself so that I could roam freely. I passed the room next to mine, Don Carlos' room, then I walked down to the kitchen where the huge bronze pots and pans were still hanging on special racks. I recalled how we would huddle there together during the cold winter days because the kitchen was always the warmest spot in the house.

Father's library was completely changed. Gone were the book cases filled with scrolls and books which had given the room its special character. Gone was the beautiful candelabra we would kindle on the Festival of Lights. Also missing were the many paintings depicting Biblical stories and scenes from the Holy Land. Despite the prominence of Don Angelo's coat of arms and the lavish displays of his hunting trophies, to me, the room looked bare. I sat down in the same chair I had sat in when I confronted my father. I felt a strange sense of well-being.

I walked out of the house, to the garden admiring the floral beds beneath the huge sycamores. Then, I lay down in the soft grass remembering the last time I stretched out there to share my dreams of being a physician with Asher.

Suddenly I was startled by a voice asking me, "You were very happy in this house?"

Don Angelo de Orgaz was sitting on the bench encircling

the big tree not far from where I lay. He apologized for startling me, explaining that he noticed how I walked around the house and could not help but realize my sense of satisfaction as I went from room to room.

"I had a very happy childhood here," I replied.

"The years you've been away matured you quite a bit," Don Angelo said. "You have grown to be quite an important man."

I thanked him for the compliment, but asked how he knew about me.

"Remember, I'm Cordoban," he replied, "and I still maintain important commercial connections in the city. My messengers leave almost daily from Toledo to Cordoba."

That evening, he arranged a splendid dinner, which he called a "welcoming meal" in my honor, and invited a small group of his friends. Senor Emilio Manzano, my father's former business associate, raised his glass, offering a toast to my return to Toledo. I also recognized Don Vincente, the duke of Cordoba, who attended the Council of Nobles. We talked about events in Toledo, about intrigues in the court, about the rise of the Inquisition. I recalled that it was Don Vincente who maintained much could be accomplished by cooperating with the Inquisition. He again boasted that neither his wealth nor his power had diminished since the Inquisition had assumed control of his city. Everyone around the tabled agreed that although the Inquisition was feared, it was wiser to recognize its power than to balk at it. I felt neither recrimination nor hostility to Emilio or to Don Vincente. I was reminded of something Andres once said to me: whenever anyone talks in company, he is aware of an informant's presence.

When the guests left, Don Angelo said with some satisfaction that the Casa Floridiana had become the hub of political activity. When we were about to go to our bedrooms, I thanked Don Angelo for the dinner and told him that the Count of Trastamara was planning a visit very soon. Don Angelo immediately offered his home to the count. Using Don Angelo's messengers, I sent letters to the count advising him of Don Angelo's offer and to Maria describing my impressions of my return to my home.

The following morning, I walked the streets of Toledo reliving many scenes of my boyhood. I climbed down the steep hill to the river where I took off my shoes and, wading in the shallow water, went over to our islet, which had been our playground. I even scaled a few stones, fondly recalling those days with Asher.

Then, I visited the Casa Zaghral, Abram Senor's former home. To my surprise, I felt none of the anguish which had once plagued me. I walked through the old *juderia* to my old school building. I sat down under a small mulberry tree in the center of its courtyard. In my student years, it seemed so large and now I saw it was no bigger than an overgrown bush. To a child, everything seems large, awesome.

"It's a pity," I thought, "as we mature, we lose our childhood's awe of the world about us."

I even went to visit the synagogue situated high above the Tajo River. The simple red-brick structure looked the same. Its front door was slightly ajar and I could see laborers working inside the building. The large central *bima* had been removed and where there once stood the Holy Ark, an altar was installed with its large statue of the Virgin in Transition. Some of the beautiful Hebrew lettering was still visible and I had the urge to step inside but I thought it best to avoid the possibility of another "Abram Senor" encounter with the Inquisition.

I wandered through the market place where, as a child, I would help my mother with her shopping. The stores and the smells of the market place were still the same, even the noise of the huckstering shopkeepers had not changed. I felt a strange delight in going into the shops, picking up fruit and vegetables, and then placing them back in their bins. Here and there I nodded to a familiar face, but no one returned my greeting.

At twilight, the shopkeepers were starting to close their

stores. I decided to make one last purchase, a gift for my host, Don Angelo. The store selling decorative tiles and statuettes was crowded but I was drawn to a very tall man who was examining a small marble statue. What attracted my attention was the tune he was humming. Although barely audible, I recognized it as the *Kol Nidre*, the prayer we chanted the eve of *Yom Kippur*, the Jewish Fast Day. I was about to greet him, but he turned away, hurrying out of the store. I followed him down the busy streets, keeping up with his pace and, when I came up close to him, he once again hummed that tune. Without looking at me, the tall stranger nodded ever-so-slightly, motioning me to follow him.

I trailed after him down the steep embankment to the river, keeping him in sight from afar. He sauntered along the river path which ended at a few abandoned huts. He quickly climbed over several boulders. I lost sight of him but he let me know where he was by throwing a branch in the air. I caught up with him just as he was entering the ruins of an ancient structure through a narrow opening completely obscured by an overgrowth of bushes and reeds. I had to keep close to him because he was leading me down an underground passage where we walked in total darkness. We were treading a sandy path; I could hear no footsteps. I lost him again when I suddenly felt his hand over my shoulder leading me down a narrow tunnel. We had to bend in order to walk through it. At the end of the tunnel, he opened a door, which creaked on its hinges, leading me into a totally darkened room.

At first I saw only a row of benches at one end of the room. Then I discerned several figures. Some were seated on make shift benches. Others stood, leaning against the wall. No one spoke. No greetings were exchanged. When the tall stranger took his place, lighting a candle on a table in front of him, everyone sat down. I looked around me but could not see anyone clearly. In the light of the just-lit candle, the tall stranger's face appeared distorted, unrecognizable.

But, when he began to chant the *Yom Kippur* prayers, there

was no distortion in his deep, rich melodic baritone. I have never heard a voice more beautiful or more distinctive than the voice of the tall stranger.

I had no prayer book, no one did, but I followed the Holy Day service with a devotion I had never experienced before. The timbre of his powerful voice echoing across the bare room gave the familiar chant an even more mysterious quality.

The service was brief. Soon, the tall stranger stepped in front of the lit candle so that we were in total darkness. He suggested that we retain our anonymity to secure our safety, warning us not to identify ourselves to one another but to leave separately without greetings. The tall stranger concluded by wishing us a Happy New Year and reciting the traditional blessing: "May you be inscribed in the Book of Life," to which he added, "and may the Holy God save you from the Holy Tribunal."

I had now become a marrano, a Christian to the outside world, a Jew in secret. And, I loved it.

When I came out of the subterranean ruins, I walked out into the darkness, marveling at the brilliant spray of stars in the dark skies. Still exhilarated by the service, I said to myself, "What a lovely way to be welcomed to Toledo."

I was now back home, in more ways than one.

In the morning, I realized the danger of fasting on *Yom Kippur* because I knew Inquisition agents were alerted to watch for backsliders who fasted on this particular day. But, despite the danger, I decided to fast, so I left the Casa Floridiana early, walking all day through the streets of Toledo.

I searched for the tall stranger throughout the city, even going down to the ruins, sauntering along the river, making certain that I was not followed. He was nowhere to be found. I sat at the entrance of the ruins hoping that someone would come by but not even one person ventured within sight. Throwing caution to the wind, I walked about the city, whistling the tune of *Kol Nidre*, hoping someone from the night before would recognize me. I continued whistling the tune but no one responded. In the late afternoon, I returned to the ruins, sitting alone, recapturing the spirit of *Yom Kippur*. My hunger grew, but the hunger pangs only increased my gratification in observing the festival.

When I returned to the Casa Floridiana after dark, Don Angelo invited me to dine with him. I told him about my plan to request Their Majesties' permission to visit my parents in Naples. He said Don Valdes was still the royal chamberlain and offered to introduce me to him so that an audience could be arranged. I replied that Don Valdes had often been to our home; I had met him on numerous occasions.

Two days later, I decided to approach Their Majesties. It was the beginning of the rainy season and the previous days' bright sun seemed in permanent hiding beneath heavy black clouds. Despite driving rains, I made my way to the Alcazar, taking shelter from the rain in various shops. Although I recognized several of the shopkeepers, I was surprised and slightly irked that no one greeted me. When I dashed into the outer courtyard of the palace, the guards let me enter, explaining that Don Angelo had alerted them to my coming and to my desire to meet with Don Valdes.

The royal chamberlain warmly welcomed me and asked, "What is the reason you seek an audience with the queen?"

"I need her permission to leave Spain so that I can visit my family in Naples whom I have not seen in almost four years."

"I see no reason why your request would be turned down," Don Valdes graciously replied. "I will set up the private audience and relay further information to you at the Casa Floridiana."

When I expressed surprise that he knew about my staying there, he said that Don Angelo had already interceded in my behalf. Then Don Valdes called one of the livery men, ordering him to drive me back to the Casa Floridiana.

I had been in Toledo almost a week and had not yet visited Don Alfonso, although I passed his dispensary several times. I finally went there one morning, noticing its orderly reception room, clean beds, and neatly stacked supplies. I had almost forgotten the stark differences between Jimenez' rural clinic in Cordoba and Alfonso's sophisticated dispensary in Toledo.

"So, you finally came to visit me," I heard Alfonso's booming voice. He approached me with his arms extended.

"I saved you for last," I said. "You know, 'the last is the best'."

He embraced me, held me, and led me by the hand around the clinic where I had once mopped the floor, the storage room where I had slept, and the large examination room where we froze in the winter months. Only when we got to his office did he let go of my hand, telling me how proud he was of my medical accomplishment. I asked how he knew.

"Your reputation as a physician spread as fast as the talk about your imminent marriage to the Trastamara princess," he said. "Tell me, Berto, does she know what a prize she's getting?".

This show of affection was so out of character for the Don Alfonso I had known. I thought him incapable of demonstrating any feelings, much less so overtly.

Was he scheming to get me to do something for him? Was it age?

Sitting across his desk, I noticed how much he had aged. His face was deeply wrinkled; his thin stringy hair was almost all white. His once-erect posture was gone; now his shoulders were stooped and his body bent forward. But, had he lost none of his arrogance as I learned from his continuing reprimand for not visiting him sooner.

"Toledo can be exciting for a young man on the loose," Alfonso concluded his harangue, "more exciting than sitting with an old doctor."

"That's not it," I replied. "I intended to visit you even when I originally planned my trip to Toledo. But, when I got here, I just wandered about visiting the old haunts of my past."

Sacred Sword

"I'm very much a part of your past," he insisted, "why didn't you come to me?"

"I can't understand," I said.

"I can," he retorted. "It's because your feelings of guilt."

"My what?" I protested.

"Your feelings of guilt," he repeated.

"Sure, I felt guilty for the death of Don Abram Senor," I said.

"Not Don Abram," Alfonso replied. "It's me. I am the source of your guilt. That's why you stayed away from me."

"Not true," I retorted. "I always speak about you with pride. Why should I feel guilty toward you?"

"Because of me, you cut yourself off from your father," Don Alfonso said, "Because of me, you remained in Spain. Because of me, you got in trouble with the Inquisition, all because I took you in as an apprentice at the wrong time."

I began to argue, but he stopped me. "How many times did you say to yourself, 'If not for Alfonso, I would have been with my father'?"

I did not reply. He got up, walked over to the window, and pointed an accusing finger at me.

"You feel guilty because you traded your family loyalty for a career in medicine," he said.

"My father said that to me once," I replied, "and I was incensed at him."

"But it's true, isn't it?," Don Alfonso asked.

"Sure. It's because of you that I became a doctor," I said. "But you didn't order me to stay in Spain."

"Why did you remain?" Don Alfonso shot back.

"Because I wanted to be your apprentice," I replied.

"Aha," Don Alfonso called out triumphantly, "so, I am the culprit, the cause for all the evil that befell you!"

He demanded that I admit my true feelings.

"Staying away from me," Don Alfonso pressed on, "was your way of salving your conscience. And, what worries me is that much of your actions in the future will also be influenced by this feeling of guilt."

I finally admitted he was right. "What do I do now?" I asked.

"If you are concerned with the future, you must not dwell on the past," he said, "Think only about the present. Be a realist."

I replied that the past cannot be easily forgotten.

"Alberto," Don Alfonso said, "returning to your father's house does not alter the past nor does flitting about your boyhood playgrounds change the present. And trying to get an audience with the queen will have little effect on your future."

I was stunned, amazed he knew so much about my activities in Toledo, wondering if he also knew of my experiences with the tall stranger. I was about to tell him of my plans to leave Spain but just then, an attendant brought in a platter of food and Alfonso urged me to eat before we continued our conversation. I ate some of the food, but I noticed that Alfonso hardly touched anything. He leaned his head on the back of the chair, shutting his blood-shot eyes.

"There are only three simple facts that must concern you now," he said sitting up. "First, you are in Spain and you cannot be anywhere else. Second, Samuel Abrabanel does not exist, only Alberto di Cadiz. Third, you are a physician and it's not only a livelihood, it's a life."

"If I leave Spain," I replied, "none of them will apply. As a matter of fact, the reason I came to Toledo was to arrange my departure to Naples"

"You will never leave Spain," he replied.

"Can you intercede with Queen Isabel to allow me to visit my family in Naples?" I asked.

"She specifically prohibited your leaving the country," he replied, "and your chances of even getting an audience with Isabel are nil."

Again I was amazed that he knew so much about palace affairs. I was utterly shocked, though, when he leaned over, grasped my hand and said, "I want you to come back to Toledo to be my assistant."

Only out of respect for his feelings did I not reject him outright. Instead, I thanked him for his offer, making the excuse that I would have to discuss it with Maria. He was upset with my response, stating categorically that he could not wait so long and that he had to know immediately whether he could count on me.

I said nothing and I knew my silence hurt him. He abruptly excused himself, saying that he was tired and needed to rest. He asked me to return later. I promised to come back the following morning and, as I was about to walk out of his room, I asked him how he knew that the queen would not grant me an audience.

He cryptically replied, "My sources of information would surprise even Torquemada."

The happiness I felt that first week in Toledo evaporated after my meeting Don Alfonso. How right he was! He correctly he analyzed my guilt feelings! Although I recognized that his insight was true, I found no peace. Admitting my guilt brought on morbidity not comfort.

Despite the cool, early winter, breeze wafting through my room that night, I felt suffocated. At midnight, I bolted out of my bed rushing down the steps to the garden where I sat in the cold damp grass. I felt a moment of relief, deeply breathing the cool air. It turned cold and I returned to my room, reflecting on the new turn of events and pondering my problem. Complicating it was the fact that I could not decide on a course of action without consulting Maria. I tossed and turned all night.

I saw clearly my dilemma: although I was known to everyone as 'Alberto di Cadiz', I had never given up my identity as 'Samuel Abrabanel'. That was my problem.

Then, I made an important decision; if I could not get out of Spain as an Abrabanel, I would do so as a Cadiz, as Alberto di Cadiz, a renowned physician, as renowned as Don Alfonso. Maria would go with me and would be out of reach of the Inquisition. I decided to accept Don Alfonso's offer. Becoming his assistant, I would then become indispensable to the monarchs or even to some high ranking Inquisition officials who would arrange my exodus from Spain. That would be my fee for being their physician.

"Nature cures. Only the doctor takes his fee," I recalled Andres' jesting remark. I smiled when I thought of Andres. That was the first time I had done so without becoming depressed. I looked out of the window where the sun burst through the ash-gray skies and I suddenly felt a unique sense of calmness envelope me. I fell asleep quite happy with my decision.

When I awakened, it was already past noon. I remembered with a jolt that I had promised to meet Don Alfonso that morning. I rushed off to the clinic where I found him nervously pacing the floor, waiting for me.

"When you didn't show up in the morning, I felt devastated," He said. "I thought I lost you."

"You didn't lose me," I replied. "It wasn't easy to make a decision. I came here to tell you that I gladly accept to be your assistant." He responded by doing something I had never seen him do before. He danced a jig and clapped his hands like a little boy. He did not ask what the difficulties were in making the decision, but simply welcomed it, saying how grateful he was to have me as his assistant.

I was grateful when he said, "I will immediately announce that you will take my place at the palace as physician to the Royal House."

Of course, I did not tell him that I would use that position to get out of Spain.

He asked me to move into the Caldera which, I soon learned, was converted into a palatial residence, since he no longer accepted apprentices. "I'm getting on in years and I can no longer take the strain of being both a physician and a teacher. Teaching a bunch of noisy youngsters who want to become doctors was never easy," Alfonso said.

"But you still have to teach me," I said.

"Teaching you is no strain," he replied. "It's a joy."

I immediately sent a letter through one of Don Angelo's messengers to Maria outlining my plans. That same day I applied myself with zeal to my work in Don Alfonso's dispensary. He referred almost all his patients to me, but was always available when I needed to consult him. Although I was his student, he treated me like a colleague and verbally thrashed anyone who called me anything but 'Doctor Alberto,' a title he conferred on me from the very first day he certified me as a physician. Within a few months, I became a familiar figure in the palace, known even to many officials of the Inquisition. Of course I was gratified with my progress and, even more so, with Maria's letters encouraging me in my work and agreeing with my plan to use my position to visit my parents.

But, despite becoming a prominent physician, I was not granted an audience with the queen. Don Alfonso was right: I was informed that as long as my purpose for the audience was to leave Spain, the queen refused to see me.

"She will give you an audience for any other reason," Don Valdes said. "However, I am authorized to tell you that royal permission for you to leave Spain is not negotiable."

My dream of leaving Spain with the help of some great dignitary would have to wait until I attained the stature of Don Alfonso. It was frustrating but, fortunately, I had become so occupied with my medical duties that I had little time to worry about it. Even my correspondence with Maria suffered because of this preoccupation, so her letters to me were full of complaints about my silence. I planned to make it up to her when she would come to Toledo with the count for the annual meeting of the Royal Council of Ministers in January, right after New Years Day.

One evening Don Alfonso invited me to have supper with him, which was strange because neither of us could afford the luxury of a free evening. That night, after congratulating me on my progress, he suggested that I take in a few apprentices so that I could taper off some of the work load. I said I felt no pressure, so I felt no need for apprentices.

"I suspect that you have another motive for working so hard," he said.

Because I did not relish the idea of getting into a debate with him, I immediately changed the subject by asking why he had not eaten anything.

"Are you ill?" I asked.

"That's why I asked you to come here tonight," he said. "I want you to examine me."

He told me that during the past six months, he had begun to feel weak, unable to retain food. He lay on the bed, and unlacing his shirt, asked me to examine his abdomen. I probed his right side, immediately below his rib cage and felt a hard lump.

"You feel it, too," he said, twisting his body away and waving me off.

"Enough examination," he blustered and glaring at me he added, "I know what you're thinking; surgery!"

I not only thought about surgery, but felt that Alfonso would have to instruct me how to do that procedure.

"Berto," Alfonso said, "How many times have you excised a tumor? Do you know any physician in Spain who has done it successfully?"

"No," I confessed with some hesitation.

"No one has," he replied. "Me? I've operated a number of times to remove an internal tumor, but only as a last resort."

I slumped at his bedside, overcome with sadness. I could not face him. I felt his hand on my shoulder. At that moment, I was not his doctor and he was not my patient. I was not his student and he was not my teacher. The bond that had developed between Alfonso and me during the past three months was more than that, almost a filial one. Now, I grieved for his imminent death.

"Berto," Alfonso said, "I called you here tonight not to sadden you with my death, but to tell you how gratified I am that you will be my successor. When I first discovered the tumor, I was distraught. All I could think about was my death, but when you agreed to work with me, I felt relieved. You're not only my successor, but someone who will carry on my work."

I did not reply.

Alfonso spoke quietly, as though talking to himself, "Death is part of life. The cycle of life is such that seeds of detachment are inherently part of every human attachment. Every 'hello' presupposes a 'good-bye'. The rising of the sun is predicated on its setting."

His impending death was not only painful to me but burdensome.

How could I tell him I was using this position only to plan my flight from Spain? How could I hurt him by saying that I did not want to carry on his work here in Toledo; that I only wanted to leave and to be away from Spain with Maria?

"It seems so strange that I should be consoling you over my death," he continued, not realizing my dilemma. "But, I'm really comforting myself. When I first discovered the lump in my stomach, I couldn't make peace with the reality of my death. I was afraid that my life was ending, a bitter end. But, with you as my successor, death is no longer frightening because, through you, a part of me will live on. And only a dying man can perceive what a consoling thought that is."

He recalled his anguish when he knew I had returned to Toledo, but did not visit him. When I finally did, he was hurt that I did not immediately accept the position as his assistant, and when I did not show up that morning, he felt devastated. So, when I told him of my acceptance, he was overwhelmed with joy.

"Now, you know how pleased I am to have you as my successor," he said breathing deeply and smiling broadly.

"Of course, I will become your successor," I said, thinking to myself that being a doctor outside of Spain, I would still be carrying his work.

I looked into Alfonso's jaundiced eyes and saw them sparkle with happiness. He covered himself with his blanket, making ready to sleep. When I told him I would do everything in my power to bring honor to his name, he closed his eyes.

He lived to enjoy the first honor I bestowed on him: I changed the name of the clinic to the "Don Alfonso Dispensary". Craftsmen inscribed his name in gilt lettering over the front of the building. At the dedication ceremony, so many people turned out we had to herd them back to the public square. Weak as he was, Alfonso attended, announced me as his successor, and told the crowd of his admirers, "Weep not for the physician, Alfonso. Greet the new master-physician Alberto."

In the following month, I assumed all his work, attending his patients in the clinic and in the many homes he would visit. I converted part of the Caldera back to a dormitory where I housed several apprentices. I won the approval of Toledo's populace both among the common people and the nobility. In surprising short order, I became the equal of Don Alfonso; I was the official physician to The Royal Court, and more. Because I did not possess his arrogance, my fame quickly spread.

I must confess I enjoyed my growing popularity, taking pride in my reputation as Toledo's leading physician. And, I must confess, too, that my preoccupation with my work gave me little time to plan getting out of Spain.

I did, however, write the count about my elevation, asking him to suggest persons in the Royal Council of Ministers who might be helpful. He sent me a list which included the name, Rafael de Adalajara, an important minister to the queen. I introduced myself to Don Rafael at a function in the palace. I learned he coordinated the exchange of foreign dignitaries for the queen and appointed her emissaries to various countries in Europe. I told him my father was in Naples and asked him if I could send a message to my family. He courteously acknowledged my request but by his tactful demeanor, I sensed nothing would come of it.

A few days later, Don Rafael's coachman woke me in the middle of the night and summoned me to the minister's home. I rushed out of the Caldera, eager to hear news from my father. It was a cold winter night and I remember rushing so fast that I neglected to dress warmly. On the way to Don Rafael's house, I wondered whether the message was a letter from my father or a verbal greeting through an emissary. When I entered, the housing minister anxiously informed me his ten-year-old son was suffering severe stomach pains. When I walked into the boy's room, he was on his bed, writhing in pain, unable to catch his breath. His face was pale white. I diagnosed his convulsions as stomach poisoning and gave him a herb purgative. Soon the lad began to vomit while I held his forehead, helping maintain his balance. When he finished, his color returned and I sat by until he fell asleep.

I explained to the parents that their son had probably eaten some poisonous berries but since he had vomited, there should be nothing to worry about. To assure them, I said I would come by in the morning to check on him. Don Rafael expressed his gratitude, pressing a gold coin into my hand.

The coin was nothing compared to the excitement I felt when he said, "Tomorrow evening, we shall be entertaining the Ambassador of Naples, and I have alerted him to bring a message from your father. It will be our pleasure to have you with us and if you wish, you may prepare a letter for the ambassador to take back to your father."

Barely able to hide my excitement, I accepted Don Rafael's invitation. From that moment on, I could not concentrate on my work. The dispensary seemed unimportant, the patients seemed unimportant, even Alfonso seemed unimportant. I could not wait for the day to pass. Time seemed to drag. I parted from my father four and a half years ago and, in all that time, I had been unable to get any word to him nor had I received any from him.

Finally, that evening, when I walked up the path to the minister's wall-enclosed casa, my heart pounded with anticipated joy. Don Rafael greeted me at the door, escorting me to his private study where he introduced me to the ambassador. He rose to greet me but, I noticed, his demeanor was grim.

"The news I have for you," the ambassador said, "is not good. I am sorry to tell you, your father died three weeks ago."

I was crushed.

I felt as though my blood suddenly drained away. I sat down timidly on the couch and, unable to contain my grief, I began to sob. I was both heartbroken and ill-at-ease in their presence. I wanted to be alone. I excused myself and was about to rush out of the house.

"I want you to know that your father made repeated attempts to bring you to Naples," the ambassador said. "He even asked the Pope to intervene. But your father's requests were repeatedly rejected by Queen Isabel."

Until that moment, I never considered myself fully detached from my father, always nurturing the hope of uniting with him. Now, for the first time, I felt completely cut off, lost, abandoned. I had been made an orphan by a father whom I had tormented.

I quickly wrote a letter to my mother, which Don Rafael gave to the ambassador. Apologizing for disrupting their evening, I left, rushing headlong into the dark streets of Toledo. I walked around most of the night mourning my father.

The shock of his death was aggravated by my inability to express my mourning. I wanted to pray, to light a candle, to tear my jacket, to express my grief in a traditional manner. I passed by a church and went in to light a candle, hoping thereby to give expression to my bereavement. It seemed so inadequate. No, it was a mockery both to my life and to his death. I blew out the candle and stalked out of the church.

I tore wildly down the street until I simply ran out of breath and stopped to rest on the bank of the Tajo River. Sitting along its darkened edge, I bitterly wept for my dead father and cursed the tragedy of my fate. I was tormented by the thought that I, who broke away from my father during his lifetime, was now seeking unity with him after his death.

Despite this nagging inconsistency, I decided there was only one thing for me to do. I had to find the tall stranger to arrange a mourner's service where I could recite the *kaddish*, the traditional prayer for the dead. Slowly, I returned to the market place but it was deserted. I sat on the steps of the court house to await the coming of the morning. I must have fallen asleep because I was jarred awake by vendors hawking their wares, women arguing with merchants, children shouting and church bells pealing. I walked everywhere, searching for the tall stranger. The thought of my father's death gnawed at me. I was overwhelmed with guilt, struggling with my own life. I went into stores and stalls introducing myself as the son of Don Isaac Abrabanel, caring little about the inherent danger, in the hope that someone would lead me to the tall stranger.

My search was in vain.

I found myself standing before the Hermandad where, four years earlier, I had reported my daily activities to the Inquisition. Suddenly all the street noise stopped, an ominous silence descended upon the square; only the church bells continued. All eyes turned toward the Hermandad where two monks marched out holding aloft the Inquisition's fluttering banner with its green crucifix. Behind them came four militia men escorting several prisoners wearing the familiar *sanbenito*, the garment of shame. The soldiers cleared a path through the crowd which suddenly began to jeer the victims as they passed.

"No wonder no one admitted recognizing me," I thought, watching the pitiful parade wend its way through the crowd, "The Inquisition is still to be feared."

I returned to the dispensary, realizing how correct Don

Alfonso was in advising me to learn to live in the 'real present,' not the imaginary one. This was Spain. As long as I stayed, I could not expect any unity with my family, even with my deceased father.

At best, I could hope the count could help me achieve accommodation with the Monarchs or, at least, get an audience to plead my case.

Don Alfonso, totally bedridden, rapidly deteriorated. Regrettably, his mind was clear so his pain was sharp. He could barely sit up. We both knew death was near. Of course, I told him nothing about my father's death. I made him comfortable, sponging his feverish body, discussing special medical problems with him, and sharing news of local events. When I told him about my visit to Don Rafael's house and described the lavish party there, he interrupted, saying, "Did the ambassador also tell you the queen denied your father's request for you to leave Spain?"

"How did you know that?" I asked, hoping that he did not know of my father's death.

"Only ignorant peasants believe in the clairvoyance of a dying person," he said, "You and I know better. A physician in the Court of Spain is privy to many secrets."

To change the subject and to avoid talking about my father's death, I told him the count would soon come to Toledo. I promised I would bring him to the dispensary for a visit. Don Alfonso turned his head away but said nothing.

He was so weak, he could barely speak and his pain increased as the day wore on. He slept only intermittently because of the constant suffering. In the late afternoon, he motioned me to prop him up on his pillows.

"Listen to me, Alberto," he said, gasping phrases, breathing heavily, talking in an almost inaudible whisper. "Time is short...You...never escape Inquisition... the count can't help. Only hinder. Detach yourself...from count, from everyone. Listen... only as my successor ... you be free. Listen to me...be a physician... like me... I give you life..."

He tried to say more, but could not. I needed no commentary on his broken phrases. I had never told him my plan to get out of Spain, yet he undoubtedly suspected. Was it intuition, clairvoyance, or knowledge he possessed that I did not?

I remained at his bedside when he died that night.

As he had previously instructed me, I arranged his burial in the cemetery in Torrijos, a small village which was his ancestral home. Many prominent people made the long trek from Toledo to honor him. His coffin was set up in front of the altar of the village church where the local priest said the mass. It seemed long to me, especially because of cold winds sweeping through the church.

Suddenly, I heard the distinctive, rich baritone voice singing the requiem, *sanctus, sanctus, sanctus*. Instantly I recognized it, the same resonance, the same stentorian depth balanced with sweet melodic timbre which moved me so deeply on *Yom Kippur*. It could only be the tall stranger. I strained my neck to look over the curtain separating the choir loft from the nave, but I could not see the singer. When the priest finally concluded the mass, I remained in my pew watching the choir members march down from the loft. The tall stranger was not among them. Standing at Alfonso's open grave, I caught a glimpse of him but he did not look at me. After the burial, as people came over to express their condolence to me, I kept looking at the tall stranger, hoping that he would not leave. I was grateful when he did come over to console me and before he had a chance to elude me, I asked to speak with him in private. When the crowd dispersed, he motioned me back into the church. We met in the choir loft.

He was a stern-looking man, young, in his mid-forties. He had a rugged looking, deeply- lined, clean shaven face with a square jaw and a mouthful of teeth. Standing close to him, I realized how exceptionally tall he was as he towered over me. We sat down on the wooden bench; I introduced myself and asked his name.

"My name is not important," he stated, making it clear he preferred to remain a stranger.

I began to tell him about myself, but he interrupted saying that he knew about me and about my past. When I asked if we had ever met before, he gave no inkling as to what his connections were with my family but I sensed that he did not know of my father's death.

"My father died," I said, "I learned of his death from the Ambassador of Naples."

"I am sorry," the tall stranger replied.

"I need a *minyan*, a group of ten men, so I can recite the *kaddish*," I said, "the memorial prayer for my father."

His reaction surprised me. Before I even finished, he violently shook his head, scoffing at me for even asking.

"To risk the lives of ten men, only to pray for the dead!" he said.

"I betrayed him in his life," I pleaded, "I want to redeem myself from that guilt."

"You not only betrayed him, you are continuing to betray yourself," the tall stranger said. "Reciting a prayer, even the *kaddish*, is no remedy for that."

I was hurt, annoyed, angry.

"Why do you reprimand me?" I asked. "Is it not enough that I can find no consolation."

"You seek consolation!" he said with scorn. "I discern in you no contrition."

"What does that mean?" I asked.

"It means regret, a resolve to make amends, an effort to undo the past," he replied.

"Of course, I regret my action. What amends can I make? My father is dead," I answered. "All I can do now is recite the prayer for him."

"Why?" he asked, challenging me, and again referring to the

kaddish as a meaningless prayer without amends.

I was so irritated by his response that I shouted, "I am still his son...despite my disobedience."

"Disobedience!" he called out. "That should be the least of your concerns. Disobedience is normal. The apple does not fall from the tree, but it falls nonetheless."

"What are you talking about," I asked. "And what does it have to do with me?"

"Disinheritance, not disobedience," he replied.

"My father did not disinherit me," I said.

"No, but you disinherited him," he said and, before I had a chance to explain my conversion, he continued, "You consider yourself Don Alfonso's successor. At his graveside, you were his sole survivor. Now you claim to be your father's heir. Which are you? You can not be both, not in Spain anyway. As successor to Don Alfonso, you have to spurn your father. The apple may fall from the tree, but it does not become a cucumber."

"I know, and that's why I searched for you," I said. "Since I learned of my father's death, I could find no consolation, no peace."

"If you want consolation, seek it not in mere recitation of a *kaddish*," he said "but in trying to perpetuate your father's heritage."

"How?" I protested.

I told him how many times I planned to get out of Spain, how the queen would not even see me, how the count's plans were foiled.

"I'm a victim of circumstances," I pleaded with him.

"You are a victim of your own dilemma," he replied almost savagely. "You still want to become a Don Alfonso, just like you did five years ago. Ambition blinded you then. It is blinding you now."

"I'm a victim of my own dilemma," I repeated to myself.

I knew that the tall stranger pinpointed my problem. His

identity no longer mattered. I was a victim of my own dilemma. I heard that before but never listened. My father said it to me more than once. Andres said it to me when he urged me to flee with the conversos, and even the count said it to me when I returned from my near-death fight with Don Luis. Yet I stayed on.

"To be an heir," the tall stranger said, "you must remember only two points. One, you must remain alive. Two, you cannot survive in Spain."

Praising me for rescuing the conversos, he reminded me that the method, using false limpiezas, was still being used throughout Spain.

I was stunned that he knew about the flight of the conversos and about our providing false limpiezas. As he refused to tell me his name, so did he refuse to tell me his source of information, but I suspected that he may have been part of the converso colony in Cordoba.

"Your problem is not getting out of Spain," he said. "Your problem is your resolve to leave. Do you really want to get out, to leave Toledo, to leave Spain?"

"You analyzed my problem correctly," I admitted. "I am a victim of my own dilemma. Now, can you give me a solution?"

"If you have to ask me for a solution," he said derisively, "it is quite evident you have yet to recognize your dilemma."

I was crushed and resigned myself to the fact that he was not going to help me with a *minyan* or with anything else. So I got up to leave trying to hide the hurt within me.

It was getting dark and from the choir loft window, I could still see the fresh mound of dirt over Alfonso's grave. The tall stranger led me to the grave. He put his hand on my shoulder as we stood there in silence.

"You can still be his successor," he said softly. "The art of healing has no geographic boundaries."

Out of nowhere, a small cluster of men appeared. They circled around me, their faces obscured by the darkness. The tall

Sacred Sword

stranger's voice chanted the familiar words:

> Yea, though I walk through the shadow of death
> I shall fear no evil for Thou art with me.
> Thy rod and thy staff, they comfort me,
> Thou hast prepared a table for me
> In the presence of mine enemies.

    Standing over Alfonso's grave, I joined the tall stranger in reciting the sacred prayer for my father: *Yisgadal veyiskadash shemey rabbah...*

11

When I returned from Don Alfonso's funeral, the city of Toledo was in a festive mood as noblemen from all over the realm gathered for the meeting of the Royal Council of Ministers. The King's Militia greeted each arriving nobleman with a tumultuous parade. The higher his rank, the more elaborate was the staged demonstration. When the Count of Trastamara, the highest ranking noble of the realm, arrived, King Ferdinand and his entire entourage met him at the city gates. After a ceremonial exchange of banners, the count and the king entered the city riding side by side on white stallions. They were followed by the count's gilded carriage which carried his family. Because of the huge crowd, I could not even get close to the procession to see Maria.

After the parade, Toledo's gentry and all the visiting noblemen gathered in the Alcazar Gardens where Ferdinand and Isabel welcomed the count. From afar, I caught a glimpse of Maria seated on the dais next to the *contessa*. As soon as the first stage of the welcoming ceremony was concluded, we managed to find a secluded niche in the palace, away from everyone, where Maria and I embraced, holding one another for a long time without saying a word.

She held on to me tightly, asking why I did not take her with me to Toledo if I knew I would be away for so many months. I hugged and kissed her, softly promising never to leave her again. I wanted to take her away where we could be alone, but she sadly told me that she would be occupied all day in other required ceremonies.

She promised to come to the dispensary the next day and we could spend the entire day together. I reluctantly let her go, watching as she made her way to be presented to Queen Isabel

Following these official welcoming ceremonies, the count's militia regaled the populace with a magnificent show. Hundreds of archers, lancers and horsemen demonstrated intricate battle maneuvers. Circus acts entertained the crowd in various parts of the city. Refreshments were distributed by the count's soldiers and merriment continued into the night. Thus, the Count of Trastamara converted the entire city into a carnival and won the hearts of its populace.

The next morning, I saw the count's carriage driving up to the dispensary. I ran out to greet Maria who had promised to come and was surprised to see the count sitting alone. He motioned me to join him. I noticed how much he had aged in the past six months. He was almost completely gray. His cherubic, once-boyish, face was pale with sagging jowls. He had lost so much weight that his skin hung loosely around his neck, making him look much older. Startled at his appearance, I asked him if he were ill. He assured me that, except for his concern for Maria's welfare, he was in good health.

"I wanted to get away so we could talk alone," the count said.

I suggested my office in the dispensary or the Casa Floridiana. The count preferred the Casa Floridiana because he knew Don Angelo from previous commercial dealings and had stayed at the Casa Floridiana previously. While driving, he described his confrontation with King Ferdinand.

"The king denied any knowledge of an assault on my power or of using Maria in any way," the count said. "He denied everything Manuel told us, calling him a bumbling old fool. But, to be on the safe side, I officially informed the king and queen that rumors of your marriage to Maria were just plain peasants' gossip and that I would never allow such a marriage."

"Yet, the queen will not permit me to leave Spain," I said.

When we reached the Casa Floridiana, Don Angelo greeted the count, repeating over and over how honored he was to extend his hospitality. The count, in turn, thanked Don Angelo, asking only to be left alone. The coachman was dispatched back to the palace to bring the countess. Our host led us to the library where he left us alone.

The count wanted to talk to me privately and that was why he had arranged for the countess to be with Maria, who would join us later. He asked me to make certain that no one was listening in. I walked around the corridors and surveyed the house and gardens, satisfied that we were not being spied on. Then I returned to the library.

"Manuel was right," the count began as we sat down in what used to be my father's retreat. "He was right on both counts. Ferdinand and the Inquisition were making onslaughts on Trastamara power."

He explained that he learned they were in league with each other, for their own interests, exactly as Manuel had described. As an example of their direct onslaughts, the count said he learned about a plot to arrest one of his knights, Ramon de Monterey, without informing the count. He had to send his militia to save his knight from the arresting agents. It was the Inquisition's first overture to assert its authority over the House of Trastamara.

The count had not yet determined if the Inquisition acted on its own or whether its officials were doing Ferdinand's bidding. The king denied any knowledge of the incident, but his assurance meant little to the count. What concerned him was that the Inquisition's assault on Ramon might presage future action against the House of Trastamara.

"We accomplished what we wanted by sending our militia," the count said. "We demonstrated that no Trastamara nobleman could be apprehended by the Inquisition without my approval. But, this defeat will make the Inquisition more subtle and probably more deadly."

"What about Maria?" I asked. "You said Manuel was right on both counts. He also warned you about Maria's safety."

"That is what I meant when I said that the Inquisition will probably be more deadly," the count replied.

He said that about three months earlier he met with Torquemada regarding the still-pending problem of placing Inquisition agents in the military units. During that conversation, Torquemada inquired about the countess' and the children's health. But he had the temerity to refer to Maria as the 'ward of the Inquisition'.

"He did so in a jesting manner, to be sure," the count said, "but Torquemada is not a jesting man."

I did not react with surprise or with shock, so the count questioned my apparent lack of concern.

"I am not unconcerned, sir, just not surprised," I said. "In this very room, not too many years ago, my father told me the Inquisition would rule both the populace and the Monarchy. He meant it would eclipse the Royal House as well as Spanish nobility."

He did not reply immediately. He paused to wipe his brow and then, throwing up his hands in the air, he said, "What makes matters worse, is that there is ample precedence for taking away children of conversos even when adopted by noble families. I investigated the implementation of the Edict of Faith and learned this practice is quite common."

I realized the torture he must be going through, and expressed my sympathy.

"Berto, Maria may be in very, very serious trouble at some time her life."

He said he finally disclosed this problem to the countess and they both agreed to arrange for Maria's safety before it was too late. He talked calmly about his getting on in years, about not having a responsible *hidalgo*, and about Enrique's youth. He emphasized that Maria had not been told about the crisis nor had she yet been told about her adoption. Neither he nor the countess had been sleeping well in the past three months because they were convinced that should the Inquisition decide to move against Maria, there was little he, or anyone, could do to spare her suffering.

We heard a creaking sound at the door and I immediately got up to investigate but found no one near our room. I suggested that it was only the wind.

"Maria simply has to get out of reach of the Inquisition," the count continued. "We have two alternatives. We could arrange for her marriage to Juan, Isabel's only son, a proposal Ferdinand made when I confronted him six months ago."

I could not hide my shock. But he explained that this had long been proposed as a way to strengthen the Monarchy. He and the countess ignored these proposals because Maria would still be under the threat of the Inquisition.

"There is only one viable solution," the count said. "Thank God, she loves you. She must leave Spain with you to Naples or anywhere we can visit you from time to time."

"This was my original plan when I went to Toledo following Manuel's disclosures," I said. "But, since the queen will not even grant me an audience, how can I take Maria out of Spain?"

"You will leave in secret with her," he replied. "And you are now the second person to know my plan."

"The second?" I asked, "Who is the first?"

"Don Carlos," the count responded.

"Don Carlos!" I replied, "I thought he was commanding the troops in Granada?"

The count explained that in the south there were several ports still under military occupation where no agents of the Inquisition were examining limpiezas. Don Carlos would personally escort Maria and me from La Caverna to the Port of Estopanna in Granada and provide passage for us to the Kingdom of Naples.

"The plan is all set for two weeks from next Monday," the count said.

"But why does she have to leave in secret?" I asked. "Why

can't she simply leave Spain as an ordinary passenger or even on a Trastamara ship?"

"We cannot chance it," the count said. "Since my confrontation with Ferdinand, the Inquisition undoubtedly knows I am aware of its plan for Maria. It can still threaten to expose Maria to bring me to my knees. And, I would probably do their bidding if only to save Maria. With Don Carlos' help, there will be no danger of exposure."

I agreed to his plan, promising that as soon as Maria and I were settled, we would eagerly await his visits.

He breathed easier, smiled and said, "As long as you do not board a ship for the colonies, you can be sure we'll be there only days after you arrive."

"You know that I love Maria," I said. "I will care for her as you have done all these years."

"Because of that love," the count repeated, "both the countess and I feel comfortable sending Maria with you."

We heard the countess arrive and we went out to greet her at the door. She embraced me and repeatedly cried out, "Berto, Berto, I love you so."

In the library, she told me that she knew about the Don Carlos plan and that she, too, was relieved to know that Maria would be in my care.

She made peace with the thought of Maria's leaving because she knew that sooner or later Maria would be married to some nobleman and would leave Cordoba or even Spain.

"Berto," she asked, "are you ready to accept the responsibility to care for our daughter?"

"Responsibility?" I replied, "That sounds as though she is a burden. I love her so, I would lay down my life for her."

The countess hugged me and said, "God sent you to protect our daughter."

"Now, where is Maria?" I said.

"Wait, Berto," the countess said, "under the circumstances,

it would be best if Maria and you did not see each other in Toledo, especially since we told Ferdinand that the marriage would not take place and that you are not seeing each other."

I had little choice.

"Remember," the count said, getting up to leave, "my plan will succeed only if it is carried out in total secrecy."

We parted with sadness but with hope.

Secrecy was now my paramount concern. I had to take special precautions not to arouse anyone's suspicion by a sudden departure. During the next two weeks, I purposely kept myself inordinately occupied, seeing hundreds of patients. It became common knowledge that since Alfonso's death, I maintained a heavy schedule, going to bed late every night and getting up at dawn every morning. I was gratified that even my apprentices noticed my busy schedule. Finally, it was they who suggested I take a rest.

At the end of the second week, I announced I would leave for a week's vacation in Andalusia. I made sure to give everyone the impression that I would return by scheduling several chores upon my return. Despite my new status, I abided by the Inquisition's rules which required me to report my plans to travel outside the city. The agent at the Hermandad instructed me that upon reaching Cordoba, I was to report to Diaz who had been officially installed as the chief investigator of the Inquisition.

The count had instructed me to meet Maria at La Caverna Monday afternoon. The following morning, Don Carlos would meet us at La Caverna to escort us to the port in Granada. I arrived in Cordoba on Sunday morning and immediately reported to Diaz who was more hostile to me than ever.

I then went about the city, visiting the many places which figured so prominently during my three-year sojourn in Cordoba. I knew that the Inquisition would track every movement I made, so I was careful to tell everyone I visited that I would be soon return to Toledo. For example, I paid to lease a horse at the stable yards, telling its owner that I would return with the horse at the end of the week. Similarly, when I visited Jimenez he volunteered to make peace between me and his son. I welcomed the suggestion, saying we would do so when I returned from my vacation.

I passed by the San Miguel Chapel but did not go in because I did not wish to see Father Pedro.

I paid my respects to Andres' family and before leaving, I told them, also, that I would soon return to Cordoba. I then rode out to the San Sebastian Monastery, visiting the room where the lovable Father Hernandez and I chatted that critical day prior to his dismissal. I had the urge to meet Nicolas to apologize for our deception. Unfortunately, he was no longer at the monastery.

On the way back, I visited the wharf at the port the Guadalquivir River where I searched for Andres' yellow-striped boat. At first I did not see her because she was partially hidden in the tall reeds in an inlet along the river. I took off my shoes, waded into the water and slid into the boat where I sat until the sun began to set.

That night, I slept in the room Andres and I had shared in the Casa Lombardia. It was the first time I had slept in it since his death. I was glad nothing there had changed. I recalled so much of our life together, especially his constant displeasure with me for my decision to break off with Maria. I knew he would be pleased with the turn of events, that Maria and I would leave Spain together. I fell asleep asking him to watch over us.

In the morning, when I awoke, I caught sight of an old bundle tucked in the rafters above my head. I brought it down and found Don Carlos' green uniform which Teresa had given me to wear the first time I had been at the castle. I took the package with me to La Caverna so that I could entertain Don Carlos with stories of that night.

I started out early Monday morning, arriving at La Caverna

Sacred Sword

just before the noon day meal. When I rode my horse to the stable, this time slowing down at the steep incline, it was obvious that the stableboy, Teresa's son Emilio, did not expect me. He was surprised to see me. I was also surprised that there were two stableboys working at La Caverna. The other one, whose face was familiar, left the moment I got off the horse. Emilio welcomed me, saying he had not been told to expect me.

I walked up the trellised path to the lodge, where Maria sat with Enrique and Teresa. When she saw me coming, she ran down the few steps and flung herself in my arms.

"You came just in time to say good-bye to Teresa and Enrique. They're returning to the castle right now," Maria said holding on to Teresa and Enrique.

Teresa embraced Maria, stroking her hair, kissing her as a mother would. They both wept. Teresa handed me a heavy basket of food, pulled me down toward her, and kissed me on both cheeks. Then, as though pushing me away she said, "Maria could have had the pick of the crop and look what she settles for."

However, when Teresa boarded the carriage, she was not laughing anymore. She poked her head out and sincerely thanked me for taking care of her Maria. She then called Enrique to get into the carriage.

Maria cuddled Enrique who was crying bitterly on her shoulder, paying no attention to Teresa's urgent calls. I put my hand on his arm and he swerved around, clinging to me, trying to stop his weeping. I assured him that, before long, we would all be together again.

When the carriage pulled away from the lodge, Maria and I went to the stable to dismiss the stableboys because I wanted no one around when Don Carlos came by. As Teresa's son was leaving, I asked about the other stable boy whom I saw when I rode in to La Caverna.

"He left earlier," Emilio replied. "He said he was ordered to ride ahead of the count's carriage to stand by in case of trouble."

Maria and I were now alone. We walked around the beautiful grounds of La Caverna. Maria wistfully said how wonderful it would be if we could remain together in these peaceful surroundings. Sitting at the edge of the lake, our bare feet dangling in the cool water, she told to me how her parents related to her the details of her adoption and how her father explained the danger she would face in the future if the Inquisition ever wanted to use her in its struggle for power. Maria wept when she told me how much lamenting and crying there was in the castle during the past week.

"But, when it came time to say good-bye," Maria said, "you should have seen me! To spare my parents, I acted as though I was leaving for a little pleasure cruise and would soon be back."

We dried our feet and walked back to the lodge. She looked about and asked whether there would ever be any chance for us to return to Spain.

"Leaving this way," she said, "I feel as though we are being exiled."

I could only hold out the dreadful hope that, at some time in the future, the Inquisition would become so powerful it would no longer need to use her as a tool to control the Trastamaras. Neither of us could sleep that night so we sat up talking about our future, reminiscing about our past.

"Do you think I will ever discover my real parents?" Maria asked sitting on the darkened porch of the lodge.

"This you will never know," I said.

"Why not?" she asked.

"When you were taken from them," I said, hesitating in my reply, "they were probably burnt to death in an auto-da-fe."

Maria gasped, bit her lips, but said nothing.

According to the count's detailed plans, we were to meet Don Carlos at dawn. He would arrive at La Caverna in a carriage, unaccompanied by military escort, with only a coachman perched atop the carriage. The coachman would know to stop at the front gate of La Caverna where we were to enter the enclosed coach and drive with Don Carlos directly to Esteponna, the military port of Granada. A military escort stationed at the first fork in the road beyond La Caverna would accompany the coach to the port.

Maria and I were waiting by the main gate when the first streaks of dawn were beginning to break through the dark skies. In the stillness of the night, we heard from a distance the fast gait of horses. We then heard them as they slowed down, making the precarious, slow descent to the turn into La Caverna's road. Moments later, we could barely make out the faint outline of the carriage as it stopped in front of us.

I opened its door for Maria, helping her to get in. She gasped with a stifled cry and fell back into my arms, flailing and pointing to the slumped body inside the carriage. I quickly jumped up and, to my horror, saw the body of Don Carlos, a dagger still in his back. I removed the dagger from his lifeless body. With the murder weapon still in my hand, I stepped down and signalled the coachman to drive on without us.

I led Maria back to the lodge. We quickly analyzed every detail of the situation. Whoever did the killing must have mounted the rear of the Don Carlos' carriage as the horses slowed on the steep hill just before reaching the entrance to La Caverna.

"Who knew that you were coming here?" Maria asked.

"No one," I said. "I told everybody that I was going to Cordoba on vacation."

"Where were you when my father told you about Don Carlos," she asked."

I told her how her father unfolded his plan in the Casa Floridiana and how he was concerned about being spied on. It may have been Don Angelo, I ventured a guess. He had once told me that he had ties in Cordoba. She then recalled all the people in the castle who knew of her coming to La Caverna.

"We're wasting precious time," I said, "trying to solve that problem. The murderer is still in the area because the stabbing was done only moments ago and we heard no horse's hoofs following the stabbing."

We went to the stable again to make certain that Teresa's son had actually left. He was gone.

"Who is the new stable boy?" I asked, remembering his surprised look and his abrupt departure when I entered La Caverna.

Maria said she did not know him, adding she had never met him before.

"Did anyone ride ahead of you when you came down in the carriage from the castle?" I asked.

"No, why?" she asked.

"It's strange that the count would have someone accompany the carriage only on its return trip," I said, telling her that Emilio told me the new stableboy was ordered to ride ahead of the carriage as it returned to the castle.

Suddenly, I felt my heart pounding as I recalled the face of the new stable boy: Reinaldo, Manuel's servant. I last saw him about a year earlier, during Manuel's amputation. He was the one who had asked what to do with the severed leg after the surgery. His presence in La Caverna was proof that the Inquisition was involved in the killing of Don Carlos.

But, at that moment, I was not interested in solving the mystery of the Inquisition. My only concern was finding Reinaldo before he could return to Cordoba to report on our presence. I took Maria back to the lodge, ordering her to lock herself in. I started out for the stable, taking with me the dagger I removed from Don Carlos' back.

As I walked out of the lodge, I saw Reinaldo coming up the trellised path with a sword in hand. He was tall, stripped to the waist, a powerful muscular body. I quickly climbed up the leafy trellises to avoid a direct assault from him. I was certain he did not see me, because he did not look up but kept walking toward the door.

When I saw him directly below me, I jumped, landing on his head with my heavy boots. He was momentarily dazed and his sword flew out of his hand. I ran for the sword, grabbed it, and charged at him with it. He recovered in time to throw a heavy log at me, knocking the sword out of my hand, and sending it flying into bushes. When he turned to search for the sword, I caught up to him, ready to plunge my dagger into his ribs. Suddenly, he turned, swinging his fist, catching me sharply on my neck. I fell back, still holding the dagger in my right hand. He kept searching for the sword but could not find it. I ran to the stable and climbed up on its sloping roof, waiting for him to get close enough for me to jump on him again. It was still dark and I strained to look out for him but I could not see him clearly.

All of a sudden, I felt myself lassoed around my neck. Reinaldo had snapped leather reins at me from below, forcing me to drop the dagger and pulling me down from the roof. Luckily, I was able to free my neck while falling and I came down crashing on top of him, strangling him with the reins. When his body seemed lifeless, I loosened my grip. That was my mistake because he suddenly jerked out of my grasp and ran away.

As he was running, I heard him coughing incessantly and trying to catch his breath. I lunged at his feet from behind and sent him sprawling on his face at the edge of the lake. With the water splashing on his face, he revived and succeeded in squirming out of my grasp. He savagely pounced on me and, lifting me over his head, he thrust me, face down in the water. I felt his heavy body crashing down on mine, pinning me in the shallow water. I could neither move nor breathe.

Just as I was beginning to lose consciousness, I felt Reinaldo's huge body slip off and I was free to breathe again. When I lifted my head out of the water, I saw Maria, a bloody axe in her hands, standing astride over Reinaldo's lifeless body.

"The last thing my father said to me was, 'As Alberto cares for you, you must watch over him'," Maria said handing me the axe, her hands shaking and her body quivering.

I held her tightly to calm her and led her back to the lodge. We sat down, trying to plan our next moves. I told she should return to the castle where the count could protect her.

Maria refused, bluntly stating, "We will both survive or we will perish together."

"You have a chance for life," I said, "I simply can't accept the responsibility of taking that away from you."

"Berto," Maria said, speaking calmly, showing no trace of hysteria, "with me, it's no longer a matter of fighting the Inquisition or of preserving the power of the Trastamaras. I love you. That's all. If you live through this crisis, I have a right to survive with you. If you die, I don't want to live."

I took her into my arms and, holding her close to me, I whispered, "We'll survive together."

"What are we going to do now?" Maria asked.

"We could both return to the castle," I said. "We'll be safe there."

"Don't deceive me," she said, suspecting my ruse to bring her back to the castle. "We can never be safe there. Not after what my father told me of the danger that will face me throughout my life."

"Then, there is only one thing to do: escape" I said, telling her about the conversos of Cordoba. "We will make our way out of Spain just like they did. We will have to get to Cadiz, and somehow get on one of the ships sailing to the colonies."

"The colonies?" she gasped, "why the colonies?"

"We have no other choice," I said, "because, under the new laws of the Inquisition, Spain has the right to request most countries in Europe to return any fleeing converso. Our goal, right now, is Cadiz."

"But my father said that the Kingdom of Naples was granting us rights of residence," Maria said.

"If the spies knew about Don Carlos' plans, they also knew about Naples," I said. "Going on to Naples now would be entering a trap."

"And how do we get to Cadiz?" Maria asked.

"On faith and on fraud," I replied. "From now on, we must think as our pursuers think and do the opposite. The Inquisition is sure that we will not return to Cordoba. That is exactly where we will begin our escape."

Maria picked up the food basket Teresa had prepared for us. She reached under the bundle of *bouretas* and drew out a leather sack full of gold coins which the count had given her to help us get settled in Naples.

"This ought to help us get to Cadiz," Maria said handing me the sack.

"Money is always useful," I replied, putting the heavy sack in my bundle where I kept Don Carlo's uniform. "But our problem is not financial. It is fanaticism and, unfortunately, fanatics cannot be bought off."

At the stable, we saddled one of the horses and together with my hired horse we rode further south. I left my horse in an enclosed pasture.

"They will think that we headed towards Granada. It will give us an extra day," I explained.

We returned to Cordoba riding one horse through the forest where we managed to remain hidden most of the day. We waited for night to fall and then headed for the inlet on the Guadalquivir where I had earlier spotted Andres' boat. Working together, we succeeded in freeing the boat from the reeds. I put the food basket and gold coins in the boat, helped Maria get in, and began to row. There were no guards, no troops, no agents to question us. But when I steered the boat into the main channel, I saw a solitary figure in a military uniform approaching us. I could have easily rowed away from him and lost him in the darkness, but I thought that he would become suspicious and might then set off an alarm. I sat in the boat waiting for the soldier to approach. It was Rodriguez, Diaz's brother. He greeted us, then asked what we were doing in Andres' boat. "Rodriguez," I said, "when Don Luis escaped from you, I kept my mouth shut for you. Promise me that, whatever happens, you'll keep your mouth shut for me."

He looked at me and abruptly turned around and left.

We took the first step of our escape from Spain.

Maria sat in the stern of the boat while I rowed away from Cordoba. She was uneasy, scanning the river banks from side to side, or peering over my head watching for militiamen. She was tense and frightened. To reassure her, I told her that when I originally planned my escape, I learned every tributary and every inlet along the route. I could bring her safely to Cadiz. I also told her of my friendship with Orlando Franco and how easily we got the conversos out of Spain with false limpiezas.

"By the time they discover our disappearance," I said, "we'll be gone."

"What about Rodriguez?" she asked, paying no attention to my attempts to calm her. "How do you know he won't report us?"

"First, he owes it to me," I replied. "Second, he's a captain in your father's militia and, most important, he was Andres' friend."

She crossed over to my side of the boat and rested her head on my shoulder. Her tears dampened my face.

"I'm so afraid," she said.

She would have been more afraid if I told her the truth. Since Don Carlos was to take us out of Spain, I had not prepared limpiezas. I had no idea how we could board any ship without them, even with Orlando Franco's help.

I rowed hard all night and most of the following day. We passed an encampment of soldiers along the river bank but they took no interest in us or the boat. I then knew Reinaldo's death had not yet been discovered. For the time being, we were safe.

The morning of the second day, we neared the small town of

Posadas where I had once solved a food poisoning epidemic. I decided to seek assistance from the innkeeper, Pablo, with whom I stayed at the time. I guided the boat along a narrow tributary and hid it under a pile of reeds and brush we gathered on the river bank.

In the pre-dawn haze, we ran across the fields to a nearby storage platform farmers used by to stack winter hay. The square, open area had no roof. Rope, tied to several sturdy posts on each corner, contained the hay. When we climbed to the top, the hay sank under our weight, providing us with a natural hiding place. Maria flattened out some of the hay around us, playfully invited me to her "dining room", and asked me to open the latch of our food basket. I fumbled with it, unable to lift its cover. My hands were too swollen from rowing. Maria noticed my bruises and, taking my hands into hers, she kissed and blew on them to soothe the blisters.

"Feel better?" she asked.

"Completely healed," I said, "no physician could have done as well."

We ate some of Teresa's *bouretas* and before the sun rose, we were fast asleep in each other's arms. We were awakened by a terrifying clash of thunder and a sudden driving rain storm. Climbing down from our perch, I found the remains of a barn door and, with Maria's help, placed it over the upright posts securing it to the posts with the ropes to make a roof.

Maria was drenched and began to shiver. I took out the green uniform I carried all the way from Cordoba and covered her with it but it offered little protection. Given no choice, I hurried Maria out of the hay storage, through the open fields to a nearby barn.

"I'm going to Posadas to get you some clothes," I said leaving her in a sheltered, dark corner of the barn.

"In this rain!" she shouted, "Are you crazy?"

"Only in this rain can I move about safely," I said. "Who would go out in such a storm?"

I was right. No one was in the streets. I circled the backs of the houses, staying out of sight, and stealthily made my way to Pablo's Inn. I slipped through an open window into the innkeeper's room where I found a woolen sweater and a long-sleeved dress. Taking a blanket from the bed and food from the cabinet, I was about to race back to the barn.

"Pablo!" I heard a woman's voice call out, "The soldiers are back. It's wartime again."

"It's not a war," the innkeeper responded, "They're from the royal militia searching for Alberto di Cadiz."

"Alberto? The physician?" she asked.

"He's no physician today," Pablo said, "he's an escaped killer. He's abducted the count's daughter."

Another voice called out, "We've got a thousand soldiers along the river looking for him and his yellow-striped boat."

I rushed back to the barn where I dropped off the bundle I had stolen from the inn. Then I darted to the river and found our boat totally exposed. The wind had blown away all the concealing reeds and branches. I worked feverishly to tip the boat over until she sank in the shallow but murky water. I then covered the spot with a pile of rubble from river bank and returned to the barn. Maria was crouched in her corner, quivering and weeping hysterically

"Don't ever leave me," Maria mumbled through her tears holding on tightly to me, "I was frightened to death."

I said quietly, "You must learn to live with fear. Until we get out of Spain, fear will be our constant companion. Remember this: in our case, fear is not such bad company. It will help us to survive by keeping us alert to the constant danger."

I candidly told her the danger we now faced: a thousand militiamen were now searching for us. I said that knowing the danger, we would not do anything to expose ourselves. She quieted down and explained that she had never had to face any moment of danger in her life.

I reassured her, "When the troops don't find us in Posadas,

they will leave the area. Then, we can continue to Seville or even to Cadiz."

She whispered a silent prayer, crossed herself, and kissed the tips of her fingers. She calmed down, saying she would try to be courageous.

The wind died, but the rains continued. I helped her spread the blanket, making our corner in the darkened barn more comfortable. I removed my wet shirt, noticing that she had difficulty changing her wet dress to the one I brought from the Inn. I helped her. Lying there together listening to the raindrops, we knew the intimacy of love.

When the rain stopped, we returned to the hay storage where we remained, waiting for the soldiers to leave the area. Every day we thought would be our last. Through the holes I poked in the hay, we could see them searching both sides of the river. They passed so close to us we could clearly hear their conversations, not only the orders shouted by their commanders. The fact that they passed us and did not bother to search our hideout made us feel secure. We also saw them standing by the river, at the very spot where I camouflaged the boat. They missed it completely. We felt safe but annoyed at the soldiers' continued presence. An entire week passed but the soldiers continued patrolling the area and each day they grew in number.

Our provisions were running low, so we began rationing our food. If Teresa's *bouretas* were enticing before, they became all the more valuable now. We ate most sparingly.

The sun came out but, to our utter disappointment, the soldiers remained.

I told Maria that until we were out of Spain, we would have to live a life of contrast: when everyone was awake we would sleep and when they slept we would be awake. At midnight when the soldiers were in their camps, Maria and I stealthily moved out of our hay shelter, romping through the fields to keep active. The clear night skies and the bright stars gave us a sense of well being that was not only deceptive but dangerous. I whispered to Maria that the enchantment we felt roaming the fields should not make us forget the peril facing us. Discovery by the soldiers would be fatal. At first, Maria was happy to run around in the open field rather than be shut in the shelter. However, when she tired, she wanted to return to the hay stack to sleep. I would not let her, explaining that she must keep awake at night because if the soldiers left during the day, we might have to start on our way to Cadiz the following night. I reminded her again that we could travel only at night, when everyone else slept. That would be our new "life of contrast".

Defiantly, she climbed up the hay storage murmuring that she had endured enough 'contrast' to last her a lifetime.

"I lost so much so fast," she said with deep resentment.

I had to do something to keep her awake, so I decided to badger her with questions.

"What do you mean you 'lost so much, so fast'?" I asked.

At first, she said she did not want to talk about it, turning to go to sleep. But then she turned back to face me saying that she must tell me all that happened. She described in meticulous detail how her father and mother took her aside, away from Enrique, to tell her that she was an adopted daughter.

"How did you feel?" I asked, "I mean, how did you react when they told you about your adoption?"

"I burst out crying," Maria replied.

"I understand," I said.

"You don't understand," she replied with a sigh. "You can't understand. No one can understand."

"Of course, I understand how you felt," I said. "After all, you suddenly lost your parents."

"I not only lost my parents," she said haltingly, "I lost everything; so much so quickly."

"Certainly," I repeated, "I understand the shock."

"Berto," she said speaking slowly, "it wasn't only shock."

"Anyone losing, as you said, 'so much so quickly' would feel the same."

"No, No," she cried out.

"What was it then?" I asked.

"I felt ashamed," Maria said her voice quivering.

"Ashamed?" I asked, "Ashamed of what?"

She hesitated a moment and then she whispered, "Ashamed of having Jewish parents, of being a Jew."

I said nothing. I did not know what to say.

"You see, Berto," she said reaching for my hand, "I told you that you don't understand how I felt. Let me explain. All my life, I grew up loving my father and mother. But, don't forget that I was brought up Catholic. I believed with all my heart that Jesus was my Savior and that the Jews crucified Him. Suddenly my father tells me that he is not my father and that I am the daughter of Jews. All at once, I lose a father and my Jesus, all because I am a Jew."

I was dumbfounded. Again I did not respond. I knew she wanted me to reply, to say something consoling, but I did not know what to say.

"You still don't understand why I felt ashamed?" she asked. "Then, listen. Ever since I can remember, the word 'Jew' was not a person. It was a bad word...everything evil. So, when my father told me about my converso parents, I suddenly had become that bad word. I couldn't even mouth it, 'Jewish'."

"You're right," I replied, "I can't understand."

"But don't misunderstand, Berto," she said, "I loved you then, when my father told me, and I love even more now. I don't want to hurt you. But it's better that we talk about this...this shame. I'm still not rid of it. I must make you understand."

I drew her close to me. I kissed her hands and, holding them close to my face, I said softly, "You have my love. All of it. But, what you're telling me now is painful and shocking. I am as shocked now as you were then."

"'I am as shocked now as you were then'," she repeated and

quietly said, "All the more reason why I must fully express my feelings."

I told her if talking about it would be painful, she did not have to tell everything. She ridiculed me, insisting on describing her feelings.

"You see, I was a good little Catholic girl. I always had Jesus in front of me. Not only in church but at home, in school, everywhere. Physically, there He was: Jesus on the Cross. There wasn't a day in my life when I didn't look at his bleeding scars, at the nails piercing his hands, at his ghastly dying face. I would be filled with pity for the dying Jesus. And, at the same time, I would feel scorn, hate, for the Jews who killed him."

"That's what being a Jew meant to you?" I asked.

"Do you really want to know?" she said. "When I was a child, four or five years old, if I did something wrong, didn't want to go to church, or told a little lie, or didn't obey my parents, I would be reprimanded by Teresa or by my mother, 'Do you want to be a Jew!' To be a Jew was worse than being bad."

I stared at her, almost in disbelief.

"You're shocked, I know. But, my father understood the shame I felt," she said stroking my face, "because, right after telling me of my adoption, he told me that since my conversion, I no longer had the stain of Jewish blood."

After thinking about it, I told her I was beginning to understand her feelings. Then, I tried to make her feel better, saying that I did not blame her for feeling shame.

"Don't patronize me," she said angrily. "I just want to talk about my feelings and I'm not interested in being exonerated."

I told her I really began to understand her and her need to share with me her true feelings. She was quiet for a long time. I did not want to intrude on her thoughts.

"That day, I asked my father who my real parents were," she spoke up, reaching again for my hand, "and he said he didn't know. But, because he understood my feelings, he kept telling me that even though my natural parents were Jewish, that did not make them evil. As an example, he spoke respectfully about your father and also mentioned other Spanish Jews who were famous statesmen, scientists, poets, and philosophers."

"One day, I will tell you about some of them," I said.

"I guess it would be interesting," she replied, "but right now, all I want is for you to understand my feelings, because when you do, you'll be able to help me."

We talked through the night, finally falling asleep in each other's arms, more in love than ever before.

The soldiers roamed the area several more days. We ran out of food. We were starving. We were thirsty; our lips were beginning to blister. I felt I had no choice but to try to enter the village again to take food. It was very dangerous, too dangerous, because the troops had recently set up their camp in the field not far from us.

"It's my turn," Maria said one evening when we were lying quietly, too weak to talk.

"It's your turn for what?" I asked.

"To get food," she replied.

"From where?" I asked.

"From the soldiers," she replied.

"We'll wait another day," I said, "they're bound to leave."

"We can't last another day," she replied. "By tomorrow, we'll be dead." I forbade her.

Paying no attention to my protest, she primped herself, combing her hair and straightening her dress, she began to climb down the hay stack. "What are you going to do?" I asked.

"No one knows me," she said. "No one's ever seen me before. I'll find some way to get food. Just tell me, am I pretty enough to entertain the soldiers."

I resented the word 'entertain' but before I could reply, she climbed down the hayloft and scampered away toward the soldiers' encampment.

Maria walked in unexpectedly to the camp, out of the shadows, before a group of soldiers eating their meal.

She began singing and dancing.

From afar, I could hear their gleeful shouting and the applause that greeted each of her songs. They responded, chanting the choruses with her and clapping their hands rhythmically to her beat.

Then, all was quiet; no more clapping and no more shouting.

I anxiously waited for her to return. She didn't. I began to worry, blaming myself for letting her expose herself to debased troops. As time dragged by, I imagined all sorts of debauchery taking place against my innocent Maria. My safety was no longer important to me and I climbed down from the hay stack to search for her.

Suddenly, out of the darkness, I heard the swish of her dress and I grasped her, helping her mount the hay stack. She triumphantly held out a basket full of food: bread and meat and wine and fruit.

When I hesitated to take any food from the basket, she said, "Silly, I only sang and danced for them."

She explained that after her singing, they filled her basket with food. They also asked her to spend the night with them, but she said that she was to visit other encampments. Only after she promised them that she would return, did they let her go. But, their captain followed her through the field as she headed back to our hiding place. She had to go through the village where she finally eluded him and made her way back undetected.

Maria's success filled her with a sense of accomplishment. She proudly announced that she had now conquered fear and could face anything that would be required during our escape from Spain. We ate our meal with relish.

Then, we talked all through the night about our past experiences and about our future hopes. Each word, every thought, drew us closer into a bond of love.

Much to our delight, the troops left the next day. That night, we carried our light pack of clothing and food to our boat. I rowed throughout the night, getting closer to Seville. For the next six nights, I rowed all night. With the coming of each dawn, I sank the boat and found a safe hiding spot, a cave, a deserted shack, or a barn where we remained, sleeping most of the day...a life of contrast.

After six days on the river, we reached the outskirts of Seville. We found an excellent hideout; a natural cave with many subterranean chambers, providing exceptional protection. We slept well all day. At dusk, I awakened Maria and asked her to help disguise me so that I could go to the city. She scraped some white clay off the walls of the cave and dabbed it on my two-week-old beard and on my hair. She tied a bundle of rags between my shoulders to make me look like a hunchback. As a hunchback, she explained, I would face the ground, thus exposing only part of my face. My hair and beard looked gray, almost white, and my crouched walk made me look like a disfigured old man. I left Maria in the cave, reminding her not to venture out. I assured her that with Orlando Franco's help we would soon board a ship to take us out of Spain, even without the limpiezas.

With the near-perfect disguise, I had no difficulty making my way to Orlando Franco's inn. Although the pile of rags slipped out of place, the disguise was so effective that people were offering me help as I hobbled across the crowded streets. I felt safe and secure.

It had been a year since I last visited Orlando Franco. Yet, when he saw me in my disguise outside his inn, he immediately recognized me and motioned to follow him. I trailed after him to the side of the building where he quickly climbed to the roof, entering a garret through the eaves. I followed him into the tiny semi-darkened room which had only slits for windows.

"When the Inquisition officials linked your name to the death of Manuel's servant and launched this search for you," Orlando Franco whispered, "I knew that sooner or later, you would be coming to me. I looked out for you every single day for the past two weeks."

When I asked what contact he had with the Inquisition, he tersely replied there was little he did not know about the Inquisition.

But he refused to say any more.

"Then, can you tell me why Reinaldo killed Don Carlos?" I asked.

He wiped the perspiration off his face with his red bandanna and, resting his head against the rafters, he told me an almost incredible story about Don Carlos and the Inquisition.

"Don Carlos was considered a heretic. The process of declaring him a heretic had been put in motion long before his murder. At the time, he was considered an opponent of the Holy Inquisition because he allowed, and was still allowing, thousands of Moriscos to leave Granada.

Torquemada warned him that his actions contravened the Inquisition's orders because the Moriscos were considered to be Catholics. Don Carlos disregarded the warnings and further ignored the Suprema by prohibiting Inquisition agents from entering military installations."

I told Orlando Franco that I was present when Torquemada threatened Don Carlos with an investigation and accused him of heresy.

"The officials of the Inquisition considered Don Carlos a heretic from the first day he took command of the Spanish Army because he blocked the entry of their agents into the army,"

Orlando Franco said. "But, he was a national hero. They could not bring him to trial."

"He became a legendary figure," I interjected, "like the fabled El Cid."

"The Inquisition could live with the legend of Don Carlos de Santa Fe, but not with the living Don Carlos," Orlando Franco quipped and then continued, "He was tried in absentia on charges of heresy at a secret session of the Holy Tribunal and sentenced to die. However, because the secular authorities could not carry out the death sentence—as they would in all other cases—Father Lopez, Manuel's successor, was charged with that responsibility. When Lopez learned that the general was to escort Maria to Estaponna, he assigned Reinaldo to impose the court's death penalty. Lopez correctly reasoned that an investigation of Don Carlos' death would bring to light Maria's attempt to escape and would tarnish the prestige of the Trastamara nobility. This would make the count amenable to negotiations with the Inquisition."

"How did they learn about the count's plan for Maria?" I asked.

"There's very little the Inquisition does not know," he cryptically replied. "If I would fault the wise Juan de Trastamara with anything, it is his utter disregard for the Inquisition's power."

I begged Orlando Franco to tell me how he managed to know so much about the Inquisition. I did not disclose to him that I knew about his former work in the Betazar dungeons. I simply wanted to know how he was privy to all the secret machinations of the Inquisition. He sternly ordered me never to question him about that. He would only tell me as much as I had to know for my own security.

"The murder of Carlos is linked to both you and Maria," he said. "Reinaldo was told to get a job as an extra stable hand in La Caverna, another example of the count's lack of caution. Reinaldo was to wait for the general's carriage at the top of the hill where the road dips sharply. There, Reinaldo would carry out the court's sentence. He was to remain in the lodge to make certain no alternate plans for Maria's escape were in effect. He was ordered to return only after he learned what Maria and you would do after the murder."

Orlando Franco related that the *Cortes* of Cordoba launched an immediate investigation centering around La Caverna where Reinaldo's body was discovered. Don Carlos body was found in the carriage only when it reached the port of Estaponna. The stable boy, Teresa's son, testified that Maria and I were in the lodge on the night of the murder and that we told him to leave the lodge. But, his testimony that Reinaldo had left La Caverna to escort the count's carriage back to the castle was suppressed.

Thus, I became the prime suspect both for the murders and for the abduction of the count's daughter. When my horse was found straying in the region of Granada, a search was organized to comb the entire area south of La Caverna.

The news of the Don Carlos' death spread like fire among the soldiers in their camps, the peasants in the farms, the nobility in their mansions, and the common folk in every town and hamlet of Spain. All were caught up in a frenzy to find the count's daughter and to apprehend me, according to Orlando Franco.

"Diaz, who was earlier named assistant to Father Lopez, argued that the Inquisition should handle the investigation itself, rather than rely on the *cortes*," Orlando Franco said. "Father Lopez rejected Diaz's suggestion, lest Reinaldos' identity be uncovered, thereby implicating the Inquisition. Father Lopez assured Diaz that when you are captured, harboring Maria, the count's complicity will come to light and the Inquisition will thereby benefit from the entire episode. Diaz taunted Father Lopez that you would never be captured.

"Lopez was right in assuming that you would soon be captured, because, when the Royal Militia found that Andres' boat was missing, hundreds of soldiers were stationed on both sides of the river. In addition, hundreds of Inquisition agents were assigned to all Spanish ports to guard against your escape."

I told Orlando Franco that Maria was with me and I described how we managed to avoid capture. I asked him to help us get passage to the colonies.

"I can't," Orlando Franco said bluntly.

I was stunned and began pleading with him.

"I am now under constant surveillance by the Inquisition," he said. "I've been charged with heretical deeds and have been reinstated with a severe warning. Quite candidly, I'm playing with fire just by talking to you."

He warned me to get out of Seville because the city was teeming with hundreds of soldiers and agents searching for me and his inn was the focus of the search. He flatly stated that the Inquisition agents knew of the conversos' escape route and therefore they undoubtedly expect me to turn to him for help.

"Seville," he said, "is like a city under siege and my inn is now closed. It's become Lopez's headquarters."

Getting up from the floor of the garret, Orlando Franco cautiously pushed aside a floor board, allowing me to see people at work in the tavern below. Replacing the board, Orlando said they were Lopez's staff.

"Yesterday, while serving their meal," Orlando Franco said, "I noticed they had an enlarged map of the area indicating where troops are stationed. The Las Marismas swamps were circled in red. I heard Lopez say with confidence that if you tried to get to Cadiz, you would be captured in the swamps."

He explained that no one except an experienced sailor could navigate the Las Marismas. I asked Orlando Franco what I could do to get out of Spain. He said he could not advise me, adding that if he faced my problem, he would not know how to proceed.

"The only thing I can do for you," he said, "is give you some food and let you stay in this garret until you find a way out of Seville."

When he left the garret, I was heartsick. To go back to Maria empty-handed would be catastrophic and I could not sit there in the garret doing nothing. I decided to go to the docks in my disguise to learn about the sailing procedures for outgoing vessels.

I actually passed Father Lopez at the port but, because of my disguise, he did not recognize me. He had probably come to the docks for the same reason I did: to determine how well patrolled they were and to see how well the ships were guarded. He was undoubtedly satisfied; I was chagrined. The port was like a prison. No one could move about anywhere without a military escort.

Without the help of Orlando Franco, without the limpiezas, and with the strict surveillance at the port, Maria and I would have no chance of boarding a ship out of Seville. And, navigating through the Las Marismas was out of the question.

Utterly disappointed, I made my way back to the cave where I found Maria calm and unafraid. She told me that, from her many trips along the river, she knew of a Trastamara garrison stationed not far from the cave. She was tempted to seek their protection, but waited for me before taking such a drastic step. I reminded her of our 'life of contrast'.

"Since it would be most natural for you to contact your father's garrison," I asked, "if you were the Inquisition, where would you station your agents?"

"At the entrance of every installation of the Trastamara militia," she replied like a child responding to a teacher's question.

This time, I did not hide my fears. I wanted her to think through our dilemma with me so we might come up with a solution. When I told her what Orlando Franco said about Seville being under siege and, when I reported conditions at the port, she also recognized the apparent hopelessness of our situation.

"As long as they suspect that we are on the river," Maria said, "they will guard the port of Seville. Is there some way to make them believe we are no longer here?"

I made no comment and she continued her analysis, "Like in

Posadas, if the troops could be convinced that we are not in Seville, they would leave the area and then we could try to board a ship for Cadiz."

"How can we possibly let them know that we are not here?" I wondered. At that moment, the cave suddenly lit up from a flash of lightning followed by a distant rumble of thunder. Another storm was brewing.

"The rain seems to be our salvation," I said, explaining that we would do exactly as she suggested.

"First, we will let them know that we are in Seville, that we have tried to bribe our way out. If the rain will just blow up into a storm for us, we could lead them to believe that we have drowned in it.

"How do we do that, drown in the storm and yet stay alive?" she asked.

"Just one step at a time," I told her. "Right now, we let them know we are in Seville."

Around midnight Maria again dressed me in my well-tested disguise and, as we were about to make our way out of the cave, Maria held back, saying that she needed a disguise, too. What would a young woman be doing with an old man in the port at midnight! I scraped off more clay and rubbed it into her hair and on her face. She ripped the dress we had taken in Posadas, making it into a shawl which made her appear like an old peasant woman. Looking like an elderly couple, we confidently walked to the main wharf in the port.

Through a window in a cargo shed, we saw an old man sitting alone in the dim room lit by a tiny oil lamp. Maria and I walked into the tiny shed and, taking off our disguising wraps, I placed a few gold coins on his table. I asked his help to get us aboard a ship to Cadiz. The man stared at the gold coins and then said that we could arrange passage only through the captain. He pointed to the bales of cargo around the dock, explaining that he was charge of cargo not passengers.

"There's enormous profit in human cargo. Can you put us in

one of those bales?" I asked, putting another gold coin in front of him.

The old man was overwhelmed by the amount of gold coins on the table.

"I can arrange it," he replied hesitatingly, "but I would have to get permission from some one."

I picked up the coins and left his shed in a huff, rebuking him for exposing our secret to anyone else.

Further down the road, we saw two drunken sailors weaving by us.

"Hey, sailor," I called out, "can you take us through the Las Marismas to Cadiz in our boat?"

"Mister," one drunk stammered, "I know this river like you know the palm of your hand. The river's my home and that includes the swamps. I can take anyone, anywhere, anytime."

"Here, see these gold coins," I said, holding them in front of his eyes, "They're yours if you get us to Cadiz."

The sailor made a grab for the coins and asked, "who are you anyway?"

"You ask too many questions," I said, pocketing the coins and hurrying away from them.

Having established our presence in Seville, Maria and I crept up to the inn's garret where we slept through the night.

Early in the morning, we heard a commotion in the tavern below. Sliding the floor board just a sliver, we saw Father Lopez questioning the old man we had confronted in the cargo shed. He kept protesting his innocence, repeating that he did not take the bribe or agree to put us aboard a ship. Lopez, trying to quiet his fears, said he only wanted our description.

When he described our appearance, Lopez nodded to his staff, satisfied the man had seen me and the count's daughter. He asked the old man if I told him where I could be contacted. Again, the old man looked around pleading his innocence, swearing by the lives of his grandchildren that he did not agree to my offer.

Soon, the two sailors were brought in by their captain to face Lopez's interrogation. They told him exactly what transpired the night before. Like the old man, they could describe Maria and me but could offer no details as to our whereabouts.

After releasing the terrified old man and the frightened sailors, Father Lopez announced to his staff, "Alberto and Maria are in Seville."

He ordered a house to house search using military men and Inquisition agents and confidently forecasted our capture. From our position in the garret, we heard Diaz arguing with Father Lopez. He criticized the manner in which the investigation was being conducted, pointing to our ability to get to Seville despite the heavy concentration of militia troops. He demanded to be put in charge of the investigation. Father Lopez warned Diaz of insubordination, threatening to return him to Cordoba. Diaz mumbled an apology. Father Lopez returned to his seat at the head of the table, inviting his staff to analyze the facts.

"Why should Alberto contact an old man to plan his escape from the city?" Father Lopez asked. "Why did he approach a drunken sailor for the dangerous task of navigating Las Marismas? It's obvious, Alberto wants to mislead us."

A staff member suggested that I want them to think we are the city so the search would be concentrated in Seville and the guards would be called off from the land route.

"That means he will try to escape by the land route?" Diaz asked.

"No, that is what he wants us to think," Father Lopez replied, "but we will redouble the watch of the river. Anything that floats down that river will be seized."

We stayed in the garret all day, grateful to Orlando Franco for bringing us food and, at midnight, we cautiously returned to our cave. After salvaging our boat, I rowed back upstream in a frenzy, reaching the nearby village of Tocino. Maria thought I was just escaping Seville, but I explained that if the rains came, we would return there but, first, we had to let the officials believe we drowned. I told her I was really following the original suggestion she made when we sat in Seville's cave. Our object was to let them know we were no longer in Seville. Maria still did not understand my convoluted plan, but she said she trusted me and she begged me just to get us out safely.

We pulled the boat along the bank near the village of Tocino and sank it among tall weeds. We hid in a barn where we took turns standing watch. A few moments after sunrise, she awakened me pointing to a man who was just walking into the barn. When he spotted me, he called me a robber and pleaded with me to take anything I wanted, but not to harm him. He seemed timid, more frightened by our presence than we were by his. He remained standing, petrified, at the entrance of the barn. I told him that I was not a robber, that he had nothing to fear.

"Then, what are you doing here?" he asked.

"We are from the town of Avdila, near the border, " I said with the Portuguese accent which was my early childhood tongue. "We were heading for Cordoba. Last night, our horse took off. He was frightened by jackals and we walked almost all night. So, we stopped here to sleep a while."

The farmer commiserated with us, saying several months earlier the same thing happened to him, but his horse returned to the farm. I then introduced myself as Armando and Maria as my wife, Clementina. We offered to work for him until we could get some means of transportation to Cordoba. Without waiting for his reply, Maria and I began to help him lift some heavy barrels he was trying to load on a wagon.

"My name is Domingo el Murijon," he said, emphasizing the Spanish intonation, perhaps in response to my Portuguese accent.

"There's much work and not enough hands to help," he said. "You can stay as long as you work. But I can't pay. I can just give you a place to sleep and some food."

When we finished loading, Murijon drove us in the wagon to

his house where he introduced us to his wife, Nina, who was trailed by her four children. She was a small woman who, despite her sickly, ashen appearance, flitted about the house, alert and full of energy. When her husband told her our problem, she was very sympathetic, offering to let us stay at her home as long as we wished.

I returned to work the olive grove with Murijon while Maria remained to help Nina with the endless farm chores and with the crying children.

Domingo el Murijon was friendly and talkative. While we harvested the olives, he told me that olives must be picked off the tree at exactly the right moment. One day too early or too late rendered them useless. He also boasted that the farm had been in his family for hundreds of years. He complained that he had too much to do for one man since his brothers had left him to work in Seville. When we finished the work in the olive grove, he thanked me, saying that he was certain God had sent me to him, otherwise the olives would have never gotten off the trees.

Looking up at the threatening skies, he said the roads might get washed out and asked me to help load the rest of his crop so that he could bring his produce to the market in Tocino before the rains. We worked hard and rapidly to load his wagon.

I offered to ride with him to Tocino. I reasoned that if he went alone he might be questioned by the militiamen who were probably still searching the area for us.

"It's good of you to take us into your home," I said as the old plow horse slowly pulled the wagon which creaked under its heavy load.

"You've already more than earned your keep. And if we get this load to Tocino, you can even demand pay from me."

"You're very generous, sir," I replied, "What you have done, taking me and my wife into your home and now offering me money, is really a noble gesture."

"I'm no nobleman," he said, "and don't call me 'sir'. I'm just an ordinary Murijon farmer who appreciates a good worker when he sees one."

"'Murijon farmer'," I repeated. "You might well be a nobleman. With a name like 'Murijon' you can probably trace your family's lineage back to the Moorish nobility who ruled over this province for hundreds of years."

"What's so important about the name Murijon?" Domingo asked.

The fact that he asked about his name indicated to me that I aroused his interest. Now all I had to do was to prove to him that he was of noble birth and he would then consider himself my protector.

"When the Moors ruled over this land, there was an eminent nobleman whose name was Abu Marwan," I said. "He was rich and powerful, and also a great doctor. Even to this day, physicians study his treatises on therapeutics and diet. As a matter of fact, the entire Marwan family had a proud noble lineage dating back over three hundred years."

"Murijon, Marwan," Domingo repeated the names several times, "Sounds the same!"

I clasped his hand and addressed him: "Domingo el Marwan.".

"Say the name of that Moorish prince again?" Domingo asked.

"Abu Marwan, " I said, emphasizing "Marwan" and stressing the similarity to 'Murijon'. Your know, everything in this part of Spain has Arabic origins. The Guadalquivir River is really made up of two Arabic words, Wadi Qabir, which means, great river. The same with other names: Guadalmes, Guadalupe, Guadaliana, Cadiz — all are really mispronunciations of the original Arabic words."

Domingo added to my theory, saying, "Our church in Tocino still has Arabic writing on its arched walls."

"You said your family owned the farm for hundreds of years, then you must be related to the Arabs who lived here then," I said.

"That's why I am certain that your name, Murijon, links you to the noble Marwan family."

Domingo was obviously impressed. He now sat erect, snapping his horse switch like a scepter. He recalled many folk tales about the early Moors he had heard in his childhood.

"'When a Moorish peasant clasps your hand'," I said, repeating an ancient proverb, "'it is worth more than the signed contract of a Castillian nobleman'."

He shook my hand, repeating his name and stressing the Moorish pronunciation, "Domingo el Marwan."

Domingo whipped his horse's flank to make him gallop, because the skies were growing darker.

"When the rains come, this road'll be under water," he said as we were nearing Tocino, "and if I couldn't have gotten these olives to town, I would have lost this year's crop. If not for you, we would starve next year, with no money for food or seed."

He patted my lap several times, calling me a gift from God. His appreciation mattered much to me because I wanted him to feel indebted to me in case of danger. I became apprehensive when I saw the large number of the troops patrolling the area. Domingo, who apparently knew nothing of the killing of Don Carlos, kept up his chatter, telling me stories of his life, obviously still seeking some remote connection with the Marwan nobility. I felt that our life depended on his loyalty to me, not just for my work, but for having bestowed on him, so to speak, the Marwan nobility.

"The real proof of nobility lay in the nobleman's concern for his wards," I said, hinting broadly that I was his ward.

The test of his loyalty to me came quickly. As we reached the gates of Tocino, a village elder and two soldiers halted the wagon to inform Domingo about an escaped killer who murdered General Carlos and abducted the count's daughter.

"Who's this man?" one soldier asked Domingo, pointing to me.

Domingo did not reply. He displayed a great interest in the fugitive, asking for more details about the killer. I did not know if he was feigning interest or trying to match me up with their description of the fugitive. They told him the details of the murder, describing me as the physician of Cordoba.

Again, the soldier asked, "Who is this?"

"He's Armando, my nephew from Avdila. He's been working with me on the farm for the last month."

The militia man waved us on. I began to believe in my own fiction; no Moorish prince could have lied with greater conviction than did Domingo.

Much to my relief, we proceeded to the market where Domingo and I unloaded the olives at the press. I helped him sell his produce at a better price than he anticipated by bargaining with a merchant who had come from Seville. There were many tradesmen from outlying areas who came to Tocino to purchase farm goods for resale. The Seville merchant was anxious to get back so I helped load his wagon. He thanked me for dealing with him first and, especially for helping him. As he left, he invited me to visit him if I came to Seville.

He said his name was Guido and his shop was near the San Estaban church.

During our brief stay in the market, the farmers talked about the house to house search in their area. The militia leader announced that if the killer was found on a farm, the farmer harboring him would face charges for abetting a criminal.

A light drizzle began to fall, scattering the farmers back to their wagons. Domingo was the first to get his wagon out of the market place. When we drew close to the guards at the gates, Domingo slowed the horse. He sat rigidly in his seat, pensive, hunched forward, leering at me and then at the guards. I was certain he suspected that I was the killer. He slowed the wagon as he passed the soldiers then, waving to the guards, he raced past them in silence.

"Thank you," I whispered when we were on our way to his farm.

He did not reply. He merely whipped his horse to a gallop. He sat in stony silence all the way back to the farm. I tried to start a conversation with him several times but he did not respond. Finally, just before we reached his house, I grasped the reins from his hands, halting his horse.

"I swear to you," I said looking squarely into his eyes, "I swear to you by the honor of my dead father that I did not murder Don Carlos. And, I did not abduct Maria, the count's daughter. She is the woman I am with and we're going to get married. Just ask her."

"I will not ask her," Domingo replied. Then, taking me by complete surprise, he added, "I believe you and I swear to you, by the honor of Abu Marwan, I shall not betray you."

We clasped hands.

The torrential downpour began just as we were entering the house. "This is no ordinary rain. It's going to last several days," he said. "It'll wash out the roads and, thank God, we got the produce to the market."

At supper, the first decent meal Maria and I had eaten in more than two weeks, Domingo told Nina about his noble heritage. He ordered me to repeat everything I told him about the Marwan lineage. When I finished telling Nina about Abu Marwan, she and the children were as pleased as Domingo had been when I first told him. I noticed that Domingo was most solicitous towards Maria, even bowing several times in her direction, behaving as though he had something in common with her.

Domingo and I were both taken by surprise when his wife got up from the table calling to Maria, "Come, princess, let's get on with the dishes."

I did not know what to make of it. Did Maria tell her about

us? Did the wife recognize her? When we were finally alone, I asked Maria if she disclosed her identity to Nina. Maria simply said yes, she did, and made nothing of it.

"Why did you tell her?" I asked, criticizing her for being careless.

"Because you taught me to 'think like them'," she replied. "What would you do if you were the Inquisition and you suspected that we were hiding with some farmer?"

It was my turn to reply like a school boy, saying "I would search every farmhouse."

"Well, suppose that while you were away with Domingo some troops came by to ask about me?" Maria asked rhetorically.

In her own way, Maria did to Nina what I did to Domingo, except she did it with no deception. She told Nina that she was the Trastamara princess and asked for help. She also told her she loved me and that when people are in love they must make their own life together. Nina was awed by Maria's disclosures, repeating the name, "Trastamara" to convince herself that Maria was there in the flesh, not a vision.

"Dearest Nina," Maria said, "you must treat me like a member of the family, especially if someone should come to ask about me."

Maria told me that Domingo's wife not only promised to keep her secret, but offered to help in any way she could. I was not worried about Domingo or his wife but I was concerned about the children, who were too little to be trusted with our secret.

"Let's not worry about the children," Maria said. "You have your rain, you have your storm, and we're out of Seville. What do we do now?"

"Simple," I replied. "We row to the outskirts of the Seville where we will crash the boat on one of the boulders in the middle of the river."

"And what would that accomplish?" she asked.

"Our only hope," I said, "is that the guards will find the

smashed boat and will presume that we drowned in the turbulent waters. The Inquisition will then call off the search for us."

"Two questions," Maria said. "First, why should they even assume that we're dead? They will probably suspect you staged the wreck. Second, how would that ensure our escape?"

"Do you see this," I said, holding up the sack of gold coins. "They will find this pouch containing 150 gold escudos in the capsized boat. No one intentionally parts with so vast a sum. No one, except a drowning man."

"My father often said that money is only useful when it is put to good use. Staying alive, I'd say, is a pretty good use," she said. "Your plan sounds fine. Just one problem: I can't swim."

For a moment, I was stunned. It never crossed my mind that with all her sailing experience, she could not swim. I had intended that she would come with me, even help me to crash the boat, but leaving her on the bank while I crashed the boat would not only endanger my plan, it would leave her totally defenseless.

"Can you stay with the Murijons?" I asked.

"Won't Domingo betray us if they come to search the house?" she asked.

"He's proved himself at Tocino," I replied.

"But you were with him," she reminded me.

"Now that he knows that you are the count's daughter," I said, "your presence is as good as mine."

I took a handful of coins out of the sack and we sought Domingo.

I told him I had to leave right away for Seville and asked if Maria could remain under his care for several days. Of course, I did not tell him our plan but I warned him that in the event there was a house to house search, he would have to find a secure hiding place for her.

He questioned my decision to go by boat in the storm but agreed to let Maria stay with them.

"She will be your ward and you must insure her safety," I said handing him five gold escudos and promising him five more when I came back for Maria.

I could not tell which impressed him more, the glitter of the gold or the grandeur of having the Trastamara princess as his ward. He called Nina and, giving her the gold escudos, assured me that they would look after Maria.

Maria and I dashed out in the storm to the river where we found our submerged boat. Domingo followed us with his tools. We worked feverishly, in total darkness and in the heavy down pour, dragging the boat to the bank and bailing out the water. With the boat afloat, I hugged Maria, thanked Domingo, and borrowed his hammer. As I began to row toward Seville, I looked back to see Maria but I soon lost sight of her in the storm.

The storm became more intense, the waters more turbulent. I could barely see to steer the boat and avoid boulders along the way. Only occasional flashes of lightening lit my way in the dark. My original plan was to use the cave where Maria and I had hidden to prepare the boat for its accident. But when I got there, I saw from afar an encampment of soldiers in the cave, probably using the natural shelter to avoid the storm. I quickly rowed out to an islet in the middle of the river obscured from sight by the heavy rains and dense fog.

I put Maria's comb, kerchief, and mirror together with the money sack into the food basket. I tied the basket to a plank in the small compartment under the seat in the stern. Then I tied the lid of the basket with a strong piece of cord and nailed shut the doors of the compartment. Using Domingo's hammer, I pried loose several planks, forcing them to come apart. I loosened the rest of the wooden panels from the center board. Capsizing the boat, I steered her splintered hull to a section of the river where several boulders jutted out of the raging water.

The swift currents slammed the capsized boat around, bouncing her from boulder to boulder.

When the broken hull came to rest on the rocks, I swam out

and wedged it securely between two huge rocks.

I took off my jacket, put seven gold escudos into its pockets, and tightly fastened it on the jagged edges of another, far off, boulder. With my surgical knife, I cut into my forearm, letting the blood flow freely onto the impaled jacket. I wedged a heavy rock between the jacket and the boulder so that some of the blood would remain and not be washed off by the rain. Finally, I flung Maria's hat among the wind-whipped reeds near the shore.

It was almost daylight when, exhausted, I finished all these preparations. I stealthily swam downstream, floating alongside a log, to one of the docks in Seville. The port area was quiet with only one soldier patrolling each wharf. The rain was beginning to let up and soon, the skies cleared. It was far too risky to make my way to Orlando Franco's garret, nor could I swim back to Tocino. Given no choice, I squeezed into the dark, slimy rafters below the dock. My body was underwater; only my head stayed above. When morning arrived, I heard an official, right over my head, barking orders, telling his men to search homes, buildings, tents, barns, caves, carriages and crates. But they did not search the encrusted upper support planks, just below the floor of the wharf, where I was perched with a perfect view of the many row boats which were sent out to patrol the river. I waited anxiously for their return.

Certainly one of them would discover my wrecked boat which was so securely wedged among the rocks and would haul it to shore.

Suddenly, aghast, I saw my capsized boat rapidly floating downstream past the port of Seville. Most of it was submerged below the water, so that it looked like the flotsam and jetsam which crowded the river after a storm. To my horror, no one noticed it. When it drifted on beyond my view, still unnoticed by the many guards patrolling the river, I knew that all my efforts were for naught. I felt devastated.

I had no choice but to remain hidden for the rest of the day hoping that, under the cover of darkness, I could make my way to Franco's garret or somehow get back to Tocino. Soon, I lifted my body out of the water, resting on a cross bar. Although the space was a cramped, unpleasant nook, I fell asleep.

At about noon, I was awakened by a babble of noise right above my head. Someone was shouting to call Father Lopez. I was petrified, certain that I had been discovered. I lay still, trying to plan my next move. Should I run out? Swim out to the river? I decided to do nothing until I understood what the commotion was about. Looking out between the boards, I saw a caravel sailing into port — my battered boat lashed to its side! The entire port area was abuzz, talking about the yellow-striped boat they had been seeking. When the caravel neared the dock, the guards prohibited any crew member from leaving the boat.

Father Lopez's marine experts boarded the boat to identify the wreckage while he remained at the wharf. I could hardly contain my excitement when one of the experts shouted down from the caravel, "Father Lopez, It's the boat! The yellow stripes are clearly visible."

Father Lopez shouted back to have the wreckage and the crew brought into Orlando Franco's inn where an investigation panel would be convened immediately.

An enormous crowd followed Father Lopez and his men who hauled the wreckage to the inn. In the hubbub, I was able to join the crowd, resuming my crouched stance to hide my face, and quickly making my way to Orlando Franco's garret. Moving the floorboard ever so slightly, I was able to hear and see most of what transpired in the room below.

First, the captain reported that as his caravel sailed upstream, a seaman spotted a capsized boat mired in the mud on the bank of river. The captain testified that he ordered the boat to be hoisted on to the ship.

Father Lopez congratulated the captain for hauling the wreckage and bringing it to Seville. He asked the captain if anything else was found in the wreckage. The captain produced a basket. One of the experts pointed to the Trastamara coat of arms woven into its warp and woof. Members of the investigating panel inspected the basket, but declared that it might have be planted there by someone.

"What did you find in the basket?" Father Lopez asked the sailor who was the first to get to the boat while it was still mired in the swamp.

"Nothing," he replied.

"If the boat was capsized and battered in the storm, how did the basket remain in the boat?" Diaz asked the captain.

"It was wedged in the compartment by these doors which collapsed against the basket and became anchored to the floorboard," the captain explained.

"And, there was nothing in the basket?" Diaz asked.

"Nothing," the captain asserted.

Lopez turned to another sailor who had tied the boat when it was towed off the sand bar, "When you reached the boat, did you see the basket in the compartment?"

"Yes, sir," the sailor replied.

"How come the basket survived the storm?" Diaz asked.

"It was tied to the plank with a heavy cord," the sailor replied. "And, when the boat crashed, the doors probably crushed down on the basket, keeping it from falling out."

The captain and crew were dismissed but ordered to remain aboard their ship. Looking down from the garret I saw Father Lopez convene his staff, which included Diaz, the ship experts, and the militiamen, to analyze the findings. They could not be sure whether the wrecked boat showed signs of having been willfully smashed. Father Lopez asked the navy to send swimmers to search for the drowned bodies.

"If they really drowned," said Diaz, stressing 'if'.

"We will soon know," Father Lopez said.

"I have a feeling that Alberto is deceiving us again," Diaz said.

"I prefer to rely on the evidence, not on your feelings," Father Lopez said, ridiculing Diaz for his suspicious nature.

While they were discussing the facts, my blood-stained jacket was brought in. Soon thereafter, Maria's hat was also salvaged. They searched through my jacket, finding the seven gold escudos and my surgical knife. An agent described finding the jacket wedged between the crevices of a boulder.

"The hat, if it can be determined to belong to the count's daughter," Father Lopez said, "would prove Maria's presence during the smashup. Of course, the jacket, the knife, and especially the seven escudos corroborate that their boat was smashed in the storm. One doesn't part so readily with seven escudos."

Diaz was still not satisfied that these finds conclusively proved that we perished, even after an investigator displayed all the evidence, summing up his conviction that both Maria and I were in the boat. Another expert testified that, after examining the boat, he was convinced the wreck could not be have been staged. Diaz remained unconvinced.

"Until their bodies are found," he insisted, "we must assume that they're still alive."

To satisfy Diaz's challenge, Lopez recalled the captain and the sailor who was the first to climb on the wreckage. Diaz questioned them separately, first ordering the sailor to stay out of the room. Diaz showed the captain Maria's basket saying, "Your sailor said that this basket was tied to a plank in the compartment underneath the seat. Tell me, was the basket closed when you found it?"

"Yes," the captain replied, reaching into the basket and producing pieces of twine. "The lid was tied with this string and over this loop."

"Who untied the cord?"

"The sailor who is in the next room," the captain replied.

"And when you opened it," Diaz asked, "you found it empty?"

"Yes," the captain said.

"Why would a basket be closed, its lid tied with this heavy

cord, when there's nothing in it?" Diaz asked.

The captain said he could not explain why. Diaz then asked him to step aside and the first sailor was brought in for interrogation.

"Was the basket open or closed when you found the boat?" Diaz asked.

"I can't remember," the sailor said.

"If I show you this piece of cord," Diaz said, showing him the cord the captain had given them, "would it help you remember?"

The sailor looked at the cord and shrugged his shoulders. He hesitated. His fingers fidgeted with the cap he was holding. He glanced at the captain.

"Sailor, you're lying," Diaz shouted, waving the piece of cord before the sailor's eyes. "We know from your captain's testimony that the lid was closed with this and that you untied it. Now, speak up, why are you lying?"

"Yes, the basket was closed," the sailor stammered. "I did open the lid."

"And, what did you find in it?" Diaz asked. "Jewelry? Money? Perfume? Tell us, what did you find in the basket?"

The sailor again hesitated; his face turned red. When he was about to reply, the captain spoke up in his defense, "The lad found some women's articles in that basket, a scarf, a mirror, and a comb. I let him keep it. He worked so hard to retrieve the wreck."

"That's all, only a scarf and the mirror and a comb," the sailor repeated the captain's words, avoiding Diaz's gaze.

The captain smiled at the investigating panel, mumbling an apology for letting the sailor keep "those trinkets." He haltingly assured the panel that he was ready to answer any other questions.

Diaz stepped up to the captain and, poking his finger into the man's chest, accused the captain and his sailor of criminal action. Diaz demanded they be arrested so the Inquisition could ferret out the facts from them. Father Lopez agreed with Diaz's demand but he urged them to confess so their sentences would be lessened.

"I don't know who you are," Diaz said to the captain, "but I am the Inquisition. You were under our orders to search for that boat, not to tamper with its contents. For that infraction, I can confiscate your ship, flog every member of your crew and send you to a fiery death. Now, start talking while you still have your tongue."

Trembling and cowering before Diaz, the captain confessed that when the wreckage was hoisted onto the deck of the ship, the crew stood by watching.

"The basket tumbled out of the wreck," the captain spoke wiping perspiration from his face, "and when we opened it, we found a pouch inside filled with gold pieces."

The captain further confessed he took half of the gold escudos and divided the remainder among the members of his crew.

Father Lopez ordered his agents to round up the crew and bring all fourteen of them to the inn with their belongings. While waiting for them, Father Lopez complimented Diaz on his interrogation technique. Diaz arrogantly replied that this entire investigation would not have been necessary had he been in charge of the search in the first place. Lopez glared at Diaz, ordering him to be silent.

When the crew filed in, Father Lopez solemnly warned them of the consequences if they were found guilty of tampering with evidence of this investigation. He repeated the captain's testimony, ordering them to return every gold piece or any other item given them by the captain.

The captain walked up to the table where Lopez and Diaz sat. He emptied a stack of gold coins from a pouch sewn into his tunic. Then, the sailor who had just been questioned produced a silk scarf, comb and tiny mirror as well as his share of the gold pieces. The captain remained at the table to make sure each crew member returned the correct amount of coins. An investigator from the panel counted the coins, stacking them in front of Lopez who ordered the crew to return to their ship to await the panel's decision.

"One hundred and twenty-seven gold escudos," the investigator announced emphasizing each number. "I can understand how such a vast sum could have blinded the captain."

The captain and the crew were hauled off and the Investigating Panel resumed its meeting. Father Lopez placed my blood-stained jacket, my knife, Maria's hat and all the items found in the basket next to the stack of gold coins. He asked every panel member to view the "mountain of evidence" and give his opinion: Was the boat destroyed by the storm or was the boat intentionally sunk?

From my perch in the garret, I saw how each one scrutinized every item on the table. They unanimously agreed that the boat was Andres', that the items found in the boat were mine and Maria's, that the boat was wrecked in the storm, and that we perished in the wreck.

Father Lopez announced, "In view of the evidence and in view of your unanimous agreement, we conclude that Alberto, the physician, and Maria, the Trastamara princess, have perished in the storm. The search for them will be called off."

Diaz objected. He admitted that the escudos found in the boat clearly confirmed that the boat had been wrecked in a storm because, "no one in his right mind would leave such a vast amount of gold of his own free will." However, he objected to the presumption that we died, insisting that the boat's occupants may have saved themselves and might well be hiding somewhere.

Lopez again asked his panel for their opinion. Each of them disagreed with Diaz's suspicion.

"The search for Alberto and Maria is herewith called off," Father Lopez announced.

Diaz got up from his seat and, facing Lopez, repeated his argument and accused Father Lopez of conducting a poor search. Diaz could not contain his anger and their bitter confrontation turned into a shouting match. Diaz screamed that as long as our bodies were not found, Lopez lacked the authority to cancel the search. He shouted his demand that the entire matter be brought to the Supreme Headquarters of the Inquisition. Lopez vainly tried to silence Diaz' ranting.

Finally, Father Lopez slammed his fist on the table and announced, "The search for Alberto and Maria is herewith cancelled."

Just before stalking out of the room, he ordered Diaz stripped of his authority and no longer considered his assistant.

Diaz retorted, "I'm going to Toledo to appeal to the Suprema and get permission to continue the search for Alberto, the heretic."

While this was happening in Seville, the search for us did not slacken in Tocino. The next morning, the skies cleared and the roads were not "under water" as Domingo predicted. He and Nina began to prepare for the house to house search which, they knew, would soon resume. As they were about to board up part of the kitchen to create a hiding place for Maria, they heard horses galloping from a distance. They went outside and saw a troop of soldiers heading for the farm. Nina grasped Maria by the hand, taking her into the house.

"Domingo," she called out, "Stall them. I'll find some way to disguise her."

Nina dressed Maria in a heavy, ill-fitting dress, dishevelled her hair, which hid most of her face. Maria ridiculed these precautions, claiming she needed no disguise because no one in the Tocino neighborhood had every seen her. Nina insisted on this get-up, instructing Maria to feign a limp so she would attract less attention. They remained in the house, listening to Domingo talking to the soldiers.

Nina recognized the voice of the *alcalde,* the mayor, asking about the nephew who had come with Domingo to Tocino.

"He's no good," Domingo replied. "I tried to get him to work with me but he kept complaining that farm work was too hard, so he took off early this morning to find easier work. He left his wife here until he gets back."

Domingo promised that when his nephew returned, he would bring him to the village. The corporal seemed satisfied and was ready to leave when the *alcalde* asked Domingo why he had never mentioned his nephew before. The corporal's curiosity was aroused and he ordered Domingo to bring out the nephew's wife.

"Nina," Domingo shouted, "bring Clementina out here."

Maria acted well the part of a cripple, hobbling as she walked out supported by Nina. She answered the corporal's questions in a Portuguese dialect.

"We're from Avdila, just across the border," she said. "There's no food and no work there. My husband came here to find work."

The corporal asked her questions about Portugal, but she said she knew little of the country. He took her for a moron and apologized for disturbing her. He allowed her to hobble back to the house.

Just then, one of the children romped out, calling to Maria, 'Hi, princess."

Nina quickly explained that 'princess' was a term of endearment the family used for their crippled niece. But, the corporal's suspicions were again aroused. He asked Maria several pointed questions about Avdila and then, warning Domingo that he was not satisfied with her answers, ordered Domingo, his wife, and Maria to follow him to Tocino for further interrogation.

"The commander of the troops from Cordoba is here," the corporal warned Domingo, "if she's lying, you're all in trouble."

Nina pleaded with the corporal not to force the crippled woman to make such a long trip because she was so weak. Maria scorned Nina, saying that she wanted to go to Tocino just to get out of being locked up in the house all day. She acted her part

Sacred Sword

superbly well, as the two women began arguing. But, the corporal was not swayed either by Nina's pleading or by Maria's insisting.

Domingo hitched the horse to his wagon and, when the two women boarded it, he followed the soldiers back to Tocino.

"You acted well," Nina said, "but why did you insist on coming along?"

"I knew that he wouldn't listen to your pleading, so I took a chance using a different approach," Maria replied.

"Suppose one of the troops from Cordoba recognizes you?" Nina asked.

"If I can keep up this act," she said, "no one will recognize me."

On the way to Tocino, Nina coached Maria about places and events in Avdila so she could respond correctly to further questioning. With this added information, Maria again assured them, that her acting would be so convincing, everyone would believe her.

The moment she was led into the small farm house which served as a military base for the investigation, Maria suddenly collapsed on the floor.

"See, I told you she was too weak to travel," Nina said, scolding the soldier for forcing her to make the long trip.

When Maria had to be revived from her faint, Nina realized that Maria was not acting and that something serious must have happened to bring on her collapse.

It was Captain Rodriguez. Maria recognized him instantly.

He was standing over her while she was helped to rise and was placed in a chair. The corporal reported his suspicions about Domingo's nephew and his doubts about Maria's claim to come from Avdila. The captain approached Maria. Lifting her shawl from her face, he looked squarely at her. Maria lowered her eyes, bowed her head, and kept her eyes glued to the floor. He pulled the shawl back over her face and returned to his desk.

"For this you wasted an entire day!" the captain rebuked the corporal. "In the time it took you to bring this hag to me, you could have searched the entire area."

He dismissed Domingo and his wife and, apologizing to Maria, gallantly said, "At least you should be flattered that you were taken for the count's daughter. She's very beautiful."

When Maria hobbled out, she heard Captain Rodriguez laughing with officers, "When I see the count, I'll tell him how much his daughter has aged."

Driving back to the farm, Nina complimented Maria for her acting but said that she could not understand how Maria staged that fainting spell. Maria made a lame excuse in order not to expose Rodriguez. She wanted to share her joy with Nina, to tell her that Rodriguez not only saved her life but that he would also report to the count that she was alive. For Rodriguez' sake, Maria kept it to herself.

He eased her worries about her parents. If Berto's scheme worked and their deaths were reported, Rodriguez' report to the count would spare her parents tremendous pain.

Within moments of Father Lopez' announcement that the search was over, Seville became a liberated city. The people wildly cheered the mass exodus of soldiers and Inquisition agents.. The inns and taverns once again opened their doors to the public; the stores and the port returned to normal. The tension that had existed for the past two weeks suddenly vanished.

However, for me, the danger of exposure remained because I could have been easily recognized as the "physician from Cordoba". I decided to find Guido, the merchant whom I had helped in Tocino and who would take a message to Domingo. I still had the five escudos for Domingo and five more which I kept from the count's purse. I waited in my garret till nightfall to go to the market place. At the plaza near San Estaban church, I searched for Guido's store. The merchants were beginning to close their shops when I sauntered into a fruit shop. I asked the owner if he remembered me from the Tocino market where I had sold him Domingo's produce. He looked up from his work, replying in the affirmative and thanking me again for my help. I asked him to get a message to Domingo on the Murijon farm. Anxious to close his shop, the merchant was annoyed with me, until I showed him a gold escudo and offered it to him, promising another when Domingo came to Seville with his delivery. The merchant was interested but insisted on being paid in advance, arguing that he would deliver the message but the farmer might not be willing to obey. Having no choice, I handed him the two escudos in advance, on the condition that he leave immediately. He grabbed the coins and took off.

My message to Domingo read, "Bring your ward to Franco."

If the merchant were an honest man and kept to our agreement, Maria would be arriving the next day in the early afternoon. I sat at the garret's slit all day, watching the door to the inn. By late afternoon, there was still no sign of her. I began making plans to return to Tocino, preparing to start out near nightfall. I began sliding down from the roof when from a distance I saw a wagon entering the city gates. My heart leaped with joy when I recognized Domingo's wagon, laden with produce, slowly trudging down the road to the port. I waited impatiently until it entered a deserted field. I ran toward it and there was Maria, almost invisible, sitting among the fruits and vegetables. Domingo explained that he loaded his wagon full of produce rather than have Maria call attention to herself by sitting alone in an empty wagon. I helped Maria get down the wagon and clinging to each other, we both profusely thanked Domingo. I handed him the five escudos and reminded him never to disclose this to anyone.

In parting, I sent my best wishes to Nina and said to him, "Domingo Abu Marwan, you're not only of noble birth but a righteous Christian, as well."

Although fatigued from the long and tedious ride from

Tocino, Maria looked radiantly beautiful despite her windswept hair and fruit-stained face. She was bundled up in a warm coat with a matching hood Nina made for her.

I carried Maria's package of food and clothing, and hurried her across the road to the garret which had been my home for the past three days. Crawling under the eaves was quite an ordeal for her but the moment we entered the small dark room, we embraced, clinging to each other unable to let go. When I began telling her of my harrowing experience with the boat, she put her finger to my lips, asking me to say nothing, just to hold her. We embraced, in silence, for a long and delightful moment.

I then told her everything that happened to me in Seville; crashing the boat, its discovery in the Las Marismas, and Lopez's decision to call off the search. I told her we could now see our way clear to our early escape from Spain. In turn, she related and acted out, her experience with Rodriguez. I commended her on her courage in the face of such a crisis.

"Rodriguez was the least of my fears," Maria said. "When you didn't return from Seville after the storm, I was certain that something dreadful happened to you."

She reminded me that just prior to my leaving for the river to crash my boat, I mentioned to Domingo that I would give him another five escudos when I returned for Maria.

"Three days after the storm, I was going to leave the farm to search for you in Seville," she said. "I decided that if I learned you had been killed, I would kill myself."

I lectured her that we were facing death each day. "If that should happen to me," I said, "you must return to your family. As a Trastamara princess, you are safe."

"Berto," she cried out, "when will you finally understand that without you, the castle, the Trastamara title, all mean nothing to me."

I kissed her, whispering, "You humble me with your love. And that's how much I love you."

She took out the food Nina had given her and we sat in that dim garret enjoying the simple repast as though it were a lavish feast. After we ate, I helped her repack her bundle and that is when I noticed Don Carlos' green uniform.

"Why the uniform?" I asked.

"Well, didn't you tell me you would leave your jacket when you crashed the boat?" she replied. "I brought this just in case you needed something to keep you warm."

We fondled the green uniform, reminiscing about our first meeting in the castle, about her family, about La Mesa, about the exciting moments we had shared.

She then brought me back to the real world by asking how would we get out of Spain. I assured her that since the search for us had ended, it would be relatively simple to get to Cadiz. In that port city, where I was not known, I could get the limpiezas in the same way I got them for the conversos. With limpiezas in hand, I said, our passage to the colonies would be assured.

Early the following morning, we stealthily made our way down to Franco's inn, which was quiet and empty. He probably saw us from his window because the moment we entered, he abruptly ordered us back to the garret.

Moments later he crawled into our room, reprimanding me for coming to the inn and reminding me that he was under surveillance by the Inquisition. He also was furious that I was so careless about my security that I openly walked through the streets. He apologized to Maria for his brusque manner, warning both of us to be careful all the time.

"But the search for me has been called off," I said.

"The danger is far from over, for you or for me," he said. "The Inquisition is still in total control of the city. The search for heretics has in no way diminished. Agents are everywhere and they are more dangerous because they operate in secret rather than in the open."

I told him how I went into the market right after the search was called off and found neither militia nor agents patrolling the streets.

"That was a four-day reprieve," he said. "now they're searching everyone and, again, the dungeons are filling up with suspected heretics."

"What are our chances to board a ship to the colonies," I asked.

"As long as Diaz is in charge, you stand no chance," he replied.

"Diaz?" I gasped. "I thought Lopez discharged him?"

Orlando Franco explained that after Diaz's summary dismissal, a high official of the Inquisition was sent to Cordoba to arbitrate the differences between Father Lopez and Diaz. Diaz filed reports enumerating the weaknesses of the search Lopez had conducted. He presented the findings of his own investigation, uncovering my tracks. He learned that I had stayed a full day in Cordoba following Reinaldo's death; that I remained seven days in Posadas; that both Maria and I hid on a farm in Tocino. Diaz claimed this proved Lopez had conducted a slipshod search. Despite the overwhelming evidence, the arbitrator decided in favor of Father Lopez but did not strip Diaz of his position as an agent of the Inquisition.

He retained his status, but would soon be transferred to another city where he would work independently, having no contact with Father Lopez in Cordoba.

Diaz was satisfied with the decision, pleading for more agents so he could continue the search in Seville before leaving for his new assignment. He was refused, but he did get permission to continue his own investigation in Seville until his transfer became effective.

"He's been around the city for the past two days," Orlando Franco said, "interrogating captains, ship builders and anyone with maritime experience.

He felt justified when one them gave credence to his theory

that the boat's occupants may have survived. Diaz has mounted a one-man campaign to search for you."

"How do we get out of here?" I asked.

Orlando Franco reiterated that he could do nothing for us, since he was still under surveillance and would probably have to account for his long absence from the inn. He could only suggest that we make our way to Cadiz on a regular ship and to try our luck from there. I asked if we could get limpiezas in Cadiz.

"No! Absolutely no!" he said. "All the churches and all notaries have been alerted to that ruse."

He also warned me not to use the hunchback disguise again when I go to the port, "because that's what they're looking for."

He took off his cap and his striped shirt, like the one most sailors wore, and gave them to me so that I would be indistinguishable from the many sailors roaming the port. I apologized for endangering him and thanked him for all he had done for us, especially for the use of the garret.

"Until Diaz leaves Seville for his new assignment, this is your safest place," Orlando Franco said, telling us that he would signal us from below the moment Diaz departed from Seville.

Just before Orlando Franco crawled out of the garret, he untied his red bandana and took out the pendant I had given him when he arranged the conversos' passage to the colonies. He gave it to Maria, saying he knew that it was her mother's. She fondled the pendant, holding it against her chest, clasping it in her hands. Then, she extended the pendant back to Orlando, begging him to keep it. He refused. Without any further explanation, he abruptly left and we only saw him briefly from above, two days later, when he threw a stone up to garret signaling Diaz's departure.

I dressed in Orlando Franco's outfit, ready to leave the safety of our garret. Maria tied up the bundle of clothing and handed it to me to carry, and then she and I squirmed out of our cramped garret, heading to the port.

"I wonder what will happen to him," Maria said as we were

Sacred Sword

passing Orlando Franco's inn.

"We'll never know," I said, "but he is precious, truly a righteous Christian."

"That's the second time you used that expression, first for Domingo and now for Franco," Maria said. "What does it mean?"

"It was my father's favorite expression," I replied. "He would often say that anyone who does a righteous deed is worthy of God's blessings."

"And when I was a child," Maria said, "I thought that just being a Christian makes you righteous."

"I can't vouch for many," I replied. "But we met some good ones, like Father Hernandez, Domingo and Nina, Orlando Franco and Rodriguez."

"And, of course, Andres and the priest who helped him with the limpiezas," Maria added.

It was a fortunate day for us when we walked down to the port of Seville. Hundreds of passengers were leaving for Cadiz that day to celebrate its annual All Saints Fiesta. Because of the crush of passengers going to the celebration, which attracted persons from all over the region, travel restrictions were not enforced for anyone going to Cadiz.

Like any other travelers, we booked passage on one of the ships sailing to Cadiz, but for an added measure of safety Maria wore Nina's hood, covering most of her face. My sailor's cap and shirt were perfect, as I was accorded immediate permission to board. We took our place on the boat with the other passengers who were already in a holiday mood. We were really fortunate there were neither militia personnel nor Inquisition agents on the ship. Maria and I felt so relieved we joined in the holiday spirit of the trip. We enjoyed the evening along the river, seeing the lights of Cadiz's festival from afar.

As we neared the port, the captain stood up at the poop deck calling our attention to new regulation which were to go into effect that day.

"By order of their Royal Majesties," the captain read from

the document he held in his hand. "Special permits will be required from all passengers and crew members sailing out of Spain from Cadiz.

"All Certificates of Limpiezas will no longer be valid unless they are authenticated in person by Diaz Delgado, Director of the Inquisition, Port of Cadiz."

I was shocked.

"What do we do now?" Maria asked, clinging to me, sensing the danger.

"I don't know," I replied. "If Diaz sees me, it's the end for both of us. It's not easy to outsmart a cunning assassin."

My first thought was to remain on board the ship and return to Seville, but when it was being tied to the wharf, the passengers were ordered to leave through a special gate for an inspection. Eager to get to the carnival, everyone rushed to get in line. We had no choice.

"If we are officially presumed dead," I whispered to Maria, who was hiding her face in the hood, "it's time to adopt a new name and get into the carnival mood right now."

We approached the official at the gate, joyful and smiling like rest of the passengers in the line. He asked us for our names. I shouted, "Me, I'm Bartolo de Cordo and this is Margarita."

"Are you together?" the official asked.

"I wouldn't trust him," Maria answered, jerking her hip into mine, and smiling broadly.

"What are you doing here?" he asked.

"Celebrating with friends," I replied, pointing to the group ahead of me.

"Keep moving! Keep moving!" the official shouted, waving us through.

12

Cadiz was filthy. It was as though the entire city was one huge warehouse serving the port. Open sheds containing mountains of produce were everywhere. Crates of fish were piled high alongside mounds of tanned leather and towering barrels of oil and wine. Heaps of rotting produce were lying about the streets and alleyways. The foul smell was overbearing.

But the rejoicing people, regaling in the All Saints Festival, seemed impervious to the acrid odor which hung over the city like a black cloud.

I hurried Maria out of the port area to get away from the prying eyes of Inquisition agents who were undoubtedly under Diaz's orders to continue searching for us. As in Seville, troops were stationed throughout the city and, wherever we walked, the fluttering green and gold banners of the Inquisition signified the presence of its agents. Most critical to us, militiamen were guarding every approach to the port.

Cadiz, like Seville, had become like a city under siege. We were safe that night only because of the carnival. The press of people churning about the city's plaza enabled us to go about undetected.

I carried our small bundle of clothing over my shoulder and we mixed with the reveling mob. The unbridled throng pressing all around us was most uncomfortable but, for us, it provided a measure of safety. Our anonymity was our best security. I held tightly to Maria as the tidal wave of humanity carried us along the streets, propelled into the jubilant crowd.

"This revelry isn't going to last long," Maria said when we finally found seats in a noisy tavern.

Time was growing short. In the morning, the populace would

Sacred Sword

awaken from its drunken stupor and we would then have to face the cruel reality of Diaz's presence.

"It has to be tonight," I said to Maria.

"What has to be tonight?" she asked.

"Our escape," I replied.

Suddenly, Maria burst out laughing, calling everyone's attention to me by shouting "loco," encouraging others to join her laughter. At first, I could not understand her sudden outburst. Then, I noticed that troops had entered the tavern. Maria suspected that they noticed us because of our sober behavior; we were the only ones not celebrating. When I realized Maria's intentions, I joined the merriment by lunging at Maria and letting her douse me with wine causing other guests to surround us, applauding our theatrics.

When the soldiers left, I told Maria to continue our merry-making, entertaining the group in the tavern, because I wanted to befriend some of the sailors in the tavern. I hoped they could tell us which ship would be sailing in the morning. We soon became the focal point of that noisy, boisterous tavern. Everyone offered drinks. Many invited us to their tables. We attached ourselves to a group of sailors who took us along as they snaked through the huge mob, stopping at almost every tavern we passed. While carousing with that group, I managed to speak to several sea captains from whom I learned that the Santa Emilia was to sail the following day at high tide.

A drunken member of our group pointed out the captain of the Santa Emilia sitting in one of the taverns. Maria and I went into our act, entertaining the guests there. We succeeded in getting ourselves invited to join the captain at his table and, after several drinking bouts and some frenzied dancing sessions, I decided to ask him take me on as his seaman and Maria as a passenger.

"My name is Bartolo de Cordo and this is Margarita. She's going to be my wife," I said. "I'm from Cordoba and don't have limpiezas because we just now decided to go to the colonies. We can't get limpiezas here because we're strangers. I can pay."

I flashed the three gold escudos offering to pay our passage in advance. The captain flung the three coins out of my hand, cursing me for annoying him. He returned to his wine and women. As I gathered up my precious coins, Maria approached him trying to persuade him, but he grabbed me by the collar and threatened to turn me over to the Inquisition.

A crowd was gathered around us, watching as the captain violently shook me. Maria, trying to free me from his grasp, slapped his face. He raged at her. My group of sailors rescued me from his grasp and helped us get out of the tavern. For a moment, we went off to a side street to collect our thoughts.

"That's the only ship leaving for the colonies," Maria moaned.

I tried to comfort her saying, "We will contact the captain when he sobers up. We'll try again."

"Try? With what?" Maria asked.

"I still have three gold escudos," I reminded her.

"What's the good of three escudos? Even with three hundred gold escudos, we couldn't get past Diaz's guards."

"There are other ways of boarding that ship," I said hoping to calm Maria's fears.

Both she and I knew I had no plan and that in the morning not only would the captain sober up but so would Diaz's agents.

Adding to our frustration and danger was the sudden rumor sweeping the crowd that an escaped heretic was loose and was being sought by the Inquisition. The official search teams who swooped down on the crowd, looking over every adult male, increased the crowd's excitement. The rumor, passed along from mouth to mouth, from group to group, stirred the crowd to a frenzy as hopes for an immediate auto-da-fe turned them into an excited mob.

I was terrified when I saw Diaz coming straight at me. He was directing the search teams, shouting orders to his agents and to the people around us.

"Diaz!" I whispered to Maria, burying my head under her

cape, acting as though I was totally drunk.

"Which one?" she asked covering me with her hood.

"The big head," I replied.

When Maria swayed me away from Diaz's direction, I collided with another agent working in Diaz's team. The agent pulled me up by my hair and studied my face by the light of his torch. Fortunately, my face was half hidden in Maria's hood so that Diaz could not possibly see me from where he stood. When the agent was satisfied that I was not the escaped prisoner, he let my head fall back on Maria's chest.

It was already past midnight. The carnival showed no signs of abating. To avoid another search, I steered Maria to one of the storage sheds where, the putrid smell notwithstanding, we quietly analyzed our problem. Despite the tension or, perhaps, because of it, Maria stretched out on the ground saying she was too tired to think and laying down to sleep.

"Don't wake me," she quipped, "until you come up with a solution."

I caressed her beautiful face, tenderly kissing her on the lips. She snuggled closer and soon she was rhythmically breathing, fully asleep, resting in the crook of my arm. After a while, it began to hurt. I endured the pain in my arm as long as I could, not moving, trying not to disturb her sleep. But, when my arm cramped shooting pain up to my shoulder, I reached over to the bundle I had carried and took out some clothes to make a pillow for her. In the darkness, I could feel the velvet cloth, stripes of braid, and metallic buttons of Don Carlos' uniform.

"Get up! Get up!" I shook Maria awake, "I have the solution." She awakened with a start, watching me as I put on Don Carlos' uniform. I smoothed out the wrinkles from the jacket and pants and then, facing her, I gave a snappy salute. Maria burst out laughing, repeating over and over, "What a beautiful monkey! What a beautiful monkey!"

"What's the matter? It's just a little wrinkled," I said, chiding her for calling me a monkey. She reminded me of our first night at the castle and we both began to laugh, recalling Teresa's reaction to me in that splendid uniform.

Then Maria asked, "Now, what's your solution?"

"It's still a general's uniform and, if you act your part, it'll get us on to the Santa Emilia, with or without the captain's permission."

"What do you have in mind?" she asked.

"Come," I said pulling her forward, "You've just been propositioned by a general."

I asked her to take off her coat and unlace her blouse to expose the top of her breasts. When we reached the port, a sentry saluted me at the guard house, but the ramp to the Santa Emilia was guarded by an armed soldier.

"Teresa may not approve of the condition of this uniform or of your dress, but this soldier will," I whispered.

She pulled one sleeve partially off her shoulder and puckered up her lips to kiss me. I walked up to the soldier holding Maria tightly around her waist. The soldier, who ordered us to halt, stared greedily at Maria's charms.

I straightened up from our sensuous embrace, showing off my green and gold uniform, which brought a snappy salute from the soldier.

"As your General," I said placing a gold escudo into the soldier's palm, "I know that I can rely on you to provide me with an adequate space for a few moments aboard the ship. And, what's more important, to keep absolutely quiet about this."

The soldier, impressed by the gold escudo and by the gold epaulets on the uniform, saluted again saying, "I understand the need for secrecy, Sir."

He allowed us to board and directed us to captain's cabin. He explained that ordinarily there were several soldiers assigned to guard the Santa Emilia, but the others were summoned by Diaz to search for the heretic. He assured me that no one would know of our presence. Closing the door of the cabin, I asked him for his name and promised him that if he kept my secret, I would help him in his military career. He smiled and returned to his post on the ramp.

Maria and I walked around the deck to make sure we were alone. The Santa Emilia was a large four-masted vessel with broad bows and a high narrow poop. Her lower deck was completely filled with cargo already stowed and securely tied down. She was ready to sail.

I selected two huge empty casks. I removed the top cover of each barrel, prying loose each wooden stopcock so the openings could be used as an air holes. When I told Maria we would probably have to remain hidden in the barrels until the ship was on the high seas, she thought it would be easy and even fun.

"Maria, our lives depend on our ability to remain in one position, crouched and cramped, for a whole day," I warned. "Staying in these barrels for so long a time will be an almost impossible ordeal."

We had to practice ways of moving about in the barrel to avoid cramps without being detected. First, I showed her how to remove the stopcock stealthily to enable her to breathe.

Maria ridiculed my warnings, but agreed to practice. I placed the barrel over her head.

She joked for a while, but soon she called out that she was all cramped up and unable to stand the pain. It was indeed an ordeal. I begged her to stay in the barrel, suggesting that she try to change positions to relieve her aches. I could hear her whimper and complain that her body ached; she could no longer tolerate the pain. When she tried to change positions, the barrel toppled over. We rested a while, then continued the experiment, sitting in several position to determine which would afford greater ease, but she cried out that the pain was excruciating.

"It's worse than the Inquisition's torture chambers," she whispered when I lifted the barrel off her.

"No comparison. Nothing can compare to the torture chambers of the Inquisition," I said.

"I'm sorry," Maria said. "I'm sorry. I didn't mean to remind you of Andres."

"I wasn't thinking only of Andres' death," I said "but of something that he said before he died. Something that could help you now."

"Help me?" Maria asked.

"When he decided to confess to the monk, he said, 'It's only a matter of how, not why, we die'."

Maria repeated the words several times and said, "What did he mean by that?"

"There's more to suffering than the pain of suffering," I said. "When you suffer for a reason, or when there's justification to that suffering, you can endure pain."

She reached for my hand and held me close. She was in deep thought.

"My suffering in that barrel is not going to be for nothing. The pain I will feel will make us free," she whispered, adding with an impish smile, "Like the pain of having a baby."

She returned to her spot, asking me to place the barrel over her. She was quiet for a long time. When I removed the barrel, I asked her how she felt.

"Like a butterfly in a cocoon," she replied.

From our position, we saw the soldier who had guarded the ship being relieved by another one. I wondered if the first guard, whom I had paid off, would keep his promise not to reveal our presence. There was nothing we could do but hope.

From the nearby storage bins, I took out enough food to sustain us though the following day and put some in both barrels. It was still dark and the port was still deserted. Maria and I sat on the floor, resting from our exhausting exercise in the barrels. I entertained her with stories of what our life would be like in the colonies. I guessed that neither her painting nor my medical

Sacred Sword

training would help us. I suggested that we would probably have to learn to become farmers.

"I had good training on the Murijon farm," she said.

"What did you learn?" I asked.

"A little about farming," she replied and, after a dramatic pause, she added, "and a lot about Jews."

"About Jews?" I asked aloud, forgetting for a moment our perilous surroundings.

I heard the guard's footsteps on the ramp and we both crouched behind bales of cloth. Apparently he heard my voice and came by inspect the ship. Fortunately, a large rat, frightened by the light of the torch, jumped up and scampered right past him. The guard returned to his post.

"What could Murijon teach you about Jews?" I whispered.

"He's not as simple-minded as you thought," Maria replied. "When you told him about his ancestor Abu Marwan, the physician, Domingo undertook to find out more about this man. He asked his priest and several of the local physicians. One of them told him that Marwan was a Jew."

Murijon told her that he also discovered that several Jews had been living in Tocino. He could not understand why they were so hounded by the Inquisition. "Domingo even claimed that he was proud to have Jewish blood in him," Maria concluded.

"Are you still ashamed?" I asked, taking her by surprise.

"Ashamed of what?" she asked.

"Of having Jewish blood in you," I said.

She did not reply right away.

"Berto," she said after a long pause, "I'm like Domingo. I don't know what being Jewish means, but on the Murijon farm I did a lot of thinking. I'm disturbed by one question: every time I think about Jews, or being Jewish, naturally I also think about the Inquisition."

"We'll soon be free of it," I replied.

"That's not what I mean," she said, "What bothers me now

is not the Inquisition, itself, but whether my father ever witnessed an *auto-da-fe*."

"He told me he knew of the burning and rioting," I replied, avoiding her question.

"I didn't ask you that," she snapped, "I asked if my father had ever been part of an *auto-da-fe*."

"Your father did not make the *auto-da-fe*," I replied. "The Holy Tribunal hands down the sentence and the secular authorities carry it out."

Maria was not to be put off.

"That's not what I asked, Berto," she persisted, "Did my father ever participate in the ceremony of an *auto*?"

"I doesn't matter now," I said.

"Help me to think through this matter," Maria said, directly challenging me.

"Berto, did Teresa, did my mother, did Enrique, did my own father ever witness an *auto-da-fe*?"

"Why plague yourself about the past?" I replied.

"Because I am part of that past," she said.

I was certain that Maria knew the answer to her question. I even suspected she had been with her father on many such occasions.

However, I assumed that she questioned me because she needed someone to confess to, someone to whom she could verbalize her guilt.

I would have preferred not to play the part. But I realized that unless I answered her question now, she would persist until she heard the truth from me.

I finally replied, "Every year, Count Juan di Trastamara would inaugurate the post-Easter carnival in Cordoba, where an *auto-da-fe* was always the opening ceremony."

"Yes, Berto, I am ashamed," she said. "I'm ashamed that my father did nothing to stop it."

"No one could oppose the Inquisition," I said in his defense.

Sacred Sword

"Andres did, Orlando Franco and Don Carlos and Domingo, they all did," she retorted.

The bleak darkness of the night was lifting. The diffused light of dawn was beginning to pierce the blackened skies. Very soon the port would come to life. Already, several sailors and stevedores were beginning to move about.

It was time to hide.

I slid down to the lower deck where I helped Maria position herself beneath her barrel.

"Whatever happens," I spoke to her through the air hole, "don't make a sound. No weeping, no crying. If you need to cry because of pain, bite down on your teeth."

I lashed her barrel, tying it to other nearby bales in the cargo area and then placed the other barrel over myself, making sure that the air hole was facing the unobstructed part of the deck so I could see Maria's barrel and ship's ramp. I was happy to see her practice opening and closing the stopcock and doing it very well. I made a silent prayer that she would be able to last the entire morning until the ship was out to sea.

It was fortunate that we got into our barrels when we did. Within moments, before the sun had fully risen, the first member of the crew boarded the ship.

From my barrel, I soon saw more of the crew members returning. The captain strutted up the ramp shouting orders to prepare the ship. The sailors were slow to react. They were still reeling from their night's cavorting. I kept my eye glued to Maria's barrel. All was well.

At about noon, a group of about fifty men, women, and children boarded the ship: emigrants to the new colonies. I looked to Maria's barrel and saw that she correctly moved the stopcock to allow more air to come in to her barrel. We had already been in the barrels longer than I had anticipated. Through my air hole, I listened to any sound coming forth from her barrel. There was none.

With the boarding of the emigrants, an unexpected danger presented itself. Several of the children began prancing about the cargo area. They were skipping and jumping from one bale to the other. They were about to climb on Maria's barrel when a crew member chased them off, warning them to stay away.

Late in the afternoon, I heard a harsh voice calling to the crew and the passengers. It was the unmistakable voice of Diaz. He ordered his agents to undertake a thorough search of the entire ship before allowing the captain to sail. I wondered whether Diaz initiated this search because the soldier had betrayed me by reporting our presence.

"If there are any of you without a limpieza, I urge you to come forward now," Diaz shouted threateningly. "We will search every nook of this ship."

Diaz's men were close to our barrels. I closed the stopcock hoping Maria had done likewise. I could not see what was going on, but I heard Diaz ordering the crew and passengers to line up for a special inspection.

"Your limpieza certificates were authenticated before you boarded this ship," Diaz shrieked. "You will all line up against the side of the ship. I will pass among you and you will show me that certificate."

After a long silence, what I feared most was about to happen: Diaz ordered his guards to inspect the cargo area. I could hear the shuffling of feet and the scraping of bales of cargo as they were moved about by the agents. I held my breath, not daring to make a sound, terrified for Maria.

Finally, after what seemed an eternity, I heard Diaz shout to the captain, at last giving his approval for the ship to depart. Soon, I also heard the billowing of the sails, the lifting of the anchor. Simultaneously, I felt the roll of the ship. I opened my stopcock and saw the passengers, giving in to their natural curiosity, lining up on the sides of the ship to look back at Cadiz as the Santa Emilia cleared the port and headed out to the open sea. No one remained anywhere below, near the cargo area, so I quickly pulled up my barrel and then lifted Maria's. I was amazed at her expression. Although she looked tired and worn out, she greeted me with a kittenish smile, mockingly pleading to stay in her "cozy barrel."

"You're still wearing that uniform," Maria gasped.

She quickly she ripped off the epaulets, the gold buttons, and braids, converting it into an ordinary ragged jacket.

Then, afraid lest the passengers might look on us as strangers and report us, we befriended some of them, acting as though we had boarded with them. Maria began to help some of the mothers tend their children as we both mingled with the colonists.

With the port nearly out of sight, a crewman started assigning a space to each passenger. He obviously had difficulty reconciling the number of passengers before him with the number of available hammocks. When he left before assigning all the spaces, I was certain he had gone to report to his superior. He returned with two additional hammocks and we breathed a sigh of relief.

But, not for long. At the stern of the ship, I saw the captain. Although he was drunk the night before, I worried that he might recognize us. I kept away from him. But, on the second day, he passed me, ogling me several times.

"Hey, De Cordo," the captain shouted, "How'd you get on this ship?"

"You have a great memory," I said, trying to hide my shock and fear at being recognized.

"Never mind that," he said. "How'd you get on board and is that bitch, your wife, with you?"

I stalled, trying to time to think up a likely excuse.

"Diaz knew us from Cordoba," I said.

"Diaz wouldn't let his grandmother on board without a limpieza," he said. "Show me yours or I'll throw you off at the Azores."

Maria joined me and began to plead with him, at the same

time apologizing for slapping him.

He gruffly explained that if Diaz should ever discover that we were allowed to sail, he would confiscate the ship when it returned to Spain. The captain insisted on the limpieza certificates. I handed the last two gold escudos to him, hoping the money would help him overlook our missing limpiezas. He grabbed the coins saying, "That's your passage fare. Now, where are your limpiezas?"

Maria reached into her bosom and brought out Franco's red bandana. She untied it, took out her mother's pendant and handed it to the captain.

He took the pendant and whistled as he kept turning it in his fingers, admiring the precious jewels encrusted in it. He threateningly asked where she stole it. Even though she swore it was hers, he told her he did not believe her. Nevertheless, he tucked the pendant into his pocket.

"Stay on board," he said. "And stay in the colonies. If you return to Spain, it's your life and mine."

The Santa Emilia was already on the high seas when Maria and I climbed to the fore deck, breathing the invigorating sea air as the ship plowed through the calm waters putting more and more distance between us and Spain.

"Senora de Cordo," I said to Maria, "the captain referred to you as my wife, so I don't have to propose marriage to you. We are married!"

"And who, my beloved husband, officiated at our marriage?" Maria asked, holding me tightly.

"The One Who causes the winds to blow. The One Who placed the stars above to guide our ship. The One Who poured out the oceans separating us from the shores of Spain."

"Senor de Cordo," Maria whispered, "I love you."

Epilogue

When we finished working on the Sacred Sword manuscript, I returned the leather-bound book to the Senora, and presented her with a copy of our translation.

"Do you know who wrote this?" the Senora asked.

"Yes, not only who wrote it but when it was written," I replied, showing her the back pages of the book.

I explained that three paragraphs were inserted in the manuscript, but unlike the rest of the text, they were written in Hebrew not in Spanish. Each paragraph is in a different hand script. For her benefit, I said, I also translated them.

"Please read it to me," she said.

I read the first insert:

"'Grandfather Samuel, of blessed memory, died today, 11 *Kislev* in the year 5379, having attained to the age of seventy. He was buried next to grandmother's grave, exactly forty-three years after he arrived in Mexico.'"

"What date would that be?" the Senora asked.

"December 13, 1549," I replied, having already computed the Hebrew date.

Before reading the second paragraph I explained to the Senora that there was no date, but it contained a historical reference.

"'Our community now numbers almost two hundred souls, and every ship load brings more fleeing brothers into our midst. It was a sad Rosh Hashana. This year the Inquisition has come to our shores.'"

Sacred Sword

The Senora needed no explanation. She knew that the Inquisition had established itself in Mexico in 1571 and had become a major force in the new Spanish colonies.

I then showed her the final paragraph and told her that I had great difficulty in reading the text because of its faded script.

"'We live with caution. Almost every day The Angel of Death is knocking on our door. The community no longer exists. For safety's sake, we have become Catholics and have assumed the name de Cordo, which brought us here almost two hundred years ago.'"